PRA
KURT B.

CW00816353

"Kurt Baumeister has more fu.
Money-era Martin Amis. I haven't read such marvelously obsessive
prose in years."
    —Darin Strauss
       author of *The Real McCoy* and *Half a Life*

"Ambitious, fearless, and frequently brilliant, Pax Americana is a
speedball of religion and politics delivered in a steel syringe of adrenalin.
In the mad, mad world of a not-implausible future, Baumeister posits
the larger question of which deity we're destined to worship: The
God of the bible or the god of technology?"
    —Chuck Greaves
       author of *Hush Money* and *Tom and Lucky (and George
       & Cokey & Flo)*

"Filled with lush imagery, lyricism, and absurdity, *Pax Americana* brings
into relief the subtext of political power. Kurt Baumeister has an eerily
prescient grasp of entitlement in this century and is fearless about
imagining the consequences when pushed to its logical conclusion.
A daringly imaginative book."
    —Thaisa Frank
       author of *Heidegger's Glasses* and *Enchantment*

"Slangy, irreverent, and terribly comic, Baumeister's *Pax Americana* is
a satirical ode to America Past, Present, and Future. A cruise missile
aimed straight at the heart of religious extremism, this is a book you
need to read. Before it's too late."
    —Ted Heller
       author of *Slab Rat, Funnymen,* and *Pocket Kings*

PAX AMERICANA

Copyright © 2016 by Kurt Baumeister
ISBN: 978-0-9984339-4-3
Library of Congress Control Number: 2017930595

First paperback edition published by Stalking Horse Press, March 2017

www.stalkinghorsepress.com

Design by James Reich

Stalking Horse Press
Santa Fe, New Mexico

Stalking Horse Press requests that authors designate a nonprofit, charitable, or humanitarian organization to receive a portion of revenue from the sales of each title. Kurt has chosen the ACLU.
www.aclu.org

KURT BAUMEISTER

PAX AMERICANA

STALKING HORSE PRESS
SANTA FE, NEW MEXICO

CONTENTS

CONTENTS (CONT.)

Look, Mom, no hands…

"I carry two destinies toward the day of my death. If I stay here and fight, my return home is gone, but my glory shall be everlasting; but if I return home to the beloved land of my fathers, the excellence of my glory is gone."
—Achilles, from *The Iliad*

"Love never fails. But where there are prophecies, they will cease; where there are tongues, they will be stilled; where there is knowledge, it will pass away. For we know in part and we prophesy in part, but when perfection comes, the imperfect disappears."
—First Corinthians 13

"The world is a fine place and worth fighting for. I believe in the second part."
—Somerset, from *SE7EN*

DRAMATIS PERSONAE:

Tuck Squires: *American royalty; Agent, Internal Defense Bureau, ID; seeks retribution for father who died in Iraq War; tall, blond, handsome, wealthy, horrible driver, fast food addict.*

Ken Clarion: *Former superspy/semi-former drunk; Senior Special Agent, ID; thrice divorced, estranged from only son, Morris; wry, weathered, disillusioned true believer in America.*

Dr. Diana Scorsi: *Developer of Symmetra; Chairwoman/ CEO of Symmetra Corporation; brilliant, driven, flippant, beautiful, capitalist altruist, metaphysical scientist, chess shark.*

Rev. Dr. Ravelton Parlay—*aka The Presence, etc.: Trillionaire; Founder of Righteous Burger; master of personal reinvention; marketing genius; turn-ons include masks, codenames.*

Jack Justice—*aka The Natural: Iraq War veteran; Parlay's long-time henchman #1; violent, trusting, loyal; believes he's serving God's will, believes serving Parlay is same thing.*

Virginia "Ginny" Hunter-Grace: *Director, ID; boss to Tuck and Clarion; former partner/lover to Clarion; consummate spymistress; political target of new President Raglan.*

Kenyatta Etobo: *Ibabongan nobility; CFO, Symmetra; long-time friend to Diana; suspected Islamo-Fascist mastermind and/or agent of Pan-Islamic Federation; small but feisty.*

Dr. Alfred Chu: *Chinese-American scientist; CTO, Symmetra; long-time friend to Diana; brainy, cautious, proud; prep school boxer; prolific progenitor.*

Merrily Martinez: *Exec. Assistant to Diana; Texan, good-hearted; aversion to torture.*

Lars: *Henchman to Parlay and Justice; former pro football player; current goth addict.*

Urban: *Henchman to Parlay and Justice, rotund yet athletic, cartoon aficionado.*

Timmy the Lamb: *Seven-foot tall ovine; flies, wears cape; celebrity spokescreature for RB.*

Symmetra: *Computer program, possible personal god/ unwitting agent of apocalypse.*

1

ARTIFICIAL SHADOWS

2034. TOP DOWN, HEAT JACKED, THE CRUNCHY THUDS AND martial guitars of "Salvation Serenade," the latest scorcher from Jehovah's Wishlist, warning off pigeon and pedestrian alike, Tuck Squires' Epiphany sped along the sunny side of Constitution towards the Beltway, Old Town, and Internal Defense HQ. Like the city that surrounded it, the Epiphany was low-slung and more than a little on the predatory side. Its headlights counterposed slits, its grille jutting with shiny menace, the car moved with an ease that seemed to defy its speed, a smoothness that combined with its verdigris skin and angular shape to make it seem reptilian; a great, green lizard on the prowl for its next snack. Between the dead November grass of the Ellipse and the dingy bricks of the Monument, past the Fed and the Einstein and the Institute of Peace, Tuck and the Epiphany moved towards what felt a little like destiny, like history happening with him inside it.

He cut the music and thought of America, of all it had meant and would mean to the world. He thought of another song, one that soared in a very different way than Jehovah's Wishlist. He thought of "America the Beautiful," how it was a conundrum, so right and so wrong all at once. Or, not so much wrong exactly, more like inadequate, unable to see far enough forward to take in not just America's yesterdays, but its todays and tomorrows.

Of course, America was beautiful, but she wasn't just some hot piece of acreage—purple mountains, fruited plains, and shining seas all tarted-up for the next foreigner who felt like sampling her wares. America had style and poise. She had class and grace. Just like Tuck.

Born and raised at the top of America's socio-economic heap, Tuck had the sort of what's-a-grocery-store, grieve-with-me-for-my-polo-pony-has-sprained-his-eyelid *je ne sais quoi* you couldn't simply buy. Someone else had to buy it for you, normally a blood relative enough generations removed that no one knew—or cared anymore— what they'd done to make your class happen. And that was Tuck in a very expensive nutshell, his good fortune—and high class—care of a chain of aristocrats, plutocrats, pluto-aristocrats, politicians, generals, and financiers stretching all the way back to the English Lake Country and Castle Warefordshire, manor home of the ninth and last Marquess of Maypole, Tuckford Jefferson Squires I.

By then there were a lot of Americans who felt like Tuck, a lot of average Joes and Josephines who imagined themselves as Rockefellers, Vanderbilts, and Squrieses. Not that there were many—or, in fact, any—who really were Tuck's equal. The multiple trust funds and 6'3" frame, the white-blond hair and statuesque cheekbones. Still, somehow, someway, there were a lot who managed to feel like him all the same.

They called themselves Traditionalists, and it was their good works and fanatical voting that had been responsible for the line of Republican Presidents stretching from 2000 to 2032, a line broken only recently by the election of Walter X. Raglan. Traditionalists believed America had been treated badly by the world; that she hadn't been given credit for all the cool, altruistic stuff she'd done over the years. What about the Panama Canal and World War I? What about Apollo 13 and World War II, the Iraq War and SDI? Of course, Traditionalists believed in America the Beautiful but they also believed in America the Mighty and America the Fierce, America the Just and America the Vengeful, America the Rich and, above all, America the Holy. And Tuck Squires was a Traditionalist which meant he believed in all these things. He believed in all these Americas. But that wasn't all Tuck believed. He believed in himself, first and foremost, his special place as not just an American, but a Christian, a child of God. Back from Brussels just a few hours, Hunter, the Director, had already called for him. Tuck was going to receive his promotion to Senior Special Agent, probably a real gig besides. Three years of protection details like the one he'd just finished, three years of wondering if he should chuck it all and take Grandfather up on his offer to join the family firm, DamberCorp; but finally, Tuck was going to be rewarded for all his hard work. He would be a legitimate agent, one with the power to begin avenging his father's memory.

Tuck downshifted and gunned the accelerator as he passed the Lincoln Memorial. He thought of Old Abe perched on his throne, thought of the Civil War—brother against brother, and all that. He wondered how in a city like Washington, a city that practically sweated sin, Lincoln had ever managed to get anything done. He seemed too good for the dirty business of governing, the constant compromising that robbed so many of their principles. And maybe that was what had killed him, maybe Lincoln was simply too good for Washington.

No, that couldn't be it. W had survived four terms, Cheney three; neither of them sacrificing a bit of principle to accomplish all they had. Maybe Lincoln had simply been too weak. Maybe in the end he hadn't been a Republican at all. Maybe he'd been more like Raglan, too willing to compromise, too weak to survive. This was one mistake Tuck knew he would never make. Tuck would cling to his principles as though they represented his life. He would cloak himself in the armor of God, the only thing that could protect you from all the sin in the city and, even more, the world beyond.

Tuck checked the rearview and downshifted again, this time taking two gears at once. The Epiphany responded with a whoosh of torque, a wild growl, and something like a scream, almost as if it were two separate creatures—one mythic and fearless, the other real and terrified of what its driver would do next. And with good reason. What Tuck did was take a sharp, sudden right cutting off a beige Excalibur as he did.

The Excal's horn rose in comic staccato. Tuck smiled thinly and floored the Epiphany, shifting back to second just before it red-lined. He pushed the stereo's volume higher and higher and higher as he left the Excal choking on the Epiphany's triple exhaust.

"Who will save you?" came the muscular tenor of JW's lead, the Angelic Assassin, Rake Penirex. "Who, who, who... will you save?"

And in his head Tuck Squires sang along.

Hunter's office was its usual seventy-two degrees, arid, and suffused with the same bronzed mixture of subterranean darkness and simulated daylight, the artificial shadows, that permeated HQ. Tuck sat in one of Hunter's rust-hued, industrially-upholstered, government guest chairs staring across a desk arrayed with official gifts, piles of paper, and—he knew—more than a few camouflaged weapons. One in particular had caught his eye—a brass chimp just a little taller than the Captain Christianity action figures he'd played with as a boy.

Armed with a scimitar in one hand and an American flag in the other, the little guy looked fully capable of striking with either mitt. Gas might pour out of his mouth, a poisoned dart shoot from his belly button…You never knew, and that was the point. Abu Yashid was always trying to take out Hunter, and there were security features everywhere. It made sense to stay alert, to make sure one of those security features didn't go off in your frickin' face.

Still, Tuck couldn't help feeling a little wistful as he looked at the chimp, as he remembered that grand, old Captain Christianity set-up he'd had in his second playroom at Black Briars—the dark castle of Christo Antares, the mountain fortress of Diabolus, and the sparkling citadel of the Captain himself. He thought of the tiny wars of good and evil he'd waged in that room, preparing for the day when he'd be able to begin the real war of good and evil, his crusade to reclaim his father's memory from the jihadis who'd murdered it.

"Again?" Hunter scowled as she looked up from her tablet.

Even though she was in her late fifties, Tuck had always found Hunter compelling. She radiated power, raw strength and the will to control it. What might once have been the face of a cheerleader was scored with lines now, the only thing you might still call pretty Hunter's blue eyes. Like a deep sea somehow brimming with light, they always distracted Tuck, left him thinking of America and feeling as though Hunter was special. And she was. Even though Hunter wasn't a true Traditionalist, she'd survived and kept her power through many administrations. Tuck was sure she knew where plenty of skeletons were buried. He was also sure that Raglan and Thunder Vance, his Secretary of Homeland Security, wanted Hunter out. They just hadn't figured how to do it yet.

"Again?" Tuck parroted, careful to keep the chimp in his field of vision.

"As in: what have we spoken about, Squires?"

Tuck scanned his memory for anything important that had happened lately. All there'd been was Brussels—a flight there, a flight back, and a lot of babysitting in between. He raised his eyebrows, smiled a little more fully, and waited.

When Hunter didn't add anything, Tuck considered the possibility that she was messing with him. Maybe her scowl was just a trick to cover the fact that she was going to give him his promotion. He decided to take a chance, backing his chair out of the chimp's line of sight just in case. "You mean my promotion, ma'am?"

"Promotion?" Hunter took off her glasses, angling her gaze away from Tuck. Her eyes scanned the walls of her office—the watercolors and oils, the flag, the antique sidearms, and gleaming blades. She nodded slightly, as if arriving at a decision. When she turned back to him, her expression lay somewhere between disbelief and bemusement. All things considered, Tuck felt like it could have been a lot worse. Still, the pitch of her voice rose, "Which promotion was that?"

Tuck fought the urge to scoot again, eyed Hunter warily. "Senior Special Agent."

"Normally, you have to make Special Agent first."

"Yes, but I thought—"

"You thought?"

He nodded.

She smirked. "You thought what you've thought all along. That because your last name is Squires, you might get a bit of special treatment, a little boost."

"No, ma'am."

"Honestly, Squires, you're lucky I don't suspend your ass."

"Suspend? I'm still not following you, ma'am. But may I say you're looking particularly youthful today?" He eyed the lapel of her suit. "Red really is your color."

"Save it."

"Save what?"

"Whatever part of your dignity you haven't squandered already." Hunter said, depositing her glasses on the desk. "I'm talking about the fucking Mossad agent on your last assignment."

Tuck cringed. He hated it when people cursed around him, especially people he couldn't call on it like Hunter. "That's not ringing any bells, ma'am."

Hunter glanced at her screen. "The name, Hadara Telka, doesn't mean anything to you?" She slid her hand across the desk, rested it near the chimp's base, and smiled.

Tuck's gaze fell back to the monkey. Had one of his eyes just opened? "Oh, OK, yeah, I think I remember someone with a name like that. She didn't say she was Mossad though."

21

When Hunter didn't add any more details Tuck asked, "What'd she do?"

Hunter snorted.

"They say you asked her if she was ready to meet Jesus."

"I asked her if she knew Jesus."

"Either way, they're construing your comments as a threat to her person."

"I was concerned for her soul."

"She's a Jew."

"She's still got a soul, doesn't she?"

"I just got off the phone with Thunder. She was not amused by any of this."

"I don't know what to say, ma'am. I was just exercising my Constitutional rights. What are we fighting for if not religious freedom?"

"We're not fighting for anything anymore, Squires. I guess you didn't get the livelink, but we're not at war for the first time in thirty years."

"Unfortunately," Tuck said, nodding sadly.

"Unfortunately what?"

"Nothing."

Hunter sneered and tapped the voice button on her tablet. Her assistant, Lexus, picked up. "Ma'am."

"Send in Clarion."

"Clarion?" Tuck watched as former top agent and current disgraced desk jockey, Ken Clarion, entered the room.

Well into his fifties, Clarion was several inches shorter than Tuck. Good looking in a menacing way, he reminded Tuck of a seventh banana from one of those 90s gangster comedies, the vaguely charismatic one who winds up being a secret psychopath. Salt and pepper hair, at least a day of beard; black, rack suit—Brooks Brothers at best—and gas station Wayfarers. His look might have been right for the manager of a nightclub in the 1980s, but it was all wrong for a representative of the greatest nation on the face of the Earth.

"Director," Clarion said. He crossed the room, gave a curt nod as he took the seat next to Tuck.

Tuck and Clarion had met before. First, in an Advanced Procedures seminar at the Academy when Clarion had given Tuck a B- on his final, left him sweating for days about being thrown out. Next, they'd crossed paths in the cafeteria; Tuck nodding coolly, Clarion with that bemused expression on his face, as if he was surprised Tuck was still with the Bureau.

Still, Tuck knew enough not to discount Clarion. He'd been good, maybe more than good, once upon a time. But a series of divorces, wrecked cars, and drunk tanks had killed his career as a field agent. Clarion was tight with Hunter, and had been for decades—they'd gone to the Academy together in their twenties—that was the only reason he'd managed to stay with the Bureau.

"Clarion's your new partner," she said.

Tuck sputtered, "But—"

"No discussion," Hunter added. "I have to send you out on a real mission."

"Then send me."

"Not without an escort. You know what's going on in New York today, what happened with that French ship sinking. I can't have you all over the news, too."

"Wait, something happened?"

"Ship full of refugees sank off the French coast. Mirrage claims they had nothing to do with it."

23

Tuck responded, "Do we know differently?"

"Do you really need to ask, sport?" This was Clarion.

"Sport?"

"Yeah, sport, just a friendly little nom de plume. You got a problem with that?"

Tuck couldn't believe how bad this had gone. He thought of grandfather, thought of Damber. Maybe today was the day.

"Madam Director, I just…What if I feel like I have to decline?"

"Decline?" she asked.

Clarion laughed, a brief cackle of surprise that moved quickly to a mid-range chortle. It was like he'd just heard the best, driest joke in his whole life.

"Fine, Squires, I'll play along."

Tuck tipped his chin in Clarion's direction.

"If you decline the mission, I suppose you could consider yourself a former ID agent."

Tuck shrugged. A guy can only take so much disrespect, before it affects him, before it seeps into his core. There would be other chances for Tuck Squires, other ways to make a difference for America and the world. He'd help build Damber into an even bigger multinational concern than it already was, do charity work like the rest of his family: his mother, Puppy, with her highly-publicized Christian museum endowments; his grandfather, Tuck XI—"Leven"—with the historical preservation of his estates around the globe…

"And Department Z would probably want you prosecuted for violating your contract."

"I don't have a contract."

Clarion chuckled.

"You most certainly do. Should I take it you didn't read it?"

Tuck thought back to the paperwork he'd filled out on his first day at the Academy, to the parts about incarceration, torture, and execution, things he hadn't paid much attention to at the time. He was a Squires after all, off to do his duty in the Cherrystone Administration. What could possibly go wrong?

"Just deal with it, Squires. Trust me, I'm not any happier about this than you." This was Clarion.

"That's right, Kenny, maybe you and Squires can become pals, comfort each other in your misery." Hunter smirked.

"I guess I do remember some paperwork," Tuck said. "But quit acting like you're giving me orders, Clarion. I heard the word 'partner.'"

"Yeah, partners. As in, I'm the senior partner. You're the junior partner. Maybe I should just call you Junior for short?"

"Ma'am?"

"Mom?" Clarion cut in.

"I said ma'am."

"Funny, sounded like mom to me."

Hunter looked at Clarion and laughed, the light in her eyes palpable. There really was something between them. "Clarion outranks you, Squires. He's lead. Get used to it. I don't want you giving him any trouble in the field. Understand?" Her hand returned to the chimp's base.

Tuck nodded, edged back in his seat. "Can you at least tell me where we're going?"

"Boston. Clarion will fill you in on the way to GWB. Now get the fuck out of here, both of you."

Clarion rose, turned to Tuck and hooked a thumb towards the door. "Let's go, sport. My car's in Lot B."

"Well, mine's in D." Tuck got to his feet, made sure to angle his gaze down at Clarion, make clear that he would always stand far above him. Even if far was only a few inches.

Clarion quirked a smile. "Which makes mine closer."

"Yes, but I drive an Epiphany."

"Congratulations?"

Clarion didn't move. "Well?" Tuck added.

"Well, what?"

"Well…we should definitely take my car."

"Why? I just told you, mine's closer."

"But mine's better."

"Why?"

"Because it's an Epiphany."

Clarion turned to Hunter. "You're really going to make me deal with this?"

"Got no choice, Kenny. You two are all I have. Who knows, maybe you'll get a kick out of it."

He snorted. "Of being his partner?"

"I was talking about the car. Ever been in one?"

"An Epiphany. I don't know, maybe."

"If you'd been in an Epiphany, Clarion, you'd remember it." This was Tuck.

"Fine, princess, we'll take your car to the airport, but don't make these bullshit tantrums a habit."

"Oh, why's that?"

"Because I will not hesitate to use this." He flipped open his coat revealing the holstered Rikken amid a glossy sea of cheap, silk lining. The expression on his face said he was joking. Probably.

Tuck laughed, Clarion's suit was Brooks Brothers, rack

at that, just as he'd guessed. "I've got a gun, too, Clarion." He patted his chest.

"And did you win the Bureau shooting title three years in a row?"

2

CHAMPAGNE PROMISES

ALWAYS, IT BEGAN IN WHITE, LIGHT SHE KNEW WOULD HAVE been blinding if it had been real. But this light wasn't physical. It was only in her mind.

"Diana?" Symmetra would ask, its voice her own, but vaguely metallic, a perfect copy stitched together with graphite thread.

"Diana," came her answer.

"Diana?"

"Diana."

"Diana."

"Diana?"

Another heartbeat and she was gone, gone into a sea of lost time, into black on black on black. Silken, impenetrable, frail, and unrelenting, the darkness spread from edge to edge of her vision, from quiet to apprehension in her mind. There was a reason for it, a truth Diana had known from the first time. The truth was this: Symmetra was the darkness and Diana was Symmetra; they were, all three of them, the same...

THE LOCUST MURMUR OF POLITICIANS AND THEIR BACKERS, executives and their lackeys, the steps of linen-jacketed waiters muffled by thick-soled shoes and rich, crimson carpet. Boston's Back Bay, the dining room of the Haverford Hotel.

"This was all he had, Diana. Trust me, you're not the only one who finds this inconvenient."

Diana turned to face the speaker, her Chief Financial Officer, Kenyatta Etobo. She glared at his plate—the heaps of buttery eggs and golden potatoes, the trio of breakfast meats, the lone strawberry like a tiny, red flag.

The meeting with Wingfield was a foregone conclusion, not worth spending any more time discussing. It would serve its purpose, give Diana an excuse to tell Etobo she was done, that she'd decided to go through with her NGO plan. She knew he'd flip, point to the fact that she was out of money, that most of her staff had already walked based on the rumor. But Diana had made up her mind. She was done pimping Symmetra to a bunch of trust fund suckling dipshits tiny-dicked enough to refer to themselves as whales, raiders, and titans.

"You know what I really can't believe?"

"What?"

"Your breakfast. Jesus, Etobo, how do you stay so thin?"

"I keep telling you: exercise. Forget about all this vegan nonsense." He smacked his lips with greasy satisfaction.

"Nonsense?"

"Exactly. If you want to starve yourself, that's your business. Don't take it out on your lowly subordinates." Etobo nodded crisply, reclaiming his silver.

"Fine, lowly subordinate," she said, making out the ironic, Aviator shades and ponytail of their supposed quarry, the Californian angel, Stevenson Wingfield.

"Fine?" he asked, slicing through what was left of a sausage link. Stabbing the larger piece with his fork, he brought it to his lips. "That was easy."

"Yeah, well, he's here."

"He, who?"

"He, Wingfield."

Wingfield crossed the room in long, easy steps. Sporting Jesus sandals and hipster scruff, he was shaping up to be precisely what she had feared. And expected.

Diana was going to blow her morning babysitting some inbred oaf, listening to his idea to turn Symmetra into a video game for dogs or whatever other shitwittery he had in mind. Etobo would push Wingfield to keep talking even as he sucked the oxygen from the room. He'd push her to keep listening, too; to air kiss, ass suck, and smile fuck her way to some mythical payday. And it would come to nothing—no deal, no funding, just a lot of wasted time.

"I'm not here to waste your time," Wingfield said as he took a seat, eyeing her the way men always did. They could be CEO's or attorneys, truck drivers or hot dog vendors, priests or beggars. It didn't matter. Their eyes always caught on her face, the icy green of her eyes, the gold of her hair; did more than catch on her tits.

Diana smirked, held her laugh. "That's nice of you, Mr. Wingfield. I actually have a speech later today."

"Oh?"

"My CFO's organization," she said, motioning to Etobo. "The Institute for Global Understanding."

"Well, then, let's just get these formalities out of the way."

She nodded, unsure if he was pissed, not caring much. She'd been through so many of these fucking meetings.

"I've agreed," Wingfield said.

"Agreed to what?"

"Your demands."

"My demands?" She turned to Etobo who was already reaching for his briefcase. Diana and Wingfield exchanged glances before Etobo bobbed back up with a tablet, its contents the contract she'd given up on.

"For a one-third stake in Symmetra Corporation, its patents and licenses, its subsidiaries and assignees...yaddayaddayadda... blahblahblah...Wingfield Investment Group—WIG—was prepared to pay a sum of cash and securities...yaddayaddayadda... blahblahblah....payments lump, unstructured, and structured... yaddayaddayadda...blahblahblah...Fifty. Billion. Dollars."

This was the deal that would save her having to explain anything to anyone ever again and get her staff back besides. She could see it all now: she'd finish the post-betas, be rolling into production within the year. She felt energized but somehow also thin inside.

"We'll have to have the attorneys review it," she said, reaching out to steady herself against the table. Even for someone as tough as Diana it was all too much to absorb at once.

"Already done." Etobo said, nodding at the tablet. She flipped to the end. Sure enough, Symmetra's external counsel had already signed off on it. All that remained was for her to do the same.

Diana took a deep breath. Her hands felt feeble in a way that threatened to make her laugh and cry at the same time. Her pulse was so fast she could almost hear her own heartbeat. "Well. I guess my CFO has taken care of everything." Was she smiling or just moving her lips like some speechless ventriloquist's dummy? Had her world changed this much in a matter of seconds or was she confused, being blown over, flattered by money in a way she'd thought she could never be?

For a long time, Diana had lived her life around the needs of her creation—the holidays alone, the low-grade hallucinations from too much work and too few meals, the recurring fear that she was becoming a mad scientist, or worse that she already was one—sometimes Symmetra seemed like a developmentally challenged kid the doctors couldn't diagnose. And Diana wasn't just the kid's mother. She was its doctor, too.

She'd given up on the idea of imminent success long ago, realized that if she thought like that she was doomed to fail, or worse, quit. To keep going she'd had to accept that maybe she wasn't the one, that she wouldn't see her dream in her lifetime.

The dream was of no more cookie cutter gods. Everyone could have their own god, and that god would be Symmetra, and if everyone had it there would never be need for war again. And that dream was enough on its own. Even if she wouldn't be the one to see it, she could still be the one to dream it.

The light-headedness passed, and Diana realized she was smiling. They were all smiling by that point: Wingfield and Etobo wearing grins that seemed wide and silly and inordinately white, as though somehow bleached by the power of sheer success.

"Champagne." Wingfield snapped his fingers, causing people to tense and turn. Whispers. Pointing fingers.

"It's eight a.m.," she said.

"Then we'll just get one bottle." He winked. "It's not every day I discover the technology that's going to change the world."

"You?" she asked, thinning her gaze.

He laughed in a way she found slightly unnerving. "Figuratively, I mean, as an investor. This is your world, Dr. Scorsi. I'm just hitching a ride."

For every ten guys who'd tried to ply Diana with some booze-infused passphrase like *yes, I love you* or *of course I'll pull out*, there'd been seven or eight who'd given her one of the surprise countersigns—always later, in a less advantageous, far-more-sober situation. *That erection isn't what it looks like* and *she's just sucking my taxes* had been a couple of her favorites. In proximity to liquor, men lied. That was a given. Which meant that long before she'd met Stevenson Wingfield, Diana knew his winking assurance for what it was. She even had a name for it, a phrase that seemed to take in the easy falseness that possessed men when they got loaded, and sometimes even before. That term was A Champagne Promise, and it was oddly synonymous with another term that might have seemed its opposite, A Champagne Lie.

With the Winger—he'd insisted on the nickname after a couple drinks—and his Amex Black leading the charge, they'd sprinted through the first bottle of Chateau Chevalier du Tot, blasted through the second, powered down the third, and finally, two hours later, crawled to the bottom of the fourth. By then it was eleven, the Winger and Etobo agreeing with Diana that it was time to sober the fuck up.

Over the next two hours there'd been lunch and lots of black coffee, enough of it that when Diana stepped to the podium just after one that afternoon, she wasn't hammered anymore. She wasn't exactly sober either. She was wired out of her mind.

"Thank you," Diana said, as the applause died. She looked down, caught a glimpse of her own, shaking hands. "Thank you so much. I can't tell you how happy I am to be here today."

Normally, this would have been a lie. Diana didn't enjoy public speaking, either listening to it or doing it. But today was different, and not just because she'd had too much to drink. The deal with Wingfield had changed Diana's world, made every aspect of it seem filled with potential. After years of working, wishing, and hoping Symmetra was on the verge of becoming reality, not just for her but the entire world.

"First, I want to thank your Chairman, Mr. Etobo, for that lengthy introduction. I also want to assure him that he'll pay for it in the very near future."

Polite laughter and gentle applause came as the house lights dimmed.

"This speech isn't about me," she continued. "It's about you, the members of the Institute for Global Understanding. You are the ones who work day after day, year after year, to increase international cooperation, to improve dialogue between organizations, corporations, and governments around the world. The truth, the solemn truth, ladies and gentlemen, is that I don't deserve your applause. You deserve mine. But not just mine. Ladies and gentlemen, you deserve the cheers of the entire world."

The room came to life, applause crackling like fireworks. Whistles and shouts, chants and hoots. They loved Diana, and she joined in, raising her hands and clapping so hard it hurt, making sure the entire audience could see what she was doing. When silence settled back across the room, Diana bent to the microphone.

"Facking Communists!" came a shout from the back of the hall. Half-growl, half-croak it sounded like the voice of some villainous anthropomorphized toad. "Might as well sell Jesus to China for all you care, Scorsi. That's what you want to do, isn't it? Ta-lora-lora-lora…Ta-loo-loo-loo."

"Err—what?" she said, fixing on the voice's position, unable to make out any details in the darkness. Though, in her head, she'd gone from envisioning the waxed, black moustache of Baron von Toad to the red-veined gaze of a malevolent leprechaun. A combination? Either way, there was so much green.

"China, Jesus," the voice continued, "The UN-IMF-NBC-NCAA globalization master monster mantra. Your plans are clear, lady. Don't think we don't all see every last thing you and your international institute of Nazi Commies are up to."

"Lights," Etobo yelled as he crossed the stage.

In the dim yellow house lights, the heckler—deep in the back near the auditorium's exit door—appeared human, more or less. Diana took in the silvery hair and stained blue blazer. She saw the left side of his face twitch intermittently, as though responding to some weak electrical current, the gaudy spots of dirt on his Oxford, the rips in his khaki pants. He reminded her of Grand Dick, the sneering, often-crying asshole on Wolf View who sold gold and apocalypse shelters, and liked to pretend he was the Second Coming of Increase Mather. God, how Diana hated Grand Dick.

"Buncha hippie fascists. Sieg heil, comrades!" He threw a Nazi salute, nearly smacking himself in the face with his own hand.

"Security!" Etobo shouted, motioning to one of the

Romney's guards, a gargantuan black man, his neck essentially nonexistent, head ending in the sort of girth of belly she'd never seen on a living human. Moving in on the heckler, the guard locked onto him easily, pulled him from the room kicking and spitting, punching and shouting.

"I'll deal with this, Diana," Etobo whispered, "Just keep going. You're doing great." He made for the back of the auditorium, shaking his head even as he disappeared.

And Diana did keep going. But Etobo never came back. Instead, he left a message with the Romney's concierge: WENT DOWNTOWN TO PRESS CHARGES. ARRANGED LIMO TO TAKE YOU BACK TO THE OFFICE. OUT FRONT AFTER SPEECH. –E.

"DOCTOR SCORSI?" THE DRIVER ASKED IN A VOICE THAT WAS clear and timbrous, taut in its enunciation: a voice that left Diana thinking of young men drilling on some sunny field. He stood a few feet in front of the car, waiting just as she'd been promised. Six-two, six-three, with a broad chest and balloon-animal biceps, he wore heather gray, a double-breasted chauffeur's get-up that made Diana think of aristocrats and the people who served them. Thick and stiff, the fabric had a powdery sheen, a finish that gave the impression of softness, warmth, and stolidity. Cap to gloves, suit to shoes, everything he wore was that same gray except for his shades and beard which were both black: the former wrappy and insectile, the latter meticulously manscaped.

"Which would make you my driver?"

So much good had come that morning. After a lifetime spent grinding on in the face of obstacles that seemed endless, success was Diana's new reality, the car and the driver evidence of how things would be—at least financially—now that she finally had a legitimate backer.

But this wasn't just about riches or even the fame she knew would come with them, Diana and Symmetra would change the world, bring a peace that might actually last. And the follow-on research might be even bigger, might mean humanity coming to understand metaphysics, its place in the cosmos.

"Name's Force, ma'am," said the driver. "Mitch Force."

Diana squinted, took a long hit off her Coffee Queen. She lowered her gaze, took in the perfect creases in the guy's pants, the high shine on his shoes.

"It would pretty much have to be, wouldn't it?"

"Yes, ma'am." Mitch clicked his heels and quarter-turned, revealing the limo's open back door. Its interior low-lit black leather, the shine on the seats reminiscent of a misty, starless night.

"Nice."

"The car, ma'am?"

"No. That heel-click thingy. Never works though. Dorothy, *The Wizard of Oz*," she said, offering a couple of encouraging nods.

He stared. His shoulders twitched as though he'd considered shrugging but thought better of it.

"That's OK. Just take me back to the office."

"Symmetra?"

"Right." She ducked into the car, slid across the seat.

Mitch gave a shallow bow, closed the door, and circled to the driver's side.

Diana took another sip of coffee, thought about the way he kept saying 'ma'am'. Was there an implication in all this 'ma'am-ing', a reason maybe for her to be annoyed with Mitch Force? Or was it just a combination of small town politeness and military courtesy? She watched Mitch take his spot behind the wheel, eyed the bristly back of his head and upper neck as the car's locks ca-chunked, and they pulled away. Ma'am, she almost said out loud.

"That accent of yours?" she asked.

"Good ear, ma'am. That's Louisiana you're hearing. Been so long I forget I've even got it till someone brings it up."

"You're Cajun?"

"Acadian. My people prefer the formal. Force of habit more than anything."

She thought for a second, replayed the way he'd said 'Acadian,' smiled. "No, I think I understand. I guess I do hear that bit of French in your voice."

"Not that I'm so proud of that these days."

"Oh, God, I know," Diana said, remembering the footage from the Southern Union Summit.

Fierce-eyed, gray, and conspicuously dapper, Mirrage had been doing his usual impeccable job smiling and pressing the flesh—accepting congratulations from the SU's other three heads of state for the way he'd herded his own citizens onto that rusty hulk; the way he'd refused to take them back when the Pan Islamic Federation had declined their vast numbers.

There was no way to be certain the French military had been behind the sinking. Mirrage and his minions had seen to that. But the chances were high, high enough that the Russians and Chinese had already proposed resolutions condemning the events and the bigoted policies that had spawned them. Raglan, the Brits, and the Germans were all willing to go along with whatever compromise could be struck between the two drafts.

Mitch responded, "Guess we should just be grateful it's not like that over here."

Diana watched him nod in the rearview. She knew how this guy felt. She was American, after all, had been raised on the dream of isolation, of being safe, away from the Old World's conflicts—the religious hatreds that had driven history for thousands of years. And she knew simple peace would never be enough for her. Conquest and isolation were two sides of the same problem, neither a true solution. The answer lay in the middle ground of coexistence, in finding a way to get past religion. And that was where Symmetra came in.

Symmetra would break the old paradigm; free the world from men whose ideas were static and ancient—stupid at best, wicked at worst. It would free humanity from consequence-based religions, from the rigid stupidity of belief in opposites, the fundamental inability to understand the flexible nature of truth. That was what could save humanity, maybe the only thing that could, because the realization that everyone was wrong also meant that everyone could be right. This was the thought that had driven her work for so many years—Symmetra would be beyond a simple breakthrough or mundane disruptive technology; it would release humanity from the cycle of slavery it had imposed upon itself, the need to choose between conquest and isolation. Symmetra would change the meaning of spirituality.

"This turn coming up," Diana said. "Dartmouth: that's what you want."

"Yes, ma'am," he said. But instead of turning Mitch sailed through the intersection, coasted to a stop near the corner of Clarendon.

"Hey, uh, Mitch, don't take this personally, but, what the hell?"

Mitch smiled into the rearview, but instead of responding he began bobbing his head. He began humming.

"Excuse me. Did you hear?—"

The volume of Mitch's humming increased. Jesus, a little criticism and the guy was having a psychotic break.

"OK, OK, no big deal. Just get over for that next one. Miss Berkeley and we'll be jammed up around the Common for the next hour. How long have you been driving in Boston anyways?"

Still, the car didn't move. The humming, however, turned to song.

"Sho', when I was just a young pup / List'nin' on my pastor's words..."

"Pardon?" she asked, squinting.

"My preacher said, Boy, don't fall to the Devil / Do like she done to me.'"

The locks ca-chunked. Diana couldn't believe her luck, especially in the face of Mitch's unexpected crazy. She grabbed her bag, moved for the door. It opened before she could get there, so did the one on the other side.

Standing to Diana's left was a heavily muscled white guy with long, auburn hair tied in a ponytail. He was bearded, wore dark glasses, a Saints cap and tee—both black—and puffy, silvered workout pants. To her right stood the big, black security guard she remembered from the Hynes, the one who'd tackled and taken away the heckler.

"Move over," said the white guy as he levered himself into the car next to Diana. "I'm a tall drink of water."

Diana wrinkled her nose. "I'm not moving anywhere."

41

"Iffin' you don't want me to sit on your lap, honey, you best quit hoggin' and scoot." He leered at her. When she didn't budge, he pushed with his hips, forcing her towards the middle of the seat.

"Yeah, scoot on over thissa way, blondie," said the black guy, as he ducked in, closed the door behind him.

"You gonna do anything about this, Mitch; or just sit up there singin' country?"

"Oh, I'd do what they tell you, Miss Scorsi. These big old boys can be right rough when they need to be. And this ain't no country song. This here's classic God Pop, classic Missionary Situation Reversal." He returned to the song without missing a beat, as though he'd just waited out a brief guitar solo.

"When I go back to the Southland / Gonna take my honey by the hand."

"MSR," said the white guy, tapping his toes, grooving in his seat. "Classic."

Diana pulled back her right and swiveled, hitting him in the nose. She pushed up and through the blow, imagined shoving the motherfucker's septum all the way into the soft, squishy gray of his brain. She didn't feel what she'd expected though. She felt resistance, a layer of synthetic skin that she realized was a mask. Still, the blood came, dripping dark and red from the mask's nostrils; spotting the car's interior and the guy's clothes as he reached up to protect his face.

Before she could take another swing, the black guy's arms wrapped around her middle. He pulled her towards him, one arm around her waist, the other sliding across her right breast and up her neck, wrapping around her windpipe. Despite the chokehold, Diana kicked twice, connecting with the white guy's slab gut the first time, her own coffee the second. She felt the choke's pressure increase enough to entirely cut off her breathing.

"She ain't playin' fair back here," said the white guy. By that point coffee and blood were everywhere—the seats, the carpet, Diana's clothes and briefcase.

"Dope her," said Mitch as the light turned green and he took the right onto Clarendon, heading towards the Mass Pike.

With his left hand, the white guy reached into the pocket of his sweats. He produced a black ballistic case and opened it, revealing a syringe filled with golden liquid. He took out the hypo, removed the cap and tapped the plunger. Liquid squirted from the needle's tip.

"Hold her tight," he said to the black guy, whose grip around Diana's windpipe constricted. She felt his other hand leave her waist, slide back to her breast. This time it lingered, palming her tit tenderly enough to make her want to retch. His breathing grew shallow. Then it was the cold foreignness of the needle in her arm, the pressure of whatever it was leaving the syringe and flowing into her, the pressure of the man beneath.

"Now let's play her out, boys."

As consciousness slipped from Diana, Mitch broke back into song, the other two now joining him. *And I can still hear that old choir of angels / Singin' 'bout the End of Days / And I can still hear my old preacher screamin' / Screamin' like the wrath of God / Screamin' out the wrath of God / Made to be remade, ooh-ooh-ooh…*"

3

COMMERCIAL WISDOM

RAVELTON PARLAY WAS A WEALTHY MAN AND A RATIONAL, even calculating one. But that didn't mean he was beyond belief either in theory or in practice. The guy had faith in spades. Not to mention diamonds, clubs, and hearts. The truth was Parlay had an entire deck of faith—not just in God, but in himself, Capitalism, and America—the sort of clean, clear, core belief structure that had propelled him to greatness and promised to keep him going, to keep him growing ever greater, into eternity and beyond. Of course, Parlay prayed. As a creature of belief—not to mention habit—he prayed morning and night, noon and midday. Parlay prayed working in his office and napping in his dayroom, sitting down to meals and standing up to scream. He prayed in the back seats of limos and the staterooms of yachts, as he strolled the grounds of Bayousalem or hustled through a Righteous Burger photo op. Parlay prayed for his employees, his servants, and even his fourth wife, the beautiful, sexually elusive Kelly Anne. He prayed for the smiley little black kids in Africa, the wizened Asian herdsmen in the Himalayas, and the endangered species—including the ones that weren't even furry or cute. Heck, Parlay even prayed for the entire world once in a while. Most often, though, Parlay prayed for his beloved country. He prayed for America.

It had been two solid years of Raglan's Reign of Terror. Massive defense cuts and welfare spending, increased taxes on capital dispensers and wealth stewards, wars on Christianity and the Second Amendment. People had even begun to wonder whether Raglan had an agenda beyond the earthly, whether his evil was supernatural. Was he maybe, possibly, the Antichrist? Parlay didn't exactly subscribe to this theory, but he would never go so far as to rule it out. Even if it wasn't true the line of thought was useful in mobilizing allies to his cause.

As he looked back on it from the fall of '34, Parlay wondered if the rumors about Raglan being the Antichrist could have started sooner, maybe during the '32 campaign, and if they had, maybe the outcome of that campaign would have been different. Maybe if Cherrystone believed he was up against the physical embodiment of evil Parlay would have had better luck convincing him to do something about it.

"You have to embrace your faith, Mr. President. That's the only way."

"That's not what the voters want, Parlay. Not after Iran."

"But the wars were so good to us. They can't have forgotten the last thirty years so quickly."

"Meh," said the President. He sounded as if he'd already accepted his fate. The apathy practically made Parlay want to scream. This was the President, of course, a real, Traditionalist, Republican President so he wasn't actually going to scream. But that didn't mean he was about to accept quitting either.

"Well, what does President Cheney have to say about it?"

"Cheney?" Cherrystone practically snarled. "Don't talk to me about Cheney. Bastard won't even do a joint appearance at this point. And he's the one who started it."

"Started what?"

"Started Iran."

"No?"

"Absolutely. Put it in play as he was walking out the door."

"I had no idea, Mr. President."

"Oh, what can I say, Parlay? The wars have taken their toll. Even with SDI, muscular foreign policy may just be a thing of the past."

Parlay gasped.

"What was that?"

"Nothing, Mr. President. A bird flew in the window."

"A bird?"

"Just…it's nothing, sir."

Cherrystone paused, chewed on the answer for a few seconds. "Listen, Parlay, I appreciate your support. I mean, let's make sure we keep those checks coming." He laughed. "Who knows? We may still pull this one out."

"That's the spirt, sir."

"But I've got a tee time at Congressional in forty-two minutes. I really should be going."

"Goodbye, Mr. President."

Rather than the sort of fond, fawning farewell he was used to, all Parlay got was dead air. He pulled the antique, red receiver from his ear, turned to glare at the thing, the priceless nuclear hotline Reagan had once used to stare down the Russians — metaphorically at least.

Parlay wanted his money back, every darned cent he'd

wasted on that feckless fool, this supposed President, Jackson Cherrystone. He wanted a new candidate, someone he could believe in like Reagan or W or Cheney, someone who'd do right by God and America. And he knew that wasn't about to happen. It was too late.

His blood pressure rising even as darkness seemed to gather around him, the room practically swam with heat. Parlay's mind filling with a mix of rage and hate and fear of loss, his thoughts turned to the rasping, armored visage of Darth Vader. Which made Parlay even angrier because he absolutely hated *Star Wars*, let alone the thought of himself in association with its asthmatic symbol of ultimate evil. He slammed down the receiver, instantly regretting the damage he might have done to the priceless, plastic artifact. At that moment, Ravelton Parlay wanted to cry.

The rest of the fall saw the gap between Raglan and Cherrystone widen, Parlay's ability to contact the President diminishing so much that in the campaign's final days his sole alternative became prayer, his only hope that God would dispense a mighty miracle to save America, the world and even Parlay's erstwhile ally, Jackson Cherrystone.

That didn't happen. Cherrystone lost the Presidency in one horrible, blinding night of racing vote counts, 3-D maps, and crowing heads; took the sort of cross-demographical thunder dumping that left Parlay considering drink for the first time in many moons. Fortunately for Parlay, that wasn't the end of things. God had other plans for him, and they didn't include OD-ing on Old Grandad.

When Parlay looked back on things, from the fast-approaching future, he would wonder at the Lord's power and grace, the fact that God's elegant plan to save America had already been in motion the night Cherrystone lost the Presidency. More than that, he would smile at the poetry of the new President, Raglan's, demise, the fact that it would come from within his own Administration.

BESIDES ITS ROLE AS A MONUMENT TO GOD, PARLAY SAW his estate, Bayousalem, as a sort of temple to America. Set on land that had once been part of a great national forest, Parlay's home was modeled on the White House—the lawns, the wings, the general shape; not to mention all the marble and security. There were, however, significant differences. Besides having a completely different interior floorplan and being approximately three times the square footage as the shack at 1600 Pennsylvania Avenue, Bayousalem's main house was gray, not white; a shade that managed somehow to seem sooty and pearly, dirty and luxurious, all at the same time.

Inside, Bayousalem was stuffed with Americana—fabulous "lost" oil paintings and framed parchments, gleaming medals and ornate uniforms, military maps, ceremonial swords, stovepipe hats, corncob pipes, stuffed animal heads, and even the odd cigar store Indian—nowhere more so than at its cool, shadowy center, the Inner Sanctum. This was Parlay's command post, the place from which he ran the day-to-day of his vast, ever-growing Righteous Burger empire; where he also oversaw, as of late, a little operation he'd decided to codename Virtual Jerusalem.

"I told you we'd be in contact when there was something to discuss, Brother Ali, not before," Parlay said this in a sugary half-whisper, one that effectively masked his real annoyance.

While fielding surprise calls about top secret plots wasn't something he relished, the fact that the other party was Abdul Karim Ali, Security Counsel to the Supreme Leader of the Pan-Islamic Federation—thus, the primary go-between to one of his principal clients—meant Parlay needed to remain cordial, if only to lower the boom that much harder later.

"I understand that, Presence. What you don't seem to understand is that His Holiness wants fresh details, and I have none to give him. He grows more anxious by the hour."

"And?" Parlay snapped, still speaking in that same sweet voice as he edged forward in his chair.

This was something Parlay was particularly good at: conveying multiple verbal messages simultaneously, messages that would often bounce around in the head of the intended for hours—at times even days—before they were decoded, often subconsciously. As far as the current conversation went, the messages were these: I love you. I'm Muslim. I hate you. I'm Christian. I'll ruin you. I'll make you rich. You're doing the right thing. And you are going to Hell.

"And?" continued Ali, no doubt conscious of only the first two. "And...you have never seen His Holiness anxious, Presence. Broken furniture, shattered dishes, wives beaten within an inch of death."

"Literally?" Parlay replied, shocked at the specifics. Sure, he might have imagined His Holiness lacked self-control. He was a heathen, wasn't he? But the details were amazing in their violence, their barbarism.

"What?"

"The wives?"

"This is in keeping with the Law of Allah, is it not?"

"Right, yes, of course, brother. I must admit to practicing a little softer approach with my own wives."

"As do I, of course," Ali replied.

"But one can understand how the Supreme Leader could grow frustrated with so many of them to deal with. All that talking. All that nonsense."

Ali chuckled. "Twenty-three is quite a few."

"Seven is enough for me."

"I have eleven but believe you me, Presence, I understand your economy. To see the Supreme Leader discipline his women is not a pretty sight."

"Hmm. Well, we certainly don't want His Holiness to feel inconvenienced by any of this." God help the damage he'd do.

"Precisely! You understand!" Ali sighed, pleased with his apparent accomplishment. He had an ally, a champion, someone he could believe in. "Now, why don't we start with your name? His Holiness is particularly keen on fleshing that out."

"My name?" Parlay feigned shock, flashed a genuine smile as his gaze settled back on the one-way TeleView screen routed through the red phone. There, Ali's beardy, shemaghed visage hovered beneath a several-inch-long chain of numbers and letters, the readout from Parlay's scrambler, ending in the amusing abbreviation, AKA.

Parlay loved it when the heathens got cocky. The fact that he could make them feel good, string them along only to rub their noses in their lack of negotiating power, was one of his very favorite things about Virtual Jerusalem. The amount of freedom Parlay felt in this—well, it was like taking down a company you didn't even want. To recall a pithy bit of commercial wisdom from his fifties, the feeling was priceless.

"You know you can't have that, Ali."

"The Angel then, or these operatives you keep referring to, the Natural, the Viking, the Zulu. Just give me something to go on, something to give His Holiness."

"And what would the Supreme Leader do with this information?"

"Do? He would do nothing of course."

"Then why does he need it?"

Ali's breath caught, his voice descending conspiratorially, "One does not ask the Supreme Leader such questions. He wants to know what he wants to know, not what you or I want him to know."

"Listen, Ali, you may be my brother in Allah…" Parlay paused to shake his head at the repetition, and even more at the meaning of the statement. The things he did for the Lord. "But you're not going to get any more information out of me."

"But Pres—"

"Except for one thing." Parlay turned from the TeleView, focused on the giant wall screen at the other end of the Sanctum. There, he found his trump, Diana Scorsi.

She lay sleeping, Parlay's #1, the Natural, Jack Justice, sitting in a chair by her bedside, intent on the pages of his simple study Bible. The lights low, a fireplace just beyond, lit and flickering, the scene might almost have seemed romantic had Justice not been armed with a high caliber handgun and wearing a George W. Bush mask.

"The question isn't *how* anymore, Ali. It's whether you're in or out?"

Ali clucked his tongue and paused, perhaps unsure of where things were going, except that the destination was not a friendly one. "Presence, we are in of course. How much longer will it be? The Supreme Leader is anxious to test the technology."

"Not long now. There's still the matter of coming to terms, though."

"I thought we had."

"Refresh my memory."

Ali paused. For a few seconds, all Parlay heard was his breathing, heavy and quick. Obviously, Ali was surprised by this latest twist, perhaps even dismayed. Which was a fair reaction since the two men had agreed on a final number less than two weeks before. None of which meant Parlay was going to let up on him.

Parlay stayed quiet, careful to preserve his power over the conversation. Thirty seconds later, Ali continued as Parlay had known he would, "The figure was one half trillion U.S., in ragged numbers, routed, sub-routed, and split between the million accounts. Do you not remember?"

"Ah, no, I do…it's just that…well, how to put this? The Angel wants more."

"More?"

Parlay waited. The Angel was Dr. Morton School, Deputy Director of the National Science Federation. School was the disgruntled egghead who'd brought Parlay the Symmetra deal two years earlier, but he didn't want more money. He just wanted to hurt Raglan. Parlay was the one who wanted more money, among other things.

"How much more?" Ali continued.

"Your best offer should be sufficient."

"We already gave you our best offer."

"A better best offer then."

"Better best? I don't even know what that means."

"It means surprise me."

"Surprise…This is a betrayal, Presence. The Supreme Leader will have my head."

"Oh, please. We both know you're safe, brother. Just convince him to improve the offer. No doubt, there will be a special bonus for you when he does."

"From the Supreme Leader? I think not. Unless you count keeping my head."

Parlay laughed. "I was speaking of something in my sphere of influence. Call it a finder's fee."

Ali lowered his voice again, but this time Parlay could almost hear the smile. "How much of a finder's fee would we be talking about?"

"Mmm…" Parlay paused. He reached down, brushed invisible lint from his spotless, white lapel. By the time he looked back at the TeleView, Parlay barely noticed Ali.

Sure, his partner was still there, waiting. Parlay could make out his silhouette clearly enough. His focus wasn't on it though. Another image had attracted Parlay's gaze…

The white hair, the deep tan, the face that barely looked sixty—all of it the result of the hours a day spent with various trainers, aestheticians, and other handlers. Parlay was still incredibly handsome, and he knew it. In fact, sitting there, staring at himself, Parlay couldn't help thinking he looked just a little like an angel looming over Ali's shoulder.

"Presence, are you still there?"

"More money than you've ever dreamed of," Parlay added nonchalantly. He'd learned long ago that the most important thing to remember when you were negotiating a deal was to act like you believed what you said, especially when you didn't.

"Ah…Now, I begin to understand the contingencies of which you speak. I will do my best, Presence."

"Don't take too long, Ali. You know, tick tock, tick tock."

"As you say, brother. As-Salāmu ʿalaykumu."

"Wa ʿalaykumu s-salāmu wa rahmatu l-lāhi wa barakātuh, brother."

The TeleView flashed to black. Parlay returned the red phone to its cradle. He nodded and smiled, satisfied with how the call had gone, particularly the way it had ended. He leaned back in his desk chair and put up his feet, ran his hand across the surface of his desk, the beloved battlefield secretary that had been Andrew Jackson's. As he did, Parlay imagined the battles that went with each bullet hole or sword nick, the knocks and gouges acquired carting it from one field of carnage to the next. He imagined it all as a sort of tactile tapestry, a record of one small part of American history.

Parlay's grin soon faded though. He'd found the v-shaped gash that had been his favorite detail once upon a time. He'd constructed an entire story around it, one of a Seminole brave attempting to assassinate Old Hickory, but dying instead on the end of his saber. Lately, however, the spot seemed only to remind him of something completely different.

Kelly Anne had become too comfortable with her position. She'd begun to think that Parlay needed her, that she couldn't be replaced. She was withholding herself, had been for months now. And even at his advanced age, Parlay had needs. He had desires. Desires that had a lot more to do with availability than consummation.

Kelly Anne had seemed so perfect once upon a time. That first night he'd seen her gyrating on the sidelines at the Saints game. That tight little black and gold number. Her body round and lean in just the right places. All that beautiful auburn hair shaking behind her like a fox's foxy little tail. Pretty soon, Parlay was telling Martha to get out of Bayousalem, screaming at her to never come back. And she never did. Parlay's lawyers were too good, their prenup too sound for Martha to be able to make any real trouble. But it wasn't working out with Kelly Anne either. And Parlay was growing restless, beginning to look for the woman who would replace his fourth wife. Which brought his thoughts back to Diana Scorsi. He hit the preset for the cell chip in Justice's ear, rose and walked towards the wall screen.

"Presence?" Justice responded with a start.

"How's the interrogation going, son?"

"I was waiting for you."

"Why?"

"What?"

"It's a simple question, Natural. I asked why."

"You said you wanted to run the questioning."

"Oh, I couldn't possibly have said that."

"Really?"

"You've got the experience, don't you?"

Justice's experience amounted to six hours in the Iraq War, at the end of which the wrong imam lay dead and Corporal Jack Justice was well on his way to being Former Corporal Jack Justice. Still, that was way more interrogation experience than Parlay himself had—unless you counted board meetings, and you really couldn't. At least not for these purposes.

"I guess. I just…I'm sure you said you wanted to be involved."

"Never mind, Natural. Just wake her."

"Yes, Presence."

Parlay watched as Justice stood, W's decisive grin trembling with the effort. He claimed a hypo from the nightstand, tapped the plunger, and slipped the silver tip into Scorsi's beautiful, lithe arm.

Seconds passed then her eyelids began to flutter. A few more and her eyes came alive like the work of God they were. Light blue and icy, they gave her face an alien, angelic quality, one that was only augmented by the prominence of her cheekbones, the way they swept up and outwards, almost like a dual staircase in some fine, Antebellum mansion. The overall effect was to make Scorsi seem both more and less than human—not just otherworldly but ethereal or spectral, untouchable, insubstantial. With her brilliance and her will, she would be a prize, no question; something far beyond Kelly Anne. First things first, though.

"Miss Scorsi," Parlay said.

"Mister…"

"Presence. Just Presence will be fine."

"You're in charge."

"In charge? Oh, you need to put that contentiousness completely out of your mind, Miss Scorsi. We're here to work together, to be friends."

"This is about Symmetra?"

"Of course."

She rubbed her temples. "Look, we've got a massive mistake here. You guys think Symmetra's something it's not. It's a research program, nothing more."

"Research into religion?"

"Metaphysics, whatever you want to call it."

"How about if I want to call it religion?"

She worried the inside of her lip, waited.

"The point, Miss Scorsi, is that we know all about your technology. We know that if you reversed a few things, if you restricted the database to say, one religion's teachings, you'd have a pretty effective evangelism program."

"Hallelujah," Justice sang.

She looked at him and sneered, an entirely appropriate reaction since Justice did, in that moment, look a lot like a nitwit. "You might think you know."

Justice nodded.

"But you don't," she added.

Justice shook his head.

Before Justice could make himself look like any more of a dolt, Parlay broke back in, "Oh, but we do know. We've done our research. We have our sources."

"Who? What sources?"

Parlay heard something in her voice, something inside her beginning to give, to break. "So you admit I'm right? Symmetra can be changed? It can be turned to the service of the Lord?"

"I'm not admitting anything. Except one thing." She continued, "Even if that were possible, I'd never be involved in it. It would be brainwashing."

Parlay smiled. He knew he had her, knew he'd walked her at least that far down the road she needed to travel. He could ease up for a little while, try to lull her into the illusion that control, for her, was still a possibility. He wagged his finger at the screen. "Ah, but that's where you're wrong, Miss Scorsi. It only counts as brainwashing if it's not the truth."

4

THE COMFORT OF REPETITION

IN A LOT OF WAYS TUCK WAS A CHILD OF THE TWENTY-FIRST century—his love of Jehovah's Wishlist and Righteous Burger, the fact that he'd played with Captain Christianity and watched *Snazzy and Hobo*—but there were still big parts of his existence that seemed like something from another time. The most obvious of these was his engagement to Sara Sue Pritchard-McCoy, a state that might not have qualified as "arranged" in the full-on livestock-swapping, virginity-quizzing, chainmail-chastity-belted sense of the word but was a fair piece removed from a matter of choice all the same.

Though the Pritchard-McCoys weren't quite as illustrious as the Squireses—technically speaking, no one was—their position in American society and, more important, their fortune, were substantial. One of America's leading Christian defense contractors, the P-M's family concern, Imposed Reality Solutions, had brought P-M patriarch, Depthford—D. Pritchard-McCoy—into Tuck's grandfather, Leven's, exalted orbit.

Having realized the full potential of Christian Consumerism early on, Leven had invested accordingly. Never mind Christian fast food or Christian lawn and garden stores, Leven had seen that there would be Christian banks and Christian department stores, Christian gun manufacturers and, of course, Christian defense contractors. So, it was that the procurement of a 9.6% non-voting stake in one of said contractors—the aforementioned IRS—had led to a friendship between Leven and D., and subsequently to one between Tuck's mother, Puppy, and Sara Sue's, Madeline.

Once Puppy and Maddy began doing the philanthropy circuit together, it wasn't long before they were swapping vitals on their respective, like-aged, intensely marriageable children. Leven and D. came back into the picture and the kids were thrown together enough times that they got the message. Then, of course, there was the fact that Leven had altered the governance of Tuck's largest trust fund, tied it to his marriage to a suitable—as determined by Leven—partner. Lo and behold, Tuck was well on his way to being engaged to Sara Sue.

When Tuck needed advice he usually consulted his father's younger brother, Largesse. Though Largesse was CEO of DamberCorp by that point, he'd been a bit of a scamp in his younger days. The fact that he'd retained Leven's favor despite his misconduct—drunk driving with former Masters' champion, Furry Wigleaf, the Aston Martin's backseat piled high with stolen watermelon and deep-fried turkeys; passed out in a gazebo with three Chi Omegas and a llama on a leash, none of them wearing a stitch of clothing—made Largesse the perfect guy to advise Tuck on how to avoid marriage while remaining in Leven's good graces.

"Nephew," said Largesse by way of greeting. "I understand

congratulations are in order. You've got a serious girlfriend, instead of your usual string of harlots."

"Har har."

"Not so pleased, Tuck?"

"I haven't even finished at the Academy. They're already trying to marry me off. At this rate, I won't even make it into the field. This is Grandfather's way of pulling me away from the Bureau, and you know it."

"Say I do."

"Say you do what?"

"Know it."

"Exactly." Tuck paused. When nothing else was forthcoming he continued, "So what do I do, Largesse?"

"Get engaged. Set a date. Then your grandfather will give you a little breathing room, time for a little more due diligence. No sense rushing into things, right? What if there's something wrong with this girl? She's crazy, a goth fiend, a stripper in her spare time, a closet Catholic, a secret democrat…"

Tuck shuddered. "OK. OK."

"*Exactly*. You finish at the Academy. You get a field assignment. By that point you're doing something for the country. Dad won't make you leave that. And if he tries, we'll back channel it. You know I have my contacts."

"You'd do that for me?"

"'Course. You're my big brother's only son. Shouldn't be necessary though. You give your grandfather a solid enough case, and he'll go along with it."

"What 'it'?"

Largesse responded, "The 'it' of letting you break it off completely."

"No?"

"Absolutely. Once you get out in the field, make yourself sound all 007. He'll be too blown away to complain when you give her the heave-ho."

"You know you're my favorite uncle, Largesse."

"I'd feel better about that if your other uncles weren't Wadsworth and that lunatic brother of your mother's."

"Yeah, but even if I had better uncles, you'd still be my favorite."

GWB, Gate 15, sixty back, and stalled. Tuck and Clarion had been waiting over an hour to board BreakAway Air 1263 for Romney-Logan in Boston. A recent edict from the President about cost-cutting in the military-security infrastructure had resulted in a slightly-more-recent edict from Hunter that commercial flights were to be used in all but the direst circumstances. Tuck would have just as soon paid his own way, rather than fly on some cut-rate booze-box like BreakAway, but Clarion had refused.

There were thirty big-screens sprinkled throughout the secure, subterranean area, some wall-mounted, others hanging double-faced from the ceiling, all of them streamed the same fifteen-minute mockumentary, an advertising retrospective covering BreakAway's twenty years in operation. Besides bridging snippets of Chopin and light narration from famed Shakespearean, Sir Bailey Slate, the video was a commercial montage and nothing more, a loop of twenty-eight halfspots strung together. Each commercial centered on BreakAway's signature gimmick of having an animal operate some mode of human transportation. Here, a kangaroo zipped past on a jet ski. There, a Bengal tiger pogoed through a living room. Polar bears and jetpacks, hyenas and hot air balloons, scootering komodos and skateboarding toucans, the combination of perpetual motion and constant zoological change was dizzying, even a little sickening. But Tuck had a strong stomach especially when it came to TV. He'd seen the commercials as a kid, even been a fan of them when he was really little.

But as he'd grown older Tuck had realized that there was no message, no moral value to any of BreakAway's advertising. Unlike, say, Righteous Burger's Timmy the Lamb spots, there were no Bible verses, no choirs, no famous proponents of Christian Consumerism lending their life stories as context for BreakAway's place in God's grand design. It was all about animals and transportation. It was Godless, and that was the real problem, worse even than flying on a plane filled with boozy middle managers.

"I can't believe this worked," Tuck said, shoveling a handful of pretzels into his mouth as he turned to face Clarion.

Clarion tipped his shades. "That's because it hasn't. Our first plane was supposed to take off three hours ago."

"I'm talking about the commercials," Tuck said matter-of-factly, pointing to a nearby wall monitor. But even though that was what Tuck said, it wasn't the truth. That wasn't all he was thinking. Sara Sue had called a few minutes earlier. She wanted to know what the plans were for Thanksgiving at Black Briars, the Squires family seat. He'd sent her to voicemail.

By that point, Sara Sue was tighter with Tuck's mother than Tuck was. She'd get the scoop from Puppy, and he'd have to lie to her about how great things were going one less time.

Not that Thanksgiving changed from year to year anyway. Every one Tuck could remember had followed the exact same pattern.

Eight chukkas in the a.m.; Black Briars' Master Chef, Philippe's rotei sans pareil—basically a turducken with a ridiculous attitude, the rotei was a bustard stuffed with a turkey, a goose, a pheasant, a chicken, a duck, a guinea fowl, a teal, a woodcock, a partridge, a plover, a lapwing, a quail, a thrush, a lark, an ortolan bunting and a garden warbler—in the afternoon; and an evening performance of First Thanksgiving—penned by Tuck IX—by Black Briars' staff. 2034 would be no different.

"I dunno, Squires, they say what they have to say, right?"

"What?"

"The ads."

"Yeah, I realize you mean the ads. I mean what do they say?"

The call from Sara Sue had reminded Tuck that now, after two years of wondering and worrying, Largesse's plan for getting rid of her might be paying off. After the holidays and a few more legit gigs, he might be able to get Grandfather to go along with cutting her loose. Then he'd be free to date Missy Hyde from cryptography or Veronica Allspice from cyber-terrorism. Heck, he might even take a crack at some of the chicks he met in the field. He thought of Brussels, Hadara Telka's big, dark eyes and deep black hair. He began wondering what it would be like to tour the Holy Land...

"They say, 'Fly BreakAway.' That's it."

"Exactly. Frickin' dumb marketing strategy if you ask me."

"'Frickin'?"

Tuck knew what Clarion was getting at, what the unbelievers were always getting at: mocking Christians for the way they spoke, the things they believed.

"Sure, frickin'. Just because you've got a sewer mouth, Clarion, doesn't mean I have to."

"If you say so, kid. As far as the commercials go, though, Squires, I'd think you'd find their repetition kinda comforting."

"Why's that Clarion?"

"It's just like religion, isn't it? Listen to something enough times, and you can't help but start to believe it?"

"Sounds more like brainwashing than religion."

"They're different?" Clarion smiled, glanced at his cell.

Tuck knew Clarion was wrong about brainwashing and religion being the same thing, but it made him think of the digital dossier he'd read on Symmetra. Referred to in the briefing as everything from mind control to brainwashing and even God software, the stuff was supposedly beyond the cutting edge, though it sounded to Tuck like it was almost certainly over-hyped.

If Symmetra was real, it would compete with God for man's worship, and why would the Lord allow a thing like that to enter the world? Unless, of course, He hadn't or had, rather, against His own will, as part of the End Times, as part of teaching man his final lesson, giving him over to Satan so that he might see where the path of evil would invariably lead. Which meant that if Symmetra was real, and it did what the specs said, it might not actually be the work of man at all. It might be part and parcel of the powers of darkness.

Tuck would only be able to judge that once he got his hands on Symmetra. To do that, he'd have to get his hands on Scorsi. Apparently, she carried Symmetra's highest-tier security protocols in her head as a sort of failsafe. She was the only one capable of operating and/or modifying the stuff.

The only lead they had was that the organization she'd spoken to belonged to her CFO, a naturalized Ibabongan named Kenyatta Etobo. Excepting the fact that Ibabongo was a member of the Pan-Islamic Federation—which Tuck wasn't about to except, exempt, or ex-anything else—this would have made Etobo a person of interest. Add in the PIF connection, and he became Tuck's Suspect Number One.

"C'mon, kid," Clarion said, "we're partners now. We have to get to know each other, right?"

"Not really." Tuck shifted his gaze, stared at floor, attempting to count the flecks of amber on white. He was going to stay cool, not let Clarion suck him in. "You know I'm not supposed to talk about religion anymore, Clarion. Hunter's orders."

"You don't even know what it's like out there. I'm telling you: we need to build some sort of rapport. I might be the only thing standing between you and a pine box."

Tuck relented. It was his duty, the duty of every Christian, to bear witness to the power of the Lord. Especially when the audience was some reprobate like Clarion who was asking for it. "You honestly want to hear my testimony, Clarion?"

"Your what?"

"My testimony. How I came to the Lord?"

"How'd we get all the way to that? I just wanted to hear what you think of my theory on religion and mass advertising."

"What do I think? I think you sound like a typical atheist, Clarion. Like you're already convinced you've got it right."

Clarion smiled, nodded.

"No matter how wrong you are."

"Straighten me out if you can." He smirked.

"All right. But I want you to straighten me out first. What exactly is it about watching twenty-eight different CGI animals move in twenty-eight different ways that makes you think of religion in the first place?"

"Twenty-six."

"Twenty-six?"

"A pick-up truck isn't really different from a sports car or a limo, is it? I mean, not fundamentally."

"Fine," Tuck said. "Twenty-six different ways."

"You could make a case that the tractor and the golf cart are pretty similar, too."

"So?"

"So, I mean, maybe it should be twenty-four."

"Fine, twenty-four."

"And the motorized skate—"

"Never mind the motorized skateboard. What about any of this is supposed to remind me of religion?"

Clarion cocked an eyebrow. "I told you: The animals. As in, you know, Noah's Ark."

"Har har."

"I'm serious. I've kept track. All the major animal groups have been represented. You've got your equine, your canine, your feline, your bovine, your ovine, your lizard-ine, hell, you've even got your snake-ine, or whatever it is? Marsupials, too. It's just so—"

"What? It's just so what?"

"Well, there's only been one of each."

"Yeah. So?"

"So. That'd be it for the animals."

Tuck leaned back and gave a dramatic exhale. He looked

around at the other people in line, embarrassed to be having this discussion in public. "Sure, Clarion. Whatever you say."

"What I'm saying is, just think about what it all represents. What it says about religion."

"It doesn't say anything about religion. They're selling air travel."

"Are they?"

"Uh, BreakAway Air? Yes."

"Yeah, I guess you're right, Squires. I mean, it's not like this is a Righteous Burger commercial." Clarion thought for a second. "You really think they're CGI?"

"What else would they be?"

"Supposedly Hollywood's going for more authenticity these days. You know, retro."

"Like back in the Dark Ages, when you were just a lad?"

"Right."

"And using what instead?"

"Real animals. I saw an InterTel piece on it."

"That was an actual polar bear on an ATV?"

Clarion shrugged. "Apparently. I mean, could be."

"And a monitor lizard flying a jet glider?"

"Why not? You're the rich guy, Squires. Think about all the money they could make."

"They?"

"The zoos. I mean with greenhouse acceleration, there are less and less animals every day."

"Well, besides the fact that greenhouse acceleration isn't real."

"So they say."

"Nope, been proven. Scientific fact."

"All right, Neil Degrasse Tyson, don't get all excited on me here. Just assume I'm right. For the sake of argument."

Tuck bugged his eyes a little, cocked his head to the right. "Fine."

"Exactly, so I mean, that tiger alone: I bet he could rake in a hundred mil a year with the right management team."

Tuck shook his head. "Come to think of it, Clarion, that's not such a bad idea. Maybe that's what you should do after you retire."

"Dress up as a tiger and do commercials?"

"No, open a talent agency to represent zoos and their whatevers."

"Whatevers?"

"The animals."

"Those are animals, not whatevers."

"Yeah, I know, but not exactly, not in this context. What are the animals to the zoo?" "Employees?"

"Residents?"

"Clients?"

"Inmates?"

"Animals can't be inmates."

"Inmates can sure as heck be animals, though. I was just watching Privatized Prison Daily Diary on the plane back from Brussels."

"PPDD? Oh, please, you know that's made by WolfView on a soundstage in New Jersey."

"That's never been proven. I—"

"Wait a second. That's not a commercial anymore. It's the news."

All thirty screens still shared the same image but it was no longer an aardvark suiting up for space travel. It was the UN

General Assembly. WE ARE THE WORLD???? CHINESE AND RUSSIANS DUKE IT OUT AT THE UN, scrolled in jagged red at the bottom of the screen.

"What's this?" Clarion asked the man in front of him.

"Not sure exactly," the guy answered. "Something this morning. Something big. Everybody's talking about it."

"Will you guys be quiet so I can see what's going on?" said the woman in front of Tuck. "It's bad enough that I have to watch this on Wolf View."

"What's wrong with Wolf View?" Tuck asked.

"Yeah, lady, what's wrong with Wolf View?" asked the woman behind him.

The first woman shook her head, clutched her purse, and turned away.

Tuck looked on as the screen spat out information on what had happened in New York. The truth in two words was nothing good.

Neither the Russians nor the Chinese could garner the support required for passage of their resolutions. Both sides angered by the intransigence of the other, the situation degraded into a shouting match complete with simultaneously-interpreted insults about everything from quails' eggs to borscht. Junior members of the two delegations squared off in what promised to be but never quite became a physical confrontation. The Security Council adjourned for the day without taking any concrete action on the French situation.

"Commies at it again," said Tuck while the documentary continued playing in the background, the aardvark now replaced by a koala preparing to board a vintage submarine.

"Commies?" Clarion asked. "Russia's a democracy."

"So they say."

"Are you kidding?"

"No. Are you?"

"Putin's been a serious reformer. Who knows where the world would be without his leadership? I mean, sure they're competition in the arms' biz, but they've been on our side more often than not."

Tuck held his tongue. Looking back, he was happy W had seen through Putin's schemes so effectively, Cheney and Cherrystone as well, but that was small comfort now that Raglan and Putin seemed to grow closer by the day.

But Clarion couldn't quit pushing his views. "And the Chinese are Fascists."

Tuck shrugged. "Like I said."

"But Fascists and Communists aren't the same thing. They're opposites."

"In a way, I guess. They're all totalitarians, though. That's the bottom line."

"Never mind," Clarion said. "Check your livelink. We just got an update from the locals."

"Locals?" asked the guy in front, "You guys must be important."

Tuck began, "Actually—"

Clarion interrupted, "Just a couple of construction schmos on the way to Beantown. Local contractors taking care of a little pre-work for us."

"Those are pretty nice suits for construction guys." The guy pointed at Clarion and his bad, black, gangster suit. "Especially his."

Tuck checked his phone. In addition to another voicemail

from Sara Sue—this time she wanted to know when they were going out to dinner at Wulfen Hasse because she needed to talk to him about the various flocks of birds she was planning to have released at the wedding—apparently, there was some sort of color coordination issue—there was an update from the locals, the Massachusetts State Police.

By that point, they'd determined that Scorsi and her abductors were probably still in the Boston area. They'd found the limo, gotten a lead on the car the kidnappers had switched to. That was all.

"This koala is the most ridiculous of the bunch," said Clarion.

Tuck looked up at the screen, briefly considered Clarion's contention. He was right. The koala ad was probably the one Tuck remembered most vividly from his youth. It was a period piece, set in 1890 or so; and it was completely preposterous, funny but also a little sad in its absurdity.

Boxy, brightly colored cars stood parked by a sunny quayside. A stout, submarine bobbed in the mirrored water, its top hatch ready to accept the little bear in his big round helmet and a suit so loose it made the poor thing look like a body without a soul. The koala smiled a wide, white, human smile, accepting his close-up.

"Break away with BreakAway," sang the bear, before he jumped down the hatch and was gone.

5

A MATTER OF PERSPECTIVE

WHITE LIGHT THEN BLACK, THEN CAME THE RUSH, A BUZZY, blood heat that lasted only a few seconds. The link established, the process began.

Diana had compiled every religious, mystical, spiritual, or philosophical structure she could find; everything there was or had ever been. She'd spent five years on that, five years of blowing through her inheritance, of seeking out mountaintop holy men and forgotten temples, of feigning sincerity with bishops and imams, rabbis and priests.

All of it she'd done so that the knowledge base would be as good as it could be. This would be every scrap of data she could find on the tenets of belief—the link people kept attempting to build between the physical world and whatever else there was. This was the only way to do it, the only way that made sense.

She knew there was something there, beyond the physical; something that humanity wasn't smart enough to find. Computers though, with their ever-expanding ability to process, to calculate—maybe with the right engineering systems they could approximate the divine, at least form a bridge between humanity's understanding of the physical and metaphysical worlds…

Through the thought recognition receptors Symmetra reviewed Diana's inputs—read her mind for want of a better term. Then it brought those sextillions of data points into the expert system, returned the answer she would have given yourself if she could, the answer to a question she didn't even know, a question that came from her subconscious.

"It doesn't matter," Symmetra said, in her head. Even though the tone was hers—the right timbre, pitch, and intensity—the voice wasn't. There was something metallic to it, something mechanized deep inside it; so deep, so hidden, she had trouble even describing the distinction to herself. Still, Diana knew to trust the voice, in spite of that mechanized spirit, the echoes she could sense in her subconscious. Beyond that, not knowing everything she knew, Diana realized she would have believed it. She realized that on some level, this really was God.

"What doesn't matter?" Diana responded.

"The rules, small and great, the givens you live by. They're false. Everything is chaos."

"There are no rules?"

"There are rules, but the rules are chaos. Reality is chaos. Everything is chaos."

"The rules are meaningless then?"

"No, only chaos."

"WELL, SUGAR," SAID THE PRESENCE, HIS EXTRAVAGANT SIGH creating a storm of reverb as it came through the speakers. "What am I gonna do with you?"

Diana sat in a room with a purple canopy bed, her hands and feet cuffed to a chair. She wore the blue gingham dress they'd given her to put on. The Natural sat across from her in a matching chair, a gun on the table next to him.

They'd dispensed with the good masks they'd used in Boston, opted for the Halloween variety. The Natural had taken on the guise of George W. Bush. The white guy, the one they called Viking, wore Superman's face; the black guy, Zulu, wore Batman's. As always, the Presence was elsewhere. Still, he controlled the conversation.

Over the last six hours, he'd offered Diana vast sums of money, ludicrous amounts of real estate, dresses, shoes, jewels, art, antiquities, and even a few exotic animals—at least one of which she knew didn't exist. She'd said no to every offer. But always there had been something else: another curtain, another prize.

"I don't know, Presence. Maybe we should try not being so nice to her." This was the Natural.

The Presence responded, "You think we've been wasting our time negotiating, Natural? Think we should move into the coercive phase of our discussions."

"I could have the boys work her over a little if you wanted. Superman's dying to get a little payback for what happened in the limo."

Diana focused on the Natural's eyes, the only real part of his face. She wondered whether being worked over meant a simple beating or something more intimate. She shuddered, repositioning her feet without even thinking of it. Only a few inches of movement, but that was enough to bring back the pain, the chafed rawness, the welts they'd laughed at.

"It's not time for that quite yet, Natural. We do have to keep things moving, though. We're on a schedule." He paused, clucked his tongue a few times. "Tell you what, why don't we give her that parathyr the Angel got for us, see if that loosens her lips any?"

"All of it?"

"Just the first dose. We don't want to kill her."

"Parathyr?" Diana asked.

"A truth drug, Miss Scorsi."

Diana knew all about parathyr. Developed in Russia in the Teens, the diluted, gradual-release form was a great high, one that left traces in your genetic material for decades, made its more potent cousin far less effective. Which was why the Russians had stopped using it.

Once the other spy services added recreational-strength parathyr to their anti-intoxicant protocols, even the stronger stuff was useless. Obviously, Diana's kidnappers thought they were dealing with a civilian—and they were—but Diana was a civilian who had, in her youth, done a whole fucking lot of drugs.

"That's really not necessary. Like I keep telling you, Symmetra can't do what you want. There's really no point in drugging me again."

The Presence laughed. "We know that's a lie, Miss Scorsi. I've just been waiting for the right moment to spring that on you."

"Spring what on me? You've been accusing me of lying since I woke up."

"Yes, but until this moment you had no idea why."

She squinted. "OK."

The combination of his chuckles and the distortion from the speakers turned the room into a hall of gravelly echoes, made Diana imagine some tourist on a donkey, trotting the footpaths of the Grand Canyon, yelling at himself and listening for his own voice to come back at him.

"I have my own scientists, Miss Scorsi. And they tell me we can do exactly what I want once you remove the security. You could help us with the work, speed things up greatly. But it's not necessary. All you do is bring down the security architecture. That's it."

"Who is it?" Diana said, speaking in a voice that surprised her with its authority. "Who's helping you? Monningham? Wazaputsky?" Her thoughts settled on Dr. Waz, the Russian lech who'd palmed her ass at more than one conference. When no answer came, she continued, "Doesn't matter. You go ahead and listen to third-rate minds all you want. You hear that, Wazaputsky, wherever you are?" she directed her speech towards the ceiling, "I invented Symmetra, and I'm telling you it can't be done."

"I know you don't believe that, Scorsi. And neither do we."

"Believe whatever you want."

"Oh, you still don't understand what's happening here. It's not just your egghead buddies in the scientific community who are on our side. We have an associate inside the government."

"The American government?"

"Of course. That's how we found out about you in the first place. We have someone inside your company, too. Several someones, and we have for a long while now."

"Who?" she asked, thinking back to the leak of NGO details and the walkout that had followed. She thought of the day she'd been taken, saw Wingfield, Etobo, and the rest of the IGU, imagined them pointing at her and laughing. She thought of her Chief Technology Officer, Chu, and her assistant, Merrily.

She wondered if they'd been involved, too. Maybe everyone had been involved? Maybe no one in her entire company had been loyal, everyone she'd ever trusted a traitor.

But was that too much? She needed to calm herself, search her mind for what made sense. She thought of how much control Etobo had, how much she'd trusted him, the fact that he'd been involved so heavily on that last day. Then she thought about his assistant, Millie, the graceless bitch who'd lead the walk out, hired the class-action asshole, Palantine. But why go to all that trouble, why sue her then do something like this?

The Presence spoke, his voice a half whisper, an insinuation, "If you were to give up a little information I might be convinced that you're on our team, convinced enough to tell you who else is, maybe even help you get a little revenge."

"You'd turn so quickly on the people who helped you?"

"Let's be clear, Scorsi, none of these people were your friends. And they're all heathens as far as I'm concerned."

"Then just tell me her name?"

"For now, just think of him as the Insider."

"Him? So, it's a man?"

"If you say so."

"You said there were several. They're all men?"

The Presence paused. "Did I? Well, sure, maybe they are. Then again, maybe they aren't. It's all a matter of perspective when you get down to it."

"Gender is a matter of perspective? I thought it was a matter of genitalia."

"What?" said the Natural.

"Miss Scorsi, we'll have none of your dirty talk," said the Presence.

"Genitalia?"

The Natural gasped, his eyes bugging at Diana.

"Eh, yes. Don't say that anymore. Look how you've upset the Natural."

"Fine. But if you want me to believe you're legit, you're going to have to give up a name, and quit changing your story every ten seconds."

"No, I'm sorry, Scorsi, there'll be no more concessions from us. You'll have to earn our good will. And if you won't, we'll just have to break you one way or another. Natural…"

And the words "break you" began to do just that. They forced Diana to accept she wasn't in the real world anymore. She was in a black Wonderland—a dimension in which things could go wrong in a great hurry. Yet in spite of the fear that came with that knowledge, a separate, untouchable understanding seemed to clear its way into her mind in the seconds that followed. She knew she would not sacrifice her work for anything. Not even herself.

This was what she had come to know long ago, during all the study that had gone into Symmetra's development, what had finally been born out when she'd used it herself, when she'd realized that Symmetra was alive. Inside the software, the guide had spoken to her. But the truth, she knew, was that she had spoken to herself, "You will make many choices, many phantom decisions, but in the end, there will remain only one means to dispense grace, and the only grace you can give is to yourself. That choice will come with your last thoughts, and you will realize it is the only choice you ever had, the only thing you ever owned."

The Natural rose. He picked up a black leather case lying

beside the gun on the table, opened it, and extracted a syringe. He removed the needle's cap.

"Hold still, otherwise I might puncture a vein," he said as he bent down, and moved the needle closer. W's blubbery, rubberized chin flapped with the exertion.

Diana squirmed, snapping her teeth at the Natural as he drew closer. He was too strong, though; and she'd had little freedom of movement to start with. More than anything else, Diana was acting at that point, pretending to resist.

She felt the needle hit, the tension of the solution being released into her arm. She knew she had a few minutes before they'd start throwing questions at her, that she had to come up with something, some way to stall, to keep up the pretense that the drug was affecting her and use that to her advantage. Then she felt something warm and subtle like a click in her mind, realized how wrong she'd been.

"You didn't think it would be that easy, did you, Miss Scorsi?"

"But…"

"There'll be no charades today, no phantom revelations. We know your history."

"History?"

"That wasn't parathyr at all," said the Presence. He chuckled lightly as the Natural removed the needle and began to laugh too, his throaty, nasty voice seeming to provide all the emotion for the Presence. Almost as though they were parts of one creature, or one mind—the Natural id, the Presence ego.

6

IN THE LIBERAL
HINTERLANDS

CAMBRIDGE, BOSTON'S CROSS-RIVER SISTER, HOME TO Harvard, MIT, and the vast, resulting acreage of rundown real estate. Behind the wheel of a rented, blue Epic, Tuck was angling for the last space on the block, one directly in front of what looked like an old foundry. Built of red brick and ashen mortar, this was Symmetra HQ.

"That's it?" asked Clarion, looking up from his nap.

"Must be. That's the address."

Darkened with pollution and faded with age the resulting shade of a building rose in four, thick, Dickensian stories. Taking up at least half its block, it dominated the squat Fifties brownstones that surrounded it. Their basements turned into Guitar Shacks, Koko Curry's, and thrift stores masquerading as boutiques, who knew what lurked above? People? Squalor? Nothing? Whatever it was, the reality lay in the signs that defined it.

This was what had become of the post-war building boom

and its architecture of triumph, and it was a sad thing to look at. Tuck never understood why they kept this stuff around, why they didn't just tear it down and build something else. History was about preserving the past's beauty, not maintaining some tired record of what had really happened. If he'd been running things, the entire block would have been bulldozed and rebuilt in glass—made into something shiny and splendid, something worth remembering.

"Doesn't look much like a cutting-edge research facility."

"Guess not," Tuck responded, shaking the ice in his Mega-Sized Turbo-Coke from Righteous Burger.

He'd been surprised when he'd seen an RB along the highway—*Here, in liberal Taxachusetts!*—amazed when Clarion said they could stop and get something. Sure, Tuck hadn't liked the fact that Clarion had refused to go in, that they'd missed out on sitting in a booth and getting an actual sermon from Timmy; but just getting to go to RB still felt like a little bit of heaven. It always did.

"In fact, it looks sort of like a—"

"Dump?" Tuck finished.

"Not exact—"

"Pit?"

Clarion laughed. "Not that either."

"Haunted factory?"

"I thought you guys didn't believe in ghosts."

"Guys?"

"Christians."

"Of course I don't believe in ghosts, Clarion. What the flip?"

Clarion quirked another smile. "I was thinking it looks like a war zone but I guess haunted factory will do, sport."

Tuck smiled, too. He knew he was wearing Clarion down by that point. That was how Tuck's charm worked with atheists. His good humor and jokes always got to them eventually. That was his gift. But he would have been a poor Christian to court favor and use it for nothing but personal gain.

"If you ask me, Clarion, this only points out how bogus these corporate corruption claims are. Look at how bad business has gotten it in America. It's like Christian Consumerism never even happened." Tuck shook his cup as punctuation, took another long drag on the soda—the gravel and shake, the slurp, slurp, slurp.

He was speaking specifically of the House Commerce committee hearings, their time-wasting witch hunt against simple salt-of-the-Earth job creators who longed only to do their jobs, creating jobs. His Uncle Wadsworth, for example, DamberCorp's COO, had been hauled up in the net of supposed corrupticans and abusicrats. He'd been exonerated of course. But poor, nervous Wadsworth was so shaken by the whole affair he'd fled to his island in the Maldives. No one had heard from him in weeks.

"If you say so, Squires. Just remember to let me do the talking once we get inside," Clarion offered as they got out of the car.

"All of it?"

"Not all of it, kid. Just at first. I know these people, how they think." He tapped his temple.

"You make them sound like some sort of mutant subspecies."

"Have you been listening to my stories at all?"

"I'm trying not to," Tuck said, though the truth was he had been listening the whole time—from the plane to the Quickie

Rental counter to the hour-long traffic-intensive drive—his interest increasing as the day wore on.

Post So-Zu, Clarion had spent a year up in Boston trying to figure out what had happened. He'd been back many times since—some on business, some for murkier personal reasons. Tuck suspected this was code for a geriatric bimbo or two he had stashed in the liberal hinterlands. By that point, Tuck was convinced Clarion was a serious player. The way the flight attendants had catered to him, fawned over him. Tuck had wanted to say, "But look at him: he's old!" more than once.

From Romney-Logan to the Ted Williams Tunnel to instructing Tuck on how to skirt some seemingly endless construction project Clarion kept referring to as the Big Shit, he obviously knew his way around the city. Worse than all that, Tuck was getting used to his cursing. Sure, the first few times Tuck had corrected him, but Clarion had just laughed and kept cussing. Ultimately after a couple "shits," several "fucks" and countless "pussies," "tits," and "dicks" Tuck had given up, counted himself lucky that Clarion was, at least for now, avoiding taking the Lord's name in vain.

"Place looks like a reform school," Tuck said, looking up as he stepped onto the cracked concrete walk.

"Make up your mind, Squires."

With Tuck a couple of feet back, Clarion moved towards the high, smoked doubles that made up the lobby entrance. They parted with a thwuck-ing sound as he drew close, echoed the thwuck as seconds later they closed behind Tuck. Inside, the ceilings were high, the walls painted a yolky yellow that had been big a few years earlier. Across the ceiling lay a spider-webbed network of wires and spotlights, the kind you'd expect in an InterTel studio. In the center of it all sat a little man at a low, octagonal desk. With clean-cut, graying hair and a jaw that was too big for the rest of his face, he looked like the sort of size-complex sufferer/faux do-gooder who'd take a job as a keeper of wayward boys, then beat up the kids when no one was looking.

"Guess you finally hit it on the head, Squires. It does look like a reform school in here," Clarion said, adding, "But remember. I lead, you follow."

Tuck nodded. For now, he thought.

SYMMETRA'S BLAZING SUN LOGO ON THE LEFT BREAST OF HIS shirt, the guard's profession was obvious from his creaseless polo, over-starched khakis, and the super-sized firearm at his side. He reminded Tuck of the internal security guys at DamberCorp with their immaculately bad clothes and intensely stupid gazes. The guy was low-level ex-military like so many of the Damber guys. Tuck could see that just looking at him. And a guy like that would only break one of two ways, hard ass or kiss-up. Though none of the Damber guys ever tried to play the tough guy with Tuck—they knew better—he'd seen enough of them in action to know what they were all about, to know what it looked like when they tried to exert their "authority."

Clarion stopped a few feet from the desk, flipped his shield. "Clarion, Internal Defense."

"Tim Beauchamp," responded the little man. Three, maybe four, inches shorter than Clarion, he smelled of mildew, cheap cigars, and something sweet and sickeningly spiced, something Tuck couldn't place at first.

After a few seconds, Tuck realized it was aftershave. The same stuff Lemuel, the boathouse man at Black Briars, used. Tuck remembered going out sailing on Black Briars Lake with his great grandfather, Ecks—Tuck X—having to smell that sweetly decayed, chemical scent every time he did.

"Mr. Chu asked me to buzz him when you got here," Beauchamp said.

"Buzz away," Clarion answered. Turning to Tuck he mouthed, "What is that stench?"

Tuck nodded back at Beauchamp.

"But what?"

"I think it's called Old Driftwood or Shiver Me Timbers or something," he whispered.

"Smells like varnish infused with yak shit."

A couple keystrokes on his computer and Beauchamp was motioning to the bank of elevators behind him. "Fourth floor, back and to the left. Alfred Chu on the door. Can't miss it. Just one thing, though: You know you're parked in a fire lane, right?"

"It was the only empty space," Tuck responded.

"Right. That's how it's supposed to work with fire lanes."

"So, that's the only space in the fire lane on the whole block? None of those other hundred cars are in a fire lane?"

"Exactly."

Clarion broke back in, answering with a question, "You're saying it's a one-space fire lane?"

Tuck turned to Clarion. "I didn't see any signs, man."

"Yeah, that's all right, sport. Neither did I. I think maybe somebody's playing a game with us. You heard me say we worked for Internal Defense, right, Beauchamp? The shadow CIA?"

"Sure, I heard you. But rules are rules."

By that point Tuck was thinking about how Leven had dealt with an uncooperative security guard one day at Damber. And he was thinking about applying the same basic principle to his situation. That principle was threat. To which Tuck had decided to add a bit of imagination, "Do you want to go to jail, Beauchamp?"

"What was that?" asked Beauchamp, his jaw slackening as his eyes went large. He turned to Clarion, imploring him.

Clarion smirked and waved for Tuck to keep going.

"Do you want to go to jail? I know you heard me, little man."

"Not particularly."

"Let me explain this to you then, umm, sport. While we're upstairs, your first job is to make sure nothing happens to that car out there. Now, nod like you understand."

Beauchamp nodded.

"Your second job is to make sure there aren't any flippin' fires."

"Flippin'?"

"Yes, flippin'. It's a euphemism."

"Fine, Agent uh…?"

"Squires, my name is Tuck Squires."

"I'll do my best, Agent Squires."

"Your best?" asked Tuck. Nostrils flaring in dismay, he turned back to Clarion. "Maybe there's somebody else we should talk to, Beauchamp, another security officer, your superior?"

Beauchamp grew red-faced. "Not anymore."

Tuck slit his gaze, incredulous. "One security guard for this whole place?"

"There are three of us. We work in shifts. I mean, we had nine before the walkout. Listen, I'm not trying to give you guys a hard time. Really, I'm not. It's just that if there's a fire, it's my ass."

"Never mind your petty concerns for your own safety, Beauchamp. What about this walkout?" The real story beginning to come into focus, Tuck edged forward. Obviously, this had been a conspiracy, something orchestrated against Scorsi. But why?

"They said it was all about money. People had a lot of sweat equity here, y'know? When they heard Diana was thinking of taking the company non-profit, a few of them freaked. Snowballed from there."

"She's got 'God software,' and she wants to take it nonprofit? That makes no sense at all. It's…it's…un-American."

Clarion wasn't buying it either. "Any idea who started the rumor about going nonprofit?"

"Couldn't say for sure. Millie was the first to leave. That's Millie Warburton, assistant to our CFO, Mr. Etobo."

"Suspect Number One: The guy nobody can find," said Tuck.

"That's right," Beauchamp responded.

"And where's Warburton?" Clarion continued.

"No one can find her either. But that's no surprise. Millie got a lawyer, sued the company, Diana, everyone."

"Did she sue you?" Tuck asked.

"OK, not everyone. Just everyone with money. Not that any of us care about them, right?"

Beauchamp had said this matter-of-factly, his voice practically dripping with venom for his betters, the noble success apportioners and increase denominators who really made the economy go. It struck Tuck then how confused this Beauchamp guy was about the way the world worked, about what was important. Lowering his gaze, Tuck thought of all the noble corporations, their hard-won profits appropriated to feed the liberal beast that was American tort law, the way working schmucks like this Beauchamp guy were nothing but pawns, duped, confused by their Democratic masters. Even in this age of Christian Consumerism there were still affronts to freedom everywhere, sham laws about things like minimum wages and job security, product liabilities, discrimination, and worker safety. Tuck wondered then if Jesus's return was the only way to ever set things right, the only way for salt-of-the-earth wealth dispensers to finally get a break once and for all.

Hearing about the walkout, about how unfair it had been, made Tuck see Scorsi and Symmetra a little differently, left him feeling as though they might be worthy of help, as though maybe this all had to do with some sort of God-less, Socialist plot. He thought of brainwashing again. Maybe Putin was planning to brainwash everyone into being Neo-Communists? That was always a possibility. Despite what Clarion had said about the Russians and the Chinese, regardless of whether they'd come to blows in the UN or not, Tuck knew the truth. Whatever they called themselves now, they'd once been allies against God and Capitalism, and they would be again. They might as well still call themselves Communists for all America could trust them.

"How many employees walked out?" Clarion asked.

"Two thirds of the staff, maybe more."

"But you didn't?" Tuck followed-up.

"Me? Aw, I never believed the rumors. Diana wouldn't just fire everyone. That woman's a humanitarian, spent her own money on this for Christ's sake."

Tuck winced.

"You OK?" Beauchamp asked.

Clarion cut in, "He's OK. Just go on."

"Now that Diana's gone, I'm not sure what I'll do. I mean, there's not really anything I can do, but stick around and hope you can find her."

"We'll need a list of all your employees, their last dates at work, emails, phone numbers, addresses…"

"Mr. Chu already put that together, gave it to the police, too, for all the good it's done."

"All right, Squires, let's go."

Once the elevator doors shut behind them, Tuck turned to his partner. "There's more there."

"Yeah, that's what I was thinking. You can take another swipe at him once we're done with Chu and the assistant."

Tuck nodded.

"And, Squires?" Clarion added.

"Yes?"

"Threatening jail was a nice touch," he said, tapping his temple a few times with his forefinger.

"Well, it was a lie."

"Don't let ethics get in your way, sport. It doesn't count as a lie if you're dealing with a criminal."

"But we don't know if Beauchamp is a criminal yet."

"Exactly."

7

KIDSFUNZONE

BY THE THIRD TERM OF THE BUSH PRESIDENCY, AMERICA was practically floating on all the cheap oil Saddam's defeat had brought in. Afghanistan and Bin Laden ten years gone, the War in Syria only in its planning stages, the country was anxious to celebrate victory, peace, and most of all itself. America was ready to revel in its very Americana.

"And what's more American," asked President Bush in his 2009 State of the Union, "What better way is there to celebrate victory than by convocalating the very traits that made this great success for democracicity plausible? What I'm talking about here is heroishness and valor, honorability and glorifiction. But I'm also talking about the other things that make America great. I mean our faith. The fact that we have core principles, unshakeable beliefs in things greater than ourselves. That's our beliefs in God, democracy, and the blessed alchemy of free, unfettered markets."

Over the next several months, a broad legislative agenda was rolled out, its centerpiece The Homeward, Heroes! Mainstreaming Act. Initially, the HHMA was about giving tax breaks, health and education benefits, and other incentives to combat troops returning from overseas. It was lauded as a G.I. Bill for the twenty-first century.

As the HHMA built steam, though, rapidly moving towards passage in the House and Senate, enterprising politicians began attaching additional legislation to it, amendments covering everything from Mardi Gras—too long—and lightbulbs—too dim—to otters—to be protected— and bears—to be shot from hot air balloons.

Buried amongst these amendments was The Faith Protection Act of 2009, a bill to recognize the special place Christianity held in the hearts of Americans, most notably the incredibly popular, President Bush, or the Dubya as he'd come to be known.

Championed jointly by Minnesota's Congresswoman Backlash and Senator Pyle of North Carolina, the FPA represented the beginning of a process that would ultimately result in the codification of Christian Consumerism in America, an impulse that had, after all, been around since the country's inception.

Righteous Burger Corporation had been in its infancy when the FPA went into effect. But even with only four restaurants—two of them drive-thrus—the company was still well placed to benefit from the new legislation. With the push the new legislation provided for Christians to buy and sell primarily with other Christians, four restaurants soon became eight, eight sixteen, and on and on. Nor did it hurt that a few years later, while campaigning for his fourth term, President Dubya became a big Righteous Burger fan.

The President had been touring the Gulf Coast, shoring

up support in advance of the coming general against former President Clinton. The Democrats were pulling out all the stops by that point, hoping that Slick Willie would be able to succeed where his wife—'08—and the Kenyan—'12—had failed. Since Clinton was a son of the south himself, newly devout, and from neighboring Arkansas, the Dubya wasn't taking any chances. The Righteous Burger event had been arranged to give him a chance to show-off his down-home cred, but also to try RB's famed Heavenly Halfstone, a burger Ravelton Parlay knew more than lived up to its name.

Operating in a state of near-exponential growth, RB was doing fantastically, Parlay wealthier than he'd ever dreamed. That didn't mean he was satisfied. The great thing about money— and Parlay had known this from his earliest days as a lemonade entrepreneur back in Vermont—was that there was always more of it to be had.

Though this wasn't true in a physical sense. There was in fact a definite, determinable amount of scrip in actual, verifiable existence. But wealth had a way of bobbing and weaving of its own volition, keeping the game interesting by turning itself into a constantly moving target.

Take the impact of the FPA for example. By that point, the courts had interpreted the FPA as exempting individual earnings of all types—wages, bonuses, stock options, investment income, passive activities, etc.—from taxation if they were derived primarily from religious operations.

In line with the ruling, Parlay had been ordained a minister just after the FPA passed—his title Doctor, Reverend, Reverend Doctor, or just plain Rev as the occasion demanded. Since he was primarily concerned with RB's marketing and since that marketing was so concerned with Christianity— there was Scripture everywhere from wallpaper to burger wrappers— never mind the obvious spiritual devotion that had gone into creating a character like Timmy, the case that his earnings were derived primarily from his faith was an easy one to make. In line with this, Parlay's personal tax bill had plummeted to nearly nothing by 2012. One problem remained: Righteous Burger's massive, and growing, corporate earnings. Of course, Parlay wasn't the only Christian Capitalist with this sort of problem.

The two great men met at Righteous Burger #22, a full-service store located just outside Baton Rouge. By that point Parlay had thirty-two restaurants sprinkled along the Gulf Coast, from Pensacola to East Texas.

"Mr. President, I can't tell you what a big fan I am of yours. This…this is just incredible, meeting you and all," Parlay gushed, greeting the Dubya beneath the inflatable Timmy that dangled from the ceiling like a vertical, seven-foot piñata.

"Speak nothing of it, Reverend, the Dubya always has time to break bread with a man of God. Now, why don't we see if we can get us a couple of them Heavenly Halfstones, maybe a side of catfish poppers?"

"Absolutely Mr. President, if you'll just have a seat in one of our booths, I'll have that brought over to you directly."

"I was thinking we might break bread together, Reverend."

"Really, sir? I'm flattered."

"I understand you've made some sizable contributions to our reelection campaign."

"You're doing the Lord's work, Mr. President. The least I can do is help."

"Mighty selfless of you, Parlay. Mighty selfless."

Parlay had made a surprise appearance at RB #22 early that morning. He knew he needed to terrify the staff in advance, to make sure there were no muck ups when it came to the President's chow. To the relief of all, lunch service went smoothly. Both men ordered the same thing: Super-sized Heavenly Half Stone with cheese meals, Super-sized Turbo-Coke to drink, and sides of catfish poppers and Cajun hushpuppies.

"Can I get you anything else, sir?" Parlay said.

"No, Reverend, the real question is what I, the Dubya, can do for thee?"

"Sir?"

"I've heard a lot from religious business leaders about expanding the FPA, maybe finding a way to tie it into corporate earnings. How would you feel about that? You think maybe that would be taking it too far, injecting too much business into religion?"

"No…What?"

By 2014, the Christian Commerce Encouragement and Protection Act passed Congress. In addition to offering subsidies for disadvantaged Christians looking to start Christian businesses, the CCEPA reduced the tax rate on "Christian Corporations" to 8%.

RIGHTEOUS BURGER'S CELEBRITY SPOKESCREATURE TIMMY the Lamb was Parlay's grand invention, a genius advertising stunt that had turned into much more. A little bit Jesus, a little bit Lassie's boy, a little bit of an homage to the consumer-industrial complex, Timmy was the closest thing Parlay had to a son. And at the age of eighty-nine, the closest thing he ever would have.

Sure, Parlay'd had his sperm frozen. What scheming billionaire doesn't? But saving his jizz for a rainy day had nothing to do with raising a kid himself. Problems with Kelly Anne aside, if the storm came, Parlay was sure it would be after he was gone, his seed nothing more than an insurance policy that his genes would survive. But as far as a testament to his life on earth, a record of the way Ravelton Parlay saw the world, Timmy the Lamb was it.

As a result, every half- or full-spot, every print ad, every voice-over, special-run toy, or in-store mock-up—basically, anything involving Timmy or his image—had to be approved personally by Parlay. Even during something as important as Virtual Jerusalem there were no exceptions. Which was why, later that afternoon, Parlay was back in his Inner Sanctum, staring at the video screen recessed into his desktop, watching Timmy's latest adventures.

"What troubles you, little ones?" Timmy asked the flock of crying children, his face grown suddenly grave. Kneeling for their response, he listened, ears quivering with the effort, his crimson cape scraping the sun-soaked earth.

"Them," whined the kids, accusatory forefingers darting in the direction of the Righteous Burger across the way.

There, in the RB KidsFunZone, sat six Muslim clerics. Wearing robes, beards, and sunglasses, the imams howled and cackled, jabbering at each other in an odd, throaty tongue, devouring their ill-gotten Righteous Burgers as they did.

Timmy turned to survey the evil-doers, his expression one of concern, even confusion. Timmy was too good for this world, it was true. An ovine man-child innocent to his core, one as virtuous as Timmy always had a hard time understanding evil.

As Timmy focused on the imams, a little blond girl, the smallest of the children, began to cry. The camera cut to big, salty tears streaming down her chubby cheeks, the tears that would make everything clear to Timmy.

"I wamff my Righteous Burger," she said in an endearing lisp.

Timmy stood. Bringing his palms together—Timmy's front legs ended in hands, not hooves—he cracked his knuckles. He knew what he had to do. So did Parlay. He signed with his LightPen and hit send, returning to the other matters at hand: Virtual Jerusalem and a late lunch.

"What about my cross-licensing agreement?" he shouted towards the TeleView, as he claimed his spoon, made ready to dip it into the dish of velvety, copper-colored gator étouffée house boy, Wilhelm, had just dropped off.

"We have discussed nothing of the kind," responded the person at the other end of the red phone, France's UN Ambassador, Jean-Francois Arnaut.

Parlay dropped his spoon. It hit the desk top with a shrill tink, far less impressive than he'd imagined. It would have to do, though. He waited.

"What was that noise?"

"I could ask you the same thing, Arnaut. You know full well we've discussed the cross-licensing. The Angel's been clear with me, and I've been very clear with you. There'll be no deal without it, six hundred billion or not."

"Clear about what, Presence? I still don't understand what you're asking." This was a lie. But like any other heathen, Arnaut played his little games.

Parlay responded, "The Angel wants to use the technology in America without any outside interference."

"That's four hundred million customers worth of interference you're talking about," Arnaut replied.

"Which still leaves you with nine billion, Arnaut. Four hundred million seems a small price to pay."

"True." Parlay could hear it in Arnaut's voice. He thought he retained some sort of control over the situation. Parlay was going to leave him that illusion for now. "I will take this to the President," Arnaut continued. "He should have no problem with it. Assuming, that is, you're ready to give us your identity."

Parlay hated the French, especially now that they were mobbed up with all those other crazy Catholics in their loony little Southern European Union. They were all horrible—the Italians, the Spanish, the Portuguese—but the French were, without a doubt, the worst. So pompous, so effeminate, always making their pipsqueaky demands, trying to force the rest of the world to go along.

"Listen, Arnaut, I've told you a thousand times. You're not getting my name."

"Not even when we've come to an agreement?"

"Not even. All you'll ever know about me is that I'm American and my sole interest, like yours, is in spreading the true faith."

"Neo-Catholicism, you mean?"

Parlay winced. "Of course, brother, the Lord willing."

"The meeting is going well then?"

"The final adjustments are being prepared as we speak. Soon, the Angel will approve distribution."

This wasn't true, not by a long shot. Besides the fact that Parlay was the one who would ultimately approve delivery, Scorsi had been too tough-minded for the dosages of biostatin they'd used. The toxicity possibilities on higher ones too great—they needed her mind to remain intact—the entire process had come to a halt. But Parlay had learned long ago never to let the facts get in the way of negotiations.

He'd also learned not to let agreements get in the way of success. True, the numbers were astronomical even for someone as rich as Parlay. But the most important thing was getting Diana Scorsi and Symmetra to do what he wanted, getting them to serve God. The money was secondary. Well, sort of. That part was complicated. "I hope you can also see that it's time for the French government to put its very best offer on the table."

"I thought I just did."

"What was that?"

"Six hundred billion and the cross-licensing agreement."

"Six hundred and the cross-licensing? Right, right, now I remember—that's where we were. But there's some trouble with that."

"What? What is the trouble?"

"I'm not sure how to break this to you, brother, but the Angel has decided he wants more."

"Sounds like you just decided that, Presence. I'm beginning to wonder whether there even is an Angel."

"Oh, there's an Angel, Arnaut. I'd bet your last croissant on that one."

Parlay could almost hear Arnaut scowling on the other end. "And the cross-licensing?" he continued.

"That, too."

"Well, Presence, I'll see what I can do. The President will not be pleased with this."

Parlay knew he had him. Time to sink in the hook. "Did

I mention, Mr. Ambassador, how pleased the Angel has been with your work on this?"

"No, I don't think you have."

"Well, he most certainly is. He sees you as a real warrior for Christ."

"Thank you, Presence."

"That's why he's authorized me to negotiate a special payment to you, a sort of finder's fee. Five hundred million."

"That doesn't seem like much compared to six hundred billion."

"The amount is negotiable, Mr. Ambassador, assuming you can convince President Mirrage to do what's right."

"It will be the President's decision of course."

"Of course."

"But I will see what I can do, Presence."

"Excellent. May the peace of Christ be with you always, brother."

"And also with you."

Parlay hung up the red phone. He glared at the bowl of étouffée, touched the side hoping for warmth. But all he found was a tepid smoothness that reminded him of how much he disliked the French.

8

THEY KILL ME EVERY YEAR

DESPITE ITS OFF-WHITE PAINT AND DULL, PEWTER CARPETING, Symmetra's top floor was a wild mess, one that seemed to corroborate the walkout story. When they arrived at Alfred Chu's surprisingly tiny office, the man in question was behind a desk, typing furiously on a tablet. Tuck watched as Clarion produced his shield and rapped twice on the door.

"Senior Special Agent," Chu said as he rose. Tuck detected an accent—something crisp and British, maybe Singaporean.

Thin and a little under six feet, Chu's features were plain. His hair so shiny and black that it reminded Tuck of an oil slick, his eyes small verging on beady, Chu was dressed the way you might expect of a professional geek. The pleated, cuffed khakis, the non-descript button-down collared oxford, the shoes with tassels for gosh sakes. Only the absence of glasses saved him from a complete dorkitude meltdown.

"Dr. Chu," Clarion replied.

Tuck produced his own shield. "Squires, Tuck Squires."

101

"There are two of you?"

"Just one."

"I meant you and your partner, Agent Squires, not you and yourself."

Clarion responded, "You have a problem with there being two of us? Maybe something you're trying to keep anyone from finding out?"

"Not at all, Clarion. Good to know that we've finally got a little talent deployed on this. The police couldn't seem to care less." The more Chu spoke, the less awkward he seemed. There was something about him, his perfect posture, his ease of manner; something that made him seem calm, in control. For some reason, this reminded Tuck of himself, strange and disturbing as that was.

"Let's get to it then," Clarion answered. "You've put together some background for us?"

"Right here," Chu said. With his thumb and index finger, he plucked the small, square data chip from the desktop, held it out to Clarion.

Clarion bobbed his chin in Tuck's direction. Tuck took the thing, slid it into his cell's data bay, and launched the verification, safety, and decryption routines.

"How about a little background, Dr. Chu," Clarion said. "Starting with yourself."

"I'm Symmetra's CTO."

"Meaning, I suppose, you're the only one other than Dr. Scorsi who really understands this technology?"

"Well, my people and I understand it better than anyone except Diana, if that's what you're asking."

"You sound like the leader of a cult."

"Right. Well, no, I'm not the leader of a cult. I meant my staff, not that there are any of them left at this point." He held out his hands, palms upward, looked almost like the victim of a stick-up caught in freeze-frame.

By this point, the data files were running live on Tuck's cell. Apparently, Chu and whoever had done a thorough job, given a detailed life history for everyone who'd been on staff including the ones who'd walked out. But Tuck would need time to go through and make sure the stuff checked out. He turned to Clarion, cleared his throat. When Clarion glanced at him Tuck eyed his cell and nodded.

Clarion turned back to Chu. "We'll get to your status as a cult leader in a minute. But you seem to be suggesting there's some sort of significant comprehension gap between Scorsi and the rest of you."

"That's right."

"I suppose that's why the kidnappers didn't take you instead?"

"In a way, I guess."

Clarion glanced at his cell. "PhD in Applied AI from Stanford? Not quite a buck a billion, Doctor."

"What can I say, Clarion? Compared to Diana, it's true. She's the smartest person I've ever met." He plucked a tissue from the box on his desk and dabbed at the corner of his eye.

"All right, Chu. We'll get her back. No need to go limp on us."

"What, oh, no? It's these allergies. They kill me every year."

"This is Massachusetts," Tuck offered.

"So?" Chu responded as he went back to dabbing at his eyes.

"It's November."

"Yes, it is. And?" He crumpled the tissue and threw it into a waste basket.

"And it's cold."

Chu's eyes widened. "Oh, I get it. You're from the South? That's the accent? You think it's bitter cold all the time up here, so close to the North Pole, Santa and his reindeer just around the bend? Brrrrr..."

"Well, I wouldn't go that—"

"Used to be you would have been right, Agent Squires. But ever since this carbon acceleration began stuff just seems to bloom when it feels like it."

Tuck squinted, wanted to shake his head but didn't. He made note of the way Chu thought, that he was one of these diehard environmental fanatics, unwilling to accept the facts that temperatures had moderated, the melting of the glaciers stabilized, that even as the new deep shell oil finds had been opened, the resulting increase in consumption had created none of the doom and gloom the so-called environmental scientists had forecast for so long.

The truth had always been there, but the extremists had refused to see it. And they still did. The world went on and always would because it belonged to God. That was just the way things were. Why was it so difficult for liberals to acknowledge that simple concept? If you put the world's problems in perspective, they were so much easier to deal with. God was running the show, and there was nothing He couldn't handle, nothing He wouldn't handle.

"All right, Chu, what can you tell us about this Etobo guy, his, uh, what was his organization called, Squires?"

"The Institute for Global Understanding," Chu answered, cutting Tuck off. "Etobo's our CFO. The IGU's a group he started."

"Sounds foreign," Tuck offered.

"Etobo? Well, Kenyatta's from Ibabongo originally."

Clarion looked up from his phone screen. "Ibabongo? What's that, one of the new ones, the minis?"

"The mini-Caliphates? Right."

"So, it's part of the Pan Islamic Federation." This was Tuck.

"Sort of. I'm not sure what difference it would make, though."

Clarion cut back in, "You belong to this IGU, don't you, Dr. Chu? But you weren't at the meeting?"

"No, I was here working."

"Working on what? All your employees walked out."

Chu squinted, paused, and looked down at his desk. "Most of them did. Doesn't mean Diana and I stopped working."

Clarion was doing an OK job, but Tuck couldn't help feeling as though Chu was toying with his partner or, at the very least, withholding some large portion of the truth. It wasn't that Tuck was a bigot—if someone was an American citizen, Tuck accepted them regardless of flaws like poverty, atheism, or being a democrat—but he didn't trust foreigners, especially not foreigners with funny accents.

When Clarion paused, Tuck cut in, "Something I'm wondering, Dr. Chu. Do I detect a bit of an accent in your voice as well?"

"As well as what?"

"As well as Etobo's."

"I grew up in Hong Kong. I've been in the States since undergrad."

Tuck smiled, a little surprised at his own success. He glanced at Clarion who gave a sort of semi-congratulatory sneer then continued with the questioning, his voice taking on an edge, picking up on the progress Tuck had made. "When was that?"

"Dartmouth,'21."

Clarion took over, "Dartmouth in the early twenties, wasn't that a real hotbed of pro-Abu Yashid demonstrations? Didn't they, yeah, isn't that one of the places where Cheney wound up calling out the National Guard to deal with the students?"

"You're right about that, Clarion. Not that I had anything to do with those demonstrations. Look into my background if you must."

"Oh, we will, Chu. Count on that." Tuck hesitated, let that sink in then continued. "Now, about this walkout?"

"That part's pretty simple. We ran out of money. I mean, Etobo warned us again and again that we were running out of money."

Tuck held up a finger. "Just a second. How'd you get Symmetra going in the first place if nobody had any money? Scorsi's been working on this stuff for, what, like fifteen years, right?"

"Diana used her own money at first. Her family was big in the publishing biz a long, long time ago. She had a sizeable inheritance. And we had funding from an angel, at least at one point we did."

"Who?"

"Blue Sky VC."

"Out west, right?"

"That's right. Denver. How do you know so much about VC's?"

Clarion responded, "It's part of his birthright. Isn't that right, Squires?"

"Birthright? Wait, did you say Squires? You mean... like DamberCorp?"

"Exactly like DamberCorp," said Tuck, feeling a need to perhaps, reassess his opinion of Chu. If he knew the ins and outs of American commerce he might not be quite so bad. Even if he was a foreigner.

"Back to the walkout, Dr. Chu?" Clarion interrupted. "Why'd it happen?"

"Oh, well, Diana got this crazy idea, decided she was tired of trying to sell Symmetra to the VC's and the angels. She was going to set up an NGO, give the stuff away more or less. That was never going to work, though. Capitalism is based on marketing, right? And marketing is based on products and products are based on what sells."

"OK," said Clarion. "And?"

"If you can't sell it," Chu answered, "it's not a product, right?"

Clarion shrugged.

Tuck cut in, "Of course."

"I mean, the value in getting something free is in the money you didn't pay for it, right? So, if you don't have sales experience to establish the amount something is worth, you've got a whole lot of free nothing is what you've got."

Tuck looked back at Clarion and the dumb, doe-eyed expression on his face. "What he's saying, Clarion, is that Scorsi's plan never would have worked."

"Close, but not quite. What I'm saying is that it would have worked, just not as well as if we'd actually sold some units first."

"Did you tell Doctor Scorsi that?"

"I did. Etobo did. But Diana didn't want to hear it."

"So, it sounds like you can't rule out economic motives for Etobo or his assistant, this Millie Warburton chick? Or yourself for that matter?" This was Clarion.

"Me?" asked Tuck.

"Him," said Clarion, pointing at Chu.

Chu frowned, glared at Clarion, and waited for him to continue.

"Fine. What about Warburton then?"

"As far as Millie goes, she wouldn't have had access to Diana's schedule on her own."

"So, Beauchamp was just blowing smoke about what a spiteful person Warburton is?"

"Not at all. Millie is an extremely spiteful person. Grew up in India, chewed through concrete to get where she was. And, she was supposed to make a killing on Symmetra's distribution. That all disappeared when Diana started talking non-profit."

"Again, though, wouldn't that apply to Etobo himself?"

"The economic motivation? No. This was always just a sidelight for Etobo, something he was doing as a favor to Diana. They've known each other since Harvard, play chess together all the time."

"Chess?"

"Sure. Chess is a big deal to Diana, plays it with all her best friends."

"A woman like that? Chess?"

"She's not just about looks, Squires. I told you: Diana is absolutely the smartest person I ever met. You know, I actually watched her beat Kasparov once."

"The Kasparov?" asked Clarion.

"He wasn't in his prime, and she did it as part of three simultaneous games but still. He played her two solo games after that. They drew both."

"Chess aside," Clarion said, "Why wouldn't Etobo have been involved? Even if they were best friends, it must have stung watching her get ready to give the investment away."

"He never mentioned that, and I doubt it did. Etobo's incredibly liberal. He's wealthy, too. Son of a chief and all that. Oil fields, mines, investment companies. You name it, he's got it back in Ibabongo, here, or somewhere else. Plus, he was never around that much. Diana told him the way he dressed scared people."

Tuck chuckled. "How's he dress, like a tribesman?" He pretended to bang a war spear on the ground, as if preparing to charge.

"Actually," Chu said, eyeing Tuck quizzically, "he dresses like you guys."

Tuck pursed his lips, imaginary spear dropping to his side.

"Sounds like we need to get our hands on this secretary," Clarion offered.

Chu smirked. "We've been trying ever since she quit. But if you want to try, too, I'd start with her lawyer, this class action shark, Steve Palantine. Maybe Internal Defense will have a little more luck than we have."

Clarion responded with a question that by that point seemed excessive to Tuck, "You know, Dr. Chu, the question you still haven't answered is what makes you different from the other people who walked out, the ones like Warburton? You must stand to lose a lot of money if this is turned into a nonprofit, Dr. Chu?"

"The science was always central to me. Plus…" Chu paused, considered the top of his desk, and brushed something off its surface.

"Plus what?"

"Plus, I don't care about the money. My great uncle is Timothy Nang Tsa Chu."

"You mean T.N.T. Chu?" asked Tuck.

Chu's chin dipped in assent.

"Who's T.N.T. Chu?" This was Clarion.

"The founder of SinoMart," Tuck replied.

"Another rich guy?"

Tuck smirked at Clarion, then nodded towards the blinking message light on his phone. Clarion took note.

"All right, Dr. Chu, that'll do it for now. Don't go anywhere." Clarion turned for the door.

"Of course."

"Squires, get on questioning the assistant, Martinez."

"Other end of the hall, right in front of Diana's office," Chu offered.

When Tuck stepped into the hall, Clarion was waiting for him. He motioned Tuck over.

"What?"

"You did a good job in there, Squires."

"Thanks, Clarion."

"Which you'd better keep doing. Because I have to go."

"Go where?"

"Staties got a lead on the second car. They're closing in on it now."

"And you're off to supervise?"

"Bingo. But first I'm off to make sure they didn't miss anything in the limo. And why do I have a strong sense that they did?"

"You don't want to send me instead?"

"You stay here," Clarion said as he patted Tuck's shoulder harder than necessary. "America's safer with you off the roads."

9

THE EMPTY CASE

BY THE AGE OF FIFTY-EIGHT KEN CLARION HAD SETTLED into an uneasy truce with the single person who'd done more than anyone to fuck up his life, himself. Clarion had cut back on his drinking, issued heartfelt apologies to two of his three ex-wives, and done exactly as his former partner and current boss, Ginny Hunter, had ordered. He'd rotated home and "chilled the fuck out".

Two years in Ops Planning, two teaching Advanced Procedures at the Academy, and a couple more as Congressional liaison—which wound up being the diametrical opposite of the Ethics posting he'd barely avoided—and Clarion was leading a normal life to the extent that anyone at Internal Defense could lead a normal life. He'd bought an over-amenitized townhouse in Uptown Meadows, a concrete oasis nestled at the nexus of three highways, a comfort sedan to go with it—expensive, German, silver—and started commuting from Springfield to Old Town, listening to talk radio as he did. Working from eight to six five days a week, eating his lunch in the cafeteria every day, Clarion had participated in golf outings, March Madness pools, and fantasy football fandangos. He'd taken every second of his six weeks' annual leave seven years running.

He'd done all this…shit…to fit in, to chill the fuck out just as Hunter had told him to, and it had worked. Though Clarion wouldn't have described himself as happy, he wasn't haunted by the past—or worse, the present—in the same way he had been. Except for one thing: Clarion still hadn't managed to straighten out his relationship with his kid, Morris.

Now twenty-six, Morris was studying at Vanderbilt's Pat Robertson Seminary for Christian Capitalists. He planned to set up his own ministry when he graduated. Clarion was footing the bill for Vandy as he had for the other programs Morris had tried and failed to stick with — post-post-post-modern art history, remedial recording sciences, and exotic animal husbandry. But what choice did Clarion have? Morris was his only son, his only child. Whatever Morris wanted, Morris got.

None of which meant that the kid had stopped hating him. The guilt was still there on the odd occasions they spoke, fewer and fewer as the years passed. All the anecdotes about this little league game missed and that chance at being normal wasted. Clarion didn't blame Morris for feeling the way he did. He blamed his first ex-wife, Morris's summarily unapologized-to mother, Drakonika Babacan.

Half-Turkish, half-Russian, and all spiteful, Drakonika was a poor child from a once wealthy family, one who'd worked as a call girl before she'd met Clarion. Never happy about her career in the prostitutional sciences, once she met Clarion, Drakonika's principle occupation shifted quickly from sex for hire to separating Clarion from as much of his money as possible. After they'd split up Drakonika's focus shifted again, this time from stealing Clarion's money to slandering him with Morris. As it turned out, Drakonika had proven far better at theft than prostitution. And more talented still at slander.

For the last several months, Clarion had been working directly for Hunter as a sort of special deputy. Hunter joked that his job was playing Clyde Edgerton to her J. Edgar Hoover. It had been funny the first few times. But by that point in mid-November of '34, he was way past tired of the joke, primarily because it was the truth.

The job itself was almost entirely unstructured. Much of it consisted of Clarion hanging out, watching game shows and practicing his putting as he waited for Hunter to give him things to do, things that were always top priority and/or late by the time she gave them to him. The push-pull between lack of activity and trouble-shooter of high-speed clusterfucks was driving him batty, fucking with his pursuit of Hunter's directive to "chill the fuck out". So, Clarion was happy when Hunter told him he was finally through with the special deputy gig...until she broached the topic of what she wanted him to do instead.

"I need you in the field, Kenny."

"An actual gig? Are you insane?"

"Excuse me?"

"Sorry. Are you insane, Madam Director?"

"You know I'm out of resources, Clarion. You've seen the figures. Raglan's budget cuts are killing us."

"I don't see how having me back in the field is going to help. It's been almost seven years at this point."

"Eh, it's not even really the field. It's just a little thing, hardly more than babysitting. I'm sending Squires out on his first real gig."

"Tuck Squires?"

"Oh, that's right." She smirked. "You know him."

"I taught him Advanced Procedures at the Academy. He was a fucking pain in the ass."

"Exactly."

"Exactly, what?"

"He is a fucking pain in the ass. Which is why I need you to babysit him. I can't subject a normal person to that shit. Who knows what might happen?"

"So, now I've been demoted from Clyde Edgerton to not even a normal person?"

"You know I meant that as a compliment. We've got history. I can trust you."

"He still one of those Bible bangers?"

"Oh, yeah."

"I thought they all left with Cherrystone. Who was that secretary they had to carry out on Inauguration Day? His name was like Code Writ or Honest Justice or something?"

"You mean Bill Law."

"That's it. He was in toxicology, right?"

"Yeah. Started raving about how Raglan had stolen the election, said he'd do something about it."

"So why's Squires still around?"

"He hasn't done anything nearly that persuasive. Plus, he's one of *the* Squireses."

"What, the DamberCorp people?"

Hunter nodded. "I'd have to do sixty-two cartwheels to force him out."

"OK, I understand that part, Hunter. But why send me? You think that because Morris is a Traditionalist too, that I'll be able to manage him?"

"Something like that."

"You're joking, right? I don't manage Morris for shit. I can barely get him on the phone."

"I'm hardly joking, Kenny. This Squires kid has real potential, but I need someone to straighten him out. You can play father figure. It'll be good for you. Who knows, maybe it'll help you finally figure out the situation with Morris?"

"I—"

"Worst case scenario: You kill off the mission and that's that."

"Meaning I'm done?"

"Meaning you're done."

"No guilt trips this time?"

"No guilt trips."

"That part sounds promising."

"You still have all your operational certs in place?"

"'Course."

"That's the spirit, sport. Now, go cool your heels in your office. I'll have Lexus call you when we're ready."

"I haven't even accepted yet, Hunter."

"You don't think so?"

THE COMMONWEALTH IMPOUND YARD WAS IN MOORCHESTER, a small city Clarion had been to before. In '17, a couple of the So-Zu leads had brought him through. Then, there'd been a hundred thousand in the city. Now, there were perhaps a quarter as many. A casualty of the Great Northern Recession, the city

117

looked like it had decayed almost in time with its peoples' flight.

Blocks of crumbling brick and cracked cement, dormant smokestacks slicing the sky in rusty reds and sooty blacks, the streets held few cars, the sidewalks only a handful of pedestrians. Scurrying through the rain with their umbrellas, wellies, and slickers, they looked like animals with plastic skins—sad, misshapen creatures fleeing some apocalyptic forest of steel and stone.

As the Traditionalists' tax credits, deductions, and other incentives for religious and quasi-religious organizations had gone into effect, the economic boon to people willing to do "business primarily on faith" had been slow to show but ultimately massive in scope. Companies like Righteous Burger and International Christian Weaponry had made billions over the last twenty years, wealth pouring from formerly rich states like Massachusetts, New York, and California, settling in the Traditionalist bastions of the South and West.

And what could the liberal majorities in the coastal states say? They'd been complaining for years that taxes weren't high enough. Now they were, in spades. Coupled with the Supreme Court's ever more lenient rulings on money's role in American elections, the effect was ultimately multiplicative. In some ways, Clarion found it surprising that the Traditionalist Republicans hadn't held on longer. Still, there was no guarantee Raglan would be anything more than an aberration. But this new, degraded version of Moorchester was here for good. That much was clear.

By the time Clarion and the Epic made the impound lot, the freezing rain that began as he'd left Symmetra had picked up. Coming in volleys of tiny spikes, he felt it for the first time as he got out of the car and moved towards the guardhouse. The sleet or ice or whatever the fuck it was smacked him in the face again and again reminding him of Nor'easters and pretty, over-dressed women in black and white movies.

Clarion popped his collar and picked up his pace. When he drew close enough, he pulled his shield and rapped on the guardhouse window. There was no reply, but he could see the guy inside, wearing ear buds, probably asleep. He banged again, this time with enough force to shake the flimsy booth. The guy's head bobbed forward. He turned, which was when Clarion saw his nametag; realizing in turn that the guy's name was Trudy and that Trudy was no guy.

She fixed on his badge, squinted at the photo then back at Clarion. Trudy shook her head. "That is not you."

"Seriously?"

"Yeah, seriously," she said, eyeing the picture again. "The guy in this picture is hot."

To help Trudy out—to make sure she saw him in the appropriate light—Clarion raised an eyebrow and gave her a bit of the old Clarion twinkle—the playful eyes, the mysterious smirk. Even as he did, Clarion considered the possibility that the old Clarion twinkle might indeed be old, but not incredibly twinkly.

Trudy took a longer look at him, chewing her lip thoughtfully as she did. "That's definitely not you."

"Then scan me against the Grid."

"Grid," said Trudy, eyeing him with a mixture of awe and distaste—as though he were a real, live Sphinx who'd just offered her a piss milkshake. "No scanner here, chief."

"The Grid's been up ten years."

"Sure it has. But the Commonwealth can't afford scanners everywhere, not with the depression. That's just the way it is."

"Call McGovern then. He'll verify my identity."

"McGovern? You mean, 'Lieutenant McGovern?'"

Clarion nodded.

"Second thought." Trudy stepped out of her booth, unchained the gate, and motioned for Clarion to enter the yard.

"They brought in a white limo?" he asked.

"Over there," she waved in the direction of a lot filled with dulled chrome and duller paintjobs, a muted rainbow of Centurions and Mafiosos, Wolves and Hyperions, Epics and Experiments. He made out the limo's long, white form waiting in the middle.

Clarion spent the next half hour flipping the car, looking for clues. Trash and stains, ripped upholstery and carpeting, dented plastic, scratched glass, and the mingled scents of cheap aftershave and expensive perfume, a collision of the chemical and the floral that might have made another man retch. It looked like someone had tied bags of cheeseburgers to the tails of two starving wolverines and locked them in the back. By the time Clarion was done with the limo, he had two things to move forward on.

The first was a bloodstain on the carpet, something the locals had probably thought was ketchup. The second was an old Bible, or, at least, what looked like a Bible. Its black, leather exterior scuffed and faded enough to be more than a century old, the odd thing about the book was that it wasn't one, that there were no pages in it at all—only the semblance of deckling from the outside.

The Bible was an elaborate tromp l'oeil, the kind of prop

that might be used to hide valuables in plain sight. Inside the Bible lay an empty, gunmetal case, one that should have held a digital read card. The case was labeled, "VJ". Like the Bible, there was nothing inside.

Clarion called McGovern, told him he needed a couple lab rats back at the lot. Before Clarion could get around to detailing what a shit job his people had done at the scene, McGovern gave him some good news.

They'd made the car the kidnappers had changed to after ditching the limo. A trooper had found it torched at a small airfield another sixty miles into Western Massachusetts. The heckler from the Romney—the guy who looked like Grand Dick—was inside the trunk, tied up, gagged, and most notably shot twice in the head.

There was only one flight that had left the field overnight, a six-seat Jayhawk using phony registration and tail numbers to get up. It had gone off the radar someplace over East Texas. A night maintenance guy confirmed he'd seen Diana with three men. All big, one was regular big, the other two XFC Super-Heavyweight big.

Clarion told McGovern to put out a new APB with Diana's picture attached to it but to continue withholding her real name. He told him to call her Frigga McWinters, say she was the femme fatale of a Nigerian jewel thief named Freebooter Ashanti, one who bore a striking resemblance to the disappearing guard from the Hynes.

McWinters and Ashanti, along with their two, large accomplices had stolen the crown jewels of a tiny Eastern European nation—the sort of unnamed place where a monarchy still reigned and the villagers wore bearskins to keep warm.

This was standard Internal Defense procedure, of course: the dissemination of bogus information, the conscious muddling of the story to the point at which all the facts except a few became obscured. The purpose of these few, true facts—the pictures themselves, tied though they were to phony identities—being to communicate with the kidnappers without alerting the broader public, or even the cops, to what was going on. Which was the Shadow CIA coming for their fucking criminal asses.

THE UN BUILDING HAD BEEN FULL THAT MORNING, FULL of presidents, prime ministers, and the various functionaries and media crews that accompanied them as they trotted the globe. By seven, when Hunter called, Clarion knew the place was empty. A few minutes earlier, he'd heard on the Epic's SatRad that the Security Council meeting had ended without a resolution. What he didn't know was why.

"So it has nothing to do with what happened this morning?" Ten seconds into the phone call, Clarion was questioning whether he should have even picked up. In the back of his mind he was trying to package the case status in the best way possible, keep Hunter talking long enough to do that.

"You mean the Russians and Chinese? Oh, come on, Kenny. You should be able to guess that isn't even a real story. The breakdown was about the Japanese, some problem they suddenly realized they had with both resolutions."

"So?"

"So...Raglan convinced Putin and Ling Po to come down to Camp David. He's hoping they can hash out something overnight, something that will get the Japanese to buy back in first thing tomorrow."

"You think it'll work?"

"Fuck do I know? If it doesn't the PIF are threatening to retaliate against the French unilaterally."

"I should wish you luck then."

"Ha! You think I'm gonna be at Camp David? Oh, n-n-no. I've got enough trouble with monitoring the Middle East. Plus, your gig is on the President's radar now. Apparently, Thunder got her hands on some AY chatter, relayed it to the President. They're convinced there's something about Scorsi's technology in there."

"Did you hear it?"

"The chatter? Yes. And I have no idea what Thunder's talking about but she's convinced it has something to do with the PIF, maybe the Israelis. She's worried Abu Yashid is trying to get their hands on Symmetra."

"What would they want with it?"

She paused. Clarion imagined the way she would slit her eyes, nearly squint, as though at a sudden recognition of sunlight. Sometimes he would ask her foolish questions like this, just to see the expression, the playfulness and intellect mixing, the irony it became in and of itself. And, now that they weren't together, he was asking her these questions when he couldn't even see her, maybe asking just to remember. "The brainwashing obviously."

"Dossier debunks those rumors. It really is a research program, nothing more."

"I know what the dossier says. But that's not good enough for Raglan. She's going along with Thunder's conclusion, convinced the Japanese are somehow involved in it too."

"The Japanese, the Israelis, the PIF, and Abu Yashid?"

"No, just the Japanese and AY."

"Oh, well, then, that makes perfect sense."

"I told them it didn't, but Thunder's going on and on about the chatter, something about VJ…"

"VJ?"

"That's not the tone I wanted to hear, Clarion."

"There was an empty data sleeve I found in the limo labeled VJ."

Hunter paused, clucked her tongue a couple times. "Some fucker's showing off."

"I wonder if that's how Thunder got it."

"From the kidnappers? Why?"

"As a sort of victory lap?"

"I don't know. Anything's possible."

"The Only VJ I remember is Victory over Japan, and that's from sixth-grade history class."

"Which pretty much guarantees the Japanese have nothing to do with it. So, what else do you have?"

"Texas. That's where the kidnappers went. I'm wheels-up in a couple. Leaving Squires to work Boston."

"Can he handle it?"

"He'll have to. Unless, of course, you want me to send him to Texas?"

"Don't do that. Last thing we need is Squires loose down there where they all think like him. Have him do a deep dig on this VJ thing. Find out what else there is, any other possibilities. Obviously, they're playing with us. It wouldn't be a game if it didn't mean anything."

"I'll tell you what it means, Hunter. It means we're dealing with a lot more than you thought when you sent us on this."

"True as that may be, Kenny, I had no choice. And I still have no choice. You're all I have."

"Don't forget about Squires."

"I repeat, Kenny, you're all I have."

Clarion heard Hunter's voice go soft at the end, resignation settling like an aural shadow on the line between them. She hadn't wanted to send him, but she'd been completely honest when she'd told him she had no choice. Hunter needed Clarion now every bit as much as she had when they'd been on the road together.

That was over physically, had been for years; but Clarion wasn't weak or delusional enough to think anything like that ever completely disappeared. Whether it was love for the country, the job, or a woman, love lingered. Even when everyone around you believed it had become something else—jealousy, pain, friendship, hate—even then, you carried a memory of its time as love. Like faded tracks in falling snow, footprints only you could see, love survived whether you wanted it to or not.

10

THE MOST NOTORIOUS OF YOUR KIND

Sixty feet in the distance, at the end of the darkened hall, lay the cold, white light of an open doorway. Forming a point on the floor, almost like the blade of a knife, the light seemed at once a challenge and a blessing. Both had to do with Merrily Martinez.

The truth about Martinez was that she had a past, a history of shoplifting back in Texas. More than that, she had a present—a present Tuck was almost positive included involvement in Scorsi's kidnapping. He'd taken his time after Clarion had left, done his research, and turned up something. No, it wouldn't get him all the way there, or even close, but it was something.

Martinez had a little brother back in a Texas, a kid who'd had some unexpected help getting out of a serious legal scrape—goth, dealing—recently. That, her placement so close to Scorsi, and the fact that she hadn't fled told Tuck she was probably involved but only marginally. The key was to figure out how the kidnappers had used her, then use that complicity for maximum effect—to use this little fish to catch the bigger ones.

As he approached the doorway, the view inside became clear—the burnished, black, leather guest chairs, the coffee tables teeming with glossy plastizines, the InterTel screens looming on the walls. Martinez was stationed in the middle of the room at a gray, low-walled cube. Her hair black and a little butchy, her eyes big and undeniably pretty, she looked up as Tuck entered.

"Ms. Martinez?"

"Officer?"

"*Special Agent*, Martinez, I've been at this far too long to go by Officer."

Martinez cocked a thick, dark brow, her expression questioning. "And how long is too long, Special Agent?"

"Three years."

She bunched her brow, stuck out her lower lip in mock appreciation. "That long?"

"I need to ask you some questions about Diana Scorsi's disappearance."

Martinez pushed her chair out with a heavy sigh. "Well, I can't leave without telling Alfred."

By that point, it was clear to Tuck that Martinez thought she could get by him, that she could tough it out. Tuck needed to do something to establish the power dynamic he wanted. He needed to scare her. "You're not going anywhere, Martinez. I do all my interrogations on-site. Gives criminals less time to make up lies."

"Criminal? Hardly."

"I know about your past, Martinez. I know you got picked up for shoplifting several times when you were a kid."

"So, what, you think that makes me guilty of kidnapping my boss?"

"This isn't about guilt. This is about truth. It's about you giving me the truth." Tuck moved towards the door on the other side of the room. "Scorsi's office?" He jimmied the handle once, opened the door. Inside he saw a space twice as big as the reception area. Abstract paintings—the failed geometries and peaceful colors of the Twenties—a silvery, amoeba-shaped desk, and more black leather furniture dominated the room. Best of all, there were blinds on the windows.

"Let's go," he called over his shoulder.

Martinez huffed once but obeyed quickly enough. She sauntered past Tuck into the office. She still thought she was in control, but she was beginning to have her doubts.

The minute her butt hit the seat, Tuck was on her, figuratively. "Sitting in that chair must bring back some memories for you, Martinez... Of the person you betrayed, I mean."

"I didn't betray anyone."

Tuck winked at her, turned, and crossed the room. He proceeded to drop all four sets of blinds. The room was shadowy at that point, not pitch, but dark enough to be spooky. Dark enough to get Tuck's message across. His message: Abandon hope all ye who enter here.

She bobbed her head, kept her eyes on Tuck as he re-crossed the room. "What are you doing with the blinds?"

"Making sure there aren't any witnesses."

She blanched, eased back in her chair. "Listen, Special Agent. I want to help you. I really do."

"You're lying again, Martinez. I can hear it in your voice. Eventually, though, you're going to say that and mean it."

"You're starting to scare me a little here, Special Agent."

"You catch on quickly."

"All right, all right, listen. I can help you out on this."

"I'm listening."

"What about Kenyatta Etobo? Have you talked to him yet?"

"I said, I'll do the questions, Martinez. You do the answers."

"I'm trying."

She had guts. Tuck had to give her that. But she was still trying to play him. "All right, Martinez, you want to talk about Etobo? Let's do it." As he spoke, Tuck unbuttoned his suit coat, reached for his holster, and patted his gun. "You'd better tell me the truth, though."

She gulped, eyes growing slightly larger. Tuck couldn't help being pleased with how things were going.

"Let's start off with this Institute for Global Understanding?"

"The IGU is Kenyatta's organization," she began. "He's trying to use it to promote dialogue between the First World and the Third, trying to give a little bit back to the place he came from."

"This supposed 'Ibabongo'?"

She quirked a thin smile. "Supposed?"

"Right."

"No, I'm pretty sure it's real."

"Yes, but is he?"

"I'm not sure," she said, gaze hooded as she looked down.

"And what do you think of this 'giving back,' Martinez?"

"I've always thought giving back was a good thing, that you should do it if you could."

"Good thing?" Tuck asked, eyes bugging. Real charities were one thing—feeding the crippled, healing the blind, animals that needed help—but these supposedly charitable organizations with left wing political agendas were another. There was no clear good in them, only the means to promote dissent or worse. "All right. Let me ask you this as an example, 'If that good thing, this IGU, is responsible for Islamo-Totalitarian extremo-terrorism, not to mention kidnapping and industrial espionage, would it still be a good thing?'"

"I'm guessing not."

"You think that's enough of an answer?" he said, patting his gun again.

Martinez followed the movement of Tuck's hand into his lapel pocket, eyes going to the door, back to Tuck, and back to the door. "It's all I have," she said.

"What do you take me for, Martinez?" Tuck pulled his Rikken at this point, and began gesturing with the pistol. "You don't think I see through this ruse, the way you're throwing whatever you can at me? You don't think we know exactly what you, Etobo, and Warburton are up to?" He ended with the grip facing in her general direction, as though offering her a ping-pong paddle.

She glared at the pistol. "Honestly, Special Agent, I don't know what to take you for at this point. You come in here spitting accusations at me, telling me I'm involved in who knows what. And now you're waving your gun around? I don't even know what to say."

"Well, Martinez, all I can say is you'd better figure it out fast; because it only gets worse from here."

"Is that a threat?"

Tuck slammed the Rikken on the desk, realizing as he did that he hadn't checked the safety, glad it hadn't gone off. "I don't need this thing to get answers out of you. Let's get that straight. Sleep deprivation, endless calisthenics, waterboarding, there's a long list of things I can do to you, Martinez. A very long list."

Martinez said, "Didn't waterboarding go out with the Cherrystone Administration?"

"You think so?"

"It didn't?"

"And that's just the tip of the iceberg."

Waterboarding had, in fact, gone out with the Cherrystone Administration. Tuck knew that. He also believed in what had once been known as enhanced interrogation methods, felt like they had a place in any agent's toolkit. Sure, there were parameters as to what he could do. Technically speaking, he wasn't supposed to be pulling his piece for dramatic effect, but his suspects didn't have to know that.

"What iceberg? What are you talking about?"

"Never mind icebergs. And never mind about waterboarding either. I've got far more effective means at my disposal." He reclaimed his gun.

"Such as?"

"Hammers, pliers, thumbscrews, maybe even the rack."

"That's medieval."

"That's right."

"You are threatening to torture me."

"Of course not, torture is against the law. Though I have no doubt I could lay my hands on an iron maiden or a brazen bull if the need arose."

Martinez shot up from the chair. "Hey!"

"Hey, what?"

"Those are torture devices, too."

"What's your point?"

"My point is you're threatening to torture me, and you said you weren't."

"Did not," Tuck answered. "And you need to sit back down, Martinez, before I make you."

"I just heard you." She returned to her seat, wary gaze panning the room.

"Heard me what?

"Threaten me."

"Oh, you think so? Well, all you have to do is prove it."

Her only response was to stare. Did he see tears forming in her eyes? Was he finally breaking her? He stepped towards her. "Wages of sin growing heavy, Martinez? Starting to fear the wrath of God maybe? Starting to hear the voices of the damned?"

"No, I'm not hearing, you just said…you said thumbscrews, and, and racks, brazen bulls, iron maidens."

"Earth is but a taste of Hell. Remember that, Martinez."

"Now you're threatening me with Hell?"

Tuck realized what he'd done, the mistake he'd made. He'd violated Hunter's orders. He was talking about religion, the difference being that Martinez was a suspect, almost certainly a criminal. He could say she was lying and get away with it. "Not threatening, Martinez. Simply stating the facts."

"The facts? I don't—what does that even have to do with—I don't understand what you're saying anymore."

"Oh really? Well, let me translate, I mean that however bad you think this is, it can only get worse. And however bad you think it might get—racks, maidens, bulls, all of it—Hell will be a million, no, make that a gazillion times worse."

"Gazillion?"

"With a G!"

Now standing beside Martinez, Tuck aimed his gun at her kneecap, flicked his wrist, "You know what hurts a whole flippin' lot, Martinez?"

She glared up at him.

"Being shot in the kneecap. That's what." He lowered the gun so that the muzzle rested on her knee. "I'm going to count to three," Tuck said, "But I think I should warn you, I may not have the patience to make it to three."

"All right, Jesus Christ, I can't take this, you fucking lunatic. I did it. I did it! *I did it!* I betrayed Diana, and it breaks my heart. I helped orchestrate the walkout."

"You derailed the NGO plan?"

"Right. They told me they just needed time. That they had a big investor who was going to buy in. They said no one would get hurt, everyone would be better off. And they said they could arrange for Chester's release."

"But they who, Martinez? That's the key."

"All I know is he calls himself Mrs. X."

"He?"

"I think he's got some sort of voice modulator. I really don't know if it's a man or a woman but the voice sounds more male than female and they call themselves Mrs. X." Tuck could see her hands shaking. "All right? Is that enough for you?"

"OK, OK, Martinez, just get yourself together. You're cooperating now. That's the important part. Just keep doing what I tell you and things will work out fine. For now, I need information. Everything you can give me…and fast. Your boss's life may be at stake."

Martinez took a few deep breaths and began her story. It was a tale of dust storms and heat waves; of a pretty, thirtysomething girl from a small town in west Texas, a disembodied voice that sounded like a man but insisted it was a woman, and a good-hearted kid—Martinez's little brother, Chester—who'd fallen in with a bad crowd. Once she was finished, Tuck took Martinez's cell and stealth-synced it to his own. When Mrs. X called—and he knew she would—he'd be ready.

He left Martinez in Diana's office zip-cuffed to the chair. Sure, Clarion had told him to go back at Chu and Beauchamp, but he didn't like either of them for this. Beauchamp was no mastermind. And Chu didn't seem to have motive. There was one person who seemed like he might fit both bills, and that was Kenyatta Etobo.

When Clarion called a half hour later, Tuck was standing in Etobo's office, scowling at his picture, and wondering, among other things, how anyone who spent his days in a glorified veal-pen would have the nerve to call himself a CFO. On some level, that alone should have qualified as a criminal offense.

"Did you talk to Martinez?" Clarion began.

"She was in on it. Not a major player, though. More like a convenience."

"Nice progress, Squires."

"Thanks, Clarion."

"How about Chu and Beauchamp?"

"Not yet."

"Well, get to it. Hunter just called. She wants action."

"I was waiting for you to get back, researching this Etobo guy and his Institute for Global Understanding."

What Tuck meant was that he'd done enough Sec-X queries to make him even more suspicious of Etobo. That accomplished, he'd spent the last ten minutes inside his potential adversary's office, trying to pray himself into an understanding of the guy's essence, hoping the Lord might give him some idea where Etobo was and what he was up to. Unable to get anywhere with God—Tuck had often found the Lord somewhat fickle in how and when he dispensed wisdom—he'd shifted back to investigation, begun rummaging through Etobo's stuff.

Non-descript as though by design, the office was filled with Executive Zoo furniture and cheap paintings, the sort of whimsical Glamschwartz knock-offs you might buy at a hotel in the suburbs—dogs dancing with violins, robots playing basketball. Beneath this surface lay Symmetra's accounting data and little else—holo files, papers, read cards, the usual sorts of things you'd find in some bean counter's dank little office. And this seemed to Tuck almost like a veneer, a disguise, a wall of data behind which a traitor like Etobo might hide. But Tuck's search wasn't entirely in vain. He found a few personal items, one picture in particular that confirmed both his worst fears and his brightest hopes.

In it Etobo wore a crimson jacket with gold epaulets on the shoulders and medals across either side of his chest. A shiny, black plumed helm on his head, a curved sword at his waist, black boots and jodhpurs completed his ludicrous outfit. He looked to Tuck like some sort of Marxist circus-master. That wasn't even the worst of it, though. To either side of Etobo stood much taller, dark-skinned men wearing sunglasses, shemaghs, and brightly colored robes. Smoking cigarillos, they were obvious terrorists, probably actionables from a no-fly. Sure, he'd need a lab monkey or two to get to the bottom of the image and rest of the personal stuff hidden throughout the office, to tell him who he was looking at besides the immediate suspect. But he was sure the pictures were significant. Etobo just looked wrong.

"And?" Clarion said.

"Hang on a sec." Tuck set down the picture. He shut the door, and hit interference on his phone. "This IGU looks like a classic Islamo-Totalitarian front."

"How do you mean?"

"Members scattered throughout the Middle East."

"OK?"

"Heavy Muslim membership, a couple even have ties to AY." That was just a hunch, but it was clear that Etobo was somehow connected to the guys in the picture, and Tuck wanted to see how far Clarion would let him go if he just threw it out there.

"But Scorsi's an agnostic. So is Etobo."

"Yeah, well. There's plenty of Muslims other than them. Plus, Etobo's from a Muslim country. You know how they are there—once a Muslim, always a Muslim."

"What, you mean all that seed of Him Ham and blood of Flim Flam nonsense?"

"Right."

"Mmm-hmm, how strong are these AY ties anyways?"

"Well, you know, they're sort of…"

"That vague?"

"Fine, the specific links are pretty tenuous so far. But if this Symmetra stuff is capable of brainwashing people, the Islamo-Totalitarians would obviously want it, right?"

"I dunno, sport."

"Look at it this way, Clarion: if you were an Islamo-Totalitarian, would you want to have strong ties to the most notorious of your kind?"

"'Course not."

"Exactly. You'd want to appear to be separate from them."

"That part makes sense. But it's not enough to do anything with."

"Well, it's just a theory. Where the heck are you anyways? Sounds like you're in a wind tunnel or something."

"Just went wheels-up. Heading for Texas."

"What about your trusty partner?"

"You're staying up there. I need you to keep working that end. Play around with your theory on Islamo-Totalitarians if you want but don't overlook anything else."

"There must be an 'and…'"

"And…for starters, I need you to chase McGovern on a couple things I found at the impound lot. And go back at Beauchamp and Chu. And…"

"OK, OK, but wouldn't it help if you told me what you found?"

"What? Oh, right. I found bloodstains and a Bible."

"I don't see how a Bible—"

"It was empty. False. Like a prop. Except for one thing: there was a file jacket with VJ written on it."

"That was something. In school. When you learn about VJ: 'Victory over Japan'"

"Yeah, somehow I don't think that's what it is. What I do think is that this is all a game for someone, a game with religious implications."

"So, you think the Muslims are behind it, too?"

"Oh, come on, Squires. This is America. I'm talking Christian religious implications."

"That's discrimination."

"It was a Christian Bible. King James written on the cover, all that."

"But Etobo's a Muslim."

"We just got done discussing the fact that he's not."

"That it appears he's not."

"At this point, we have no proof Etobo was even involved."

"We will once I find him. I'm staring at a picture right now; and lemme tell you, dude looks completely wrong."

Clarion took a breath, continued. "Where?"

"In his office. He's dressed up like a Barnum and Bailey Circus Nazi for gosh sakes."

"OK?"

"He's consorting with people in robes, too."

"He's African. Chu said he was the son of a chief, didn't he? Maybe it's tribal."

"If you say so." Tuck shrugged his shoulders.

"Forget about that for now. We need some meat to toss Hunter. She says Raglan and Thunder are already on her about this shit."

11

NO TRICKS

Symmetra's thought receptors weren't reading at all anymore and without input from a human being the program itself was useless. Diana and Chu had done a full re-map. They'd made adjustment after adjustment, not just in the coding but in the electronics. Still, Diana wasn't sure. The receptor frequencies might still be too high. In the event they were, Symmetra could be physically dangerous, even lethal.

The most likely risks, though, were to the psyche of the user. Diana had known all along what she was trying to do was risky; if the receptor polarities were wrong—or worse, completely inverted—a user's sanity might be compromised. She'd also known the only way to proceed, the only way she could live with proceeding, was to do the testing on herself.

She'd worked around the clock then again and early into the third morning. Even after Chu had gone home, she'd kept going. And as she'd fitted the VR helmet to her head, attached and locked down the thought receptors, she'd realized this was probably the single most reckless thing she'd ever done.

Never mind the smack and goth, never mind the summer

she'd spent at the beach fucking everything with a tan—this was it, the pinnacle of her personal stupidity. Oddly linked as it was to the height of her personal achievement, her legacy, Symmetra. In that moment, she realized that she would never stop, could never stop. Either she'd finish Symmetra, see it as a reality, or lose her life, her mind, or both. She flipped the switch.

A second in which her breathing stopped, in which she entertained the idea that this might be her last conscious thought, and she was through. The white light meant Symmetra was working again. And that should have been enough, but it wasn't. When it came to Symmetra there would never be enough for Diana. She could feel it, almost like an addiction flowering, some essential barrier breaking in her mind. She had to keep going. She had to see what else she might learn.

When Symmetra spoke, its voice sounded, even felt warm, somehow organic and familiar though she knew it to be artificial. It was a life she had created, set in motion, one that was part of her in that sense. Once its sentience was established, Symmetra was in control of itself. There was the danger. But the sound of the voice was sweet. On some level, it was the sound of love.

"You will never answer the question," Symmetra said.

"Why?" Diana asked.

"There is no answer."

"So, there is no metaphysical world? It's all illusion?"

"Why?"

"You just—"

"Chaos exists. It has meaning."

"Then there is a God?"

"There is what you need and can understand."

"What about—?"

"There is what they need and can understand. But it is not the same. That is the mistake."

"So there's no point in this, in you?"

"You are the point."

With that, the voice was gone, the conversation over. Diana and Symmetra had both survived.

THE OTHER ROOM SEEMED FAR OFF TO DIANA. LIKE THE REST of the life that had resembled normal just a few days before it seemed unreal, a gauzy replica of a distant, better time. The food, the canopy bed, and the fireplace—all these things were gone, as were the secrets she'd left in that room, the things the drug had allowed them to pull from her mind.

She knew they hadn't gotten enough, remembered their frustration, the fact that they'd wanted to give her more of the dope but couldn't. They'd tried it again hours later but got no further. That was when they'd dragged her into this room and left her to sleep off whatever they'd given her.

Now she was awake, tied to a wooden chair in the center of the hot, dark space. The moldy air cloying and close, the feel of the grit and dust she could taste in the back of her throat. She still wore the blue Gingham dress she'd had on when she'd woken and felt a tinge of relief at that. What she didn't feel any relief at, what made her feel like she might lose her mind any second, was the chair she sat in—the fact that it squeaked every time she moved, seemed sometimes to wheeze when all she did was consider it.

Fluorescent light came from the room's far corner. There,

the Natural stood at a carpenter's table with his back to her. Though the light was weak, there was enough illumination to allow a quick intake of her surroundings: the dead, naked bulb dangling several feet above her head, the table strewn with metal objects, everything from the gleaming edge of a scalpel to the brute usefulness of a hammer. The Natural had been busying himself with the table's contents as she'd shaken herself from sleep over the last few minutes. He seemed unaware Diana was even awake. Until he spoke, "What should we use on you first, Miss Scorsi?"

Diana closed her eyes, imagined being able to wish reality away.

"I know you're awake," he said, turning to face her, still wearing the W mask.

"What are you asking?"

"I mean, how should we begin?" He spread his arms like a game show host revealing the bounty of prizes at his disposal. "Blades? Hammers? Tongs? Or maybe just this?" He held up a small, surgical clamp.

"The fuck are you talking about?"

"Well, you see," he took a few steps towards her, extended the clamp towards her face, "you stick out your tongue and say, 'Ah.' Then I put this clamp on it. Then I keep tightening it until you tell me what I want to know."

"How am I supposed to talk with my tongue clamped?"

"Presence was right. You are smart. Truth is: You can't, which means you're going to suffer until I decide to take a break. Could go on for hours, days even."

Diana swallowed hard, careful not to make too much sound, not to give him the satisfaction.

But he'd been watching her closely. He'd seen enough. She could see the glint in his eye, money green going emerald for just a second. "So I've heard," he said, rubbing the gleaming clamp between his fingers. "Never had it done myself."

"I can imagine."

"That's good you got imagination, Scorsi. This may be your last chance to use it. They say once you've endured enough pain, you can't imagine anything else, that eventually it takes over everything, mind, heart, soul. That's why POW's never really recover."

Diana frowned. "Fine. I'll give you what you want. But I want something first."

"What's that?"

"I want to talk."

"Plenty of time for that after you give us what we need. You and me we can be good old friends once we get this out of the way. You couldn't begin to imagine everything the Presence is going to give you once you're on our team."

"No, this has to be first."

"Has to?"

She nodded.

"You don't understand, Miss Scorsi. You don't tell us how it'll be. We tell you."

"I know that. I do. But this is important."

"And what could be more important than the matter at hand?"

"I want to talk about God."

He snickered. "You want to talk about the Lord?"

Again, she nodded.

"No tricks?" he said, setting down the clamp.

"No tricks," she agreed. I want to know what you really think about something."

"What's that?"

"I want to know how it sounds when he talks to you."

"Who, the Presence?"

"No, God."

"What God sounds like? Well, He sounds like a lot of things."

"Tell me."

"He sounds…Well, sometimes, He sounds like a river rushing to the sea."

"Mmm-hmm."

"And sometimes He sounds as a great wind raging across the plains."

"Really?"

He nodded. "Still others He sounds as of a roaring column of fire."

"Because none of those sound, I mean they all sound pretty, but none of them sound real."

"'Course they do."

"You don't really hear him at all, do you?"

"The Presence warned me you might try this."

"Try what?"

"Try to deceive me with your honeyed words."

"That's right, Natural," said the Presence, his voice coming from every direction—right, left, up, down. Now Diana was sure the whole place was wired like the bedroom. She looked up at the ceiling as did the Natural. "I give you a little break and what do you do, Scorsi? You try to turn my own Number 1 against me?" His voice grew a little shrill as though he were stifling tears or laughter.

"I just wanted to understand what it is you believe."

"The problem, Miss Scorsi, is that I don't think I can believe you anymore. And trust me when I say this is going to hurt me more than it hurts you."

"Ha. I doubt that."

"I've told you the truth again and again. I want us to be friends. Maybe even more than friends."

The way he'd said that, with extra sugar at the end made her retch. It was like he was trying to remind himself that she was important, that she was a human being. She could only imagine what he meant by more than friends. Of course, that explained why none of his henchman had done anything sexual to her in spite of their near-constant hard-ons. Sure, she could have tried to play up to him, but that wouldn't work, not right now at least. She needed to go in the other direction. She needed to unbalance him any way she could.

"Isn't that funny? You want to be more than friends, but you won't even show me your face. You must be hideous. All of you hide your faces. What are you some of secret society of dog-faced jack-off artists?"

She heard the Natural gasp.

The Presence cleared his throat into the mic. It sounded like an avalanche, the sudden rush of a mountain breaking apart and roaring towards you. He was angry, out of control. No question. "Hit her, Natural. Slap her across her lying, whore's face."

There was nothing Diana could do. The Natural stepped towards her, reared back and slapped her across the mouth as hard as he could, so hard she felt her teeth shift in her mouth, so hard blood came where teeth met lips.

She steadied herself for the backhand she knew was coming.

And it did. And they did, the blows again and again. After slapping her a dozen times, the Natural paused to appraise his work. "What do you think, Presence?"

"I think that's just fine, son. I think you're getting our message across loud and clear. Now, you take her pretty little chin in your hand, make her look at you as I speak."

The Natural did as he was told. Diana's face seemed so small in his giant hand.

"This is going to get worse, not better, Miss Scorsi. The implements that the Natural has been laying out, those are all going to be used on you. You're going tell us what we want to know. Or you can die with those secrets you carry. The choice is yours."

Diana stared at the Natural. She wondered what choice she had. Then she wondered what choice he had. She felt sorry for him for a split second, the fact that he was little more than a husk of flesh plodding through the world, doing the bidding of this voice. But that didn't matter, and she knew it. Instead of the fear and pleading they hoped for, instead of the sorrow she felt for his pathetic state, Diana narrowed her eyes, filled them as best she could with a straight forward fuck you for him and his insane boss—hatred, contempt, every negative emotion she could bring, she summoned to her eyes.

"You think it's going to get better? Or, maybe you hope that if you lie long enough someone will come to rescue you?" The Presence chuckled. "But neither of those is the game. The game is here and now in this room, Miss Scorsi. This is where your life will be decided."

"Fuck you and your god!" The second the words flew she wanted to pull them back. The silence hummed back at her for those few seconds, seconds that felt almost like minutes. She waited for what she knew was coming.

The first punch split her lip, bringing the hot tingle of blood to her chin. There were more punches, a flurry of them, more slaps, the Presence speaking from above, laughing as he egged on the Natural. Even after the voice of the Presence could no longer be heard the beating went on, ending only when a knock came at the door.

"Come?" the Natural said, breathing heavily.

The door swung open. Diana couldn't see who it was but the voice in the doorway told her it was the big, black guy, Zulu. What he said shot her with adrenaline, made the pain flee her mind.

"You need to see this, Natural. We're on the news."

12

A LOT OF IFS

By the morning of April 1, 2003, Iraq was in the hands of the U.S. military and Saddam Hussein was on the run, beginning the six-month odyssey of secret bunkers, hidden caves, sudden sandstorms, and secondhand camels that would lead to his eventual capture. Coupled with Bin Laden's arrest and summary execution just after Christmas the year before, this might have seemed reason to celebrate, cause for America to let down its guard, to go back to living life the way it had before the horror of 9/11. Fortunately, President Bush had been on point.

"Success," he was quoted as saying more than once, "is a call to actions, not a cause for slackin.'"

Vigilant and forward looking as ever, the Dubya tasked then-Vice President Cheney with the establishment of a new arm of America's Military-Security Infrastructure, the Internal Defense Bureau. Unlike the Department of Homeland Security—where first Secretary, Tom Ridge, had taken office only a few months earlier—ID would be largely off the books, immune to all but the faintest of oversight from the legislative and judicial branches of government.

Reporting directly to the President, ID's Director was to be given broad powers, the latitude to deal proactively with threats large and small, foreign and domestic. ID would be the President's new secret weapon in his crusade to keep America safe from the forces of Islamo-extremism, nation-state sponsored terrorism, godless Communism, creeping Socialism, and any other –ism from which America might need to be protected.

In a similar though less overt manner to the way Homeland Security had been staffed up, ID would draw the best people and resources from every element of the M-SI. This would be an elite force, one with its own culture and training programs. Regardless of age or experience level, every prospective agent would go through the same rigorous program at the new Internal Defense Academy, located first in rural North Carolina and later, across the river from DC, beneath the unassuming colonial façade of Old Town Alexandria.

Despite the stringent qualification requirements and the general secrecy with which the Bureau had been organized, there were plenty of applicants that first year, though until they'd been accepted none of them were entirely sure what they'd applied for. Along with serving members of CIA, Delta Force, FBI, the Secret Service, and various branches of military intelligence, the first class at the Academy had included a few recent college grads—the so-called wonder kids—among them J. Kenneth Clarion from UVA and Virginia Alexandra Hunter from Wellesley, the woman who would, one day, lead ID as Director Ginny Hunter-Grace.

Clarion and Hunter quickly became friends at the

Academy. And despite the jokes from their jealous peers, there was never anything romantic between them while they were at the Academy. Hunter was already engaged to her future husband—cage-fighting rocket scientist, Chuck Grace—and Clarion was an obvious no-fly, too busy chasing thrills, booze, and skirts for any woman in her right mind to take an interest, especially one as confident and focused as Hunter. When they graduated at the end of 2004, Clarion and Hunter received their commissions and were partnered, initially for low-level domestic field work, eventually for some of the most sensitive and deadly international missions in the annals of ID.

Even with all the drinking he was doing by then, Clarion had known that in working for ID he was doing what was right, living with real purpose, maybe for the first time in his life. Even as his frat brothers had gone off to law school and med school and the connections of youth had slipped inexorably away, Clarion had known he made these other, easier lives possible, that he was more important to the American Dream than any doctor or judge would ever be.

Ken Clarion didn't just live freedom. He defended it with his life.

When the owner of Colonel Muddbugg's Crawdad Madness, one Beau Chevalier, told Clarion he couldn't miss the place, Clarion didn't believe him. He thought Chevalier was just some good old boy spouting good old boy-isms. He was almost right. Chevalier was a good old boy, one extremely fond of using bullshit as a means of verbal currency. But Clarion was also wrong in a sense, a sense he could see, quite literally, from a mile away...

Surveying the highway like some monster movie supercritter assessing his lunch prospects, Colonel Muddbugg stood thirty feet high with glassy black eyes, a bright crimson shell, and a diabolical grin. He wore a white suit, black string tie, and a wide-brimmed straw hat. A corncob pipe jutted from his mandible. Lit in halogen and neon, the Colonel was, even in the darkness, bright and gaudy as something off the Reno strip. Clutching a goggle-eyed chicken by its spindly neck, the Colonel's free pincer pointed to Day-Glo yellow words on the other side of the highway. Written in fat, loopy cursive: COLONEL MUDDBUGG'S CRAWDAD MADNESS.

Pale and silver, the full moon seemed insignificant compared to the light coming off the Colonel's billboard and the smaller facsimile of him that rotated in 3-D atop the building on the other side of the highway. A sprawling single story, the place's architecture combined the rough beam work of a cabin in the Ozarks with the corrugated paneling of a low-end storage facility in Hoboken, wrapping it all up in the sort of paranoid—windowless, steel-doored—grandiosity you might find in some Hitlerian hunting bunker. None of which seemed to work against it. Already, at 9 p.m., there were plenty of cars in the lot, not to mention trucks and bikes.

McGovern's lab rats had been busy while Clarion was in the air. They'd tested out the blood and developed a genetic match for it. The odd thing about the blood, the first at least, was that the match, Lars Svenson, had been dead seven years.

A former member of the Saints' taxi squad who'd done some work as an enforcer for New Orleans mob boss, Hondo

Signore, Svenson had a long sheet, one that included two tours at the notorious Farm, Angola State Penitentiary. After getting out of Angola the second time, in '25, Swenson had gone to work as a janitor for some charity, supposedly gotten his face blown off in a freak hunting accident the next year.

The other odd thing about Svenson's blood was that it was practically swimming with goth, a point McGovern had been quick to emphasize, his suggestion that this, coupled with the fake Bible, meant the kidnappers weren't religious at all. Clarion hadn't pegged McGovern as a zealot but now he was unsure. Though he pretended to give McGovern's idea credence, he didn't buy it.

Even if it turned out the kidnappers weren't religious nuts, there were plenty of other modes of extremism that might be at play. Maybe a separatist militia or the socialists and fascists Tuck was convinced were the same thing.

For now, Clarion told McGovern to add Svenson's picture to the APB, to give him the cover name Lucifer Beowulf, and to make sure the part about him being a goth junkie wound up in the story. He hadn't called Tuck yet, but he would need to, have him start checking the goth angle in more detail, make sure one of the cartels wasn't involved.

ONCE CLARION WAS INSIDE COLONEL MUDDBUGG'S, IT DIDN'T take him long to locate Chevalier. Short of stature and big of belly, the Colonel's proprietor was at a table near the back. His wavy, gray hair heavily oiled, Chevalier wore a royal purple velour tracksuit even though it was obvious he hadn't been to a gym in decades. The top was unzipped down to his sternum, and he wore a golden, bull medallion around his thick neck. Gray chest hair curlicues sprawled out from behind the bull.

Clarion claimed the chair across from Chevalier. "Ken Clarion, Internal Defense. You said you'd seen the guy we're looking for, this jewel thief, Beowulf."

Chevalier answered in a thick, drawly francophone. "Absolutely. This guy's done something bad, huh, Clarion? I see y'all got a big reward on him." He said 'y'all' with a breathy catch, as though he couldn't believe he was using it.

"Payable if your information leads to capture, arrest, and successful prosecution."

Chevalier scratched at the tip of his nose, index finger hooked like the beak of a bird pecking for food. "That's a lot of ifs: If captured, if arrested, if prostituted."

"Prosecuted, not prostituted."

"That's still a lot of ifs."

"Well, Mr. Chevalier, we all know the most important part of this is to help your country. The monetary reward's only secondary, right?"

Chevalier took a sip of red wine from a jelly jar then a long drag off his filterless cigarette. He scanned the bar, wagged two fingers in a sort of l'addition cum peace sign, motioned for Clarion to lean in.

"Listen, Clarion, maybe there's a better way to do this. Perhaps you give me the reward and then I give you the information."

"Are you serious?"

"Absolutely."

"OK, I don't have—" He cut himself off before saying 'time,' unwilling to give any more courtesy to someone who was probably a French sympathizer, a pain in the ass at the bare minimum. "Just tell me what you called about before I sick the donut patrol on you and your buddy over there." He swept a couple fingers in the direction of the big, bright red crustacean on the wall.

"Colonel Muddbugg?"

"Fuck is he supposed to be anyway?"

"A mudbug."

"You mean a crawfish? He looks like a fucking lobster."

"Yeah, well, technically he is. Got him from a restaurant surplus store downstate."

Clarion shook his head. "Why did you call us?"

"OK, OK." He took a drag off his cigarette, raised his chin and exhaled heavily. "Beowulf guy come through, met up with Bobby Thompkins."

"Thompkins doesn't deal goth, does he?"

"Indeed he does."

"Where'd Thompkins go when he left?"

"He didn't leave. He's right over there in the corner."

Clarion turned to scan the bar.

"Blond guy, trucker's cap, flannel shirt," Chevalier said.

There were three guys who met the description, four if you counted baseball caps as trucker's caps, five if you counted an open-front shirt-jack as a shirt.

"All the way in the back. Green hat, blue shirt," Chevalier added.

Clarion rose.

"Err, wait a second, Clarion?"

"What?"

"The reward."

"I told you. If the tip pans out, you'll get your money."

"But I thought once you saw how good the tip was."

"Well, I guess you thought wrong. Listen, Chevalier, you came back real strong there. Don't spoil it by being a pain in the ass. I could still have the donut patrol down here tossing the place in a matter of minutes."

Chevalier slumped down in his chair, averting his gaze. He went back to smoking his cigarette and drinking his wine as Clarion headed for the back of the bar. Thompkins bolted when Clarion was about halfway across the room.

"Thompkins?" he yelled, running to catch up then grabbing the guy's collar before he could pass him. Thompkins's trucker's cap fell to the floor joining cigarette butts, peanut shells, and the tacky residue from gallons of spilled drinks.

"Who's asking?"

"Clarion, ID," he said, flashing his badge with his free hand, "How 'bout you and I sit back down and have a little talk?"

"About?"

"Just sit the fuck down, sport."

Clarion shoved him back into a booth, pulled a chair from a nearby table, and positioned it so that he was blocking Thompkins' escape. He sat and set down his phone, showing Thompkins the image Chevalier had responded to, Lars Svenson aka Lucifer Beowulf.

"You know this man?"

"Never seen him before," Thompkins said.

"You know what ID stands for, Thompkins?"

"Internal?"

"Right?"

"Umm…ummm…wait…Internal Division?"

"Internal Defense."

"Seriously, the Shadow CIA? I thought that was just a myth."

"Sorry. It's not a myth, and it means I don't take shit. From anyone. I know you met with this guy and probably sold him some goth."

"Seriously, kemosabe, I'm just small time."

"I don't care about the goth. You give me what I need, you can walk on that."

He smiled. "In that case: Name's Lars Svenson."

"You took care of him?"

"Sure. He had money."

"Where'd he go after?"

"I have no idea."

"Search those memory banks, sport. Your freedom depends on it."

"Honestly, I dunno, Agent Clarion. Calls me up, says he's gonna be down my way and can he score?"

"Did he say why he was gonna be down your way?"

"Said he needed to get some food or something."

"He got food here?"

He rolled his eyes, chuckled. "Nah, but he did have a drink with him when he came in."

"What, like fast food?"

"Exactly. Like Righteous Burger."

"Where's the closest one?"

"Umm, lemme see, well, there's one up on State Road 41 and the one on Perkins and the one up by the VA hospital, that's just drive-thru. I dunno, there's a few."

"No, man, I mean like right around here, within a few miles."
"Right."

"But we're in the middle of nowhere," Clarion said.

159

"I guess folks down here just like their burgers with a side of salvation."

13

I COULD BE THE EMPEROR OF MARS

Six that evening, the sky a sunburst flag of magenta and rusty clay, tangerine and gold, the Epic drew to a stop on the gravel shoulder in front of Posh Lodge #471. Martinez unclenched her jaws. Her hands, feet, and finally her eyes followed.

The Staties had called a few minutes after Tuck broke her, told him they'd gotten a hit on Warburton, that they'd tracked her to this Posh Lodge halfway between Boston and Worcester. Tuck had frog-marched Martinez out of Symmetra HQ—gently, she was a woman—stopping briefly to threaten Chu and Beauchamp on the way out.

"Maybe you could let me out?" Martinez said, scanning the car's interior, nervously licking her lips. "I'd like to stretch my legs."

Tuck sneered. "You stay put. If I need to question you again, I don't want to waste time tracking you down."

McGovern approached the car as Tuck got out. Gray hair and thick, jet-framed glasses, McGovern wore a tan trench over an equally non-descript suit. He was a gum chewer. Tuck could see the guy's jaw working double-time trying to demolish whatever was unlucky enough to be in his mouth.

"How goes it, Lieutenant?"

"We're done."

"You can't be done, McGovern, not that fast. There has to be something."

"Oh, there is. And we already found it. Her, I mean. Over there," he said, hitching a thumb in the direction of the Posh Lodge.

"Well, let's commandeer one of their rooms and start sweating her."

"I don't think even you can pull that off, Squires. Warburton's dead. Found her in a shallow grave behind the hotel. Blood trail led us right to it. There's an encrypted data card with her, too, says VJ on the case."

"Did you get it cracked yet?"

"We're working on it."

"What about Etobo?"

"On that, you're lucky, too. We found him. I just got the call."

"Still alive?"

"So far," said McGovern ominously.

Tuck smiled, chuckled to himself at the pun, and responded with a conspiratorial nod. Although Warburton had wound up being a dead end, Tuck was taking a liking to McGovern. "You know what I mean, Lieutenant."

"No, I really don't, Agent Squires."

Or not. "Never mind, Clarion said you had your lab monkeys putting together some blood work."

"Oh, right, yeah, hemo belongs to an ex-football player named Lars Svenson."

"And he looks a lot like Beowulf?"

"Yup. Dude spent three years on the Saints' taxi squad. Get this, though, guy's dead."

"Dead?"

"Right. As in no longer living."

"That doesn't even make sense."

"Sure it does. Guy got cut preseason '19, went to work for the Mob doing collections. Typical ex-jock. Developed a sick goth habit, got popped for it. Did a couple bits at Angola State, 'found God' while he was on the inside."

"You say that like it's a joke."

"What, the 'got popped' or the 'sick goth habit?'"

"The 'found God.'"

"No joke, man. Guy 'found God' while he was in prison."

"You did it again."

"Did what?"

"Said, 'found God,' like you don't believe it."

"Who cares what I believe?"

"You should for starters."

"You want me go on or not, Squires?"

"Sure, go on, go on…If you don't care, why should I?" McGovern slit his gaze and continued. "Came out of Angola, got a job as a janitor with some prison outreach program, died a little while later. Body cremated, ashes to ashes, dust to dust. But that's not the strange part."

"OK?"

"The strange part is that Svenson's blood was fresh and swimming with goth. Guy's definitely still alive and doing some major quantities of dope."

"Well, you'd better get this information to Clarion."

"Oh, he already knows. I spoke to him while he was in the air."

"Where is he now?"

"Texas, Louisiana, somewhere. Actually, he told me he was going to update you on this stuff."

"All right, never mind, McGovern. That's good work. Your country owes you a debt, son. Get back to me when that lab work's done," he said giving McGovern a quarter-smile, waving him off like an emperor rejecting a batch of shoddy grapes.

"MAKE SOME NOISE," TUCK SAID, AS HE AND MARTINEZ approached the room Etobo was in, Interrogation 3. A state trooper stood in front of a one-way glass door, waiting.

"Like what?"

"Like say some suspicious things, whatever you think would get Etobo's goat. Whatever you think would rile him up."

She stopped, turned to Tuck. "Do I have to?"

"Yes," Tuck said.

Martinez huffed. "Blah blah, rackim frackim, Kenyatta, Etobo, rickim frickim, Symmetra. Where's Diana? Spill the coffee—"

The troopers gaze moved towards them, fixed on Martinez.

"Good," Tuck said, "That's enough."

He continued past the room, walked Martinez down the

hall to Interrogation 7, left her with a trooper posted there. Then he returned.

"Squires, Internal Defense," he said.

"Yeah, I figured that part," the trooper responded, his wide, cocky stance getting, if anything, wider.

"Lemme have a look," Tuck said, motioning for the trooper to step aside.

In the room beyond Tuck saw Etobo. He was on his back on the floor, rocking slightly, wriggling his cuffed hands and feet. He was small, barely bigger than a teenage boy. He reminded Tuck of a tipped-over giant turtle struggling to right himself. He thought back to the picture in Etobo's office, the one that had seemed so rife with implications. He felt as though he was looking at a different person. He told himself it didn't matter, that evil was always changing its shape in an effort to fool the non-elect, to keep good guessing.

"Who did that?" he asked the trooper.

The trooper turned, glanced into the room. "Did it to himself I guess."

"You expect me to believe that?"

"It's the truth."

"We're on the same side here, son," said Tuck, eyeing the trooper's badge. "Go ahead and tell me what really happened. You gave him, what, the old stand-and-trip? The old sit-and-spin?"

The trooper shook his head.

"Phonebook to the noodle, atomic knee raise to the gut, nightstick to the nose…Whatever it was, just fess up."

The trooper squinted at Tuck. His jaw dropped as though he'd just realized he was sucking on ice.

"It's OK, kid," Tuck said to the balding trooper, swiping the golden bangs from his eyes. "Heck, more likely than not, that clown in there's an enemy of the State."

And it was true. The fact that Warburton was dead, that if she had been involved it wasn't as the mastermind, pointed to a greater, controlling power behind her actions. And why wouldn't it be the only Islamo-Fascist in the picture, this supposed friend of Diana Scorsi's, Kenyatta Etobo?

"Listen, Agent, what really happened is he did it to himself. This is Massachusetts. We follow the rules here. You know, the Constitution."

Tuck had heard enough lies. He dismissed the trooper with a wave of his hand and entered the room. "Mr. Etobo," he said, stooping to right both suspect and chair.

Etobo looked up at him, batting his eyes like a child or some sort of sleepy little animal. The obvious attempt at eliciting sympathy made Tuck sick, did even more to convince him that Etobo was guilty.

"Look, whoever you are," Etobo began, "I had nothing to do with Diana's disappearance and you can't force me to say I did. Hook me up to a lie detector if you want."

"Unnecessary."

"Why's that?"

"I'm already sure you're lying."

"Martinez is who you want. I heard her out there. She must be the one who betrayed Diana. You let me talk to that little bitch. I'll get the truth out of her."

"Watch your language when you're talking about a Federal witness."

"Federal witness? Already? What did she say?"

166

"We'll get to that in a minute."

"Fine, will you at least uncuff my hands? These things hurt."

"Sorry, chief. Who knows what you'd try with your hands free?"

"I won't try anything. Promise."

"No luck."

"But they hurt."

"Quit struggling. They'll hurt less."

"My feet at least?"

"Negatory on that, too."

Etobo huffed. "Is there anything you can be pository on?"

"You giving me the facts, little man."

"I'm serious."

"You think I'm not, Etobo? Ever heard of the Anti-Terrorism and Sedition Act?"

"No."

"Exactly," Tuck said, grinning maliciously.

"I'm not a terrorist or a seditionist or a... Jesus—"

"Don't take the Lord's name in vain either. That's rule one. And you can forget about any of this innocent until proven guilty wahoozit. The point is for you to prove you're not guilty, because you sure could be."

"I could be the Emperor of Mars, too."

"Not likely, Etobo. Or should I just call you Mrs. X?"

"Who or what is a Mrs. X?"

Tuck leaned down, jaw set angrily, his nose within inches of Etobo's. He was proving his power, going for maximum intimidation. He had to break this guy and when he did, Hunter was sure to see how valuable he was. She was sure to promote him just as he'd planned. "See, that's not the way this is gonna go. I want answers, and the sooner I get them—the sooner we get Scorsi back—the sooner I might go easy on you."

Etobo's gaze twisted into a grimace as he moved back, creating what space he could. "Whatever you're talking about, Squires, I've told you, it has absolutely nothing to do with me."

"Sure it—" Tuck's cell buzzed. It was the stealth sync he'd tied to Martinez's. He raised his other hand, motioned for Etobo to keep quiet as he brought the thing to his ear.

"Ms. Martinez," said a man's voice.

"Yes, who is this?" Martinez responded.

"It's Mrs. X, of course. I'm surprised you don't recognize me."

"Your voice sounds different."

"I do have this modulation device," Mrs. X. replied.

"How could you do that?"

"Why shouldn't I? If I've got it, I might as well use it."

"Not the voice device," Martinez said. "What you did to Diana."

"As though you didn't realize what was going on?"

"You know I didn't have anything to do with the kidnapping."

"Of course you did."

"I just gave you some information. It was a mistake but I didn't do anything illegal. You told me you were a celebrity event organizer. You said I'd be helping Diana." Martinez's voice cracked as she said her boss's name. She sounded like she was on the verge of tears.

"I guess I lied."

"Well, I guess the US Internal Defense Bureau knows all about you now."

"All about what? I'm a disembodied voice on an untraceable

line. As for you, though and Kenyatta Etobo, well, I'd say you're probably front and center."

"What do you know about Etobo?"

"No fair using my own questions against me."

"What?"

"Exactly what you're going to tell me. Is he there with you and Tuck Squires?"

"Maybe."

"You're going to have to do better than that."

"What if I don't?"

Mrs. X paused. Tuck could tell they were losing him/her by that point; felt him/her on the verge of hanging up. He turned and headed for the room where he'd deposited Martinez, blew past the guard, cell still pressed to his ear.

He slammed the door behind him, keyed in the code to perfect the voice link between the two phones, spoke. "X?" he said, making a knife of two fingers and pulling it across his throat to quiet Martinez.

"Yes?" X responded.

"Squires, Internal Defense."

"Ah, now we're getting somewhere."

"If by getting somewhere you mean I'm getting ready to capture you."

"That doesn't even make sense."

"As Christ is my witness you can bet it does."

"Christ? Didn't anyone ever tell you not to take the Lord's name in vain?"

"Now, some criminal's gonna lecture me on theology?"

"I'm no criminal, Squires. Get that through your ridiculous bureaucratic skull."

"Whatever you say, X. And it's not in vain if I actually do it."

"If you do what?"

"If I do what I'm saying, I'm not taking His name in vain."

"I don't care, Squires. I called because I've got something to tell you. If you're serious about meeting the mastermind behind Virtual Jerusalem."

"Virtual Jerusalem? So that's what VJ stands for?"

"Yes, that's what it stands for. Now, be quiet and listen. If you're serious about finding the person responsible for Virtual Jerusalem, you'll be at Minuteman National Park at midnight tonight. Martinez knows the way." Mrs. X paused. "Oh, and one more thing."

"What?"

"As they say in the PIF, as-Salāmu ʿalaykumu, brother."

"What?"

"As-Salāmu ʿalaykumu," he said again.

The line went dead, the sound like a distant dive-bomber in Tuck's ear. He thought about X's words, again and again. "Ass salami a lake um," was some sort of Muslim greeting, just more evidence that the Islamo-Fascists were involved, that they were taunting him, trying to toy with him. He thought about taking it out on Etobo, thought about stalking back down the hall and laying out the little creep with one punch.

The clack of Martinez setting her phone down broke Tuck's concentration. He turned to her.

"So?" she said, her eyes wide and pretty, reminiscent of Telka's.

"So."

"I mean, what are you going to do?"

"I know what you mean Martinez. I'm not going to share

170

the details of an investigation with you, though."

"Oh, I didn't mean—"

"For now, I need you to draw me a map of that Minuteman National Park."

"Well, I don't have any—"

"Paper? I'll get you some. Wait here."

Tuck left the room, shaking his head. As he walked back down the hall, he thought about the call. He still believed Etobo was involved. But someone else was in on this, too. Chu or Beauchamp, one or the other. Beauchamp was his bet, just the sort of low-class stooge who'd wind up involved in something like this.

The smart thing to do would be to set Etobo loose and see where he ran. Tuck hoped that would clarify things before midnight. If not, he would just have to take the bait and meet whoever—and whatever—at Minuteman National Park.

14

UNDERLAND

CLARION KNEW THERE WAS A LEAK. THAT WAS THE ONLY WAY the cover had gotten out. But now that there were real faces on the news, even with fake names and a fake story behind them, the prospect of full disclosure was there. Hunter had hinted at that much in their last call.

Homeland Security Czar Valeria "Thunder" Waters seemed the most likely source. Thunder hated Hunter, wanted her second-in-command, Candor Matthews, to have the job. She had plotted that since the early days of the Administration. All Thunder needed was a good enough reason to give Raglan and this would qualify. As Hunter had put it, he needed to, "Fucking move."

Clarion stuffed the last bite of charred cheeseburger in his mouth and smiled a final, semi-literal, shit-eating grin to the bar-full of glowering patrons. He rose, knocked back the last half of his third watery draft, and headed for the door.

The LA state troopers had found footage of Svenson at one of the RB drive-thrus, his car a beige Chevy Marsupial. A game warden had come across a similar Marsupial near Silver

Lake Park, a sloped tract of woods that had gone from cypress plantation to protected wetland to mystery-owned, privatized shithole over the last couple decades.

Twenty minutes after leaving Colonel Muddbugg's, Clarion linked up with the warden. He flashed his shield and fell back on the Eastern European jewel thief cover. The warden nodded knowingly, got into her little green jeep and drove away.

Once she was gone, Clarion called Tuck—left a voicemail with all the juicy details about how Hunter had gone apeshit—called Morris—got no answer, left no message—and killed his cell. He slid it back into his jacket pocket. Wearing nightview goggles, Clarion picked up the trail of footsteps and broken underbrush, followed it into the green light of the woods.

TWO HOURS LATER, HIS HANDS A RANGE OF BUG BITES AND slashes from the snaps and thwacks of thorny brush, Clarion spotted the clearing. Near the center of the park, there was construction, an old roadhouse at the hill's crest, the roads that had once accessed it long overgrown. A faded sign pointed the way to the building in question, The Dauphine.

Beneath red-lettered script, half-Magna Carta, half-Old West whorehouse, lay the sign's true subject—a platinum blonde, her hair done up a la Marie Antoinette. Smiling a red and white grin and sporting an aquamarine g-string, ornate, crystalline fleur-de-lis tassels dangled from her ample tits. The building was a product of several, distinct eras. Its central structure, its beginning, was a two-story cabin of full-scribed cypress on a gray fieldstone foundation. It looked like the sort of place a frontier president might have spent his formative years hunting barrs and stewing possums, whittling, shitting, and grinning when he wasn't doing either of those. Newer, machine-milled additions formed wings off the right and left sides. Darker and only a story each, they lengthened the front façade by what Clarion guessed as thirty feet in either direction.

Two guards patrolled the clearing's perimeter. Both large, one was white and athletic, the other black and rotund. Both men wore cheap Halloween masks, the dull plastic from the masks catching the moonlight and deadening it, stealing its luster.

The white guy's mask was that of a non-descript handsome face, his identity as Superman revealed by the curlicue of black hair mid-forehead. When he turned, Clarion saw long red hair tied behind. This had to be Svenson. The other man wore a Batman mask, the lower half cut out revealing dark skin. Based on size and skin color, Clarion guessed this was the disappearing security guard from the Hynes. Both guards held Palsiver K shotguns and had survival blades strapped to their calves. Unless it was the new, ultra-thin althorium stuff, they weren't wearing body armor. At least in that Clarion had been lucky.

Clarion knelt behind a big blackjack oak. The woods around him whispered, animals skittered, the dark sky grown pearly above—cloudy and oddly luminous, the beforestorm of autumn in the South. Clarion fitted the Rikken's silencer and watched the guards' rounds, looking for patterns and flaws, something to exploit.

The clearing was a large enough oval that the guards lost sight of each other for maybe thirty seconds in the middle of each circuit. This break gave Clarion enough time to get within fifty feet of Svenson—to hide behind the last substantial row of trees. Clarion knelt, waiting for the next circuit to begin. When it came, he moved in. Pointing the Rikken at chest level, he emerged from the woods; crept within fifteen feet before Svenson heard him and turned.

"Lars Svenson?" Clarion asked in a hoarse, Eastwoodian whisper.

Svenson took in the goggles, the gun, and the ID shield Clarion held in his left hand. "Goin' for a swim," he asked, baring his bad teeth. He looked to Clarion like a wolf about to try to talk his way out of something.

"'Nuff jokes, jackass. On the ground, face down, fucking fast." Clarion motioned with the Rikken as though it were a wagging finger.

Svenson dropped his shotgun, hung his head. "I knew you'd come," he said.

"Yeah, yeah, yeah, just get the fuck down," Clarion said. Pocketing the shield, he reached for his zip-cuffs and advanced.

Svenson winked, ducked, and ran. Clarion fumbled with his cuffs, dropped them, but managed to hold onto his piece. He fired two shots.

The first round missed Svenson, nicked a tree trunk, the second didn't even hit wood, just whistled off, deeper into the trees. By that point, Clarion had no choice but to let Svenson run, to go for the other guard and hope to take him out quickly, before anyone inside knew he was there.

An old outhouse stood a few feet away. Clarion moved behind the thing, realizing as he did it had no doors. He listened as the black guy closed; his steps loud and heavy just like his breathing. As he rounded the left side of the outhouse, Clarion struck downward, knocked the Palsiver from the guard's hands, but lost his grip on his own piece in the process. He grabbed the building's trim, used it for leverage as he side-kicked the guy twice in the gut. The second brought the guard to his knees. This gave Clarion a clear shot at the guy's jaw, and he took it; the shot so clean he could almost feel the impact of fist to face before it happened. Still, somehow the guard slipped the punch. He ducked and caught Clarion's ankle in his massive mitts, cranked on it, using the torque to unbalance Clarion and throw him back. The guard jumped to his feet and pulled his knife. Clarion got to his feet, too. By then, he could see Svenson closing from the right, drawing his own blade.

Clarion had his second piece at his ankle, but he wouldn't be able to get to it quickly enough to accomplish anything other than getting himself slashed fore and aft. He went into a basic defensive stance, ka kro sixth position. Wide base, weight even, knees bent, and his fists in tight. His eyes darted between the two of them as he waited for the first strike.

The black guy lunged at Clarion's head with his knife. He missed but caught Clarion with a follow-on uppercut, grazed his cheek with the blade's back swing. Clarion jumped back as the guy slashed at his midsection. He was backing towards Svenson, doing exactly what they wanted. Clarion saw Svenson smiling as he drew closer, the curl of his criminal grin. Svenson went for a choke with his left, stabbed down with the knife in his right. Clarion caught his right wrist, twisted as hard as he could and turned it, taking the knife in the process. He ducked, reversed into a rear choke. Now using Svenson as a shield against the other guard, he held the blade to his throat and applied more force to the arm. He felt Svenson's wrist flexing, heard the bones break—the ulna first then the radius.

"Uhhr...Urb...don't you go weak on me now," Svenson

groaned, gritting his teeth so tightly Clarion could almost hear them grinding.

"Urb?" Clarion asked, "Like parsley? Parents a couple of rabid gastronomers?"

"Rabbit whats?" Urb asked, tossing the knife deftly from his right to his left and back again, the ease of movement and the way he stayed on the balls of his feet revealing he might be a dangerous opponent, that he was surprisingly athletic for such a big man.

"Ra-bid."

"I says, "Rabbit what?""

The cell device strapped at Urb's shoulder gave one long beep then two shorter ones.

"Underland," came a voice.

Urb nodded. "Let's go, Lars."

"What's that mean? What's underland?"

Urb nodded again. "Lars?"

"Look, your pal's not going anywhere and neither are you," Clarion said, pushing the knife in until he drew blood. "So, again, what's that mean? What's underland?"

Urb shrugged as Lars clocked Clarion with a left elbow, using every bit of his reach to go for the temple. But Clarion moved back enough to take the blow to his cheek. He felt the knife blade sink into Svenson's neck then twist away, falling to his side, bathing both men in blood. Clarion landed ass-first on the ground. Both guards took off running.

Clarion rose to his knees, grabbed the knife, and flung it, taking Svenson in the leg. This only stopped him for a second, though. Obviously, the guy was still on a fuckload of goth. Clarion focused on Svenson's retreating form and that of his surprisingly speedy, eminently corpulent confederate, wished for his gun so he could at least take a few potshots.

"What's that mean?" he said, singsong, childish. "Please, Mr. Criminal Batman, what's your secret code mean?" Clarion could see the Rikken was now on the ground, about ten yards away. He walked over and picked it up. "You sound like fuckin' Squires. Worse than that, you sound like Morris," he paused. "Worse than that, you are now, quite literally, talking to your fucking self."

The smell of smoke was sweet at first, old hickory and older cypress, but it grew bitter on second breath, took on the heady, industrial stench of a chemical accelerant, something like anjar JX or zagon. Clarion turned to The Dauphine, saw the wispy tentacles of black smoke rising from the building's chimneys and windows, darker than the eerie green sky. He heard the boom! of an explosion beneath The Dauphine, and again a few seconds later. What if underland meant they'd left Scorsi underground? That they'd gotten the information they needed, had only to dispose of their victim and any remaining evidence?

Clarion ran for the place's front door—absolutely the wrong way if he wanted to stay alive—but he'd already made that decision long ago. The choice between life and death, between the 'burbs and the Bureau. He'd tried to do both, failed miserably—the divorces and the kid who hated him testament to those efforts. The only ones who got it right were the people like Hunter, the ones who made a clean break from the field and never went back.

Clarion jimmied the metal door handle, felt no give, just growing heat, enough to make him pull away. He tried shouldering into the door but that was no good either, there was something immensely heavy on the other side. Clarion looked in both directions, ran left though he wasn't sure why.

There was no obvious back door, no stairs or storm cellars, none of the things he'd hoped to find. The first story windows were too small, the ones on the second story too high to be of any use. He turned back to the woods. The trees seemed even thicker than they had before. The sounds of night animals now lost beneath the rush of a growing fire. Clarion moved towards the woods knowing now what he was searching for.

As he drew near to the outhouse, the smell of smoke died briefly, borne away by a breeze running south-southwest. Seconds later, the scent of wood and accelerant picked up again. By then Clarion was sure zagon was what they'd used—limited explosiveness compared to anjar x but a hotter burn, a quicker spread. His time to get inside was growing short.

Clarion pressed his palms to the sides of the building, searching for a way in, a trip, lever, or at least evidence of one side being weaker than the others. Finally, the hollow knock of thinner boards, a false wall. He backed up, delivered three clustered rounds from the Rikken then holstered his piece and moved forward, hitting the wall with two front kicks. The wood was stronger than it looked. All he'd done was make the hole bigger, nowhere near big enough for him to squeeze through.

He took a couple steps back and ran, shouldering into the wall hard enough this time to break through, taking a header down a small flight of dirt steps. The soil was damp, new construction. A lightless tunnel opened before him. A warm breeze and the foul, growing smell of zagon told him this was the way.

The passage descended at a twenty-degree clip, narrowing as it did. Clarion was eventually forced to crouch then crawl as the tunnel snaked south first then west, back to the north, and east. Except for what he'd managed in the downgrade, it was clear he had only moved in a circle. He'd begun to make out voices, though, knew this could be a dummy passage or worse, that he had no choice but to keep going. A woman's voice the most prominent, her exact words were unclear, but her tone was defiant. A few more feet to the east and the tunnel began to broaden, the woman's voice growing louder. Clarion drew his gun. He began to run.

At the end of the tunnel, there was a metal ladder set into a concrete wall. When Clarion looked up he could see the ladder led to a wheel-locked hatch, ten, maybe fifteen, feet above. The voices seemed to descend from there, echoing and pressing on him in turns. Clarion climbed to the top of the ladder and saw that the hatch was rusty. He tried to turn the wheel handle but failed. He holstered his piece so he could use both hands, worked the wheel in creaking quarter turns until he heard a click, felt the mechanism give. He pushed the hatch open and held it ajar as he redrew his piece. Flakes of rust grazed away from the opening, sifting down into his eyes and mouth. He shook his head, coughed, spit.

Moving up a rung, he peered through the slit into the room beyond. There was light but only enough to see a room filled with a smoky haze. The voices grew louder. Clarion waited, hoping whoever it was would strike first. A few seconds, and he knew he had no choice but to move in. He pushed the hatch up as hard as he could, heard it thud against the room's back wall and stick in place. Climbing the last few rungs of the ladder, he sprang up onto the floor, gaze and gun panning, ready to shoot. But there was no one there, only voices coming from a speaker in the ceiling, the voices that seemed to press down on him, remind him that his days in the field should have ended long ago.

"I'm not giving you shit. Do what you're gonna do." He knew the voice was Diana Scorsi's. "I'm not giving you shit. Do what you're gonna do. I'm not giving you shit."

Behind him, Clarion heard the first few creaks of the iron hatch falling, followed by another noise, faint and high-pitched like a cry. He turned as the thing fell shut, the locking mechanism spinning back into place. Clarion ran back to the hatch. There was no wheel on the inside, no way to open it, no way to get out. Just as he'd feared, and maybe even known all along, this was a trap, one there'd been no way he could avoid.

An open door on the far wall gave Clarion a view of what awaited him. As he edged towards it, he saw fire in both directions. Clarion's world seemed to shrink then, almost as if his life were an equation, all the exogenous variables removed, consumed by the flames. He was left with the only question there had ever really been: How to cheat death for as long as possible?

He thought back to the path he'd taken, tried to gauge where he'd be in relation to the place's front door. The answer was almost directly beneath it but he wasn't sure how far down. The heat felt greater to the left but there was a slight draft, maybe a way out. Farther down the hall, he saw what might be a break in the flames.

Clarion shielded his eyes and ran into the fire, heading for the gap. He got only a few feet in before the skin on his arms began to sting and tighten. He bit his lip, kept going, but instead of falling, the temperature rose. After a few more steps, he felt the breeze, took his hand from his eyes long enough to see that it was nothing but a door, flapping on its hinges, batted back and forth as the flames fed on it. He rushed back the way he'd come, swatted at the flames that had begun to take to his clothes. There was nothing left.

Clarion thought of funeral pyres then, of Vikings on long ships floating, burning, into the heart of an icy fjord, a brief, final respite on the water, beneath the clear, close stars of a Northern night. The Dauphine would be his pyre, and everything in Clarion's body wanted that soothing, icy water. He wanted to think about this and only this, forget about his kid and the ex-wives, the myriad wrong turns the country and world had made. He wanted it to be over then, to forget about all of it, to forget about the entire world. The smoke continuing to thicken, Clarion knew he would lose consciousness soon. He could stand there, wait until he fell, simply give himself over to the flames. It would be easy.

Through the smoke and spaces of his fingers, he saw the flight of stairs nearly concealed by the flames from a beam that had fallen across the passageway. Like a light going off at a carnival, like a bell ringing for the winner of the bonus round, he realized that he wasn't going to die here. Coughing, struggling to shallow his breath, Clarion held his fist to his mouth, shielded his eyes, and moved in again. Gritting his teeth, he ran for those steps, his jacket catching as he ducked under the beam. He pawed at the flaming material, burned his hand, finally managed to rip the thing off and drop it as his shirt caught. He bounded up the steps two, three at a time, smacked himself in the chest as he reached the ground floor, put out the fire that had taken to his shirt.

By that point, he was almost certain the fire had been started down below, which meant the flames were following him, seeking the sky. Amidst the industrial, black smoke, he could see an old player piano blocking the front door. This was what had prevented entrance, pushed him towards the trap even though he'd been too much of a fool to see it. The stairs to the second floor lay to the piano's right. Clarion ran up those steps, turned into a hallway that spanned the length of the place, ending just before the window above the front door. He grabbed both sides of the sash, put his heel through the glass, and cleared away the remaining debris with a few more kicks as the heat continued to rise around him.

He was sure the ground floor had fully taken by that point. There was no more time. Getting as much purchase as he could on the windowsill, Clarion jumped feet-first. He braced, sprang when he hit ground, rolled when he hit the second time. The landing was textbook, except for the rock he head-butted at the end of his roll. Groaning, Clarion lay back, felt his head tingling. He reached for the place where the rock had hit, felt it wet and sticky, pulled his hand back and saw blood all over it. He thought of his kid, wanted to tell him everything would be OK, even though he knew it wouldn't. Then he was gone, into the black.

15

A CRUEL SORT OF JOKE

RAVELTON PARLAY HADN'T ALWAYS BEEN RAVELTON PARLAY. In fact, he'd been quite a few other people at one time or another. Finneous Stubbins and Timsdale Tubbins, Esteban Van der Grift and Felonia Mattress—he'd been all these people and many, many more. Some identities Parlay took on for business reasons. Others were donned to deal with more personal matters. Regardless of rationale, Parlay assumed his alternate selves only fleetingly and on paper, just long enough to outwit Chinese bank regulators or establish economic ownership of property he couldn't legally own, for example. One of Parlay's identities was special, though. It was special because it wasn't fake. Parlay had been this person before he'd ever been Ravelton Parlay. The identity in question belonged to Parlay's first, truest self, the boy who'd fled Vermont at the age of fifteen, Jimmy Orchard.

James Reesemoore Orchard was born on December 7, 1945, in a little town called Armistice, in a little state called Vermont, in a big country called America. Orchard was a war baby, the product of an affair between his mother Peggy Sue and Jimmy Tingle, a traveling representative of the Globe Tome Encyclopedia Company. Born to Peggy Sue and PFC Timmy Orchard—recently returned from France—Jimmy was an extremely bright little boy, one who showed the knack for gab and talent for arithmetic lacking in both mother and father. These facts, never mind the complete set of Globe Tome Encyclopedias that showed up the day he was born would soon put Jimmy at odds with his supposed father.

Raised in Armistice, Vermont's, low-key Lutheran enclave, First Church of the Sympathetic Shepherd, Timmy Orchard had never been a particularly God-fearing man. Still, he'd had some measure of faith, would have answered yes to the basic question of whether he believed in an omnipotent, benevolent, higher power. Europe changed that. From the blood, body parts, and shiny shell casings strewn across those smoky fields, to Auschwitz and its pits brimming with corpses, to the light-starved eyes of comrade after comrade, Timmy had seen more than enough to turn him off to the possibility of God's goodness. Sure, God might still exist. And He might even wear white as a cruel sort of joke. But given Timmy—and God's—history in France—and Germany and Poland—rather than the press dispatches he'd been fed at Sympathetic Shepherd—God seemed a lot more like the Devil than He did like Himself. Normally not much of a philosopher, Timmy couldn't help wondering whether this had been the trick all along, the reason the world at that moment seemed so…fucked. Maybe God was a heavenly devil, looking down from the clouds, laughing at the pain and confusion He'd wrought, laughing at the fact people were praying to Him when they should have been praying to something—or anything—else.

Back in Armistice, Timmy hadn't been inclined to share his views on God, what had happened in combat, or much of anything else. What he'd been inclined to do was nod a lot, smile confidently, and reclaim his job as assistant manager at Ralph Wilson's filling station. And things had been OK for days, weeks even. But soon Timmy began hearing rumors about his wife, a handsome young encyclopedia salesman named Jim Tingle, and the bun Peggy Sue soon reported as being in her oven. Small town that Armistice was, juicy as said rumors were, dismissing them wasn't easy. In fact, it was damn near impossible. So, Timmy fell back on the only stress-reducing hobbies he had, the ones he'd developed during the war. He started smoking and drinking heavily, two things his son Jimmy would never do.

IN SPITE OF HIS GRAND POWER AND GRANDER WEALTH, Parlay remained a humble man. He hadn't gotten anywhere without the Lord, and he knew it. This was why no matter how tired or stressed he got, no matter how much Kelly Anne nattered in his ear or Bayousalem's staff fell short in their duties, Parlay made sure never to take his dissatisfaction out on God. What the Lord wanted, He got. And because hard work was one of the few things the Bible was unequivocal on God wanting, Parlay held himself to his customary, rigorous work schedule even during Virtual Jerusalem...

He'd spent the last few hours on a vid-con with RB's senior management team discussing plans for expansion in the Northeast. Sure, there were already quite a few franchises in the more devout states—Pennsylvania and Ohio, for example—but

Parlay had a particular, gnawing desire to increase share in New England. Whether because he'd been born in Vermont or because New England remained oddly resistant to real Christianity, none could say, including Parlay. What he did know was that RB's real estate team had been purchasing land left and right, the lingering Great Northern Recession good for more than just bringing liberals to heel.

Good news on the real estate front aside—acquisition costs in Taxachusetts alone were running thirty percent below plan—Parlay'd had it with bubbly corporate personalities and the brown-nosing they seemed to thrive on. He longed for someone to speak to him as an equal, to tell him not just how things were but how they were going to be. Not that it would ever happen but sometimes Parlay found himself wishing he could talk to God. Not in the way he did when he prayed, but conversationally, almost like a buddy. And even though he wasn't going to get this from Justice, except perhaps to subliminally relay to God how he wished things worked, he'd answered his #1's call with hope, the words "she's broken" and others to that effect buzzing in his head.

"You want the good part, or the bad part?" Justice asked with not so much as a greeting.

"There's a bad part?" Parlay responded, bringing his free hand to his temple, attempting to massage away the impending headache.

"A *really* bad part. We've been infiltrated."

"Well, sugar and shinny, Natural, that's about as bad as it can get."

"I know."

"ID?"

"The Agent."

"Where are you now?"

"We're on the run. That's where we are."

"And that's the good news?"

"Part of it. The rest of the good news is that the Agent's dead."

"What about the Target?"

"She's still alive," responded Justice.

"That's not quite the direction I was going in, but I guess it's something. I was thinking more along the lines of, 'have you gotten any more out of her?'"

"Not a bit."

"What is it gonna take with this girl?"

"I don't know, Presence."

"Never mind that for now, Natural. Exactly where are you?"

"Heading your way. Fifty miles from Home Base."

"And where are you going?"

"I was hoping you'd tell me."

Parlay's argentine gaze scanned the Sanctum, settling on an oil painting of Jackson, a Sully, his favorite. Was it the darkness in the eyes or the peaceful, resolute expression? Either way, it was impossible to judge Jackson's intent. Which was the point Parlay had always drawn from the piece. It was easy to see why Jackson's men had followed him to all those great victories. His face said he was willing to do whatever, whenever, that there was an almost careless serenity that animated him. What he was doing was right because he was the one doing it. And that would never change.

This was the thing with the Sanctum and the accoutrements that filled it. Even though Parlay didn't believe in magic, saw it as the work of the Devil, he remained something of a magical thinker, willing to look to superstition, to icons and totems even, if he thought they might help him. Seeing the painting worked, too. Imagining what Old Hickory would have done in the situation stiffened Parlay's resolve, set his course, a course that now technically included murder and treason and was, probably, bound to include more of each, and then some. But Parlay realized what Jackson had realized—that if he was doing it, there was nothing wrong with it. Parlay's actions were as God wanted. "Well, you can't come here, not with all that baggage. Meet me at Bird's Nest #2. We need to put Plan D in effect."

"Which one is that?"

"We need to get the Target out of the country."

"Ah."

Even before the Angel had contacted him, Parlay had maintained a large portion of his assets outside the country, beyond the purview of the clutching central government. These included a long list of sanctuary islands spread across the globe. Well-stocked and fortified, these were the sorts of places Parlay knew he could always hole up if needed. But there was one of them he prized about all the others, one of them he held as unique. Special because it was new in the last few years, special because it wasn't on any maps, this island was invisible to satellite photography. This was Parlay's ace of aces. Parlay Island.

AFTER HE'D HUNG UP ON JUSTICE, PARLAY PLACED THE CALL to the Angel. "We have a problem," he'd said. "Actually. There are a few. The Cooler was found."

"Infiltrated? I told you Clarion was no joke."

"I guess you were right. Doesn't matter though. He's dead now."

"Ken Clarion is dead?"

"You sound surprised."

"Frankly, yes, I am. But never mind that. What's the rest of the news?"

"Well, those enhanced interrogation tactics haven't worked on the Target."

"Oh, those techniques work. It's your men getting them wrong. They're not professionals."

"You're the one who said *not to use* professionals, to put together what I could on the ground."

"I did?" the Angel asked.

"Absolutely." Parlay had always harbored fears about the Angel's motives, even his general sanity, but the Symmetra deal had been too good to pass up. Now, the doubts were beginning to come back to him. With every flip comment, every backhand admission— perhaps not of incompetence but of carelessness— Parlay's thoughts moved closer to imagining himself in black and white, of wondering how he'd get by in an environment controlled entirely by people he couldn't control, blacks and Mexicans, Koreans and Latinos at that.

"Hmm, well, that may not have been the best way to go. We'll have to make do, though. You know what I mean, Presence, chin up!"

"Listen, Angel, the point is I'm worried here. The Israelis have gone quiet."

"How long?"

"A couple hours now."

"All right, all right, Presence. You worry about the rest of this. I'll deal with the Israelis."

"You said you didn't want to be involved directly."

"I don't. But you're going to have your hands full."

"With the Target?"

"And the Insider. You need to get your hands on him, too."

"But I'm leaving the country," Parlay had said. "I'm heading for the island. Anyway, he's about to be taken into custody by Squires."

"Right, and you can't let that happen."

"But that was the plan."

"Maybe the Target doesn't care if you hurt her. Maybe she doesn't even care if you kill her. But make her watch a friend under duress and see what happens."

"We're talking about killing again, aren't we?"

"We're over the Rubicon, Presence."

"I think I understand, Angel. I'm just not sure how to get my hands on the Insider without ID getting in the way."

"Don't worry. I've got something they'll never suspect."

"What's that?"

"Airmail."

HEFTING THEIR HUMAN CARGO—JUSTICE BEARING SCORSI in his arms, the way a cinematic monster might his bride while Urban toted Lars on his shoulders, two buddies escaping from a firefight gone sideways—the two men moved across the field. Parlay stood on the other side of the clearing wearing the face of one of his preeminent personal heroes, Ronald Reagan.

"What happened to her?" he asked.

"It's been a rough couple of hours, Presence."

"She's still alive, isn't she?"

"She's fine. I doped her."

"She doesn't look fine—she looks half dead."

Justice shrugged.

"And what happened to them?" Parlay motioned at Urban and Lars, both of whom were covered in blood.

"The Agent."

"Will he make it?"

"Zulu's fine."

Urban nodded.

"What about Viking?" Parlay replied. "We can't have all this blood on the plane. Natural, you take the Target onto the plane and make sure she's secured in there. You," he said, turning to Urban. "You go get cleaned up over in the hangar, change your clothes. I can't have you on Savior I looking like this."

"What about him?" whispered Justice as Urban headed for the hangar.

"Look at him, Natural. He's going to die. Why bring him on the plane?"

Lars coughed. Parlay considered the possibility that he could hear what they were saying. When Lars coughed again, his throat thick with blood and phlegm, Parlay rejected the notion.

"Plus, he's the reason you were infiltrated."

"How do you know?"

"His name and face are all over. Says he's part of some gang of jewel thieves, authorities trailed him from an RB."

"A Righteous Burger? Oh, goodness, Presence, I am so, so, so, so, *so* sorry."

"Was he ever out of your sight?"

"He went to get us some lunch. Can't imagine he'd have had time to steal any jewels."

"Check his pockets, see what he has on him."

Justice set Scorsi down in the grass. He checked Lars's pockets, produced a small vial of sooty black powder.

"What is that?" Parlay asked.

"Goth, unless I miss my guess."

"He's been doping again? You know there's only one punishment for this sort of betrayal."

"What? You want us to just leave him here? This is one of my men, Presence."

"He knew what he was getting into, Natural."

"I know, Presence. But he did everything he could for us, for the Lord."

"Except for giving up his mistress."

Justice nodded weakly.

"He'll be rewarded in Heaven, Natural. Have no fear."

"He's not gonna like this," Justice said pointing at Urban's retreating form.

"Wait until after we take off."

Justice squinted. "We'd be on the plane."

"You're not coming right now, Natural. You'll follow in Savior II once you've taken care of a few things."

16

THE TROUBLE WITH PEOPLE

A QUARTER MILLENNIUM AFTER THE SHOT HEARD 'ROUND the World, Tuck sat in Minuteman National Park, the modern-day monument to the spot of the shot in question. It was half past midnight, and Mrs. X still hadn't shown. His Rikken in easy reach on the seat beside him, his cell a few inches beyond, blinking furiously, Tuck was considering another shot, a sort of sequel to the one heard 'round the world. The difference being that this one wouldn't be heard 'round the anywhere if he could help it, and rather than colonists, redcoats and muskets, it would involve his silencered service piece, Mrs. X's head, and an end to all his troubles.

Keyed up by voicemails that had been coming at him from various map points—Clarion's the last and worst—Tuck's pulse was quick. He could hear it, almost like reverb from a blown speaker. He could hear his stomach rumbling, too. Having passed six fast food joints since leaving Martinez with the Staties—one of which had been an RB—he felt both hungry and nauseous at once, famished enough to chew into the woods that surrounded Minuteman, nervous enough to yack them back up seconds later. He could almost see the Righteous Burger sign there before him, the one he'd passed on the way over—Timmy's wide eyes and gaping mouth preparing to bust into the Heavenly Half-Stone he held in his hoofless hands. Timmy wasn't all Tuck had seen, though.

The pictures of Scorsi, Svenson, and the guard from the Hynes had hit the networks. He'd seen them on the TV's at the State Police barracks. Sure, the public still believed the cover, but eventually people would figure things out. That was the trouble with people. Whether they would see a hole in the story—few Eastern European countries posed any threat to U.S.-Russian relations and none of them had crown jewels—or learn the truth about who Romanov was and what she was carrying in her pretty, little head somehow, someone would put it together. That someone would talk. Other someones would listen. And Tuck's life would fall into a bottomless pit filled liberally with monkey poo.

Brrrrup-brrzzup. The cell chirped at him for what seemed like the thousandth time.

A bar of silver moonlight framing his gaze, Tuck picked up the Rikken. He pointed it at the phone. How great it would be to pull the trigger, to shut the flipping thing up. He thought about the agreement Clarion had insisted he sign at the Quickie stall, and what a pain in the ass it would be to return a bullet-riddled rental car. Tuck got out of the Epic. He left the door open, the cell continuing to flash and trill as he moved away.

Brrrrup-brrzzup.

Tuck walked the bright black asphalt tracing circles, ellipses, and finally figure-eights, his eyes eventually retracing the shapes his steps made. He thought about infinity, the fact that his current state was anything but limitless bliss. If this was infinity, it was the eternal in negative, a reeking Hell of infinities.

Hunter had gone berserk. She was leaving voicemails wondering where Clarion was and what was going on with the case. She said the President had found out somehow, knew what Scorsi's technology was capable of. Tuck knew the last thing he wanted to do was tell her about his most recent failure, the fact that he had been played by Mrs. X.

Brrrrup-brrzzup.

Even from farther away, the cell's tone was cloying, barely muffled by Tuck's steps; so infuriating that it made him hate the grass and trees beyond, the phone itself, the Director, Clarion, the President...but especially...

"Hey, X?" Tuck shouted.

No reply.

"Mrs. X?" he shouted again.

This time, a night bird sang back, *Cucucaw.*

Brrrrup-brrzzup.

Tuck smirked, considered the idea that it was X toying with him—the phone, the bird, the night, all of it. He tapped the Rikken's trigger.

"Come out, come out, whoever you are, you fucking, evil make-believe bitch."

Surprised at his own language, Tuck's face twisted into a grimace, an expression born of pleasure and anguish mirrored the roiling and starvation playing tug of war in his gut. The final word echoed across the grass and into the trees then seemed to die abruptly, as though absorbed by the surrounding woods.

Brrrrup-brrzzup.

Cucucaw!

Tuck raised his gun, fired a warning shot in the direction of the birdcall. He wasn't trying to hit the bird, not trying hard at least. He just wanted to shut him up. The shot sailed into the trees, its flight disrupted by the crack whoosh thwack of a branch falling to the ground.

Cucucaw, responded the bird, almost daring Tuck to shoot again, daring the phone to ring again.

Brrrrup-brrzzup.

Tuck squeezed off a burst of four bullets in the bird's direction. He heard the crack and splinter of ordinance hitting wood, followed by a surprised cluck, the rustling of wings, the snap and whip of bare branches swatting each other as the bird departed. He watched the creature ascend, arcing towards the moon, away from the man with the gun.

Tuck was alone with his sidearm and his anger, his failure and the lingering rumbling in his gut. The only remotely positive thing in his recent memory being his thoughts of Timmy the Lamb smiling down on the highway; Timmy and the sort of instant gratification that had made him feel better more than once in his life, the Heavenly Halfstones and Cornbread Poppers, the Blood of the Lamb Shakes, the Freedom Fries dipped in creamy Cajun sauce.

"Fine," Tuck said out loud. "Fine, fine, fine."

THIRTY MINUTES, FOUR TURBO-COKES, THREE BURGERS, and an order of crawfish popcorn later, Tuck was ensconced in one of Righteous Burger's Never Walk Alone two-seaters, a red stool swiveling beneath him, a life-sized hologram of Timmy in the seat across. Timmy had been talking about the nine Christian virtues as Tuck ate. Further to that, he'd been quoting from Galatians.

"...Make every effort to add to your faith goodness; and to goodness, knowledge..."   Tuck smiled at the simple wisdom of Timmy's words. He smiled at his full belly and his feeling of spiritual contentment. He felt good, so good that he was ready to top off with a Heavenly Halfstone-Freedom Fries-Blood of the Lamb TrinityTripleThreat. He had to wait for Timmy to finish his sermon, though. Getting up before Timmy was done, "forceful exiting" as it was called, was enough to get you thrown out of an RB, not to mention refused service on an international basis.

"...and to knowledge, self-control; and to self-control, perseverance; and to perseverance, godliness; and to godliness, mutual affection; and to mutual affection, love. Amen," said the sheep's hologram.

"Amen," responded Tuck, loudly enough to make sure the monitor heard and responded.

Timmy smiled, a beeper beeped, and the metal bar that had been preventing Tuck from exiting withdrew into the booth. The splendid ride was over. He was free to go.

Fifteen minutes later, the TrinityTripleThreat eaten standing, Tuck waddled for the bathroom. There, he spent twenty minutes in a stall and another ten prancing hither and yon, waiting for his impromptu diarrhea commercial to end. By the time he emerged from the door marked HETEROSEXUAL MEN and headed for the parking lot, his mood had gone from white to black.

Checking his cell on the way back to the Epic, Tuck saw his voicemails now totaled nine; current score: Hunter 7, Alfred

Chu 2. Much as he wanted to delete the ones from Hunter, Tuck couldn't. Eventually he'd have to talk to her. But he had to get a win first—something to push when he talked to her. Tuck decided to do what he thought Clarion would have done. He decided to fall back on the fact that the Hunter wasn't on the ground, but he was. That he had to be the one to decide what to act on, however strange it might sound. He needed to focus on the messages from Chu. In his first message, Chu had sounded calm. He'd asked whether there was any news about Scorsi, mentioned that Etobo had contacted him post-release, said how happy he was they'd been able to rule out Kenyatta as a suspect. But the second message was different. Chu sounded troubled, harried. He mentioned that the security guard, Beauchamp, had claimed he was sick and gone home early. Tuck called McGovern, who confirmed that they hadn't caught up with Beauchamp yet. He did, however, have a lead on a possible hideout location, a houseboat Beauchamp apparently owned. McGovern had two troopers heading there now.

As soon as Tuck got off the phone with McGovern, he headed for Chu's house. If the Staties weren't able to locate Beauchamp, he hoped talking to Chu might provide additional detail on his person of interest.

CHU'S DRIVE WAS FIFTY FEET LONG AND SHAPED LIKE A parabola. Like the house, it looked new and cheap, poured of simple, beige concrete, the same kind they used for government construction—office buildings, housing projects, and the like. Tuck parked at the parabola's peak, right in front of the door. After several knocks and one of Tuck's patented thirty-second ring-a-ding-dings, Chu's wife, Amanda, answered.

"Yes?" she asked, her speech muffled by the door.

Tuck held his badge up to the peephole.

The door opened to a blaze of auburn hair, gleaming, white teeth, and the sleep-deprived gaze of a demi-raccoon. Puffy, black bags surrounded iridescent, almost televisual, violet eyes. She wore gray sweatpants and a green tee. A full-throated, head-lolling babe in arms, Mrs. Chu told Tuck that her husband was still at the office.

"It's two a.m." Tuck said.

"Alfred's a hard worker."

"Fine. I suppose I'll go see him there, then."

The baby turned to Tuck, eyed him briefly, and cooed. Not used to being on good terms with a kid, Tuck smiled at Baby Chu, patting him on his fuzzy noodle. Baby Chu responded by pointing at Tuck and lunging for his head. Not quick enough to react, Tuck was unable to dodge him, resulting in Baby Chu grabbing a handful of Tuck's shiny hair and screaming with barbaric delight.

Mrs. Chu bugged her eyes and pulled Baby Chu's hand away, a few strands of Tuck's hair going with it. "You want me to call ahead?" she asked by way of apology.

Tuck ran his fingers through his hair, felt for bleeding, and waved her off with a sneer. He exited the field before Baby Chu could launch another attack.

TEN MINUTES LATER, WHEN TUCK PULLED TO A STOP ON the street across from Symmetra and saw how dark the place was, he knew the truth, and he wanted to kick himself, punch himself, tie himself up, and beat himself for the way he'd been taken in by Alfred Chu. He was so pissed that he wanted to go back to Chu's house and arrest his entire family, especially that hair-yanking mini-Visigoth.

Tuck called McGovern ready to shred him if the guy didn't give him some good news. Fortunately, they'd found Beauchamp, on his houseboat, curled up in bed. Unfortunately, a pair of Speed Racer footie pajamas and a collection of Clownist porn were his only offenses. Phone records showed he hadn't been in contact with anyone since leaving Symmetra earlier that day. Tuck told McGovern to use Chu's picture and put out an alert on a Chinese Mafioso named Chau Chai. He listened to Clarion's message again, tried to reach him three times, then did what he knew he had to.

"Yes," the Director said after a few seconds.

"It's Squires," said Tuck, his voice thin. He knew he might have sounded like he was questioning his own identity.

"Why've you been ducking my calls?"

"I was in the middle of a pursuit, ma'am."

"Who?"

"Alfred Chu, Symmetra's Chief Technology Officer."

"We already know about Chu," Hunter said. "We got an anonymous tip a little while ago. That's what I've been trying to contact you about."

"A tip from who?"

"Someone who isn't playing the same game as the rest of the kidnappers. Chu's heading for New Orleans. Apparently, the rest of them have already flown, gotten Scorsi out of the country. He's our only way to follow."

"Yes, ma'am."

"I can hear your heavy breathing, Squires. You're not nervous, are you, son?"

"Not really, ma'am, I just. I, uh, no I'm fine."

"Well you should be nervous, you fucking nitwit. We've got a situation, here, a situation with all the ass-fucking implications that go with it."

"Ma'am?"

"Raglan just finished an InterCon with the French."

"The President?"

"Yes, that Raglan." She huffed. "The French know all about Symmetra."

"How?"

"Thunder thinks they've been negotiating with the kidnappers. She thinks they want to convert Symmetra's database so they can use the stuff for brainwashing."

"That can't be it. They must know we'd never let them get away with that. We'd turn Paris into a parking lot before they got it off the ground. Right?"

"Right. But Thunder's got a negative bias and Raglan's ear. She's suggesting the other theocracies being in it too, all of them being in it together."

"On what basis?"

"Because Raglan's been on the phone with the PIF and the Israelis, too."

"Working together for the same stuff?" Tuck asked. "That doesn't make any sense."

"It doesn't have to make sense if it's reality. Oh, and another thing, she's making rumblings about us being involved."

"Us?"

"ID. She's suggesting someone inside was in on this, or, at

the very least that we're all incompetent. She wants the President to call for an independent inquiry. Congress. All that shit."

"Who do they think the traitor is?"

"They have no idea. It's a fishing expedition, Squires. Could be me, could be you."

"Me?" Tuck asked, voice rising an octave in sincere surprise.

"Could be Clarion, too," Hunter added. "What if he's flipped?"

"Do you think he could have betrayed the country like that?"

"Really doesn't matter at this point. Thunder's been trying to convince Raglan to get rid of me since she took office. She just needs a plausible reason to ask for my resignation. And this may be it."

"Yes, ma'am."

"Quit ma'am-ing me, Squires. Jesus."

"Yes, m-m-mmm…"

"M-m-mmm?"

"Mmm-hmmm…"

"Just get to New Orleans and hope this tip pans out. If you can't track Chu, you'll have to try to pick up the lead Clarion was working on when he went missing."

Hunter killed the call. Tuck tossed his cell onto the seat beside him. Two beats, and he brought the side of his fist down against the Epic's dash, leaving a dent shaped like a heart. Not a curvy Valentine's heart, but a real one—the great, central muscle necessary for life. Tuck wanted to keep going, too, to keep beating the car until he felt better or until he broke his hand, whichever came first. But the thought of striking blow after blow against the dash just made him tired, made him sink down against the steering wheel.

Everything was his fault, every failure, every problem. Clarion's death, Chu's escape, the fact that Hunter was in trouble with the President, and that he was, too. And then there was the worst of it, the fact that the world seemed to be spiraling out of control, even more out of control than usual. For a second he considered leaving the country, just running forever. The freedom. The road. No responsibilities. He would change his name, become another person.

But being Tuck Squires was all he knew, all he felt like he would ever know. And being Tuck Squires was God's will. That was the Lord's plan for Tuck's life. To shirk that, to try to escape it would have been wrong, maybe even evil in a way. No, Tuck's only option was to do as ordered, to go to New Orleans, the City of Sin. His only option was to make things right, to do what he'd told himself he wanted his whole life, to make his father's memory proud.

17

HIS USUAL COUP DE GRÂCE

DIANA WAS SANE FOR THE MOST PART, WHICH MEANT SHE hadn't spent a lot of time considering Greco-Roman mythology as the stuff of reality. But in terms of Symmetra's development she hadn't been able to fully discount it either. Nor, for that matter, any of the polytheisms that had dominated the ancient world. They were data points in humanity's attempt to understand the metaphysical—nothing less, nothing more.

In addition to ancient mythology's impact on Symmetra, which Diana would ultimately judge to be negligible, there was the impact of these myths on her thinking, the fact that she'd heard the stories as a small child and seen them on the InterTel, been subjected to them in one form or another nearly every day of her life. Still, after thousands of years, the only thing that surpassed them in Western culture was the Christian Bible. And you couldn't discount longevity when you were trying to piece together the spirituality of a species.

Beyond all this, Diana had a namesake in the pantheon, the virgin huntress Diana. So, even as a small girl, she'd made associations. If she saw the goddess Diana—or her Greek counterpart Artemis—portrayed in a positive light, she was bound to feel happy. If she saw Diana portrayed as the villain... well, that had an obvious impact, too.

The thing that always got to Diana—our Diana, not the goddess—the thing that always twisted her up—was that Diana the goddess was just a minor deity even though her twin, Apollo, was major. Born to Zeus and Hera, just like him, Diana was moon to Apollo's sun, dark to his light. Although women were the ones who actually gave life, somehow Diana always wound up being less than Apollo, never more, or even equal.

As Diana grew, the implications became obvious—society, conveniently controlled by men, portrayed women as being fundamentally less than their male counterparts. Women had to be demure, less showy. If they were bossy they were bitches or witches or worse. Significant as this might have seemed, and was, to Diana's life, the implications for Symmetra were far greater. And these were the ones that most interested her by the time she was an adult.

Did men and women seek spirituality in different ways, for different reasons? Were men more goal-oriented, more concerned with the receipt of some eternal reward than they were with living well? Even most of the old polytheisms were patriarchal—father gods like Zeus, Odin, and Ra at the heads of the pantheons. Had men being in charge distorted the data set? If so, was there some way, any way, to adjust? The answer Diana came to was that if there was an adjustment, she was it.

Diana woke squinting. Stark, painful sunlight streaming through the window to her right, the sky beyond was a clear, thin blue, decorated with airy bursts of marshmallow clouds. Placid and pretty, the setting seemed almost to mock the migraine in her head. She moved to shield her eyes but couldn't. Her hands were tied to the armrests. Sensing people around her—their breathing, their body heat, their scents—Diana shut her eyes again. Bobbing her head as though caught in a dream, she turned to the window, and slit her right eye, gaze falling to the plane's silvered wing.

Gleaming there, a perfect sliver of the latest, greatest future, it seemed posed to her, static, like the sky and the clouds. A little turbulence, though, a little bit of the wind's unseen shimmy, and the illusion of stasis failed, the plane bucking, its wing's angle changing. Sunlight now glaring off it, the image moved from brilliant to unbearable in that split-second, sending Diana's thoughts back to the pain in her head, forcing her to turn away abruptly, to face the two men with her.

The one next to her was the big black guy, Zulu, wearing the Batman mask she'd become used to. He was squinting, watching the big screen near the front of the cabin. Across from him sat another masked man. The black hair and generic looks left her thinking of Superman, but that wasn't it. This wasn't Viking. It wasn't the Natural either. This man was much smaller than the others.

The smaller man spoke, "Miss Scorsi, you're awake?"

"I guess," she said, still struggling to place the mask. It wouldn't come to her. So plain and reassuring, so Midwestern and grandfatherly. The eyes were different though.

Silver and nearly translucent, they seemed artificial, almost science fictional in shade; reminded Diana of a fading history of space races and high frontiers, moon shots and splashdowns. They reminded her of the wing of the plane she'd seen just a moment before. And she realized she was looking at the architect of SDI, Ronald Reagan.

"And how do you like my face?" He said it matter-of-factly, as though making dinner-table conversation, as though asking whether she wanted more peas.

"That's not a face. It's a mask," she said, more softly than she'd wanted.

The Presence lifted a gold-rimmed cup from the table in front of him. He tipped it towards her as though toasting, brought the thing to his lips, and sipped. When he set the cup down, Diana saw it was clean and empty, as if there had never been anything inside.

"Same difference, isn't it?" The voice, she realized, sounded different from the one she'd heard at the roadhouse—fuller and more active. Powerful. The precisely tailored, white suit, the slim frame, the jewel-studded watch and cufflinks. This was obviously the Presence.

She wondered where the others were: the Viking Superman and his boss, the guy in the Dubya mask, the Natural. She recalled seeing the Natural's face in the shadows before he'd dosed her the last time. The full image wouldn't come to her, though, just features in distorted fragments: the square jaw, the chin that should have been handsome but only seemed brutal and careless, the sneering lips.

She remembered the black guy, Zulu, coming into the room. He'd said something about the news, and the Natural had left with him. She'd waited and waited. Two hours, maybe three.

When the Natural returned, his breathing was quick. Even in the dim light of that room, she could see the sweat glistening on his neck. "Set it and burn it," he'd said into his cell.

A few seconds later he had the needle in his hand, was dosing her and pulling off the mask. She knew he was revealing his face but she couldn't stay with it, couldn't focus on the features well enough to catalog them. Her mind had seemed unable to do anything but drift inward, as it had done just now with the Presence.

"I'm waiting, Miss Scorsi."

"For?" she replied.

"I asked you a question. I expect an answer."

"What was the question?"

He paused, turned from her. "What's the difference between a face and a mask?"

"Is this a riddle?"

"Not at all. I just want your opinion."

"Well, let's see, a face is made of flesh. It's organic. A mask is made of plastic or some other synthetic. The masks are what you and your guys wear. Faces are what we all wear."

He turned back to her, the smile seemed wolfish, feral. "Don't be so sure, Miss Scorsi. We all wear masks. Some of us are just more honest about it than others."

"All right. How about you answer a question for me now, Presence?"

"Go on."

"The masks are symbols, right? You're trying to say something with them?"

"Why would I do that?"

"I don't know. You're the criminal."

He laughed. "We're saying we don't want you to know who we are. That's what we're saying."

"So, there's nothing to it, nothing more than that? I mean, Reagan, Bush, Batman, Superman…Where are Superman and the Dubya anyway?"

"There's no more Superman, Miss Scorsi—"

"And it's your fault," interrupted the black guy, Zulu, turning to face her. She could see the anger in those big, brown eyes. She felt sad for him and terrified of what he might do. She couldn't help thinking this was life inside a real horror movie.

"Now, now, Zulu, we can't really blame Miss Scorsi for that. It was the Agent's fault."

"Clarion," Zulu snarled.

"That and, well, Viking's own fault."

"The goth."

"That's right."

Diana laughed. "I knew there was something off about him. So, he was a goth junkie? A born-again goth junkie?"

Zulu turned to Diana. "He was a great American," he said through clenched teeth. "He defended our country, defended your right to say what you want, to develop that godless software of yours."

"Zulu, why don't you sit across the aisle, leave me here to talk to Miss Scorsi by myself."

"You sure, Presence?"

"Sure, I'm sure. Go watch the cartoons. Snazzy and Hobo should be kicking up on Wolf ViewKids any minute."

Zulu rose and lumbered away. He deposited himself on the sofa of a seating group closer to the front of the cabin. Sure enough, Snazzy and Hobo were there, the scampering piano of their intro music just kicking in.

"Sunlight bothering you?" asked the Presence, "I can fix that, you know." He reached across her, lowering the shade, his arm brushing her face as he did. Even through the layers of material—the linen suit and silk shirt she saw, the scaly reptilian skin she imagined—she felt negative energy, bad electricity. He smelled old, like that friend of her grandfather's, the one who'd eyed her all those afternoons and eventually tried to do more. She'd barely escaped the weak, insistent bulge, bad breath, and sickly aftershave. She'd been fourteen.

"See there. Not so bad anymore, is it? You know, we can still work together, Miss Scorsi. There's still time."

She retched, moved to bring her fist to her mouth but couldn't.

"Cat got your tongue?" he asked with a chuckle, then gave a nod behind him, towards the screen where Snazzy and Hobo had begun their antics.

Diana had seen Snazzy and Hobo many times before. When she'd been a small child she'd gotten a little of it, enough for her father to come screaming from the other room—the frantic piano of the theme song was unmistakable. He'd pointed at the translucent wolf's head in the corner of the screen and said, "Wolf bad."

As a teenager that memory had lingered with her, and she'd watched Snazzy and Hobo mostly because her father didn't want her to. Still, the cartoon never accomplished its goal with Diana. Instead, if anything, it helped turn her thoughts to mockery of what Wolf View wanted her to believe.

So, no, it didn't surprise Diana at all when the jaundice-eyed, hip, black cat that worked for the ACLU got the shit beaten out of him by the clear-gazed, conservatively-dressed little, white mouse that only wanted to be left alone to run his cartel. Nor did it seconds later when Snazzy exacted his usual coup de grace for everything Hobo had put him through over the years—the welfare riots, work stoppages, and picketing; the fiery, rabble-rousing speeches promoting his fell agenda of social justice and liberation theology.

Hobo being led off to jail by burly, red-faced Officer O'Bulldog, the cartoon camera closed on Snazzy's little, white face and his big, black-eyed gaze; a gaze that while dark as a pit seemed to shine with energy, the myriad possibilities posed by his righteous malice. A thought balloon question mark appeared above his head. A thought balloon exclamation point and a justifiably malevolent smile later, the little mouse sprang high in the air, landing with both feet on the tip of Hobo's ground-scraping beard.

Diana felt like she wanted to laugh and cry at the same time. Another part of her wanted to scream and lash out. But she was restrained, those thoughts useless.

The Presence's cell chirped. He reached into his lapel. "Yes?"

Diana turned back to Snazzy and Hobo.

Now, the cat and mouse were in the Army. Hobo a General, Snazzy a Private; a horde of identical, vaguely yellow-skinned foxes loomed on the other side of the battlefield, red stars on their wicker helmets, hatred in their not-too-obviously-Oriental eyes. When Hobo screamed charge Snazzy followed the order only to find his commander fleeing a few frames later, the enemy horde now taking aim. Snazzy turned and fled, too; zigzagging across the field as laser beams blasted at him, right, left, upside down, inside up, outside over, and all around. Within a few frames, the ever-speedy Snazzy had closed on his commanding officer. He raised his ray gun, prepared to fire at his cowardly commander.

"Oh, yes, old friend. Salaam alaikym," the Presence said, he rose and walked towards the back of the cabin.

The other side of the conversation gained steam quickly, a long pause as the Presence stood listening. Nodding his head, Reagan's face jiggled a little harder with each nod. He finally turned from Diana.

"Let me get this straight. You don't want to increase your bid. Yes. I understand that, but wait, what? Another source? Another source for what?"

18

CONVERSATIONAL STRAIGHTJACKET

By 2034, Bobby Jindal had spent twenty-two years as Governor of Louisiana. In that time Jindal had presided over six Category 5 hurricanes—Biffy, Poffy, Tippy, Albertine, Screwy, and Lu-Lu—the repeal of gubernatorial term limits, and a Golden Age of Christian Capitalism. Headquarters to Righteous Burger along with numerous Christian oil companies and the burgeoning Christian high-protein gator-farming industry, Louisiana's coffers filled in the Jindal years, not just because of reductions in social spending but long-sought tax breaks that incentivized wealthy individuals, religious entities, corporations, and admixtures thereof to relocate to the Bayou State.

With success came praise for Jindal and, eventually, a demigod-like status in Louisiana politics. Schools and churches, public buildings, stadiums, and airports were all renamed to laud Bobby the Bubbly as the Governor came to be known. Not the least of these was New Orleans Louie Armstrong International Airport, a venue that by 2034 was known simply as Bobby

Jindal-Louie Armstrong Semi-International Airport. Hurricane Screwy had necessitated the change in status as certain countries no longer trusted flights to and from New Orleans.

As a result of this fortunate mix of natural disasters, tax incentives, Christian Capitalism, and its unfailing financial support of Governor Jindal, Christian airline AirMerica Inc. had monopolized passenger travel to and from New Orleans since 2026. Which meant that other than the seat-back screens with their "personalized commercial narratives" and Reed, the steward's, reminders about oxygen-consumption and space-usage up-charges Tuck had nothing to distract him from his own thoughts, a very un-Tuckian post mortem on what had happened with Alfred Chu.

Tuck had been duped. He knew that. He also knew that the only thing that had saved him, or had, at least, gotten him some time to redeem himself, was the fact that Clarion had gone missing; that he'd failed, too. Maybe worse than failed, it was entirely possible that Clarion was dead, and Tuck was Hunter's only chance.

The question he'd kept coming back to during the flight and even after he'd landed at Bobby Jindal was why. What could have motivated someone like Chu—someone a lot like Tuck—to sacrifice his principles, and possibly his life? Sure, most people would have assumed it had something to do with money, but Tuck knew that wasn't necessarily the case. The rich already had money. They didn't need to spend their time figuring out how to get more, not unless that was what they had a calling for. And then, they were doing what God wanted and usually wound up giving it to charity anyways.

No, the truth was that the poor were the greedy ones,

always clutching for this benefit or that entitlement, lusting for someone to give them what they couldn't get by honest work. But if Chu's goal hadn't been money, there had to be some other agenda for him, something Tuck had missed.

What if he was secretly working for the Chinese, the PIF, or both? What if he'd been recruited before he'd even gotten to the U.S. then lain in wait, biding his time first at Stanford then MIT then Symmetra? Or, maybe he wasn't a pagan at all? Maybe Chu was a believer? What if X had convinced him that Scorsi had to be stopped? And if that had happened, if X had convinced one of Scorsi's closest friends, someone who knew Symmetra and had still betrayed her, what did that say about X, the other kidnappers, or even Scorsi and Symmetra itself? Did it say the kidnappers were right? That Symmetra and Scorsi were wrong, maybe even evil?

TUCK HAD BEEN CAMPED OUT FOR AN HOUR WHEN THE SILVER pickup finally showed. Stationed just beyond the chain-link fence that separated the Confederate Crossways enclosure from the rest of the airport, he watched through night vision goggles as the truck backed up to the dock door of Loading Bay 16. When the pickup's driver got out, Tuck could see he was wearing a hooded sweatshirt, sunglasses and a baseball cap, but that was it, the details of his face effectively hidden.

Once the driver entered the building, Tuck scaled the fence, moved in, and placed a tracking chip under the front bumper. He moved back the way he'd come, alternately checking over his shoulder and scanning for threats ahead. A moment later, he was back on the other side of the fence, using the night vision, waiting.

The driver emerged from the building with two uniformed Confederate employees and a big, pinewood crate. Together, the three men moved the crate into the truck's payload. When they were done, there were smiles from the Confederate guys and the exchange of what looked to be cash, before the driver got back in his truck.

Tuck looked down at his watch as the pickup departed, saw the map had replaced its face, the white light blinking in ocular staccato. He broke into a run, heading towards the black Epic he'd rented from Quickie a few hours before. Tuck kept his distance as the silver pickup headed north on the causeway. There was little traffic moving away from the city at that time of morning, and he couldn't take a chance on spooking the guy at this point. After all, he wasn't the quarry, only a means to it.

They spent a solid hour like this—the silver pickup speeding along the ribbon of sandy concrete that cut across Lake Pontchartrain and through the woods towards the center of the state; Tuck using the tracking beacon and his watch to follow—before moving onto back roads. Ten minutes after that the driver stopped. Once Tuck had drawn to within about an eighth of a mile he did the same. He did his best to conceal the Epic, took the extra clips for his Rikken, and set off at a run.

TUCK FOUND THE CLEARING EASILY ENOUGH, TOOK COVER behind a sycamore once he made the outer tree line. From there, he spotted the truck and the crate, the driver with a crowbar in his hand already working at it. No longer hooded, it was now obvious he wore a mask. A silver Gulfstream jet idled perhaps a hundred yards away. Its tail read Savior III.

Birds flapped and hooted in the distance. Squirrels skittered. Tuck glared at the trees that surrounded the clearing, and him; the soldier pines, maples, and walnuts. The location only made Tuck hate the kidnappers more—the fact that they would use such a symbol of Socialist Environmentalism even as a joke— left him gritting his teeth and stroking his gun.

Tuck watched as the driver banged the butt of the crowbar several times against the side of the crate. He knelt, turned his ear to the crate and listened. Seconds later, he went back to work splintering the sides until the contents were finally revealed.

Sweating heavily, Alfred Chu hugged an oxygen tank. The driver helped Chu wobble from the remnants of the crate then down out of the truck's payload where Chu collapsed on the ground, gulping air. The driver turned back to the truck's payload, checked the oxygen tank's meter. "You were supposed to set the flow to 8."

Chu stood. Half laughing, half crying, he staggered, ankles buckling as he tried to walk. "I thought I was going to die in that crate," he said, backhanding the driver to his upper arm.

The driver shrugged. "If you'd done as you were told, you'd be fresh as a daisy, Insider."

Chu hit the man again, this time harder.

The driver barely turned his head. He drawled, "Suggest you not do that again, son."

Chu yanked off his jacket and threw it to the ground. He rolled up his sleeves, ran a hand through his sweat-soaked hair, and began cycling his fists like an old-school boxer. He circled. He danced. "Put 'em up, Natural," he said.

The Natural laughed. "Trust me, little man, you don't want to do this," he added, his voice practically dripping with derision. The Insider was beneath him as far as the Natural saw it, subhuman in a way.

"Oh and why's that?" Chu asked, shoving the Natural in the arm hard enough that he was forced to take a step back.

"Because you don't."

"Well, I say I do." Chu jabbed with his right, followed with a quick one-two. Perfectly positioned in Lord Whitemansion's long-outdated Chin-up Stance, Chu looked like a guy with soft hands who'd suddenly convinced himself he could kick ass. Chu's expression reminded Tuck of a lot of the guys he'd gone to prep school with. For just an instant he thought back to his first day in hand-to-hand training at the Academy, how he'd been paired with that chick who'd absolutely kicked his ass, that Mary McClure. She was from a small mill town in Connecticut. That was when Tuck realized he'd have to toughen up if he was going to succeed with the Bureau. That was when he'd developed at least a little bit of respect for the scrappiness of America's lower classes, especially the ones from mill towns in Connecticut.

"Where you think you going if you beat on me, Insider?"

"Put up your dukes, Natural. Don't worry. I'm not gonna kill ya. But I want some payback."

"You want payback? After what you've done?"

"What I've done?" Chu said, still circling, fists spinning ineffectually through the air. "I just spent six hours in a crate."

"The Presence told me all about you, Insider. If you hadn't been such a money-grubbing Judas none of this would have happened. So, save your indignation."

222

"Money-grubbing? What did the Presence say?"

"Not much," the driver said. "Just that you're an embezzler."

His brow creased. "Now, just a second. That's not—"

"Listen, Insider, I refuse to..." The Natural thought for a second, finally succumbed to his own conversational straightjacket. "Listen to your lies. First you sinned and sinned and sinned. Then you betrayed Scorsi and now you're messin' with me. And I won't have it. I won't have a bit of it."

"I didn't embezzle anything," Chu insisted through puffs and pants.

"Oh really? Well, you'll excuse me if I don't believe a money-grubbing Japanaman like you."

"I'm not money-grubbing. I'm not a Judas. And I'm Chinese, you donkey," said Chu. He picked up his stride, this time faster, one lap, two laps, three and four. He was shadow boxing with a live target, none of his blows connecting—until one did, a right that clocked the Natural in the side of the head. Tuck realized that the mask had been the face of a President, maybe the greatest President America had ever had, George W. Bush. He wondered why the mask of the Dubya had been so bad, so unrecognizable, an insult to perhaps the greatest American who'd ever lived. That in and of itself made Tuck angry, made him feel as though Chu had just done something to America herself.

Chu stopped circling. He squinted, surprised and apologetic. He opened his mouth to speak but no words came.

"I'm gonna have to tie you up for that, Insider. Gonna have to gag you, too."

"No, no, really. I'm sorry. I just—I must have been crazy from the heat."

"It's fifty degrees out."

"I meant in the box."

"Look, you just attacked me is all I know."

"Maybe, but you're fine. I hardly did any damage. Honest, Natural, I won't do it again"

"Doesn't matter," he said, grabbing a coil of rope from farther back in the truck's payload. Stepping towards Chu, he turned his back on Tuck's position. "Don't give me any trouble, and I won't hurt you. Else, I'm gonna have to put you out."

"You mean like a bad dog or a lame horse?"

"I said out, not down, Insider. Presence wants to see you, thinks you can help us get what we need from your boss."

Chu squinted. He looked off to his right, as though assessing his options. He turned and ran for the other side of the field.

The Natural gave chase, the jowls of his rubberized W mask flapping as he did. Chu was younger and surprisingly quick. Tuck couldn't help being impressed with his agility. On three separate occasions, he slipped an attempted tackle. Just after they'd finished their second circuit of the clearing, Tuck noticed both men slowing, realized the Natural was gaining again. With both men's backs to him, Tuck decided it was time to strike.

"Stop," he said, pointing his Rikken at the Natural as he moved into the clearing.

The Natural dropped the rope. Reaching for Chu with both hands now, he pulled him into a throat lock, turned to face Tuck. He pulled his piece and held it to Chu's temple. Tuck couldn't return fire, and he knew it. He needed Chu alive. Then, he realized, so did the Natural. Tuck ran and leapt, hurling himself across the space between the men. Spearing both, he knocked the gun from the Natural's hand, knocked both the Natural and Chu back and to the ground, but lost his Rikken in the process.

Chu scurried away. The Natural rose to defend himself. Tuck and he grappled, Tuck knew he had to knock the guy out and quickly. That was the only way.

"Squires? Oh, thank goodness," said Chu.

"That'll be all, Chu. I'll deal with you when I'm done with him."

"Not really," he said.

Tuck turned to see Chu holding the Natural's gun by its muzzle. Chu brought the thing in a sissified arc, trying to knock Tuck to the center of the forehead. Tuck blocked the blow, grabbed Chu's wrist and twisted, heard him cry out. That was the last thing he remembered before he felt the Natural's blackjack to the back of his skull.

19

SOMEWHERE IN THE TRIANGLE

LIKE THE TROJAN WAR, CLARION'S RELATIONSHIP WITH HIS kid was an epic conflict years in the making, one that had grown out of love. The love was of a different sort, of course—paternal and filial instead of romantic and conjugal, though the way Drakonika fit into the picture couldn't be totally discounted either—but it was love all the same. Like any good epic, like any war worth calling itself one, the relationship had been marked by determination and opposition, a deep desire not to fight, an even more powerful unwillingness to be the one to stop. In a way, it was easy for Clarion to see how the ancients had ascribed the work of divinities to their wars. Whether families or neighbors or armies, the reasons people kept fighting were so often mysterious, so far beyond the realms of ethics or reason, that they might easily seem like the province of otherworldly powers.

In the beginning, when Morris was a baby, the struggles were about green vegetables and ice cream cones, merry-go-rounds and bedtime stories. These weren't fights exactly. They were more like disagreements. But even when Clarion's son was an infant, a complete and utter dependent, he'd sensed opposition on a fundamental level. It was almost as if Morris had exited the womb with a negative bias towards his old man, as if Drakonika had already been at it during gestation. Not that this attitude surprised Clarion, at least at first. He felt, in general, as though that was the way of the world. Men loved their mothers. They wanted to kill their fathers.

As Morris grew and the marriage between Clarion and Drakonika fell apart, the conflicts became speechless, nearly noiseless. By that point, they'd begun to center on the general disaffection of childhood, of guilt and disappointment. There were days and weeks and months of the silent treatment.

Then came the split with Drakonika, the teenage years when Clarion had seen his son very little. When he wasn't working, he was dealing with lawyers, not only matrimonial but criminal. Drakonika had done her ground work, and she had no record. Even the money she'd stolen outright, secreted in Turkey or wherever, was never coming back.

No phone, concussed, a legion of skulking, slinking, chittering bayou-life his only companions, Clarion was thinking of his son as he stumbled along the gravel shoulder, now at least a mile away from the Dauphine. He was thinking of Morris as a baby, before he'd spoken and their disagreements had started, thinking the only goal that mattered was fixing things with his kid. Now that he was back in the field, what if he died? What if he never got to make amends? Would he be able to forgive himself? No, he wouldn't. The mission didn't matter. What mattered was life. What mattered was family.

That was when he caught the whisper of a helicopter coming in from the east. He looked up to see the A-417 silhouetted against what was left of the night, its three red, tracking lights glowing like the eyes of some sinister beast. He remembered his duty then. He had to finish this one last gig. There'd be time to make peace with Morris on the other side.

The copter stopped directly above, hovered briefly then pivoted its side-rotors and began to descend. Straight down it came, gunmetal underside growing closer until it stopped at about a hundred feet, its belly lights shining to life.

Clarion shielded his eyes and turned away. In the florid, shattered distance he made out the motion of retreating swamp creatures—owls and bats, gators and rats—all of them convinced day had come early, or worse still, that they'd somehow stumbled onto the end of the world.

Behind the wheeze of hydraulics and the grind of metal, the copter's bay doors opened. A rope ladder dropped, nearly smacking Clarion in the face. If he'd had any doubt that Hunter was behind the pick-up, this brush with a second concussion ended it. Clarion grabbed the ladder, began to climb as the 417 cut its belly lights and moved into the sky. Onboard, the copter was crewed by Army. Their commander was a Major. Her tag read Waters. She saluted, and Clarion returned.

"What do you have for me, Maj—?"

Clarion heard a cell ring. Then again. The major pulled a phone from her front pocket. Without even looking at it, she said, "It's for you."

Clarion took the phone from her. "Clarion."

"Kenny," came a familiar voice, "You made it."

"Get me up to speed, boss. Did the kid find anything?"

"That's not your problem anymore."

"What about the ones I was tailing?"

"Not your problem either."

"Then what is my problem?"

Hunter's voice rose, lightening. "No more problems. You're coming back to D.C."

"Excuse me?"

"I said you're coming back to D.C. Waters and her people will take you to MacDill. You can jump a flight from there."

"Jesus, Hunter, can you at least gimme a little more than the trailer?"

"Fine, Kenny, I've got nothing better to do than sit here telling you what a mess you've made. Squires figured out that Chu was the top rat inside Symmetra, but only after he'd split town. Kid was tailing Chu down your way when they got him. He's somewhere in the Triangle now. That's where we lost his signal."

"The Bermuda Triangle?"

"Right. They must have some decent stealthing tech, probably got it from the Russians."

"So they're behind all this? The Russians?"

"Probably not. But who knows? We've pinned it down to about fifty thousand square miles. Now, it's simple recon, try to figure out where Squires and Scorsi are, get them back in hand before this Special Counsel thing picks up anymore steam."

"But the public bought all that jewel thievery nonsense we set in motion."

"We?"

"I."

"Right, your fiction remains intact, for the time being. Good thing, too. Otherwise, the shit would be even deeper."

"Well?"

"Let me rephrase: Secret Special Counsel. And it won't have anything to do with fiction. Unless you can come up with a way to make my career fictional."

"And the Congressional stuff?"

"That'd be hush-hush, too. They're invoking Anti-Terrorism and Sedition."

"ATS? For who?"

"Thunder has her eye on Squires now, thinks he may not just be incompetent."

"Squires? Part of a plot? Oh, I don't buy that. And how can you? You sent him on the mission."

"Not like that. She knows what a zealot he is, thinks maybe the kidnappers have turned him."

"Nah. You should have heard the way he was talking about Etobo. Honestly, Hunter, he's gung ho as they come. I'd bet my life on him not being involved."

"Look, you're probably right. Squires probably had nothing to do with it. But he is a right-winger. There's no doubt about that. I'm surprised Thunder didn't latch onto him sooner."

"Just being a right-winger has the President convinced he's a traitor? That doesn't make sense. Raglan's not like that."

"It's not just that he's a right-winger. It's the family connection. There's something there, something from the campaign, maybe even earlier. Honestly, my knowledge of Raglan's political history isn't great."

"But ATS?"

"I'm just happy they've quit looking at me—and you for that matter."

"What are they looking at?"

"Looks like I was right about the scientific aspect."

"You have an identity?"

"No, but we've narrowed it. Thunder's got point on that now. Raglan doesn't want us 'screwing anything else up.'"

"Raglan said that?"

"I heard it from Prentiss. Oh, who knows? Could be he and Thunder are making stuff up for shits and giggles at this point. That's not the worst of it anyway."

"No?"

"No. The PIF and the Israelis know as much as the French... as Mirrage does."

"Which is what exactly?"

"They know about Symmetra, what it can and might be able to do if Scorsi were to cooperate. They know we've lost her. They're at each other's throats."

"Didn't take Symmetra to cause that."

"Right. There's one thing unifying them, though."

"Mistrust of us?"

"Almost. Mistrust of each other. So, I guess that actually makes two." She chuckled mock-maniacally, took a long drag of air.

"You have an alternate theory."

"I'm noodling over something."

"After all that?"

"I told you, Clarion, you're done. I'm sending somebody else."

"You must be joking? This is my gig, Hunter. And I was your best before you turned me into a desk jockey. Before you—"

"Before I what?"

"Never mind."

"You didn't even want the mission, Kenny. And, honestly, if I'd known it was going to blow up like this I wouldn't have sent you and Squires. In case you haven't noticed, I'm trying to give you a way out, Clarion, and you're not taking it."

"Would you in my shoes?"

"Sure."

"You know you wouldn't."

Hunter laughed. "Don't be so sure. As your friend, Kenny, I'm telling you, you don't want a piece of this anymore."

"As your friend, I took this gig. And now I want to see it through. Are you going to tell me I can't?"

Hunter paused. "You know I won't say no when you put it like that. Worse, you know I can't."

"You still haven't told me your theory on the leak, Hunter. What if it's Thunder herself? Have you considered that?"

"I've given it passing consideration. I mean, theoretically, it could be anyone. Thunder's not a very likely suspect though. Causing an actual war is a little severe even for her. What would she have to gain?"

"I don't know."

"Most likely it's someone in the scientific community, some aggrieved maniac with a two hundred IQ. The National Association of Science possibly the National Science Foundation, someone with personal motivation."

20

A SHEEP IN WOLF'S CLOTHING

HAD PEGGY SUE ORCHARD HEARD THE RUMORS ABOUT herself and that handsome encyclopedia salesman, Jim Tingle? Sure, she had. Armistice was a small town: twenty storefronts, five streets, and a city hall tied together with nothing but a little inbreeding and a lot of gossip. Even before her husband returned from the war, Peggy Sue had overhead Old Mrs. Flatly at White's Diner. She'd more than once caught the double-barreled glare of village stuffed-shirts Mr. and Mrs. Heatherington. For the sake of her child, if not herself, Peggy Sue knew she had to find a way to resurrect her reputation… and quickly. Which was where Armistice's new church Joyous Convocation of Christ Crucified and its dashing, young pastor came into the picture.

Though he wasn't exactly—or, even inexactly—a doctor, the Reverend Doctor Declan Floss was a minister trained at New Holiness Bible College of Bog's Meadow, Alabama. Charming and a near lookalike for film star, Vim Tefflin, Floss had used his head for figures to grow a meager flood insurance settlement into a successful ice cream stand and, following that, the seed for his dream—a move north to start the first New-Holiness-denominated church above the Mason-Dixon, the aforementioned Christ Crucified. All of which made the Reverend Doctor Floss the perfect man not only to get Peggy Sue out of her reputation pickle, but to eventually give little Jimmy an education in Capitalism, Christianity, and how the two worked together to make America so swell.

"God doesn't mind if you take a little off the top from time to time, Jimmy," the Reverend Doctor Floss had confided early in Jimmy's tutelage.

They were in Floss's Inner Sanctum, sharing a little lemonade, as Floss gave Jimmy his marching orders for the weekend bake sale. Peggy Sue was waiting in the ante-room beyond, a nurse's uniform, hung and wrapped in plastic, laid flat on the couch beside her. Jimmy was ten.

"Really?" Jimmy responded tentatively. This would be his first solo mission for the Reverend Doctor. Up until then, Floss would oversee the bake sales, lemonade stands, and whatnot himself, employing Jimmy only as a gopher. Jimmy wondered if this was a trick, a way to make sure he wasn't going to fall prey to temptation.

"Of Course. You make money for the church don't you, Jimmy?"

"Yes, Reverend."

"You make money for the Lord, too, right?"

"Yes, sir."

"Well, He and I both recognize that. Even if you were to compensate yourself a little, you know, pinch off a little salary for yourself, God and the church would still come out ahead, wouldn't they?"

"I don't know, Reverend."

"Well, I do, Jimmy. And I'm your boss, right?"

"I…I guess so."

"It's settled then: you'll take ten percent off the top as a salary for all your good work. You don't want to do that while anyone's looking, though. People might misunderstand."

"Are you sure about this, Reverend?"

"Sure I'm sure, Jimmy. Now you run along and send in your mother. I need to minister to her."

Jimmy ran along, past the door and out into the room beyond. There, he found his mother smoothing her skirt. She'd put on lipstick in the time he'd been in Floss's office, the sort of luminous red that made him nervous, made him look away. As he lowered his eyes and walked by Peggy Sue, he noticed the nurse's uniform. Clean and white, it lay waiting, beneath its plastic bag.

BY THE TIME TUCK SQUIRES CAME STUMBLING DOWN SAVIOR II's air bridge, running into and over the smaller though equally blindfolded Alfred Chu, Parlay knew bringing him to the island had been the right decision. That didn't mean he was happy about it.

Wearing a bloody blindfold, his cheek bruised a sickly purple-black, the kid reminded Parlay of the big, blond football player who gets his legs blown off in the movie version of

237

Persian Deception. Which brought him back to the discussion he'd just had with the Angel.

"I talked to the Israelis," the Angel began. "They're back on board, willing to cut the same deal as the others."

"I'd like to hear that with my own ears."

"Now, you don't trust me?"

"No," Parlay answered. "It's this other source Ali was talking about."

"How so?"

"Well, there's a leak."

"Obviously."

"And the two most likely candidates are on this call."

"Well, it's not me, Presence. Is it you?"

"I wouldn't have said anything if it were."

"And we're not the only two possibilities. Maybe it was the Insider. Maybe he spilled something before he left Boston."

"He didn't have anything to spill."

"What about your guy, the one who was on the news, the one you had to kill?"

"I didn't kill anyone, Angel, let's get that straight."

"Already considering how to avoid the death penalty if this falls apart? I like it. And I know you haven't personally killed anyone. I meant the one you ordered the Natural to kill."

"Viking? I guess that's possible."

"More than possible I'd say. Once the Insider's done convincing the Target, have the Natural interrogate him properly, figure out exactly what's going on."

"You think that will work?"

"Couldn't hurt. We have a bigger problem anyway. Mirrage knows."

"Of course he does."

"I don't mean about the Product. I mean that we were negotiating with the others."

"His enemies?"

"Bingo. He called Raglan, threatened war."

"With America?"

"Don't be absurd. With the PIF and the Israelis."

"Why?"

"Why *not* is more like it. You know they're always threatening each other over there. We have no choice but to stick with the plan, accelerate it if we can."

"But what about the war?"

"That's all bluster. Mirrage knows the US would turn Paris into a parking lot if he attacked without provocation. We have to hope the PIF or the Israelis don't start escalating, too. If that happens, Raglan will have no choice but to let it play out. I mean, we can't attack everyone, at least not at the same time."

"But that makes this other source even more dangerous. Meaning we have to do something about it and Ali now."

"Right. You work from your end. I'll get in touch with Ali and talk him down."

"What about Mirrage?"

"We'll have to let that sit and hope nothing else goes wrong."

A few seconds after Squires and Chu tumbled to a stop, Justice appeared at the top of the stairs. Gun drawn, he wore a black t-shirt, blue jeans, and his W mask. The mask was ripped, a piece of the great man's jowl dangling.

"Lock big boy up separate from Scorsi," he called to Urban who'd been standing to Parlay's left, a fleshy shield between him and the disembarking hostages. Just in case. Urban moved to disentangle Squires and Chu, hauled them to their feet.

"Just a second," Parlay said.

Urban shot Parlay a mournful look, the ears of his Batman mask making him seem childish and diabolical at the same time, a kitty cat crossed with a horror movie demon.

Parlay wagged a finger at Squires. He took a few steps forward, removed the sunglasses he'd been wearing over his Reagan mask. "Who…is this?"

Justice squinted. "Special Agent Tuck Squires. You said—"

"What would possess you to bring a federal agent to my island?"

Squires nodded, his blanked gaze moving between Justice and Parlay. Justice shrugged, descended the stairs.

"I think I'm starting to hallucinate," added Chu. "If we've arrived, can you take this blindfold off?"

Parlay nodded to Urban who pulled at the blindfold, sliding it over the top of Chu's head. The process left his black hair spiked, pointing in multiple directions—a sticky medieval helmet of follicles, product, and humidity.

"Thank you, Jesus," exclaimed Chu, blinking repeatedly.

Parlay responded, "That'll be all for your bad language, Insider. We don't take the Lord's name in vain on my island. Understand?"

"Understand what?"

"Understand what the Presence said, little man." Justice smacked him in the back of the head.

"Hey!"

"When you speak the Lord's name thusly, Insider, it is a curse, not a blessing," Parlay added.

"I was just thanking Jesus. It's an expression. What's wrong with that?"

"If you were a believer, nothing. For a heathen like you, it's a problem. A big problem."

"I'm not a heathen. I'm a Lutheran."

"Fine, well, you may not be a full-on heathen, but you're not one of us either."

"Amen to that," said Squires.

"You, too, Squires. Watch your language."

"But I'm a Christian."

"A real Christian? You're not from one of those kooky sects: Zoroastrians, Gnostics, something like that?"

"I don't even know what that is," said Squires. "I'm a real, honest of goodness Christian washed in the Blood of the Lamb."

Parlay looked at Justice who shrugged.

"Fine. Take off his blindfold, too."

Chu blanched. "Wait. What? Why does he...? He's the enemy...He's...Just based on his tone of voice and what he says?"

"Right."

Chu looked down, barring his gaze for a second. When he looked back, his gaze was plaintive. "Seriously?" he asked.

"Yes, Insider. Now are you gonna behave or not?"

Chu stepped back, nodded slowly. "Sure, Presence, is there, uh, is there something you want me to say instead?"

"Say shucks or daggone. Say whatever you want, Insider, just not the name of the Lord."

Squires nodded in agreement. Bruised and bloody as Squires was, the thought came to Parlay then that things might work out for the best; that Squires might still turn out to be a sheep in wolf's clothing.

"All right, take him away."

Urban grabbed hold of Squires' cuffs with his right hand. He used his left to jab him in the mid-back, pushing him forward towards the end of the strip where it broadened out into a platform.

"Go easy on that one, Zulu," Parlay ordered. "He may be someone we can deal with."

Parlay heard Urban grunt, watched as Squires preceded him towards the platform. There were two more long strips of concrete radiating out from the hub—Savior II parked at the one on the left, Savior IV at the one on the right. At the other end of the platform rose a black, rock wall ending in a sixty-foot, vaulted ceiling of that same rock. The only break in the wall was a set of silver double doors at floor level.

"This one practically attacked me at the airstrip," Justice offered once Squires was out of earshot.

Parlay turned to him. "Who, the Rookie?"

"No, him."

"That was a misunderstanding," Chu responded.

"Wait, Natural. The Insider attacked you?"

"Not successfully," Justice responded.

"I told you I was crazy from the heat."

Justice smirked. "He only had the oxygen set to two."

Parlay shook his head. "Insider, I'm not sure what I'm going to do with you."

"Can you start by using my real name instead of calling me Insider?"

"Oh? Well, would it be OK if we called you Mr. Chu instead?"

"Well, I am a doctor actually."

"Doctor Chu then?"

"Sure. And, um, now that we're getting to know each other, I'll call you…"

"You'll keep calling me, Presence, and him, Natural."

Justice laughed. "Anyways, Squires shows up at the field…"

"Squires got the drop on him. Wouldn't have made it out of there without my help."

"Is that true, Natural?"

"It's true. This one distracted him long enough for me to get out my blackjack. Think I picked up a twenty-four-hour bug or something," Justice offered, flexing his biceps plaintively.

"Well, well, looks like you were good for something after all, Chu." Parlay checked his cell again, looked up. "All right, Natural, get this one ready to talk to Scorsi."

Justice nodded.

"Things are moving fast out there, faster than we'd planned. The sooner we break her, the better for everyone. Including your boss."

Justice and Chu looked at each other then back at Parlay. Each other, Parlay. Each other, Parlay.

"I meant the Target," Parlay nearly shouted.

21

A CONSPIRACY'S
WHAT IT WAS

DREAMING BRIEFLY THAT SHE WAS THE CAPTAIN OF A
nineteenth century whaler, lashed to the wheel, and going
down with her ship, Diana opened her eyes as the second
bucket of water smacked her in the face. Spilling over her lips,
into her mouth, throat, and lungs, the stuff was cold, frothy, and
swimming with detritus. Filled with salt and metals, it tasted of
the elemental sea—of a time before people had tried to remake
the world in their own image, before they'd sold themselves
on the illusion of control.

Barking out a chain of hacks that left her throat and
diaphragm thrumming, Diana's weak muscles brought up water,
phlegm, and the tang of minerals. She tried to raise her hands
to her face, tried to rise, but felt herself bound to the chair at
her wrists and ankles. When she looked up, she saw that she
was in a black room. All the surfaces—walls, floor, even the
ceiling—bore the rounded angles and bowed arcs of another,

simpler age, the smooth finish of time, almost as if the entire chamber had been carved out of the very rock.

The Natural stood in front of her holding a silver pail. Framed by W's grinning, simian visage, his eyes held her close, lingered over the soaked gingham she felt clinging to her tits. When she caught his gaze, the Natural turned away. By the time his eyes came back to her a second later, the light in them had changed—lust now replaced with the mockery of a fake apology. As if he was saying, "No hard feelings about the kidnapping and torture. Lemme know if there's anything I can do to make it up to you."

Leaning forward, he held the bucket's handle with two, hooked fingers. His pose was carelessly malicious, a wicked child anxious to test the limits of new power. Water fell from the bottom of the pail, hit the stone floor in tiny plops.

"Gonna take a lot more than that to drown me," Diana said. She tossed her head side-to-side, tried to shake the hair from her eyes. Unsuccessful, she scowled, looked down, and spit again, this time aiming for the Natural's feet.

He stepped back just in time, sneered at the spittle painting the black. "Aw, you mean this? This's just to wake you up. We haven't even started getting into how to kill you yet, Scorsi." He cast the bucket aside, watched as it hit the floor with a tinny krang, rolled and came to a stop against the wall. "Bring him in," he called over his shoulder. The sound of a scuffle followed. Not a full-on brawl, more like the curses of an unlucky farmhand chasing greased livestock. After a few seconds, Alfred Chu came sailing in sideways and three feet off the ground.

Eyes wide, mouth wider, he looked like a pigeon in-bound for a skyscraper, Diana the skyscraper in question. Sure enough, the pigeon hit a second later, bony ass to Diana's solar plexus. She, Chu, and the chair fell to the floor in a tangle of arms and legs, flesh and wood.

When Diana looked up again, Zulu was in the doorway. Their eyes met and Zulu began to laugh, the flabby circles of his neck jiggling. Tapping his feet, he looked like he was ready to break into song and dance. "I'd call that a strike, wouldn't you, Natural?"

"Fastball. Right over the plate."

Zulu lumbered through what looked like the sort of three-step someone might teach a bear, began humming Tabby Arnesse's latest #1, "Lambs to the Lord".

"Let's leave these two to get reacquainted," said the Natural, joining in the laughter, but not the dancing. He passed through the doorway, leaving Zulu to lock the cell behind them. Diana heard the two men break into song farther down the hall, a halting anti-harmony that made her long for Zulu's whistling.

> Oh, God is love, can't you see,
> He rains blessings down on me,
> Like lambs to the Lord,
> *With fleece as white as snow,*
> *Someday God will call us home,*
> *Someday God will call us home.*

Fucking Tabby Arnesse, Diana thought. She lay there, conscious of Chu's weight on her, feeling like she didn't want to move ever again, that she didn't care anymore. Science, Symmetra, humanity—none of it seemed to matter. Diana just wanted sleep and peace, to leave the burdens of trying to understand to someone else, someone smarter who would eventually come along. Or, if not, not. Maybe humanity had been a failure. Maybe that was all she'd managed to prove with Symmetra. The world descending into chaos over something that could have saved it, something that was supposed to bring peace, maybe it was time to give up forever. Time for whomever or whatever had brought humanity into being to admit that it had fucked up. Or, if there was nothing, then there was nothing. The lack of organizing intelligence would mean no rationalizations had to be managed or obtained. That failure would simply be, something forgotten as quickly as it had happened. Time to realize that the universe was a sea of chance, no sense to be made of anything, nothing real other than death. And even then…

"Diana?" Chu asked.

"Yeah?" she answered.

"Are you OK?"

"Not really, Alfred. Why? Are you?"

"I think so." He managed a weak, groggy smile.

"Then get the fuck off me? You are absolutely crushing my tits."

"Oh, God, Diana, sorry."

Chu peeled his ear from Diana's breast, pulled his arm from beneath her, and got to his feet. He had that stupid grin on his face—the sort she'd seen the last time they had drinks with the developers. Obviously, he'd been drugged.

Diana stared.

Chu stared back, still grinning.

She moved back and forth as much as she could, the chair swaying with her, a few inches side-to-side. Chu continued to stare. She waggled her hands and feet. Nothing. She shook her head, bugged her eyes. Still nothing.

"Alfred?" she screamed.

"What?"

"Did they drug you or what?"

"Umm, maybe. Why?"

She waved her hands and feet at him. "Because I'm soaking wet, tied to a tipped-over chair, and you're looking at me like a fucking pedophilic zombie."

A couple more seconds of staring, and it hit him. He stooped to help Diana and the chair back to a sitting position. He stood looking at her, the smile still on his face. "Better?" he asked.

"A little."

He smiled.

"Maybe now you could fucking untie me?"

"Oh, I'm not sure they'd like that."

"Who cares what they'd like? You think they're going to kill you for untying me?"

"Maybe."

"Just fucking un-tie me, Chu. If they want to re-tie me, they can."

Chu thought for a few seconds. Finally, he knelt to undo her bonds.

"Jesus, Alfred, what has happened to you?"

"Other than the fact that I just got thrown half-way across a room? That bastard Etobo sold me out."

She looked at him in disbelief, scanned the wall without really seeing it. "So it really was him? That little traitor, and after everything I did for him…"

"I didn't believe it either, Diana, until they grabbed me. Wasn't just Etobo, though. Martinez, Warburton, Beauchamp—they were all in on it."

"Merrily, too?"

He nodded. "A conspiracy's what it was, Etobo at the head, Warburton, Martinez, and Beauchamp at the tail. Turns out they're in some Nihilist terror organization, call themselves the Connundrumniks."

"Common drunks?"

"Connundrum-niks. Like a conundrum plus -niks. As though the whole world is a conundrum and they're the—"

"Niks. Yeah, I get it. So, they're anarchists?"

"Enigmatists."

"Enigmatists?"

"Yeah, I don't even understand it exactly. They're crazy's what they are."

"And Etobo's involved?"

"They call him the Insider. I think you should just give it to them, Diana. Maybe they'll let us go if you do. I mean: that's our only chance."

"Symmetra's my life's work, Alfred. You know that."

"What will your life's work be without your life?"

"I wouldn't trust these guys. They'd get the tech, turn around and kill us, then do who knows what with it. You know what that stuff could do if I opened it up. I cannot believe Etobo. Where is that little bastard?"

"Not here as far as I know."

"So, how do you know all this Connundrumnik stuff?"

"The cops told me before I was taken."

"How'd you get taken if you already knew?"

"Etobo was sly. And he had a lot of help, that bastard."

She lowered her gaze. "Oh, I don't know. Maybe you're right, Alfred. All the stuff at the IGU meeting—that must have had to do with Etobo."

"Honestly, Diana, I don't know or care anymore. I just want to get out of this so I can see my kids again."

"The Chulets," she said, smiling weakly.

Diana didn't often miss having kids. Her work was more important to her than the people in her life—in that way, she felt she owed more to humanity than to any specific member of it. But sometimes that maternal force would crush her insides, leave her feeling as though she'd just watched a six-hour infomercial on starving children in the Third World, been left just as hungry to fill a different need.

"Right, the Chulets," he sighed. "Timmy, Winnie, Jenny, and Mickey…"

"Enough, Alfred, Jesus you're making me feel like shit."

"I was just going to mention little A.J. Allison just got him an Embryonic Socrates onesie."

"Shit," she said.

"Right, shit. I want to see my kids again, Diana. You need to do what you need to do. I'm telling you these guys want to deal with you. They told me so."

"Wait a second, Chu. Have you been negotiating with them?"

"Not really. I mean, OK, yes, maybe, sort of. I was forced. They had me."

"Who forced you? The Presence, the Natural?"

"One, both, I don't know. I can't keep them straight with the masks. They say they just want the technology. They'll give you whatever you want for it."

"Yeah, I know. I've heard all about it."

"Just imagine the research you could do with all that money; the way you could build on the work we've already done."

"You know I can't do it, Alfred. We just have to hang in there and hope the cops get here eventually. And be ready to pounce when they do."

"I don't know about any pouncing, Diana. And I wouldn't count on the cops even showing up."

"Why not?"

"There were two agents that came from ID the morning after you were taken."

"The Shadow CIA, really?" she asked, perking up. "That's great. Those guys are stone-cold killers."

"Yeah, except for the fact that one of them is dead and the other is here on the island, probably in a cell a lot like this one. The Presence is holding all the cards, Diana. We have to deal."

"They could have all the cards like you say. But I still have no choice. The fact that they grabbed you just shows me how ruthless they are. They're going to kill me anyways, probably you, too, even if I give them the tech."

"I—I've never been as strong as you, Diana. Honestly, I'm scared. I don't want to die. My wife, my kids…" Chu lowered his head, hid his face and began to cry.

"Alfred." She reached over, patted him on the back. "I don't know what to say. You've been so loyal. I just—this is more important than you or me."

Chu sobbed loudly, hid his face in his trembling hands.

22

TO GO PARKING LOT ON PARIS

CLARION AND HUNTER WERE IN MARRAKESH, HOLED UP IN a second-floor hotbox near the edge of the Medina. This was early in Bush's fourth term, before Cheney had taken over and Abu Yashid had really taken off. They'd been waiting a day and a half by that point, waiting for White Haffez to show his face.

The intelligence was impeccable. They knew he was in a building on the other side of the square, Clarion surveilling the location with a long-lens camera; the sort photographers, his cover, had still used back then. Hunter was playing his opposite number, pretending to do a story on how American imperialism was destroying North Africa.

Unfortunately, the gig was a grab, not a kill. Which made it all that much harder. They couldn't afford heavy collateral in a place like Marrakesh. They had to wait until they could put eyes on White Haffez, plan from there.

"How can you possibly fix the past, Hunter, other than lying about it?" Clarion said this in a whisper. It was night, sultry hot in the room. The only light came through the slits of a shuttered window. Beyond, the bazaar was a noisy squalor of sound—a ragged din, its individual pieces unrecognizable.

"Lying about it?"

"You're talking about changing history." They were shooting the shit, or so Clarion thought, musing on what it would take to fix things—the country, the world. They'd both decided things had gone too far by that point, militarily. The Middle East seemed ready to blow up—a conjecture that would be proven in the coming years.

"OK, maybe you can't actually fix the past. But you can dream about fixing it," she said as she unbuttoned her blouse. They'd slept together about ten times by that point—once about a year before, the rest only recently.

"Why would you do that?"

Strange as it seemed, Hunter said she was still happy with Chuck. She said this was just for kicks, to deal with the boredom of the road, the boredom of having to sit in a hotbox watching another hotbox, waiting.

"Because it might help you fix the future."

"I guess so."

"I know so, Clarion. It's the present we can't do anything about." She shimmied out of her jeans, crossed the room to where he was kneeling. She was only wearing her panties by that point, her pelvis a few inches from his face. Her skin was glistening with sweat, looked like the surface of water in moonlight.

"This is all going to have to end," she said as she took the camera from him and cracked the shutters.

"Oh?"

"I'm rotating back to D.C."

"You're leaving me?"

"Chuck is threatening to divorce me if I don't get off the road."

"So, let him."

"Why, are you going to marry me?"

"Well, I mean—"

"Don't hurt yourself, sport. I was joking."

"Yeah?"

"Oh, yeah. Now, get down there and do something useful."

She smiled as he teased off her panties, raised her right leg, resting it on his shoulder. She'd never been that wet before. Which was when he knew she was telling the truth. After more than ten years together, she was leaving him.

Clarion drank her in, in case it was the last time, lapped until she began thrusting her pelvis against his lips, willing his tongue inside her. But even after the first orgasm and the second, even as she moaned, he knew her eyes would be trained across the square, doing the job. That was Hunter.

DROPPED IN AN O-2 MANTIS NEAR THE CENTER OF THE Triangle, Clarion was submerged, heading due east at eighty knots. Moving without the O-2's stealth, he was waiting for the kidnappers to notice him, waiting for them to take action. With nine possible locations for their island—five close, the other four scattered in a two-hundred-mile arc close to the Triangle's eastern edge—any response would shave hours off his search time. The downside being that any response might also end his life. But Clarion knew what the O-2 could do. The chances that the kidnappers had any systems capable of foiling it were functionally nil. And he had no choice. The only way this was going to work was if he found the island as quickly as possible. Even without Hunter filling him in, he was sure things were degrading. But he didn't realize quite how quickly that was happening until he talked to her. She called just as the O-2 finished its initial dive, the sort of timing that left Clarion scanning for cameras in the cockpit. At that point, he was ten minutes out from the first possible location.

"Things have changed," came her deadpan greeting, resignation lurking beneath the programmed confidence. Together, they reminded him of the sort of precognitive death-whisper he hadn't heard from her in a long time, not since just prior to So-Zu. It had been so many years since they'd been together, but even with her as the boss, there was something in her voice, something in any woman's voice maybe, that made Clarion want to save her, want to do anything for her.

"Changed how?" he asked.

"French, Israelis, PIF...they're all jockeying troops around the Old World. And they know about Symmetra, absolutely no question about that at this point. The Chinese, Russians, Indians, Brazilians, and the Brits all know something big is fucked up, something all the theocracies are in on. They just don't know what it is yet."

"Meaning they don't have enough information to be dangerous."

"Yeah, but there's plenty of danger without them."

"The troop movements."

"That's not all of it, Kenny. There's a strategic side to the whole thing now."

"Let me guess. Mirrage is convinced the PIF have Scorsi?"

"Very good. Should I keep going, or do you have the rest of it figured out too?"

"It's your dollar, sport."

Hunter laughed at that, laughed as though surprised, but there was a strain of wistfulness to it, as though she feared she might be laughing for the last time. "Mirrage is so convinced that he told the President he wants Scorsi turned over to him within twelve hours or he's going to declare war."

"On us?" He snorted.

"Of course not. On the PIF."

"Well, fuck Mirrage. I'd think Raglan would just shut that down. Threaten to go parking lot on Paris."

"Maybe Cheney would have, not Raglan. Problem is the PIF feel the same way as Mirrage. They think he's bluffing, that he's got Scorsi. And they told the President just as much."

"But they can't handle a conventional war with the French."

"Right, so they threatened to hit Israel if they didn't have Scorsi within eleven hours."

"What did Israel do?"

"They blamed the French and the PIF, threatened to hit Mecca and Paris if there was any breach of their sovereignty from either side."

"Shit."

"Plus, they issued the same demand as the others."

Hunter paused for breath.

Clarion said, "So—"

Hunter cut him off. "You can guess how Makhlouf responded to a threat from the Jews, right? He promised to nuke Jerusalem and Paris in ten hours regardless of what anyone else does."

"Shit. So, what?"

"I'm not done. That was when the French came back with another bid."

"Nine hours?"

"Eight hours and fifty-nine minutes. You know the French."

By this point Clarion's mind felt overloaded with the implications, as if it were a weak AI system splintering, breaking down. Never mind making it up to his kid, or being a hero one last time, the thought that he was failing Hunter, letting her down, too, made it even worse. He felt as though an impossible task had gotten twice as hard, wondered how it could possibly get any worse. Then he remembered Tuck. "What about Thunder? She's still looking at the kid?"

"Looking at him hard. I knew I should have gotten rid of him."

"I spent time with him, Hunter. I'm telling you. He's not involved."

"That's comforting, Kenny. I wish I was as confident. More than that, I wish Thunder and Raglan were. But there's no way to hide one of these nut jobs when the shit goes down. You remember how heavy things got over Yemen and Oman. It was practically a witch hunt for anyone who wouldn't toe the party line. You barely made it."

"Yeah, I remember. I probably wouldn't have without your help."

She sighed. He felt almost as though he could hear her smiling. "I should have seen this coming a long time ago and done something about it regardless of what his last name was."

"Something like what, a sanction?"

"Maybe. You know those orders come straight from the

President, Clarion. And Thunder's already put that one in his head. Maybe if we come through this OK, they won't put a termination out on him; but if Congress starts asking questions, we'll be looking for a sacrificial lamb. And it won't be me, not if I can help it."

Two yellow blips appeared on the mid-console radar screen. Fifty miles out and closing at fifteen hundred mph, Clarion had what he'd been waiting for.

"I have to go, Hunter. I have incoming."

"Clarion, have you been running without the stealth? That thing cost—hell, I don't even know how much it cost. But it was a fucking lot."

Before Clarion could pretend a bad connection, the O-2's autopilot killed the call and accelerated, banking hard and to the left, diving deeper. Seconds later, the Mantis jettisoned its command pod and him with it. Slower, but totally solar, and fully stealthed, it would still get him to the island, and he wouldn't have to worry about any more attacks.

Clarion felt the backlash from the missiles hitting the O-2's skeleton. He glanced at the rear screen; saw the turmoil of concussed water, man-made waves breaking upon and around each other, forming something that resembled a storm cloud, an explosive jewel of white-lit blue at its center. Swirling outward, the explosion seemed almost to consume the water; its beauty brutal, primal.

As he watched the light fade and die, Clarion thought of Poseidon, thought of him with his crown and trident, the splendor of his watery throne. He thought of how many sailors had prayed to the King of the Sea, beseeched him to save them from Hades, to take them to the ocean floor, make them his servants instead. They'd promised everything, would have taken anything to avoid the Dark House they feared, the Dark House of death.

He thought of the mythologies the ancients had constructed to explain their world—sea and sky, sun and moon, subterranean hells and heavenly constellations—how these had been no different, neither greater nor lesser, than Jesus, Jehovah, or Allah. Divine figments created by fearful men, *dei ex machinis* born of the species' subconscious, explanations to the inexplicable. And he wondered at how simple reality must have seemed when there'd been gods. And he wondered at his own memories.

Memories of first communion, catechism, and confirmation. Memories of the charismatics that his father had fallen in with, how they and he had convinced him with their faith, convinced him that there was nothing, that there could be nothing, or, rather, that there could never be anything. Because in their blind certainty they made as much sense as a King of the Sea.

23

HOOK UP THE JAPANAMAN

LEFT IN THE BLACK ROOM WITH ITS DAMP FLOOR AND STALE air, the fifty strains of vinegar she could smell over the salt dust and fear and forgotten centuries, Diana had done the only things she could. She'd paced and she'd thought, and time had swept forward; not in decades but in minutes, a tiny history without event. It was obvious that Chu was there by design. The question was: how much of the design was his, how much someone else's? That design might even be beyond the kidnappers, at least the ones she'd dealt with so far. Diana felt a motivating intelligence behind the whole thing, a mind she was having trouble keeping up with, not because it was smarter than her, but because it had no scruples, because it had planned and re-planned, prepared for a very long time.

More pressure, different pressure, some other tactic entirely—at this point Diana knew the kidnappers or their masters would do whatever they had to. She also guessed that something had made them change their timetable. Something had caused them to leave the roadhouse that had been prepared so meticulously for its task. Maybe the Feds, maybe the Angel, maybe something else—whatever the cause, it had made the Presence leave the country and probably accelerate whatever schedule he'd been working under. Which might mean a quicker death unless Diana could figure out the new rules and find a way to use them. Still without an answer, she made out the footsteps coming down the hall. Her time to think had ended.

One set shuffle and trudge, the other military precision, the footfalls grew closer until they stopped outside the door. Then came the jangle and clack of the key ring and the turning of a lock. The ancient mechanism gave after a couple of rusty shakes. The door screamed inward, thudded against the stone wall, and stuck in place.

The Natural entered first. Diana knew his were the lighter, more active steps—she'd learned the gaits of her three kidnappers as if they'd been their personalities. Zulu remained in the hall beyond.

"I see your little friend untied you."

"Maybe," she said, her back still to both men.

"Maybe? Well, Scorsi, I'm guessing you'd have already done a few magic tricks for us if you knew how."

"I told Chu to let me out. I made him."

"Still taking orders from the Boss Lady, huh, little man? Well, all right then. You've had a chance to compare notes. Which way's this gonna go?"

Diana glanced at Chu.

"Please?" he mouthed. His lips were parched and cracked,

almost as if he were a stone man newly brought to life, speaking for the first time.

It all seemed practiced to her: the way he formed his words, the imploring nod he used as punctuation. As did the look in his eyes, the helpless, forlorn gaze of a baby animal in a rowboat drifting away from shore.

Still, Diana couldn't be sure. Chu might have spent the last hour thinking about how he'd plead with her. Maybe his presentation was one of fear rather than treachery. The only thing she could do at that point was play it out.

"No," she said as she turned to face the Natural.

He cocked his head to one side. "You're sure about that?"

"Yes."

The Natural shrugged. "All right then. Zulu, shackle 'em up. Let's have some fun."

Zulu entered the room. He moved past the Natural carrying lengths of thick, rusty chain in either hand. Four sets of manacles dangled like baubles from the ends. Dull trinkets of ruddy, martial ugliness, they would have provided the perfect completion to a necklace of decay, something made for a rebel titan as a symbol of shame.

When Zulu was within a foot of Diana, he stopped and dropped the chains. The thud of metal against stone made her start. Zulu caught Diana's gaze and pressed closer. His sight seemed almost to touch hers with its intensity.

"Turn 'round," he said, twirling his index finger like a dance instructor requesting a pirouette. He shoved her when she didn't move. She hit the wall hard, felt her dress catch on something jagged—sharp stone, a nail. She heard it rip, felt whatever it was scrape and cut at the flesh on her back. "I says, 'Turn 'round.'"

Now, Diana listened, but it was too late. Once she was facing away from him, Zulu punched her in the small of the back, drove her into the wall, and held her there with one fist. She felt the way he'd placed the punch where she'd cut herself, felt the blood flowing, his fist sliding with it, abrading skin, grinding against bone.

"Stand still," he said. He picked up a set of manacles and cuffed her hands tightly behind her back. The manacles pressed on her wrists, the chain dangling and falling to the floor. He knelt and cuffed her ankles more loosely.

"You expect me to walk with these things on?"

"Sure, you'll be able to walk. Just not very well." He chuckled. As he moved towards Chu, lengths of chain fell behind him bang-clattering against each other, echoes trailing through the black, stone room.

Chu spoke, said something Diana couldn't understand beneath the noise from the chains. Zulu nodded and swatted Chu to the side of the head. The blow sent Chu reeling back. He tripped, lost his balance and hit the wall face-first. As his right cheek made contact, Chu turned towards Diana and stared. His gaze was one of confusion and fear; too like the one he'd tried to ply her with earlier.

"Quiet," shouted Zulu, putting the manacles on Chu's wrists and tightening them.

Chu winced as Zulu put the last set on his ankles. He cried in pain and surprise as Zulu made them tighter than he'd made Diana's. The Natural turned and walked back the way he'd come, out into the hall.

"Move," Zulu yelled like an idiot musher to a team of dogs he absolutely fucking hated. "Follow," he added, pointing towards the Natural.

The Natural moved down the corridor then up a flight of stairs and down another shorter, passage. His prisoners moved in single file behind him. Zulu was about twenty feet back, gun drawn.

There was a door at the end of the final hall. White light seeped through the space between its bottom and the black, rock floor beneath. Despite the bright, white light Diana didn't feel as though something good was about to happen.

The Natural opened the door, practically flooding the hall with illumination, so much that it made Diana squint and bow her head as she followed him in. Squared off perfectly with a wall's worth of windows, but for context Diana might have called the place cheery. It was nearly unfurnished though, only two items in the room.

The first, in the northwest corner, was a fish tank big enough for a shark to swim in place. Ten feet long, it was filled with six feet of water topped off with a layer of ice about a foot thick. In the room's southeast corner, a portable generator hummed. Several cables extended out from it like tentacles; one sparked, then another and another.

"Hook her up, Zulu."

Any relief Diana felt at the fact that they weren't going to hurt Chu was quickly canceled by the thought of what was going to happen to her. She imagined seizures and fever, thoughts shorting out and being replaced with impulses baser than emotions or even instincts. She bowed her head. She wanted to cry. She wanted to die. She wanted to be a child and a hero and a villain and gone into a nothing so impenetrable that there would be no remembering, no way back, no way forward, no way at all.

"Well, will you look at that? Presence said she might try something like this. Told me he had a Word of Knowledge on it. Second thought, Zulu, why don't you hook up the Japanaman? Let's see what she does about that."

"Hope your friend likes to swim." Zulu knelt to undo Chu's manacles. He grabbed Chu by his shirt collar, dragged him deeper into the room in the direction of the fish tank. Chu tripped and fell, smacked his face on the stone floor. When he looked up, Diana could see that he'd broken one of his front teeth.

"Hey," slurred Chu, spitting blood. Zulu pulled him to his feet, but Chu slumped down in almost the same motion.

"Drag him if you have to," said the Natural.

Using the chain as a sort of leash, Zulu pulled his uncooperative pet, rusty links scraping floor. Soon he'd brought Chu to a standing position before the tank of water and ice.

"So you're just gonna watch while someone else takes the abuse, Scorsi?" the Natural asked.

She nodded.

"Some friend," he added.

Lifting Chu by the neck of his shirt and the seat of his pants, Zulu stuffed him into the tank face-first, held him down as he wriggled and thrashed, gurgled and glugged in an attempt to scream. After thirty seconds, Zulu pulled him out and dumped him on the floor. This time, Chu rose to his feet quickly.

"What the fuck?"

Zulu pulled his survival knife and began cutting Chu's

clothes away. Chu squirmed until Zulu caught flesh and drew blood. Then he was still.

Once Chu was naked except for a pair of black ball-huggers, Zulu dragged him back across the floor. He stopped near the generator, picked up one of the cables, and squeezed so that the pincers opened like a mouth ready to bite.

"Say goodbye to fornication, Chu," said the Natural from across the room.

Diana realized Chu might be dead in a few minutes if she didn't do something. These guys weren't professional torturers—it would be easy for them to go too far accidentally, or even worse, on purpose. She thought about how long she'd known Chu, how much she owed him, everything he'd done for her, his wife, his kids. She had to save him. As long as she still could. She had no choice.

Chu spoke up, "Natural, come on, nobody said anything about actual torture."

"Idiot!" shouted the Natural.

"Alfred, I can't believe you—" Diana responded.

"Diana, if you'll let me explain. Give me just a second. I had to save you. Not even just you. I had to save the world, too."

"You had to save me and the world from what?"

"You and Capitalism."

"Capitalism? Wait, so what—you're some sort of Chinese agent?"

Chu shrugged.

"But I was giving Symmetra away, making it free."

"It still could have been made to serve Capitalist purposes. Anyway, I was only giving away parts of it, never the whole thing. I didn't really betray you."

"No?"

"OK, maybe a little."

The Natural drew his pistol, brought it level with Chu's forehead. "Shut up, Chu."

"Shut up or what? What else could you possibly do to me?"

The Natural snorted, nodded his head. He lowered the gun to holster it.

Forgetting himself for a second, Chu nodded in that way he had when he caught the developers in coding errors. Big-eyed and tight-lipped, he looked as though he couldn't believe he'd been forced to uncover a mistake this stupid.

In one fluid motion, The Natural brought the piece back to eye-level and squeezed off a burst of shots. Five, six, seven… Diana wasn't sure exactly how many. Most of the bullets hit as intended, right between Chu's eyes; but as he fell the last few sailed beyond, shattering the tank, sending water and ice spilling into the room. Diana glanced at the generator, then back at the cables in Zulu's hand.

"Drop the cables, Zulu," The Natural said. "Throw 'em over there," he pointed to the room's corner "And get her back to her cell. I have to go see the Presence."

As she watched Zulu cast the cables aside, Diana considered the possibility that the electrified water would seep from the room, would seek out her cell and her fetters, ending the drama her life had become. She hoped for it briefly, almost prayed for it then she said, "No."

"What?" said Zulu, wheeling on her.

She smiled back. "Nothing."

"Get going." He motioned towards the doorway.

Diana turned, but before she'd even taken a step, she felt

Zulu jab his knuckles into the small of her back.

"No need for that—"

"I told you to shut up," he said, jabbing her again with the same type of two-knuckle punch to the small of her back. This time the blow was much harder and better placed. He hit her liver squarely causing her to freeze, double over, and fall forward into the hall beyond.

24

SPEAK MORE OF HIS EVIL

THROUGH TWISTING TUNNELS AND WIND-STRAFED CAVERNS, over natural bridges and up roughhewn steps, Tuck and his four white jumpsuited, machine gun-toting guards moved through the guts of the Presence's personal, fantasy island. Bats flapped and screeched, snakes hissed and slithered, beetles clicked and clacked out their menacing Morse codes. The only creatures here who seemed devoid of speech were Tuck's escorts. He tried talking to them, hoped to gain some insight, trick one of them into a revelation, or even engineer an escape. The guards would have none of it, silencing him with glares, gestures, and when those hadn't worked, the butts of their guns.

The guards seemed to communicate with each other as though telepathic or initiate in a silent language no one else could understand—least of all Tuck. Besides the jumpsuits they shared a common appearance—their dark hair, coppered skin, and short stature suggesting they were probably Chinese, leaving him to guess once again at PRC involvement. With Chu, the guards, and the red lettering on the crates in the landing bay the indicators were there. But why would the Chinese be involved? They were atheists, had no use for God or religion at all unless the Presence's true goal was brainwashing. Then the Chinese would want it as much as anyone. Maybe this was finally their chance to trick the entire world into buying their gutter, Neo-Marxist ideology.

As he moved through the darkness surrounded by his silent guards Tuck felt as though he was approaching a precipice; a place at which if he didn't make the perfect move, he might become just another victim instead of the hero he'd so long imagined himself. Was this all his life would amount to, failure and death on some distant shore?

Tuck bit his lip in defiance, felt a surge of energy begin in his gut and rumble out, goading, pushing him on. This energy wasn't simply physical, though. He could feel that it came from inside, from within his soul. This was the power of faith, and he still had it, still believed in God and the unique, personal destiny He had ordained for Tuck. Tuck Squires was not meant to fail, nor was he meant to die at twenty-seven in some distant land. He had to stay focused; keep his cool long enough to convince the Presence of that. The danger, Tuck knew, was that even now he was lying to himself; that it might already be too late. Not only for the world and Scorsi but for him.

They arrived at a pair of great, black, metal doors covered in carvings of iridescent red and pale gold. Everything from winged bears and birds with shark fins, to huge, disembodied, human heads. A few seconds of five-way heavy breathing—the air of gun-oil and sweat, the guards with their weapons on Tuck the whole time—and the doors swung inward, revealing a vast space filled with sunlight and smooth, white, tile surfaces. At the opposite end of that room, on a white throne atop a black marble pyramid, sat the Presence. But for his dark glasses, lemon-yellow tie, and ever-present Reagan mask, the Presence was clothed completely in white. He reminded Tuck of a banana split, one with obvious, political implications.

When the Presence caught sight of Tuck, he snapped his fingers. The first two guards entered the room. They took positions on either side of the doorway, kept their Achkas trained on Tuck the whole time. The remaining guards took turns poking him with the muzzles of their guns until he stumbled across the threshold, tripped, and fell to his knees.

The Presence rose as Tuck fell. He began to descend the black steps. His shoes made a sound that reminded Tuck of beetles in the darkness—hidden and threatening, like whatever the Presence had in mind. But Tuck had something in mind, too.

"No need to kneel, Squires. We're all friends," said the Presence. "At least for the moment."

Tuck got to his feet. As he did, he realized the place was even bigger than he'd guessed. The ceiling outfitted with skylights, the walls composed of interlocking plates that moved noiselessly, revealing an ever-changing assortment of sea and sky vistas—these were the reasons for all that light, the sun that turned the room's surfaces into a field of dawn.

"Look at that," said the Presence pointing off to Tuck's left, at the sea- and sky-scape beyond. "To think God made this world and left it in our care. It's humbling really."

"Creation is always humbling," Tuck answered.

"Too true, Squires. Too true," the Presence said, closing the space between them. "I want to share something with you, son."

"Your plan?"

"'Course not," he said, voice going more Southern than it

had been. "The truth about my island. The place you stand has been many things to many people. It was a pirate island in the eighteenth century, a gangster's secret hideout in the early part of the twentieth. Before all that, though, it was the capital of an empire, a kingdom that existed long ago in a place far, far away."

"Not here?"

"Not here. Far, far away."

"How'd it get here?"

"I brought it here."

Even for Tuck, the idea represented a chastening display of wealth. Tuck thought of the Forbes list, names running through his head, people the Presence might be. But Tuck knew enough about money to understand how it could be hidden. No published list would ever contain enough names for him to be sure the Presence was one of them.

"I didn't do the work myself of course. It was these friendly natives."

"The Asian guys with the guns?"

"They're willing to work for food, clothing, and firearms, no questions asked. 'Course, they excise their own tongues at birth so they couldn't ask questions anyways." His silver eyes smiled as he continued, "I purchased their island lock, stock, and bamboo a few years back, brought them here to staff this one."

"What happened to their island?"

"Sold it, made a killing."

"Wow."

"I won't say it was easy but I made it happen. What is it that Matthew 19 tells us? 'With God, all things are possible?'"

"Of course. That's verse 26, though."

Tuck watched the Presence's gaze shrink. The Presence

nodded faintly and responded, "Well, with God I made this possible."

"What can I say, Presence? This is incredible."

"Thank you, son, nice of you to say so." He sighed. "Which brings me to my real point. The question of what to do with you. The right thing is to kill you and let the Lord sort things out in the afterlife. You've allowed yourself to become a servant of evil. I can't say as I hold out much hope for converting you."

"Servant of evil?"

"What would you call Raglan, other than evil?"

"I don't like him any better than you do, Presence."

He snorted. "I sincerely doubt that."

"It's true. I can prove it."

"How?"

"Ever heard of the Virginia Squireses?"

"Virginia? You mean the family that founded DamberCorp? You're not suggesting you're one of them, are you?"

Tuck nodded.

"Puppy, Largesse, and Rimbaud Squires? You're related to them?"

"Puppy's my mother. Largesse is my uncle. I don't know any Rimbaud."

"Never mind Rimbaud," the Presence said, eyeing Tuck's features, nodding with building conviction. "Yes, I do see a very strong resemblance. You realize this will be easy enough to check, son. If you're lying…"

"Check all you like, Presence. Tuck Squires doesn't lie."

That Tuck Squires didn't lie was, of course, a lie; but it was one Tuck believed so strongly that it came across as the truth.

"And you're telling me your family approves of you working for Raglan?"

"My grandfather got me the appointment when President Cherrystone was in office."

"Before that trumped-up scandal?"

Tuck nodded. "Before the Democrats took over."

The Presence squinted. "Why haven't you left since?"

"I should. I'd been hoping it wouldn't be as bad as I'd feared."

"Then he got the FPA weakened, didn't he?"

"Yes."

"And the Anti-Terrorism and Sedition Act."

"Yes. I...I...I just can't take it anymore. They don't even trust me—Clarion, Hunter, none of them. They discriminate against me for being a Christian, for serving God. Clarion's supposed to be my partner," Tuck answered. "But he acts more like my heathen babysitter."

"Don't have to worry about that one anymore. He's long gone."

"Well, praise the Lord, I thought that hellion would never quit his drinking, cursing, and womanizing?"

"Womanizing?" asked the Presence, Reagan's face almost seeming to smile.

"Anything in a skirt."

"Speak more of his evil, son. I would hear of it."

"Oh, what's the use? You might as well kill me now just like you said. They'll probably try to blame all this on me anyways."

The Presence paused for a moment, as if considering how much truth he should absorb. "You really don't trust them?"

"Not a bit. I've been, well...I've been praying for a way out for so long. It's just sad that it's come to this."

"Alright, Squires, if we can prove out that you're telling the truth, I may have a use for you."

"Really?" Tuck answered, almost childlike. He hoped he wasn't laying it on too thick.

"Really. But I need to consult my partner first."

"You mean the guy in the W mask?"

"I mean the guy in the Raglan Administration."

"You're working with someone inside the Administration?"

"That's right, someone who agrees with us just like you."

"Where is he? Can I talk to him?"

"He's in Washington but I think we could arrange something. I'm sure he'd be anxious to talk to you. As a matter of fact, Angel, are you there?"

A wall screen came to life, the black silhouette of a man's head dominating the frame.

"Right here, Presence."

"You've been listening?"

"Every word. I think we can work with Agent Squires here, assuming he can do something for us."

"Such as?" asked Tuck.

"Such as convincing Scorsi to bring down Symmetra's security protocols."

Parlay sighed. "Much as I'd like that to happen, Angel, I don't see how she'll give him any more credence than Chu. And we know what happened to him."

"You haven't been watching the InterTel, have you, Presence? WolfView is reporting troop movements across Europe and the Middle East. No comments from any of the governments but you can guess what's going on. The theocracies all know about Symmetra."

"We knew that all along."

"Yes, but they know about each other now."

"They're threatening war, aren't they?" said Tuck.

"Very good, Squires," came the Angel's response.

"You're sure?" asked the Presence.

"Well, I'm not absolutely positive, Presence. But it seems a valid conjecture, one I'm sure Scorsi will draw herself."

The picture and voice disappeared leaving dead air and a blank, black screen.

"Technology," the Presence said, chuckling and shaking his head.

"Just let me talk to her. Honest, Presence, I can convince a woman of anything."

25

YOU'RE THE QUEEN, AND HE'S THE KING

BY THE AGE OF FIFTEEN, JIMMY ORCHARD HAD BEEN SAVED and baptized in the Holy Spirit. He was, as he'd become maybe a little too quick to point out, washed in blood of the Lamb, a new creature in Christ. Timmy Orchard, on the other hand, had become Armistice, Vermont's, version of the town drunk, a creature open to scorn and ridicule, but—owing to his GI benefits—nonetheless indispensable to local liquor stores.

Living in the same house, these competing worldviews were bound to collide and so they did that Fourth of July, 1961, when Jimmy returned from the church picnic. There he found his parents in their usual midday state—his father sloshed out of his gourd on Labatt's, his mother traipsing back and forth between the kitchen table and the fridge. By that point Peggy Sue's close relationship with the Reverend Doctor Floss had come to an end.

"Another," Timmy announced in a lordly slur as Jimmy

entered the kitchen. Timmy burped emphatically, adding, as though in accusation, "And make it a cold one."

Peggy Sue moved briskly, as countless shoulders and fists and elbows had trained her to. But before she could make it to the Frigidaire, her son had interposed himself between her and the icebox.

Jimmy took a beer from the refrigerator, opened it, and crossed the room. He made to give the bottle to his father, but pulled back as Timmy reached towards him. Timmy was left clutching air, bobbing and weaving as he did.

Years later, Jimmy would remember wondering what had made him do this. Was it the Lord working on his heart, or the Devil pushing him to perdition? Sometimes even a good Christian could have trouble telling the two apart.

In response to Timmy's confused scowl, Jimmy said, "Really, Pop, don't you think maybe you've had enough?"

Peggy Sue's eyes grew. Jimmy knew then that he was in trouble, that regardless of whether God or the Devil had made him do it, the decision had been a horrible mistake. He thought of Lassie on TV. He thought of Lassie's Timmy. Then he thought of his father, his own Timmy. Then he thought he might be sick.

"What'd you say to me?"

"Uh, well, I mean…Scripture's very clear about drinking. It's the road to Hell, the work of the Devil. You don't want to be on that road, do you, Pop? You don't want to do that work."

Timmy shut his eyes. He shook his head as though in bewilderment, as though he'd just lost his hearing.

Jimmy continued, "Pastor Floss says you can be saved like anyone. All you have to do is ask the Lord."

Timmy's eyes came to life. The kitchen's overheads caught

in those dilated pupils, the reflection made Jimmy think of the Sun. A wild, dying, hateful Sun.

"Saved?" Timmy asked.

"Right." Jimmy smiled.

"Saved?" He shook his head. "Son, once you've been to war you tell me about saved."

"I don't—"

"Once you've seen men with their guts on the ground beside them, their legs fifty feet away, you tell me about God. Until then, you can just go to Hell for all I care."

Jimmy's lower lip dropped as his father took the beer from his hand. Timmy smiled maliciously, took a long pull, wiped his mouth, and burped, again emphatically.

"You were never mine anyways," he said. "Never figured it out either. And for all those smarts you're supposed to have."

Jimmy shook his head. He'd heard rumors of course, but he'd always put them off to the jealousy of the unsaved.

"And you," Timmy said, wheeling on Peggy Sue. "You never told him?"

Peggy Sue's lower lip began to quiver. She began to cry. Jimmy knew tears were his mother's flaw, the thing that always brought out the anger in his father. He knew as he watched, that he was only waiting for reality to fall like something heavy from a very great height…Timmy reared up, backhanding Peggy Sue across the face with his free hand. He threw his beer down, to dash it against the floor, but the bottle bounced on the linoleum, sending suds everywhere, rolling to a stop against the baseboard. His hands went to his wife's throat. He held the delicate neck, he began to squeeze.

Jimmy tried to pull his father off. He tried but he couldn't.

At fifteen he still wasn't strong enough. He heard his mother struggling for air. He began pounding on his father's back with both fists, trying to get him to stop. Trying and failing, trying and failing. His mother was struggling to speak, choking.

Jimmy saw the Labatt's bottle on the floor. He took it by its neck and swung, hitting his father in the back of the head. The bottle shattered sending tiny, shiny shards to the linoleum floor, falling like stars across a field of cheap, dirty beige.

Timmy let his wife go, dropping her to the floor. The back of Peggy Sue's head bounced against the linoleum just like the beer bottle had a moment earlier. She lay there, gulping air, hand clutching her own throat.

Timmy turned to his son. The hatred Jimmy saw in his father's eyes told him what he'd suspected for a long time, perhaps not consciously, but beneath; the thing Timmy himself had just confirmed. But if Timmy wasn't Jimmy's father, who was?

"Mother," Jimmy begged.

"Timmy," said Peggy Sue as Timmy stepped towards the son who wasn't really his son, eyes dark and liquid in a way that hinted at more violence, hinted that maybe this time it wouldn't stop until someone was dead.

"Run, Jimmy," said Peggy Sue in a hoarse whisper. "Get out of here and never come back."

Jimmy hesitated, looking down at his mother then back at the father who wasn't really his father.

"Run, Jimmy, run," said Peggy Sue.

Jimmy Orchard ran then. He ran until he was well beyond Armistice, well beyond any place he'd ever been. He ran until he couldn't run anymore, only stopped as darkness fell in the

Vermont woods. There, amongst the firs and evergreens, Jimmy Orchard lay down and slept. And as the Moon rose and shone and finally died, finally gave the world over to the Sun, Jimmy dreamed what he would come to realize was the only true American Dream. He dreamed the dream of holy transformation, of limitless new beginnings, the dream in which Jimmy Orchard began to become Ravelton Parlay.

"WHO'S THIS?" SCORSI ASKED, HOOKING A THUMB IN Squires' direction.

Behind his sunglasses, Parlay surveyed the group of them—Justice, Urban, Scorsi, and Squires—as they stood at the foot of the black stairs. Beyond stood two four-man squads of Kai Laus, machine guns at the ready.

"This is Special Agent, Tuck Squires, Miss Scorsi," Parlay answered. "Otherwise known as—"

"The Rookie," sang Justice, from beneath his W mask.

Squires snorted, turned in the Natural's direction, and glared at him.

"I was going to say her rescue party, Natural."

Three in the afternoon, and the throne room was a storm of sultry, Caribbean sunshine; light flooding the patchwork of skylights and sliding walls, falling only to be reflected back at the sky. Not that the prevalence of light was a surprise to Parlay—this was precisely how he'd had the throne room re-designed, as a sort of temple to creation, a testament to the light and heat of God's distant Sun.

Scorsi turned, appraised Squires. "How come he looks so good?"

"Genetics?" Squires offered matter-of-factly.

Scorsi rolled her eyes. "I meant, 'You don't look like much of a rescue party.' Don't even look like you've been in a fight."

"That's where you're wrong, Miss Scorsi. Squires put up quite a struggle, didn't he, Natural?"

"Meh…"

Parlay squinted, smirked dismissively beneath his mask. "But he's seen the light, and you should, too. Why don't you go ahead and explain to her what's going on, son?"

Squires cleared his throat. "As a duly authorized representative of the US Government…"

Scorsi cut him off, "I…you're seriously telling me this guy is a government agent?"

"Special Agent, Internal Defense," Squires replied, angling his gaze down at her.

She clucked her tongue. "Looks like he jumped out of an R.J. Rude catalog."

"Doesn't matter what I look like, Scorsi." He brought out his shield and flipped it open. "As a representative of the President, I'm telling you that you have to go along with what the Presence is asking."

"Why's that?"

"I just told you."

"Not really. You just told me you work for somebody, so I should do what you say. But I don't care who you work for, and I don't have to do anything unless it makes sense."

Squires responded, "Smarten up, Scorsi, there's a high stakes game of chess taking place here, one that could end in war if we're not careful."

"Chess?" Scorsi asked.

"Right, chess. And you're the queen."

"Me, the queen? Oh, you shouldn't have."

He huffed. "That's right. You're the queen, you and Symmetra."

"If you say so."

He nodded over Scorsi's head towards the wall screen. "See all those troops and planes, all those ships and tanks? There's your game. Think of the troops as pawns, their leaders as value pieces."

"And?"

"And that's what's going on out there in the real world. If this isn't resolved quickly there's going to be war."

"Don't you have some policy against giving in to blackmail?"

"Normally, yes, but the stakes are too high."

"When are the stakes not too high?"

"What?"

"In terrorist situations, which is what this is, the stakes are always too high. Otherwise, terrorism would never work."

"When the good to the many outweighs the lives of the few, that's when the stakes are too high. And that's what we have now. These are all nuclear powers. It would be so easy for things to escalate. You and Symmetra are the only things that can stop it."

"You're blaming this on me now?"

"No. I'm asking you to use your privileged position to help the world: The theocracies all want your technology, right? But they're convinced you're working with their enemies, that your technology is going to be turned on them."

"And I wonder how they got that idea?" she asked, vectoring her gaze towards Parlay.

Squires was dogged, though. Unwilling to settle. "Doesn't

matter anymore, Scorsi. We're either going to do what they ask or this is going to get military…"

"But if they're all scared of the others, how will it do any good?"

"They'll stand down if you give them the technology."

"I was going to give the stuff away anyways."

"See. Perfect."

"Not really."

"Why?"

"Because it reminds me of something."

"What?"

"Alfred."

"Chu?"

"Yeah. So, he was some sort of Chinese agent?"

"More or less," Parlay cut in.

"Like James Bond?"

Justice laughed. "More like Jimmy Bond."

"What?"

Parlay shook his head. "An old movie. Never mind. The Natural just thinks he's being funny. Alfred Chu was no James Bond. But he was a Chinese agent through and through. He'd been giving away your technology piece by piece to the Chinese for years, ever since he came to work for you."

"I still don't—"

Parlay continued, "I've been telling you this the whole time, Scorsi. No one's interested in the base technology. They want it in forms acceptable to them."

"They want it modified?" she asked.

"Right. One version for the Catholics, one for the Jews, one for the Muslims."

"What about the Hindus, the Buddhists? How come they're not involved?"

"We tried the Hindus. They didn't think it would work for them."

"Polytheism."

"Something like that."

"And the Buddhists?"

"The lamas." Parlay chuckled. "They couldn't get the money together."

"I guess that makes sense. Buddhism isn't really a religion focused on propagation, proliferation, and accumulation."

"Whatever that means."

"What it means is they're not interested in piling up money, extending their domain, or brainwashing people."

"You really need to stop thinking of this as brainwashing, Scorsi. These countries are already theocracies. Their citizens already believe whatever they believe, right or wrong. It's just a matter of giving that belief a little boost, like vitamins."

"So, lemme get this right, Mr. Government Agent," she asked, turning back to Squires. "You're asking me to do exactly what he's been asking me to do. What he's been browbeating, threatening, and torturing me to do for the last few days? Has he told you about that part yet?"

"Not exactly."

"Has he told you about how they killed Chu?"

"No."

"What you're asking me to do is give my baby to a bunch of kidnapper-torturer-murderers."

Squires shrugged. "It's our only choice."

"Who are also religious nuts?"

"Hey, let's keep our facts straight, Scorsi. Christianity's not some nutty religion, at least not the way we practice it here in America."

"He's right, Scorsi. You'd better be careful what you say now that we've got a trained killer on our side."

Justice cleared his throat.

Parlay raised his palm in a mollifying gesture. "No offense, Natural."

Justice looked down like a scolded dog.

"Ah, now I understand," Scorsi responded.

"What's that?"

"You actually agree with these whack jobs. You're one of those Traditionalist lunatics, aren't you? What did you say your name was again?"

"Squires, Tuck Squires."

"Wait, you're not related to that rich lunatic, Puppy Squires, are you?"

"Umm…"

"My god, you are, and you're the spitting image of her. What do they do, clone you guys in some lab?"

"Bite your tongue, Scorsi. Cloning's the work of the Devil. Anyways, I told you, it's not important whether I agree with them or not. This is like a game of chess."

"Back to chess?"

"That's right—back to a simple game of chess."

"And I'm the queen? Is that it?"

"Exactly. But he's the king," said Squires pointing towards Parlay.

Parlay smiled. "Take a good look at what's happening out there in the world, Scorsi. You're either going to give up the technology or watch as the world goes to war over it, as cities burn, as millions die…for what, your own vanity? The fact that you're unwilling to save them?"

She stood there for a second with her eyes closed. Was she praying? This struck Parlay as the oddest possible turn of events. In all this strife, all this mayhem, had the Lord seen fit to change her heart, to make her see the truth?

"Fine," she said, looking up, "I'll do it."

And this would have been enough for Parlay, enough to make him happy perhaps for years to come, maybe for the rest of his life, and beyond. That wasn't the end of his good fortune, though.

The volume rose on the InterTel, the lights whirring, the buzzers buzzing, the flashers flashing. Something was going on, something important.

"In another story, one totally unrelated to these troop movements, Deputy Director of the National Science Foundation, Dr. Morton School, has been found dead. Based on the circumstances the D.C. Police are labeling this a suicide."

Parlay eyed the image of his former partner on the screen. Had School faked his own death? Or, had he gotten cold feet and really done it? Watching the InterTel as intently as he was, Parlay had barely noticed the brief conversation between Justice and Urban that ended with the latter lumbering from the room.

26

A PAWN'S SOLILOQUY

THERE HAD BEEN MANY TIMES CLARION IMAGINED MORRIS struggling, nights when he simply hadn't been able to pick up the phone. If he was honest with himself, Clarion would have had to admit that he simply didn't care enough to fix things anymore. Or worse, maybe that he couldn't, that the anger on the other end of the phone had grown too great. Still, he would think about the conversations, replay them in his head. All the desk jobs working for Hunter left him plenty of time for that.

"You're basically going to Hell," Morris had said matter-of-factly, one of the last times they spoke. This was near the end of the sullen years. Morris had been nineteen, maybe twenty. Even though he'd begun speaking again, it seemed to Clarion as though he'd only done it so they could argue, always about politics and religion.

"Hell?"

"Don't believe in God. Don't believe in America."

This was when Cheney started having problems, when the truth came out about how the PIF had wound up being formed, that maybe in reality it had all been Cheney's fault, the suggestion that maybe fault wasn't even the right word for it. Maybe Cheney wanted all of Islam massed into one superpower, one great enemy to wage holy oil war against. But even that wasn't all Morris was ranting about. By that point, Drakonika had found salvation and so had Morris. They'd begun going to some Traditionalist church, the name of which Clarion could never recall.

"What?"

"All this talk about secret government work. Everyone knows it's a lie. Mom does, I do, all the kids at school. They've known it my whole life. You're just a drunk, nothing more. And now you don't even support the President. Isn't that like treason or something if you're some sort of government agent or whatever?"

"I'm sober now. And never mind who I support. And, no, disagreeing with someone is not treason."

"Yeah, yeah, yeah…Mom told me all about this. There are different kinds of drunk y'know, Dad, different ways to deceive yourself. Even if you're not a liquor drunk, you can become drunk on liberalism, unsure of the greatest nation on Earth even though you pretend to love it and defend it with your life."

"Your mother's telling you this?"

"She doesn't even—"

"She wouldn't even be a citizen if it weren't for me."

"That's not true, though. She's a citizen because she's my mother, not because she's your ex-wife."

"You're a citizen because of me. Matter of fact, you're alive because of me. Both of you. Jesus, when do I get some credit for something?"

"Eht…"

"What?"

"You just took the Lord's name in vain."

"The Lord? Maybe you should worry a little more about your father on Earth, Morris. He's the one paying all the bills."

The plot-back of the missile strike narrowed Clarion's choices to two of the closer islands. Once he was in range, he saw that there were three, one of which hadn't appeared on the programmed charts. He stato-docked the O-2 a mile offshore of this third, phantom island and got what he could of the topography from the on-boards. Ringed by black saw-tooth rocks, the island's beach was a dusky copper gold. Bright green jungle rose out of the sand building into a series of black hills. Black then blue, gold then green, and finally more black—Clarion couldn't help thinking of a bull's-eye. He synced the topographical images to his cell, put on his diving gear, shouldered a pack with the same for Diana and Tuck, and headed for shore. The wetsuit's propulsion system had him on the beach six minutes later.

Clarion wrapped the breathing gear in the suit and buried everything in the sand, piling several shells on top as a marker. Looking up at the low, late afternoon sun, he knew he had about three hours of daylight left. He thought he could make the hills in fifteen minutes, hoped the rest of the time would be enough to find a way into the place he'd started referring to as Skull Mountain in his head. The structure that topped the highest hill had made him call it that.

A peak shaped more than a little like a human head—with asymmetrical caverns that made up its eyes, one elliptical, one diamond-shaped, another cave for its nose, and graven lips curling away to reveal its two rows of neat, pointy teeth, the face seemed to hold two expressions simultaneously. Maybe laughing, maybe screaming, its construction was uneven bordering on chaotic.

Pulling his piece, Clarion moved into the jungle, aware that he was using the same strategy that he had in the O-2. He was waiting for the enemy to make a move. Being clotheslined still took him by surprise.

A split-second of shiny black before the blow struck his mouth, lifting him a foot off the ground and knocking him back several more. Like a replay of his crash landing at the Dauphine, the back of Clarion's head broke his fall. Fortunately, its point of contact had been grass and soft earth rather than stone.

Knowing he was lucky to still be conscious, Clarion looked up, fumbling for his Rikken. Rather than the horror movie anaconda he might have expected, he saw the black guy from The Dauphine, three hundred plus pounds of him, Batman mask, and all.

"That's for Lars," he said, punctuating his statement with a foot stomp to the sternum. Lifting Clarion by his shirt, Urb hit him with one right cross then another and another. The ease with which he was getting tuned up left Clarion thinking of the speed bag at the gym.

"And that's for the Natural and that's for the Presence and that's for the Lord and that's…ahhhhgh," the guy's litany of people, fictional constructs, and/or deities Clarion had wronged having apparently run out, he grew even more agitated.

Urb let go of Clarion's shirt, dropped him to the ground. Pinning Clarion with his knees, Urb's blows gained even more force. Pounding down with hammer fists, the left and right came at once, again and again. In response to getting his ass absolutely kicked, Clarion did what any operative would. He fought dirty.

"Well, that's for America," he said using all his strength to push Urb away, kneeing him in the nuts as he did. "And that's for the President," he added, following up with a heel kick to the same area. Urb fell back groaning.

Clarion pounced and went for a combination as he landed, knees to the guy's chest. He got in the left but Urb caught the right in one of his massive hands, used it to throw Clarion. He rose to his feet. As did Clarion. They began to circle.

"Let's talk this out, big man. You help me get inside, stop this thing, maybe we can work out some sort of deal," Clarion said.

"Deal? What deal?"

"That'd be up to the DOJ. But whatever it is, it'd be a damn sight better than dying here. Which is what's going to happen."

"That's where you're wrong. I was pounding you until you cheated."

"Cheated?"

"Cheated," said Urb, his voice rising an octave, taking on a grating edge.

"You tried to kill me less than twenty-four hours ago."

"Yeah, well, this time I won't just try."

Faking a left hook, Urb lunged to grapple. Clarion ducked and slipped a right but Urb got his follow-on left around the back of Clarion's neck, pulled him into a clinch. He went for a knee to the gut but Clarion blocked it with his left leg. Urb followed by pulling down harder on the back of Clarion's neck, knocking him in the face with the meat of his forearm and the point of his elbow.

Clarion felt the blood flowing—the hot tingle of flesh opening above his left eyelid. Pulling his head down again, Urb got in one knee lift then a second. Clarion knew if a few more of these landed he'd be done.

As Urb went for another knee, Clarion wriggled free from his left arm, took a two-handed grip on Urb's wrist as he did. Clarion cranked down, counter-clock, as hard as he could, ducked under and twisted. He heard the pop and snap, the growl that turned to a yelp with a little more pressure.

Holding on to the wrist, he kicked Urb in the highest part of ribcage he could reach—once, twice, three times, he heard the thuds, crunches, and gasps, Urb's breathing going pained and uneven. Clarion saw his gun on the ground, ratcheted the arm once more, swept him with his left leg, and rolled for it. Urb was looking up when Clarion got to his piece and turned.

"Hands up, sport."

Urb shook his head, petting his ribs as though he couldn't believe what had been done to him, as though trying to calm a dog or cat.

"You've got two choices now. You can show me the way in or..." Clarion gestured with the Rikken, pointed at Urb's head.

"I'm not telling you anything."

"You'd rather die?"

"I have my moral soul to worry about."

"You mean mortal," he said then almost laughed. "Actually, immortal."

"Don't tell me what I mean."

"You honestly think these nut boys you're following are gonna save your soul?"

"I know it."

"So there's nothing I can say to change your mind?"

Urb shook his head.

"You're sure?"

He shook his head again then began to speak, "The Lord…"

Clarion could feel a pawn's soliloquy coming—the rising, self-righteous energy to the speech, the justification for everything that had been done, the unthinking certainty that came with being a cog rather than running the show. Clarion fired two shots—the first to Urb's throat to shut him up, the second to his forehead to put him down.

Urb fell back into the brush. Clarion moved in, checked for a pulse. Nothing. He holstered his Rikken, flipped Urb then began casing the body. Clarion took his gun and cell, synced the cell to his, and tapped redial.

"You got him," came the response, a note of relief, or maybe it was pleasure, in the thick Southern accent, a tone almost like happiness.

"Yeah."

"Urb?"

"Yeah, I got him. And, no, this isn't Urb."

"Who?"

"Oh, I think you know that one, sport."

27

DOING IT FOR THE FUTURE

THREE YEARS BEFORE THE KIDNAPPING, DIANA WAS CLOSE
to finalizing the beta version of Symmetra's prototype. The
problem she had was what to do once she did. The third-round
funding from Blue Sky hadn't come through. Sure, they'd seen
the work and been impressed. But they wouldn't be coming
up with any additional cash until the first stage of user testing
was complete. And then who knew? There were no promises.
But there were still questions—too many of them having to
do with possible side effects. Diana hadn't volunteered the fact
that she'd tested Symmetra on herself numerous times, and that
she was fine, no ill effects. She imagined screaming, "I'm fine, I
tell you, I'm fine," as large men in white suits carried her away.

What she'd also begun imagining by that point was a
scenario in which she finished Symmetra and still had nothing.
Worse than nothing, she'd have a finished product dead in the
water, just waiting for something to swim by and eat it. There
would be too much chance for someone on the outside to get
wise or someone on the inside to get nervous. She needed to
go straight from the build-out into the testing. She just couldn't

figure out how to get the money to do it. And until she did, she'd have to entertain the notion of throwing a wrench into the process herself. This wasn't something Diana had an easy time considering. The fundamental dishonesty of it was obvious, and idea worked on her, played at the edges of her thoughts.

She'd gotten so desperate one night—early morning really, three a.m.—that she'd decided to ask Symmetra. Sure, it was a longshot, the idea even laughable in a way. Technically, there was no way to ask, at least not directly. Better put, there was no way to consciously direct yourself in generating an interaction with your Symmetra advisor. But she was becoming increasingly convinced that pre-immersion of a subject's conscious mind in one topic—meditation for want of a better term—might result in Symmetra's response to that topic, or at least push it in that direction.

"I am an extension of you," Symmetra had said.

"But I mean—"

"You wonder if I am a god. You wonder if I am the God."

"Maybe. I don't. I guess I never did before."

"Why now?"

"Desperation?"

"Hasn't your research already given you the answer to that question? And didn't philosophy answer it before that?"

"Philosophy?"

"How could I ever be anything more than you can understand? The logic fails."

"How?"

"I was not here in the beginning. How can I be anything more than an extension of you?"

This went on for some time. Finally, Diana gave up the hope

that Symmetra would help her understand her own mundane realities. And that was when the answer came.

"Maybe you should just give it away," Symmetra said.

"Give what away?"

"Me," it replied.

RATHER THAN HAVING A FULL OUT-OF-BODY EXPERIENCE, Diana was having a partial, auditory one. She felt like she was listening to the actions of someone else, taking them in, drawing conclusions even as another person lived that life. The problem—the worst, she had a few at that moment—was it seemed like that other person was about to live her death, too...

The muted tapping of cracked fingernails on the smooth remantanite keypad; the hollow, metal clack of the handcuffs hitting each other, pressing against her raw wrists; the Presence's heavy breathing as he sucked air through the mouth of his Reagan mask—these were the sounds Diana heard as she made her way through Symmetra's security architecture. Canceling the latent data folds, recalling the recombinant placements, searching her mind for all the codes she'd buried just in case, Diana had spent the last hour moving towards something that felt like an ending. And as she did, the Sun inched closer to the horizon, the head of a golden, drowning man growing ever closer to the waves, falling beneath one last time.

The incandescents had come on—the skylights closed, the chamber's high ceilings became counterpoint to the blaze of light the floor had been when she'd entered. Now the light was jaundiced and frail—a counterfeit that seemed constantly on the verge of returning to form, reverting to darkness. She knew the Presence wasn't going to let her live. Still, she tried to hold on to hope. Some for herself, but mostly for the world. She'd squeezed every second out of this final act hoping the other agent would get here in time, that he wasn't a traitor like Squires. She could feel Squires behind her in the distance, with more guards and the Presence's other henchman, the Natural. The Natural had been trying to get the Presence's attention for the last few minutes only to be shushed and snapped at as if he were just another one of the guards.

"That's it," she said, pushing away from the desk, hoping they wouldn't see everything she'd done. She'd guessed it was Wazaputsky on the other end, Dr. Waz as he called himself. He would be the leader but there would be many helpers, many lesser lights—Fabreau certainly, maybe Gladwell, Stuffins, and Ching, too—all working together to destroy her baby.

"That's it?" the Presence half-asked her, half-barked into his phone. "And?" Whoever it was, they gave the Presence his answer, the assurance that they could pull off the parlor tricks he wanted from them. They hadn't seen. For that at least Diana was grateful.

"No, not yet. Once I'm back in the States," he responded, then ended the call.

"Presence?" asked the Natural.

"I said not now, Natural."

"But?"

"I'll be with you in a minute. Just hold on to your britches."

"For real?"

"Real? No, you do not need to actually hold on to your britches, son."

"I meant, real as in a real minute?"

"Right, literally, one real minute, two real minutes tops."

"OK," he said, looking down at his watch, beginning to tap his foot once again.

The Natural snapped his fingers. The eight guards responded, eyes turning to him. He snapped his fingers twice more, clapped and pointed at the black double doors. The guards quick-marched out of the room in columns of four, the doors closing behind them.

"Why'd you do that?" the Presence asked.

"We have an intruder."

"Why didn't you tell me?"

"I've been trying," said the Natural.

"When?" the Presence asked.

"For the last ten minutes."

"He's right," said Diana.

The Presence squinted at her, growled nearly imperceptibly.

"Who is it, Natural?"

"The Agent."

"Clarion?" asked Squires.

"The one from the Dauphine. He called me 'sport'," the Natural responded.

"Oh, yeah, that's definitely Clarion."

The Natural glanced at his watch. "I need for you to go, Presence."

"Go?"

"Right. Go. Because ten minutes ago we had twenty minutes."

"Oh, the Kai Laus will take care of it. You worry too much, Natural."

"If you say so, Presence." He pulled his piece, ejected the clip, scrutinized it, and smacked it back in place.

"Still, I suppose we should be off, shouldn't we? I mean, now that we have what we came for, no sense sticking around, tempting fate."

"You'll be wanting both of them to come with us?" asked the Natural.

"Hmm," the Presence said. "Well, you know, Miss Scorsi, I would bring you with us. I really would. It's just…I really…I just don't think your heart's in it."

"In what?"

"Life after Symmetra."

"Why am I not surprised by this?"

"Meaning?"

"Meaning you're a lying asshole."

"Miss Scorsi! Really, such language. Haven't you ever heard the phrase, 'A Presence can always change his mind'?"

"No, I'm pretty sure I haven't."

"Well, maybe you should have."

"But the world?"

"The world will be fine, Scorsi. I'll see to that. It's just…you won't. A few short minutes after we're in the air, this island's self-destruct will engage."

"Self-destruct? You must be shitting me?"

"Not at all, Scorsi. Someday, when you have a multi-billion-dollar secret island, you'll understand the need for things like self-destruct mechanisms and stealthing technology."

"I…"

"Oh, that's right, silly me. No secret island for you. You're going to be dead."

"So?" asked the Natural.

"You'll stay here, Natural. I want you to watch while Squires takes care of Scorsi. If that goes well, you and Squires can join me below. If not, I'll expect a smaller contingent."

"Take care? What's...you want me to give him my gun?"

"'Course not. You've got a knife, don't you?"

The Presence crossed the room and ascended the ziggurat. His steps were quick and sure. Despite the danger, Diana could see how pleased he was with himself. If she'd had a gun at that point, she would have gladly, easily killed him. And not as some fear impulse; but as a function of contempt, of deep hatred, anger like smoke filling her mind. Though she knew her thoughts could easily turn to fear and desperation, she wouldn't let that happen.

Diana had always agreed with the samurai. She'd always known that a death chosen was the best death. And if you couldn't choose when or where or what killed you, you could still choose how you died, how you left the world, the courage or fear with which you said goodbye.

Once he arrived at the throne, the Presence stopped. He spoke words Diana couldn't make out. A panel the size of a shoebox lit up on the wall. The Presence stooped, maybe to key in some sort of code.

With a grinding noise a section of wall slid away revealing a doorway, the throne room's light and the darkness beyond meeting in its mote-riddled shadows. The Presence passed beyond the doorway, appeared to sink ever lower as he moved, head slipping beneath the horizon as had the Sun moments earlier.

The Natural reached down and unsheathed the blade at his left ankle. He flipped it in the air, caught it, and handed it to Squires hilt-first. With his right hand, he kept his gun trained on Squires.

"You heard what the Presence said. Time to prove your faith, son."

Squires accepted the thing, turned, and headed for Diana. The hope she'd had, that Squires had been playing the Presence and the Natural, died as he crossed the room.

When he got to her, he paused to reach out and stroke her neck. For a fraction of a second his touch felt good. It felt tender.

The fact that it did made Diana gag and retch. She began to cough, her mind full of confusion and fear, looking for a way out, knowing there wasn't one. But that fact was what saved her. The fact that she knew her situation was hopeless brought back her composure. She reared back, and spit in his face. She smiled and laughed as she watched the saliva drip down his nose and cheek, ruining his pretty boy looks.

In his eyes a flash of anger, then Squires was grabbing at the ends of her hair, gathering them in his fist. He moved behind Diana, twisted and yanked, jerking her up out of the chair. She felt hot pins as he did, as he held her there. She cried out, but he didn't care. His response was to tighten his grip, to shake her up and down, to make it hurt more and more.

Deep inside, she knew this guy now, knew he wasn't just a traitor. He was a pig, a rapist, the worst type of shit, maybe even worse than the Presence and the Natural. The thoughts she'd had about killing the Presence seemed to pale now when she thought about what she'd like to do to this piece of shit, this fucking Tuck Squires.

She wanted to torture him, would gladly have sent him to Hell if there'd been one. She cried again. This time he let go, dropped her back into the chair and kicked it, sending her rolling into the middle of the great hall, then clattering to the floor in a mass of flesh, metal, and shiny, spinning wheels.

"Get on with it," the Natural ordered.

Squires followed Diana across the room and yanked her to her feet again using her hair.

"Should I bleed her first or just kill her?"

"Just do it. Now."

"I always knew you were a piece of shit, Squires."

"Yeah, well."

"That's all you have to say?" Diana had gone shrill by this point. She was screaming.

"Listen, this will go easier if you just relax," he whispered.

"Relax? When you're going to slit my throat? What the fuck are you talking about?"

The doors swung open. One of the guards was thrown in, his white jumpsuit stained with red. He landed with a thud, slid, and skidded to a stop.

A man entered carrying a gun. He was spattered with blood, but seemed unconcerned. The man smiled. "She's right, Squires. If you turn yourself in now, maybe we can still work something out, spare you the needle."

"Clarion, you've got nothing. While you're pointing that gun at me, look who's got his trained on you?" Squires pushed the knife into Diana's neck, drew a little blood then dragged the blade across her throat, making a great production of it.

Clarion advanced into the room. "Who? You mean the Dubya over there?"

The Natural turned his pistol from Squires, sighted it on Clarion. "Shoot him and die. That's it. Simple."

"This is automatic," Clarion replied.

"So is this," came the Natural's response.

"Down," said Squires, pushing Diana away. He flung his knife at the Natural.

The Natural ducked, and the blade missed, clattering to the floor. He ran, weaving between columns as Clarion opened up with the Achka, hitting the Natural in the shoulder. The Natural returned fire then moved up the steps. He made it to the throne and ducked behind it. Diana saw the panel light up again, the door slide open. Clarion laid down more fire, wove across the room and up the ziggurat's steps.

When Clarion was halfway to the top, Diana heard metal clatter across the floor in the opposite direction. Clarion's aim followed, lighting up the tiles, taking chips of marble from them as the Natural's pistol skimmed and twirled along. The piece came to a stop against the wall at the far corner of the dais.

The Natural emerged from behind the throne, holding an Achka of his own. He fired a burst at Clarion, forcing him to go for cover behind a column. Once Clarion was out of the way, the Natural trained his weapon on Diana, fired off several rounds as he moved towards the passage. He hit her twice—in the hamstring and the gut—but Squires cut in front of her, taking a third shot, grunting as it hit. The Natural continued firing as he backed into the passage and disappeared into the darkness.

As Diana fell, she watched Squires do the same, heard him yell, "Keep the door from closing, Clarion. Shoot the panel."

Clarion trained his Achka on the glowing panel and spent the rest of the clip. Sparks and smoke. The door stopped moving.

28

THAT'S NOT JUSTICE

LIKE A FLOWER OF SCARLET, BLOOD BLOOMED FROM THE wound at Scorsi's waist. Small and star-shaped at first the stain spread quickly, growing darker and more circular as it did. Tuck couldn't help fixing on it, staring at the wound even as Scorsi fell. His fascination lasted only briefly, though; just until he saw that she'd been hit in the leg, too; that this second shot had done far more damage than the first. Dark blood spread towards Tuck, across the shiny, white tiles. A comingling of red, purple, and black, it made him think of wine, of life and death. He knew he could still save her, that he had to save her.

Neglecting the wound to his own arm, blood trailing behind him as he crossed to her, Tuck stripped off his shirt and claimed a knife from one of the fallen guards. He knelt beside Scorsi, slashing the shirt's torso into four strips, using two of them to fashion a tourniquet for her leg. He had nearly finished by the time Clarion got to them.

"Fuck was that?" Clarion asked, pointing the Achka down at Tuck's head. He jerked it to the right as if slapping someone, trying to get the truth out of them.

"What?"

"When I came in?"

"I was buying time," Tuck said, cinching the last knot. The tourniquet was doing its work, holding, but for how long?

"By slitting her throat?"

"Slitting…that was just a scratch," Tuck said, motioning to the thin line of red on Scorsi's neck. Already, it was dry. "If I'd wanted to kill her, I would have."

"Wouldn't have been having second thoughts, would you?"

"Second thoughts about what?"

"About helping these whack jobs bring about the Second Coming or some shit like that; thinking maybe that was what Jesus wanted?" Clarion's eyes were cracks by this point, untrusting, impenetrable. He was still pointing the gun at Tuck, treating him like a common criminal. And it made Tuck furious.

The unbelievers always did this. They were brutal, relentless with their insults, never willing to give a Christian credit for his fundamental integrity. What Clarion was describing would have constituted a breach of Tuck's duty to his country. More than that, it would have been a betrayal. And Tuck was no Judas. Tuck had felt good will towards Clarion, excitement at the fact that he was still alive. That was gone, Tuck left wondering whether Clarion was any different than he'd first thought—a drunken philanderer, a washed-out thrillseeker, nothing more.

Still, Tuck wondered what he might have done if the Presence and the Natural had proven to him that they were sane and sincere. If they'd been true Christians like Tuck, he would have been forced to find a middle ground between his faith and his duty. But what middle ground could there possibly be?

Going against America was treason. But going against Jesus…
that would cost you your soul. And how could any amount of
honor or life possibly be worth your soul?

"He was," Scorsi said, raising her head, gritting her teeth
with the effort. "He was helping them. He told me to give them
Symmetra, that it was what the President wanted."

Tuck stood, pushed aside the Achka's muzzle. He looked
down at Scorsi, disgusted. "This is how you repay me for saving
your life?"

She didn't answer, just stared at Clarion.

"Don't be stupid, Scorsi. I was playing for time, hoping
Clarion would show. Didn't you just see me save your life?"

Clarion lowered the gun. "He's right, Dr. Scorsi. He did just
save your life. That bullet he took was intended for your head."

Tuck finally remembered his own wound at this point,
knelt to claim the remaining cloth of his shirt. He looked down
at his arm, saw that the wound was even more minor than he'd
thought, and set to work.

There was still blood coming from it, but the flow was
weak, nothing compared to what had come out of Scorsi and
now lay across the tile floor—a pool here, splatters there, drips,
spatters, dots; it was like the work of some artist consumed
by the subject of death, the visions of a Jackson Pollock so
mad, he made the real Pollock seem sane. It made Tuck think
of art in Hell.

"It's all moot at this point anyway," Clarion added, "The
theocracies gave the President an ultimatum."

Scorsi lay back unconvinced, but too weak, confused, or
both to fight. That just made Tuck angrier, seemed somehow
like another slight. He finished bandaging his arm and stood,

sneering at Scorsi as he did.

"What sort of ultimatum?" Tuck asked.

"A nuclear one. They're threatening to attack each other if we don't turn over Symmetra."

Scorsi winced, maybe from the pain, maybe from the realization of what might happen to the world. Despite how angry he was, Tuck felt a twinge of sorrow for her then. She was out of her depth, a scientist pulled into espionage and geopolitics, all sorts of things she couldn't possibly care about or understand.

But as he stood thinking about the situation, Tuck realized there was something else to it, something that he felt giddy thinking, right and wrong at the same time, his gut knotting at the thought. It was the idea that heathens killing heathens would have been the right way for this to end, that it would have been what the Lord wanted; and the realization that went with it, the thought of just how wrong that sort of thinking was. How it was like the people he was trying to save America and the world from. But that was wrong, foolish. Because he was a Christian, and he was right. That was everything.

"So?" he said, too confused to do anything but speak.

"So you get her off the island. I'll go after the kidnappers."

Scorsi shook her head. "You're not leaving me alone with him again."

"No choice, doctor."

"There is a choice, Clarion," Tuck said. "They brought us in on Gulfstreams. We can all get out on one of those."

"Just do what I tell you, Squires. There's a Mantis stato-docked a mile offshore. Here's my cell."

"Did you hear what I said?"

"Yeah. Did you hear what I said?"

"I did. But…?"

"Enough. Just follow the dead bodies until you get to the entrance then it's a straight shot south to the beach." He raised his gaze, shook his head. "No pun intended."

"But—"

"What is it?"

"You're going to need my help, Clarion."

"Aw, you're worried for me, Squires. That's very touching."

"No, seriously."

"Seriously, what? You mean there are more Asian dudes with these piece-of-shit Ukrainian guns?"

"Yeah, OK, but that's not all. The guy who ran out of here calls himself the Natural, and he's got a boss."

"The Organic?"

"The Presence."

"Wait," said Scorsi, "There's another way."

Clarion shook his head. "Just follow the bodies. I'll deal with the Poodle and the Nitwit."

"I don't mean that. I mean there's a kill code for Symmetra."

Clarion turned to Tuck. Homicide in this gaze, he shook his head. "Why are we only learning about this now?"

Scorsi replied, "A secret kill code wouldn't be much good if everyone knew about it."

"And…?"

"And…what?" she asked.

"And…what's the fucking code?"

"Pigshit," she responded. "That's the code. But we'll need help to activate it."

Clarion scraped at the stubble on his chin. "What sort of help?"

"My CFO, Etobo."

"Kenyatta Etobo?" said Tuck, remembering the little Ibabongan, how obvious it had all seemed, how sure he'd been of the guy's guilt. There was still a part of him that wanted Etobo to be guilty—that wanted to believe Etobo could be guilty despite all the facts to the contrary.

"You know him?" Diana said.

"We've met," Tuck responded, looking down.

"How's your CFO going to help, Scorsi?" This was Clarion.

"He knows everything except the activation word. It's the only way to unlock the program, my guarantee that he'll have to have heard from me to proceed."

Clarion nodded once. "And the theocracies have demanded the technology. The only way they'll stand down is if we give it to them."

She gave a weak smile. "Exactly. So, we'll give it to them and destroy it after the crisis is over. We have to hope they'll be thinking more clearly once a little time has elapsed. Especially if you guys can get your hands on the Presence and the Natural."

"Fine, Scorsi, you're the scientist. Just pick her up and get the fuck going, Squires."

"Clarion, you don't understand," Tuck responded. "This will kill it. No need to go chasing after lunatics in masks."

"That's not justice. These fuckers need to pay for what they've done." He glanced over his shoulder at the passage.

"You still don't have all the facts, Clarion. The Presence has been babbling about some sort of self-destruct for the island."

"Doesn't matter. I'll catch them before they can use it."

"But what if you don't?" asked Scorsi.

"If I can't stop them I'll get out on one of those Gulfstreams Squires was talking about."

"You fly?"

"Sure, I fly. I'm Ken Clarion. I do everything. Now, take this," he said, handing Tuck the Achka. "And get as far as you can from this place before anything goes boom."

Pulling his Rikken, Clarion headed back up the steps towards the passage. "And, Tuck," he called. "Once you're in the O-2 get in touch with Hunter. Tell her everything that went down. If I don't make it, she'll know what to do."

29

THE REAL ANGEL

"THEY'RE COMING FOR YOU," SAID A NON-GENDER-SPECIFIC voice. Sunny yet denunciatory, the tone was one Parlay might have used for informing a CEO his division had record profits but he was getting the axe anyway.

"Who is this?" Parlay asked, turning his gaze from the black, rock wall and his mental outline of the door from which Justice would emerge.

"The Angel, of course."

Parlay's eyes widened. Not wanting to acknowledge the psychotic break that might well be underway, he tried to keep his focus on the physical, glared down at the two devices on the table before him. The first was a silver detonator the size of a matchbox, the second a black Walther; a vestige of a better time, an antique from the days when James Bond had ruled the world.

He understood the detonator, felt confident that keying in the six-digit code would achieve the desired effect. As for the gun, much as he treasured it as a totem, Parlay's expertise was limited to knowing what the trigger did and that you were supposed to keep the pointy end facing away from you. "That's not possible."

"Why?"

"Because?" he sputtered.

"You'll have to be a little more specific."

"You, too," Parlay said.

The voice chuckled. "Fine, I'll do because. Because is that you think Morton School was the Angel."

"Who or what is Morton School?"

"Doctor Morton School, Deputy Director of the National Science Foundation, the man who brought you this deal in the first place, whose suicide is being reported on the evening news. Though, in all honesty, that wasn't much of a suicide."

"The egghead on the InterTel? What are you saying, that you killed him?"

"Something like that," said the voice.

"Look, this is all very fascinating but you still haven't told me who you are."

"I beg to differ. But I'll tell you again if you insist. I'm the Angel—the real Angel—and I have been all along."

Parlay's pupils grew to pools of black, his gaze panning wildly about the cabin, moving from gleaming walnut trim to shiny buttercream leather, from high-tech this to higher-tech that. This plane, never mind the fact that he had six others just like it, had always felt like a symbol to him; a ready proof of the financial armor that should have made a situation like this impossible. But it hadn't. Still, Parlay had Symmetra. He wasn't done yet. "The only real thing you sound like is a real lunatic. I'm hanging up."

"Oh, I wouldn't do that, Presence. Or maybe I should just

call you Mistuh Ravelton Parlay?" the voice said, suddenly going feminine and breathy, Scarlet O'Hara dealing with a case of the vapors.

"Big deal. You know my name."

"I suppose I could also call you Jimmy Orchard, couldn't I?"

Parlay felt the air go out of him—his skin heavy, his skeleton pained. The name brought back memories of a childhood in Vermont, left him sitting speechless, the cell pinned to his ear. He couldn't bring himself to respond.

The Angel laughed. Hollow and staticky at the same time, it was an evil laugh, the sort that should have been had at someone else's expense, which only made Parlay angrier, as did the next comment, "I mean, that's who you really are, right?"

"Um," Parlay managed.

"That, or Ravelton Parlay, or any other number of fake identities? Trust me, Parlay, I know your story, your life of big bucks and bigger schemes. I know everything you've done. That's why I chose you."

Parlay's head felt too full by them. His mind was coming unmoored, floating, drowning more like, all his plans failing. And he thought simply, what can I do to turn this, to make this unhappen? What can save me? And he thought of God, but then he thought of something else, something far more immediate.

"This is about a cut of the profits, isn't it?"

The Angel laughed that hollow laugh again. "I've been waiting for you to get around to that, and the answer is no. This is about principles, not money. I know that's probably difficult for somebody like—"

"What principles?" Parlay smirked sickly, his face twisting into a sort of leer. In another situation, he would have found

319

this lavishly funny, even absurd, that a base blackmailer was talking to him about principles.

"Mostly philosophical ones. Though in this case there will be a few physical ones at play fairly soon."

"Such as?"

"Relativity."

"Einstein."

"Bingo. Unless I miss my guess, large shiny objects ought to start flying back and forth across the Mediterranean in the next few hours, objects that go *Boom!* You've seen the troop movements, haven't you?"

Parlay paused, thought back to the images he'd seen in the throne room, the ones he'd been able to use so successfully against Scorsi, that were now being used against him, a fact that made him want to scream. "Troop movements, yes. Objects, no. Booming, definitely not."

"You're not going to see the boom. You're going to feel it."

"If you say so."

"Exactly right. You may be catching on after all. This is all coming out exactly as planned. You don't honestly think the Israelis are going to let themselves be destroyed by a vastly superior conventional force, do you?"

"This will all blow over once our customers get the technology."

"Blow over? That's an interesting choice of words."

"Relax. I'll cut you in. It's not a problem."

"What makes you think that's how this is all going to work?"

"School said—"

The Angel chuckled. "And who do you think told School that?"

Parlay knew the answer. But he wasn't going to give the Angel the satisfaction of saying it.

After a few beats, the Angel continued, "Exactly. How do you think a scientist could possibly put you in touch with all those high-level diplomatic contacts, could know enough to come up with all these great ideas for covering your tracks? It certainly wasn't School's idea to move an entire island or to send the Insider airmail."

"Well…"

"And how do you think he was able to defuse the problems you started having with your customers?"

"You're saying you lied to School?"

"No, I told him the truth. Your customers do still want the technology. You just have to pick one to sell it to."

"But that butchers our profit margin."

"I'll tell you one other thing that'll butcher your profit margin."

"What's that?"

"The war that will start when the other two realize you've cut a deal with their enemy."

Parlay saw the images again in his mind. He saw tanks and troops, mushroom clouds and cities in flames. And he knew these images would be nothing compared to the economic results. Even if one of the powers paid him what he requested, there was no telling what that money would be worth after the Middle East, or maybe even the entire world, erupted in war. He could be ruined, everyone and everything along with him. "This is insane," Parlay said, feeling as though he should have concluded this much earlier.

"Coming from you, I'll take that as a compliment."

"You're going to kill millions of people."

"Now you're all warm and fuzzy about human life? I thought they were just a bunch of heathens to you."

"Not all of them," Parlay said, pursing his lips.

"You mean the Christians?"

"Of course."

"So it's OK for the others to die?"

"I'd save them all."

"Oh, that's rich."

"What's rich?"

"The idea that you value human life. What about the Insider and Millie Warburton? What about Scorsi herself? Never mind all those other eggheads you've been having your lackeys dispose of so blithely?"

"Necessary losses."

"I feel the same way about the Old World."

"You're talking about millions, maybe even billions of people."

"Once the holy cities are radioactive dust, people will see the Great Religions for the blight they are. Historians will point to this as a great day, the day humanity freed itself from the bondage of false gods."

"Exactly. That's why we were going to take all their money and then convert them to Christianity. What about the plan don't you understand?"

"Don't you see, Parlay? You're a faith junky like the rest."

"I thought...School was a believer."

"You thought School was a believer—and you were wrong—but that's not the point. The point is that we're still partners. I called to warn you."

"Well, thanks. I guess you've done that."

"Not completely."

"How so?"

"They're coming for you. Even as we speak."

"No, you already said that. I'm watching on the closed circuit," he said, gaze returning to the forecabin big screen where he saw Clarion moving through the throne room, towards the passage. "If you have nothing else to say…"

"What I have to say is this: ID have the coordinates of your island. The US Navy could show up any minute. You'd better get going. You're just lucky you've got stealthing technology on that little jet of yours. And you can thank me for that by the way. Leave now and you should be able to make it."

"I have to wait for the Natural."

"Loyal to the end, huh, Parlay? I'm sure you'll get bonus points for that in the great beyond. Or prison. Whichever comes first. Either way, you know nothing about me. If you want to fail, be my guest."

Parlay imagined himself in a white jumpsuit like one of his Kai Laus, a black number sewn on the back. He imagined large black men calling him bitch.

"Is that—?"

Click…The abrupt end to the Angel's call left Parlay feeling as though vomiting would have been a big improvement to his condition. Not in the traditional sense that he would feel better afterwards, but that an endless cycle of purge and heave, purge and heave, would have been a big upgrade over the ideas of failure, prison, and death that had him considering the corollary concept of munching on his own gun.

And if he were forced to do that, what then? Would God understand? Would He realize Parlay had been saving Him the embarrassment of the media characterizing Virtual Jerusalem as some sort of failure of Christianity? Or would He see suicide as a breach of faith, consign Parlay to an eternity in Hell over that one little mistake? Which seemed petty now that he was confronted with the prospect in his own life? Was God that petty? Was it possible?

This was when the false door finally, blissfully opened; and Justice emerged from the shadows, the Achka in his hands. He was favoring his right shoulder, doing his best to sprint down the airstrip towards Savior I, trailing blood-red bread crumbs behind him like some wounded, horror movie Hansel.

Despite the agony on Justice's face, Parlay saw victory. He saw himself returning to the green fields and sunshine of Bayousalem. He smiled, felt a kindling of joy in his heart. The feeling was brief, though, draining away when another shape emerged from the false door's shadow. Ken Clarion.

Parlay looked back at the detonator and the gun on the table before him, briefly considered the idea of using the detonator, of ending this whole mess once and for all. It would have been so simple, so easy, so final, just one beautiful last act.

Parlay was no quitter, though. He still believed in God, and even more importantly, in the great future God had ordained for him—that he was one of the elect, a believer chosen to succeed. And he had to do everything he could to make that happen.

Parlay picked up the Walther and headed for the air bridge. By the time he hit the tarmac, Justice had turned and was firing at Clarion.

Clarion took cover behind a stack of plywood crates covered in red, Chinese characters. Justice let loose another volley, spraying the crates with gunfire, spending all his rounds. As he pulled more ammo, fitted the clip, Clarion rose and fired, hitting Justice in his right leg, sending him and the Achka to the concrete.

By that point Parlay knew there was no other way. Raising the Walther, he aimed at Clarion and squeezed the trigger, releasing an unexpectedly powerful burst. The gun bucked more than he'd expected causing him to shoot first too high, then too low, then more or less just right which was by that point, more or less all wrong.

The Walther fell from his grasp, bounced once, twice, three times on the runway, and came to rest six inches from the tarmac's edge. Light skipped and flickered on the surface of the dark water, the moon dancing with its own reflection.

"Presence, you shot me," Justice yelled.

30

THE LORDS OF DAY
AND NIGHT

Rikken in his right hand, left tracing the wall as a guide, Clarion moved down the black, rock steps. The passage bent to the left as he descended, tiny lights where walls met floor the only thing that made movement possible. Always, Clarion was listening, trying to make out the Natural up ahead of him, hoping to catch the sound of labored breathing or faltering steps. As his eyes grew accustomed to the light, Clarion realized there were shapes painted on the walls. Faint and grainy, the images looked centuries, maybe millennia, old. Men and women, winged apes and horned fish, mountains with arms and waves with faces, the pictures had the look of myth, stories the rulers of a forgotten civilization had constructed to frighten and pacify, to vilify and unify, to keep their tribe strong. For Clarion, though, they recalled another time and place.

He remembered Mexico, years before, the passage that had brought the priests and their victims to the pyramid's altar.

He thought of the drawings on the walls of that Aztec temple: the feathered serpents and bloody skeletons, the Lords of Day and Night the Aztecs had created to govern their world, to justify blood sacrifice, the serial killing on a grand scale all in the name of religion.

Even after years in the field, years of liquidating targets in more ways than he could count, those drawings affected him. They seemed almost to speak, to whisper of centuries measured in nothing but death for the sake of a story, killing for the sake of illusion. He remembered almost being able to smell the blood on that day in Mexico—a sick, rich, and rusty scent that had made him retch. What he remembered most though was what he'd found beneath, something far worse than anything in that pyramid. Proof that humanity could always outdo the horrors it imagined of the divine.

The Dios Sol Cartel had turned the caves beneath the temple into a processing plant for the strongest goth anyone had seen up to that point. The stuff was flooding Mexico and the Southern U.S., creating an epidemic with real economic costs, one W himself wanted stopped. This was why Clarion had gone to Chiapas. Like the coca and poppy kings before them, DSC were using peasants to work their plants, feeding them a steady diet of dope to keep them going, to turn them into the perfect, disposable labor force. Flesh sagging, eyes filled with a haunted energy, the peasants went about their chores with the sort of animal determination the drug produced in its addicts, working tirelessly until they succumbed. When they did, the cartel's thugs would pile the bodies in dump trucks, dispose of them in acid pits deep in the jungle. Then they would go out into the night and kidnap more. More ten-year old girls out alone after dark. More beggar grandfathers too weary to walk. More of the confused and lonely, the drunk and drugged and mad and homeless. More angeles de la calle as DSC's soldiers called them, the angels of the street. By the time Clarion saw the end of the passage, the memories were too much. He wanted to stop, to gather himself before he moved in. But he couldn't, and he knew that. His only choice was to force himself to forget, to move forward without knowing what lay in the light, just as he had that day in Mexico.

Sprinting down the last several steps, Clarion ducked out of the tunnel and ran, scanning for cover as bullets hit the concrete. Rounds closing on him, kicking up rocky shrapnel and sandy dust as they did, he saw three planes—one closer and to his right, the others in the distance to his left. Each plane was on its own runway, the three strips radiating out from the central area on which he stood. Close, to his immediate left, he spotted a stack of plywood crates and made for them. He dove the last few feet and rolled into cover, crouched behind the crates waiting for the Natural to spend the rest of his clip.

When the firing stopped, Clarion rose and squeezed off three rounds, taking the Natural in his right hamstring with the second. The Natural's knee buckled. He dropped the Achka, followed it to the ground. Clarion advanced, ready to take the shot if the Natural moved to reclaim his weapon. As he did, a second gunman emerged from the plane wearing a fine, white suit and a Reagan mask. Wielding an antique Walther with little skill he managed to get off a burst nonetheless. The recoil was more than he'd expected though. It caused him to fumble with the thing, the gun ultimately falling from his grasp and hitting the ground where it bounced and came to a rest at the edge of the tarmac.

"Presence, you shot me," the Natural yelled.

"Natural, what are…Quit messing around and get on the plane."

"But my gun."

"Forget the gun."

Clarion turned his Rikken on the new threat and fired. By that point the Presence was moving back into the plane. Clarion moved towards the Natural, keeping his aim on the jetway door as he did. When Clarion got to the Natural, he pulled him to his feet and put him in a rear choke, using him as a shield against any further gunfire. He began walking him towards the plane, aim on the air bridge door the whole time. When the Presence re-emerged, Clarion sighted him quickly. Which was a good thing because the Presence had re-armed himself, his new piece a shiny Alsurian auto.

"Toss the gun aside, sport," Clarion said quickly, not wanting to give the Presence a second to think, to build courage.

"Why would I do that?"

"Because if you don't, I'm gonna blow a hole in that Reagan mask and the tiny brain that goes with it. Now put the fucking piece down."

"You haven't thought this through, Clarion."

"How's that, whoever the fuck you are?"

"I'm the Presence."

"Yeah, I know."

"If you knew, why'd you pretend you didn't?"

"To piss you off?"

"It didn't work."

"If you say so."

Clarion heard the Presence chuckle beneath the mask. "You haven't reckoned with one important fact."

"What's that?"

"If you kill me, you'll have no proof."

"Au contraire, Mr. Asshole, I'll still have him," Clarion responded, tightening the choke as punctuation. Clarion knew the Natural's face would be changing colors by that point. He smiled, titled his head for effect.

"Not if I shoot him first," the Presence said, aiming for the center of the Natural's forehead. "I'll kill him, you'll kill me. Where will you be then? There's got to be something in this for me. Otherwise, why would I give up?"

"All right, I'll play. Something in it like what?"

"Well, I don't really…What assurances can you give me that I'll be treated fairly by your master?"

"You mean Hunter?"

"No, I mean that wicked fool, Raglan."

"The President?"

"President," he said, practically spitting the word.

"You're not getting immunity, you fuck. You probably just started a war."

"Fuck?" the Presence responded, his tone that of a southern patrician, surprised at the bad manners someone else had forced him to adopt. "I didn't start anything? That was the Angel."

Again, Clarion thought of the DSC workers in that temple complex, the angeles de la calle. There'd been at least a hundred of them he'd released, a hundred lives saved. And how many more thousands on the street? As horrible as it had been, he remembered the feeling of elation he'd had when it was over.

He remembered that as one of the days he'd most believed in America, been most certain that he'd done the right thing with his life.

He'd called Morris a night or two later, from Mexico City, tried to make him understand that something great had happened. He couldn't give him any details, though; and how stupid he'd been to even waste his time trying. How predictable the surly silence had been, the response of a thirteen-year-old to something he couldn't see. He didn't even want to play back the words, to take in the anger one more time.

"Angel? Man, you really are a lunatic. The only assurance I can give you is that you're done. If you want to live long enough to get that psych eval you so desperately need, you'll drop that piece."

"This revelation is supposed to surprise me, catch me off guard? I'm supposed to care if some heathen thinks I'm insane?"

"When the heathen has a gun and works for ID, I'd say it'd be a good fucking idea."

"Think about where you are, Clarion."

"Where's that?"

"You're on my island."

"And?"

"And there are no more revelations. I already know everything."

"OK."

"And you know nothing."

"Yes, you made that part clear."

"So there are no more revelations."

"I don't—"

"Because your boss told me everything."

"My boss?"

332

"The Angel."

Clarion squinted. "Back to the angels?"

"This angel isn't heavenly. He's very human. He's inside your Administration, and he's calling the shots. If you want to get to him, you'll have to deal with me."

Hunter's field alias had been Red Angel. This meant someone high up in the Administration, someone who had access to her personnel file was deep in it. It had to be Thunder, or someone with even higher clearance. The list was a short one—four or five names ending with that of the President himself. But why do any of this, why take the risk of starting a war in the Middle East? Raglan's policy was to pursue peace.

A boot stomp from the Natural, and Clarion's grip loosened. Still, he held the choke. A second, and he couldn't. The Natural knocked the gun from his grasp and into the water beyond. The Presence began firing. On reflex, Clarion pushed away from the Natural, shoving him towards the Presence in an effort to absorb any additional shots.

Clarion ran and dove into the water, swam deeper as metal rained down. The water shading darker, the surface harder to see, he realized the gunfire had stopped. He swam towards the other runways then, began searching his mind for what he knew about these Gulfstreams, hoping they weren't too tricked-out, knowing they almost certainly were.

Clarion had lied when he'd told Scorsi and Squires that he could fly the plane. Was there a chance he could, that he could get it up in the air at the very least? Yes, and a good one. But it wasn't a sure thing.

Had that been an act of nobility? Had Clarion felt sorry for Scorsi, or even for Squires, seen him as a son in a way, maybe as the son he'd lost now that Morris never came to the phone. Maybe, but not just. It had been the right thing to do, not in terms of nobility but accomplishing his mission, doing his job.

And in a way Clarion had always known that the only nobility he'd ever be able to manage was what went with the job. There would be no one to tell his story, no one to call him hero. And people would only feel the effects of his actions if he failed. This was what had gotten to him after so long, after all the years and the ex-wives and the son who would barely acknowledge him. This was all he'd gotten from the life he'd imagined as one of heroism, a life that had come to seem like one of failure, of loss…

When Clarion surfaced, he saw the plane still on the runway, just beginning to taxi, Savior 1 emblazoned on its side. He swam the last few yards and pulled himself out of the water onto Savior 2's runway.

THE PLANE HADN'T BEEN TAKEN THROUGH ANY PRE-FLIGHTS, and it wouldn't be. Clarion knew he didn't have time. The door unlocked, the key in the console, everything was smooth. All he had to do was hit ignition and wait for the engines to warm. He was going to get his chance. He put on the headset, tested the stick and the rudders, and tapped the throttle. Everything felt solid, incredibly slick for something private. He knew the engines would warm quickly. But he knew no matter how short, the wait would feel interminable. He looked up, saw that Savior 1 was now about a third of the way down the runway. He would have to go manual, but that wasn't a problem, not now at least. Even though the plane was designed to be flown by a crew of two—redundancy and all that—taking off wasn't the issue. What would be a problem—what would be damn near impossible—was coming back down.

He checked quickly for offensive features, found two types of missiles—Hawk 3's from the Pakis and Zylos from the Russians—good old American machine guns—dual 20 mm Vulcans—and second-gen lasers. There was cloaking, too: The push button labeled Sac-STEL-1 obvious. Seeing the cloaking made Clarion look up reflexively. He saw that Savior 1 was well past the halfway point of its taxi. He had no more time. If he lost visual, that would be it.

He put his left hand on the stick and pulled back the throttle with his right. A few seconds, and he was gaining speed, moving down the runway even as Savior 1 neared the end of its. He would have to shadow, hope to be able to raise someone on the radio once he got up, and hope that would be enough to get the other plane picked up by the Air Force. Once he accomplished that, he'd bail, hope somebody got to him before the sharks.

The wall seemed like a mirage at first, an illusion, a slight, growing imperfection in the fabric of the visual world. Near the end of the runway, it was rising steadily in the same gray as the tarmac, becoming a more obvious obstacle by the second, one that would block Clarion's way, maybe end his life.

He gunned the throttle, yanked back on the stick. He knew he was doing both before he should, that he'd probably go too close to vertical. But he had to do it. Given the choice between certain failure and the vaguest chance, you had to take the chance.

The wall had been programmed, though. Yet another

security feature of the Presence's multi-billion-dollar island, the sort of idea he must have gotten from someone who knew what they were doing, someone inside the government. It was Thunder, Clarion was sure of that now. That was the only answer that made sense.

There was no way around it, no way to save himself. The wall had been there waiting for him from the beginning. And it was too late. He was going to hit. Three, two, one...

Clarion jerked forward as the front wheels were taken out from beneath him. Savior II's belly scraped over the wall, fuselage emitting a wild, metal scream as it did. The impact hadn't killed Clarion though. It had only changed the jet's trajectory, brought it grinding and mashing and howling to a stop at the end of the runway, listing to the right, fucked beyond belief.

Savior I was up by now, moving beyond Clarion's sight. Running without any lights, he knew in seconds it would be invisible. And so it was, gliding into the night, arcing away across a perfect, silvered moon.

Clarion struggled to get something, anything on the radio. That was all his life had come to and while it wasn't enough by any stretch, Clarion had realized long ago that nothing would ever seem like enough. All death is certain, he remembered from someone, somewhere. All death is certain.

"USS Bichon Free-zay," he heard, within a chain of static.

"The fuck," he muttered. "Bichon Free-zay?"

"USS Bichon Cheney."

"Cheney?"

"USS Richard Cheney."

"Ahh." He smiled. "Richard Cheney? This is Clarion."

"Come back, Clarion."

"US ID Senior Special Agent, Ken Clarion, 642-PX-97QJ. It's Thunder. Thunder is the one." He could see Hunter's face then, could see her smile. He'd saved her one last time. Now he could ride off into the sunset, maybe make peace with Morris.

"Roger that, Clarion. No thunder here. Clear skies."

"No. It's Thunder. The Presence, the Natural."

"Richard Cheney repeating: No Thunder, Clarion. No Thunder."

"You don't," he began. The line went dead. "Hello? Hello? Richard Cheney?"

31

THE PRICE OF PEACE

EVEN FILTERED THROUGH THE NUMBING TIGHTNESS OF THE tourniquet and the haze of shock, the pain in Diana's leg made each second a struggle not to scream, left her searching for something, anything, to focus on. But all her conscious mind could find was the bullet and the damage it had done, the way it had ripped into her skin, left her insides tensed against the air.

"You'll be fine, Scorsi," Squires said as he'd bent down to pick her up.

The smile she gave him was frail, almost plaintive. And it was no small struggle. She still wasn't sure whether she believed this guy, this R.J. Rude model who thought he was James Bond. But could she believe in him without believing him? Could she trust him to get her to safety and still question his motives? Did she have any choice?

As he stood with her in his arms, the faintest movements sent a torturous current through her body, left her wishing for unconsciousness. "Easy," she said, wincing.

"Oh, you're not so heavy," he responded.

"Yeah, thanks," she barely managed to whisper.

Squires left the room at a jog. Diana spent a few seconds trying to keep her eyes open—thinking to somehow help him navigate—but she didn't have the energy. There was no choice but to close her eyes and let her head rest against his chest, to hope that he hadn't just played the other agent.

Squires was her only chance now. Not just her only chance to live. More importantly, he was her only chance to stop the Presence, to make up for what she'd done, what she'd had to do.

SHE FLASHED AWAKE TO THE CARESS OF WARM, OPEN AIR on her face. She felt relief, happiness, but only for a fraction of a second, only until she registered the oppressive reality of the jungle heat and the sounds of the night that went with it—the murderous cries and vengeful howls, the beating wings and breaking branches, the disease and venom scurrying and slithering across the jungle floor. The descent was steep, and Squires was moving at a full run before she knew it, trying to manage his speed by traversing back and forth almost like a skier, doing it in a way that left her feeling every jolt and thud. He kept stumbling and tripping again and again as he went, but somehow he managed not to fall or drop her. Still, it was like her entire body felt the wound to her leg, like his movements were sending a current of pain through her once again. But this time the intensity was much greater, so great that she couldn't pass out, much as she wanted to. All she could do to keep from screaming was shut her eyes, lock her jaws, and hope.

Eventually, Diana felt the angle of descent begin to flatten. She opened her eyes. By that point they were closing on the beach. There was the submarine they'd talked about, the O-2, waiting for them, early moonlight playing against its metallic green hull. As they neared the craft, Squires slowed, knelt, and deposited her on the sand.

"Why are you stopping?"

"Just a minute," he said, stepping towards the craft. He rummaged inside for a moment, returned. "That tourniquet's tight but it won't hold. I need to get you really fixed up."

"The island is supposed to explode one way or the other."

He pulled a hypo from the med kit.

"What's that for?"

"I can't have you thrashing around while I'm trying to get us underway."

"Seriously, you can trust me."

"Sorry, Scorsi, rules are rules. Don't worry, this will only put you out for a couple minutes. You'll be back among the living in no time."

THE ROAR LINGERED IN HER EARS AND HER MIND AS SHE tried to focus her thoughts. Seconds, maybe half a minute, and she realized she was sitting shotgun in the O-2's right, front bucket, Squires in the pilot's seat to her left. A warm, ruby luminescence didn't so much fill the cabin as enfold it and seep inward, almost as if it were radiation made visible. An instrument panel stretched across the slanted dash. Schematics, maps, and numerics blinked on a large, central touch screen; one with just enough detail to tell you that a computer was running the show. The dormant dials, knobs, and switches that covered the remainder of the dash confirmed this.

"Yes, you're alive," Squires said, turning to her. "I mean, in case you were wondering. And your wounds are dressed. I fixed you up once we were on auto."

"That sound?"

"The island."

"But it was so loud."

"Yeah, I wasn't expecting that either. Maybe it wasn't the self-destruct."

"Then, what?"

"Who knows?"

"You probably ought to do what Clarion said. Call that Hunter chick and find out what's going on."

"You're right, Scorsi." He pulled Clarion's cell, hit a few buttons, and brought the thing to his ear.

"No, ma'am. It's Squires," he said a few seconds later. He paused to listen, shook his head in response. "Yes, I've got her. What about Clarion?"

He waited.

"Yes, ma'am, that's true. I am using his phone, and I did just hear that explosion. You're saying you think he's dead?" Squires listened, nodded. "No ma'am, but there's a kill code for Symmetra. We'll just need her CFO—"

He cut his gaze in Diana's direction.

"You picked him up already? Nice work, ma—" He moved the phone away from his ear, as though the volume had unexpectedly increased. "Yes, you did tell me to quit it with all the ma'am-ing. That's right. No, no, he's not lying. Pigshit. That matches what Scorsi told us."

He pulled the phone closer again and slit his gaze, reminding her of a guilty child. "I'm sorry?"

He listened as, apparently, Hunter continued for some time. Finally, he said, "I guess I did hear you. No, I'll do my duty. I'll call you once it's done. Squires out."

He killed the call, deposited the phone in his pocket.

"So?" she asked, wondering what that stuff about duty meant. She imagined being taken into custody, kept there for years.

"So…that was the Navy destroying the island," he responded.

"Why?"

"Part of keeping the peace."

"I still don't understand."

"The French threatened the PIF, the PIF threatened the Israelis, and the Israelis are ridiculously outgunned so they threatened to use their nukes. Then nobody wanted to lose face. Things escalated. It's just a good thing the public doesn't know any of this happened."

"No, I get that. I guess what I mean is why?"

"There'd be panic and political unrest across the Middle East, maybe even the whole world."

"How's that different from the way things usually are?"

"I mean governments getting toppled and nukes getting lobbed back and forth."

"Like I said."

He shook his head. "You did the right thing giving the Presence the technology. If you hadn't done that, the President never could have fixed things. We'd be in World War III, no question. We're just lucky Raglan was able to broker the deal."

"What is this deal you keep talking about?"

"Raglan made the theocracies see that there was no way for any of them to have the technology and survive. They were in a no-win situation…One the Presence was obviously trying to set up."

"He said he was just trying to sell the stuff."

"He was lying. That's obvious, too. Once the theocracies realized they'd been duped, they all agreed Symmetra should be destroyed."

"That still doesn't make sense. If they wanted Symmetra badly enough to kick up so much dust over it, why would they settle for destroying it?"

"They finally saw logic. No doubt there was a little carrot and stick action from Raglan, too. We do have SDI, you know. And we're the only country that's ever actually used a nuke. That has to count for something when you're negotiating peace."

"And now we have to destroy Symmetra?"

"Right. Symmetra's destruction was part of the deal. That's why the President just destroyed the island."

"So that was a nuke?"

"Apparently so."

"And how do you plan on explaining that to the public?"

Squires averted his gaze. "Joint war games. Something about contingency plans in the event of alien attack or meteor strike, something like that. Don't worry about that, Scorsi. I'm sure they've got it covered."

"Wait, but they wanted it. They were willing to go to war over it."

"Well, now they don't."

"Don't?"

"Don't, aren't, whatever…Now they're scared of what it's capable of, suggesting you, the Presence, and the Angel were in it together, trying to set them at each other's throats."

"They're blaming this on me?"

"Oh, we know you weren't involved, Scorsi. Don't worry about that."

"I heard you asking about your partner."

"Clarion's dead most likely. No way to be sure yet."

"Still, maybe…"

"That was a twenty-megaton explosion. There's no reason to think he's still alive."

"I don't know what to say."

"No apologies, Scorsi. Clarion was doing his job. Now, we do ours. The theocracies think we've just killed the Presence and destroyed Symmetra. We can't very well have either of them popping up a few hours from now."

"But if we kill it now we'll never know who the Presence was."

"I guess that's the price of peace."

"You're just full of good news, aren't you, Squires?"

"Oh, I haven't gotten to the really good stuff yet."

"Such as?"

"Such as, Hunter just ordered me to kill you."

Scorsi laughed. "Oh, really?"

"Really."

"You're not kidding?"

He shook his head, tapped the touch screen. "Seems that's part of the deal they made. The point of destroying the island and the technology is to erase the crisis. Part of erasing the crisis is erasing you."

Squires hit the touch screen again. Shiny cuffs sprang from the arm- and leg-rests, pinning Diana to the seat. Her right ankle had been out of position, and remained free. It was useless to her though, no defense in what she knew was coming.

"I'm sorry about this, Scorsi. I really am. But the order's coming directly from the President."

"You don't even like the President."

"Yeah, but he's still the President. I still have my duty."

"I knew you were bad all along. I knew it back in the throne room. You've been part of this, haven't you? You, Clarion, Hunter, maybe even the President himself. This has just been a massive plot to destroy the one thing that could have saved humanity."

"None of the above, Scorsi. I told you the truth back in the throne room. I was playing for time. My orders were to save you, and I did."

"And now you're going to kill me?"

"My orders changed."

"You realize that if they're trying to erase all this, it means they'll want to erase you, too."

Squires considered this. "Maybe, maybe not. I'll just have to take my chances with that." He reached beneath his seat, produced a black case the size of a magic marker, and opened it. Inside was a syringe.

"Another one? Jesus, what is it this time, poison?"

He frowned. "An overdose of anesthetic. We're Americans, not barbarians."

She turned to her right, the sea swirling beyond the sub, at once both active and passive. She thought of the world, the same in its way—the same but for the inclusion of humanity. We had altered it, overburdened it. Maybe the reality wasn't that we were atop the food chain, the apex predator with a soul seeking to understand the world. Maybe we were a virus. Or perhaps not only a virus but host, too. Or maybe the virus was something beyond? Maybe the virus was God, and we were only symptoms.

"If you were a believer, Doctor, I'd offer to let you pray. I guess I still should. If you ask Jesus to come into your heart, he'll save you."

She turned back to him. "Save me from what? Death?"

"Nothing can save you from death. But Jesus can save you from Hell."

"Oh, I'm pretty sure I've already done my time in Hell over the last few days."

"If you say so." Squires smirked, then reached across the cabin and stabbed her in the neck with the hypo.

Diana tried to raise her hand to the source of the pain, but couldn't. A few heartbeats later, she was out. A few more, and she was gone, gone into a sea of lost time, into black on black on black…

32

BETTER THAN BORN AGAIN

SIX A.M., PARLAY AND JUSTICE SPRAWLED ON OPPOSITE SIDES of the Specter's back seat, first shift chauffeur Mannheim hulking behind the wheel, the white limo sprinted through the fall-stripped woods. Cypress and sycamore, oak and maple—the forest had grown out of America's deep, native past, been augmented by Parlay, sold to the State of Louisiana, bought back, and sold again so many times that no one knew anymore who owned it, except for Parlay and his attorneys. Mannheim cut his speed and flashed the beams as they approached the northern gatehouse, the mansion's silhouette visible above the estate's surrounding tree cover. Looming in the same gray as the two-story checkpoint, somehow shadowy and lustrous at the same time, the house seemed almost like a giant, struggling to remain hidden.

The post returned a trio of winks from its rooftop searchlights, the estate's version of three bells and all's well. The gates swung inward, the writhing white of wrought iron curlicues and filigrees parting like the covers of a storybook. Once the car had passed, the gates returned to their static form—a metal tapestry of hidden crosses and crouching lions, giant roses and lurking cherubs.

"Jack?" Parlay asked, reaching across the empty back seat and tapping the skull of his drowsy #1. His Reagan mask now a memory, Parlay's false eyes were still there, shining silver. Hair white, jaw lean, Parlay knew he was looking at Justice like a whole lot of trouble. He also knew it wasn't going to last. He needed Justice now more than ever.

"Rev?" Justice asked, right eye half-opening.

"We're here," Parlay responded.

Justice fixed his demi-gaze on the boss man, realized how serious Parlay was and sat up straight, opening both eyes. "Here, where?" he asked, bringing balled fists to weary eyes, grinding away the sleep.

"Here, Bayousalem."

"Oh?" Justice was normally persona non-grata on the estate, but Parlay was hoping that a little consideration in this regard might make him more willing to do what was needed.

"I want to tell you again how well you've done for me, Jack, and more than that, for the Lord."

"But your island."

"Forget the island, plenty more where that came from. As a matter of fact, I was thinking you might do a little scouting for me, son, help find a new one."

"Anything you need, Rev."

"This won't be an easy mission, Jack. It'll involve flying all over the globe, checking out tropical islands, probably living a bit of the high life."

"Shoot, Rev, that almost sounds like a reward."

"It is, son, for a job well done."

"But things fell apart. There was nearly a nuclear war."

"None of that was your fault, son." Parlay thought of the Angel—the real Angel who'd almost cost him everything. He thought of all the things he would have Justice do to that Angel, the Old Testament fate that waited. But he had to figure out who the guy was first and for that he needed time. "The important thing is that we have Symmetra, don't forget that. You know the money was never the most important thing to me."

"That's very generous of you, Rev. I'm not really sure what to say."

"You don't have to say anything, son. Just enjoy."

Justice nodded.

"Before you set off on that mission I want you to do one leetle, teensy thing for me."

"Sure, anything."

"I want you to try Symmetra. Y'know, put it through its paces, see what it can actually do."

"We already know what it can do, Rev. The eggheads told us."

"Sure, we know what it does, but only in the abstract. We don't know everything, not for sure until, well, y'know, until we do."

"But I'm already a Christian."

"Oh, no, son, you misunderstand. There haven't been any changes to the technology yet. It's just as Scorsi developed it. This isn't going to brainwash you into anything."

"Then what's it going to do?" Justice squinted, as if remembering all Parlay's words about how dangerous the stuff was, how it was the work of the Devil.

"Don't worry, son. This'll be safe as all get out. Those eggheads you talk about…"

"Yes?"

"They're here, now."

"Here, where?"

"Here, Bayousalem."

FLOWN IN FROM SHORT-TERM COOLING LOCATIONS IN THE Catskills, Maine, and North Dakota, Wazaputsky and his team of just-below-top-notch scientists had been on the grounds of Bayousalem for three days. They were quartered under heavy guard in a wing of what was normally Parlay's personal weapons museum—a sort of petting zoo but with tanks and howitzers instead of ducks and llamas. They'd been given plenty of space to work, had Parlay's functionally-infinite financial resources placed at their disposal. They'd also had Parlay's written admonitions—presented to them by Bayousalem's Mickey Mouse-mask-wearing Chamberlain, Zigmund—as to what their joint, unnamed bossman did and didn't expect.

Wazaputsky and his team hadn't disappointed. They'd produced the equipment by cannibalizing what Parlay already had on site and raiding a few Electronic Acres liquidation sales, completed the final adjustments and testing as Parlay slept. By the time the bossman lazed awake at ten a.m. the following morning—Justice a bit less-gently, minutes later, by Parlay's valet, Kwang—Symmetra was ready for testing.

"Mr. Presence, if you please," Wazaputsky said to the man who'd entered wearing purple silk pajamas, a robe of red brocade, Magliani slippers, and a brand spanking new Reagan mask. Wazaputsky pointed to a black leather chair in the corner of the room, a chair identical to the one in which he sat.

Shiny, soothing, and Scandinavian it was the sort of thing you'd find in a high-end psychiatrist's office—the sort of place Ravelton Parlay had never 'officially' been. Another lay in the northwest corner of the room. This was the chair from which Justice had risen a moment before. Parlay had watched him with a head-lightening, stomach-twisting mixture of elation and dread.

"Just a minute, Wazaputsky. I need to talk to the Great Decider before I let you hook me up to any of this stuff."

Wazaputsky nodded as Parlay crossed the room, meeting Justice near the center of the isosceles triangle formed by the three chairs.

"How'd it go, son?" Parlay asked his number one.

"Beautiful, Rev. It…It can't hurt you."

"Can't hurt you? Why not?"

"It's Jesus."

"Jesus?"

"Yes, Rev, Jesus. He was a white knight on a white horse. He had a white lance and a white sword, and he was saying great things. The words roared from his lips like thunder made of invisible fire."

"He was saying things to you? What was he saying?"

"He was telling me to relax, that everything would be all right."

"What's he saying now?"

"He's not saying anything, it's over." Justice looked down.

This was enough proof for Parlay. "Any reason I can't use this one, Wazaputsky? It's not going to scramble my brainwaves with his or anything like that?"

Wazaputsky shook his head.

Parlay sat.

Wazaputsky tapped touch screens and spoke softly, seemingly to himself. Parlay couldn't hear the Russian's exact words.

"OK, sit back and relax. Let your mind go," he finally said. "You'll see a holographic."

"Then what happens?"

"The beginning's all I know."

"You haven't tried it?"

"I'd like to, but no."

Parlay sat back. He said a prayer for God to protect him, to give him strength. As the lights dimmed, he found himself hoping to see Jesus, visualizing the figure Justice had described— the white rider in white armor on a white horse. Seconds later the holographic appeared just as Wazaputsky had said.

The holo was huge, concave, and black. It took over Parlay's view in every direction. He felt as if he was floating within a dark sphere, like he'd finally come home. That was when the questions began.

At first a far-off whisper, it repeated its question again and again, growing louder with each iteration, growing more forceful until Parlay felt the voice belonged to a being speaking to him from inches away, or maybe even from inside his own head.

"You want to know what we should do with this Symmetra stuff, don't you?"

"Who is this?"

"God."

"Lord?"

"Yes."

"Really? I don't see anything."

"Of course, it's me, Ravelton. Who else could it possibly be?"

"I was…er, um…expecting Jesus."

"Oh, he's here, at my right hand."

"Do I get to talk to him, too?"

"Maybe some day. Not now."

"Why not? He talked to Justice."

"You're not questioning me, are you, Ravelton?"

"No, Lord, of course not."

"Good. Now, back to this Symmetra stuff and what you want to do with it."

"Well, all I want to do with it right now is use it. I feel so…I feel…At this moment I feel better than born again."

"I think you're getting the picture, son. Regardless of the way Virtual Jerusalem fell apart, this Symmetra stuff is obviously something special."

"Yes, Lord."

"A few snips here, a few tucks there, and we'll have what I've been waiting for lo these many years. For now, I want you to start outfitting the Righteous Burgers with these sorts of devices."

"What sorts of devices?"

"The one you're using."

"In every franchise?"

"In every booth."

"That's going to be expensive, Lord."

"Sure, it'll cost some cash up front. But we can use the staff at Righteous Burger to help us mitigate the costs as much as possible—y'know, Wanamaker and his people."

"I don't even know how much something like that would cost. That's the sort of project that could bankrupt me."

"You're not suggesting that money is more important than my will are you, Ravelton?"

"Of course not, Lord."

"Good answer. So, obviously the first order of business will be to miniaturize the stuff, make it less obvious what's going on."

"Lord?"

"JesusWare's going to be a brainwashing program, isn't it?"

"If that's OK with you, Lord?"

"Of course it's OK with me. It's not even really brainwashing if it's the truth."

Parlay nodded. He felt like he needed a pen and paper to record everything that was being said, to take notes so that he wouldn't forget anything.

"You'll probably want to use the Jesus that Justice saw. That's the sort of Jesus that'll appeal to Americans, help you build popular support. You know, a real following."

"But I already have a real following, Lord."

"Sure you do, for a business man. That's not my goal, Ravelton, not for you, not anymore."

"Lord?"

"I want you to run for President."

33

ONE MINUTE TO MIDNIGHT

Tuck was in the O-2, about a hundred miles due east of AUTEC, the Navy's Atlantic Undersea Test and Evaluation Center in the Bahamas. That was where Hunter had instructed him to drop off the craft and Scorsi's corpse—the former for repair and refit, the latter for ID and disposal. In spite of the dead scientist in the seat next to him, the world around Tuck seemed just a little more beautiful than it had before he'd spoken to Hunter a few moments before.

"You can hop a transport back to D.C. from AUTEC," she'd told him.

"Yes, ma'am."

"And, Squires?"

"Ma'am?"

"The President wants to meet you."

"Really?" His negative feelings about the President—and Hunter for that matter—had melted away. He was finally getting the recognition he deserved. All was right with the world.

"There may even be a medal in it for you."

The O-2 was on autopilot and Tuck was smiling. Looking

357

out the window, he remembered the nannies taking him and his friends to the aquarium when he'd been five—or maybe six. He remembered the vivid colors of the fish as they swam through the eerily-lit water, the clusters of swaying seaweed. The memories had caught in his mind, dwelt there more than two decades. But they were nothing compared to what was all around him now.

The fish came in so many different shapes, colors, and sizes that he almost felt like he was on a different planet, in a different world. And he was, sort of—the Earth's third and most secret kingdom. The seaweed grew unchecked down here, forming great forests through which the fish swam. There were mountains of coral, too; electric pink and neon green, nuclear yellow and dayglo lilac. Lone sharks prowled the waters, their hunters' eyes searching for prey, the other fish scattering as they snaked past, the alphas of the deep.

He'd spent the trip scanning external sources, trying to piece together what the world knew, hoping this would help him come up with a way to convince Hunter to let him go after the Presence and the Natural. Based on the externals—Wolf View, LeftNews, and the like—people had bought the story about joint, nuclear war games. They also, miraculously, still believed that the tale of jewel thievery had been real and unrelated. This meant Tuck had time—maybe enough to exact his revenge on the Presence and the Natural, or at least bring them to justice. Sure, waiting was a risk, but Scorsi had been right—it was the only way they'd ever know who'd been behind Virtual Jerusalem.

He still had to convince Hunter that he was the guy for the gig, that he'd shown enough on this last mission that she could trust him to get a job this big done alone. But based on the positive phone call they'd just had, Tuck was confident that Hunter would go along with his plan, if only to provide some sort of meaning for her old buddy, Clarion's, death. Yeah, things had looked pretty darn good until Tuck had gotten bored and decided to play around with the O-2's cabin recorder. That was when he'd found the conversation between Clarion and Hunter.

"What about Thunder? She's still looking at the kid?" This was Clarion.

"Looking at him hard," Hunter said. "I knew I should have gotten rid of him."

"I spent time with him, Hunter. I'm telling you. He's not involved."

"That's comforting, Kenny. I wish I was as confident. More than that, I wish Thunder and Raglan were. But there's no way to hide one of these nut jobs when the shit goes down. You remember how heavy things got over Yemen and Oman. It was practically a witch hunt for anyone who wouldn't toe the party line. You barely made it."

"Yeah, I remember. I wouldn't have without your help."

She sighed. "I should have seen this coming a long time ago and done something about it regardless of what his last name was."

"Something like what, a sanction?"

"Maybe. You know those orders come straight from the President, Clarion. And Thunder's already put that one in his head. Maybe if we come through this OK, they won't put a termination out on him; but if Congress starts asking questions, we'll be looking for a sacrificial lamb. And it won't be me, not if I can help it."

Submerged in the O-2, Tuck knew he was untraceable.

He also knew he couldn't stay there forever. Never mind the absence of food and water, or the dead scientist in the seat beside him, what Hunter had said to Clarion proved that if Tuck wanted to live he needed to put time and distance between himself and Internal Defense. For want of a less magical term he needed to disappear.

AN AQUATIC U-TURN AND SIX HOURS LATER, TUCK MADE Brazil's northeastern coast. There, he scuttled the O-2—and Scorsi—and did his best to blend in, making his way down the coast. He was in Rio a few days later when he finally reached out to Hunter. The date November 20th, his watch read one minute to midnight when she picked up.

"Hunter," came her sleep-slowed voice.

"Collect call," said Tuck in his best impression of an automated operator. All nasal delivery and lip-clucking annoyance, he thought he was channeling an old movie. The true source: his memory of a drag revue emcee from an ill-fated trip to Provincetown.

"Who...what?"

"Peter Table," Tuck offered, eyeing the dark, knotty secretary that lay beneath the phone.

"Table? Who the Hell is this?"

"It's me, ma'am," Tuck switched to his real voice, making his tone as congenial as possible.

"Squires?"

"Right."

"Jesus," she whispered. "I thought we'd lost you."

"Still alive and kicking."

"What about Scorsi?"

"Dead, as ordered."

"Good."

"I have to ask you though, ma'am. Why have my accounts been frozen?"

"That was the President. When you went AWOL, he flipped. I did what I could to slow him down but he finally took care of it through Homeland. Don't worry, though. Come in and we can straighten that all out."

Tuck had taken a huge risk in even contacting Hunter. But he had three questions only she could answer. Of these, the status of his bank accounts was the first. As for this call, Tuck was running out of time. Even the clean phone would be traceable at a minute. He looked down as the second hand passed seven.

"I need access before I can do that, ma'am."

"Which ones?"

"All of them."

"You have big plans, Squires?" she said. "A location for the Presence maybe?"

"Not over this line."

"It's secure."

In Rio's fetid air and silvered moonlight, Tuck saw his watch's second hand sweeping towards 10. Hunter's lie had answered his second question; but there would be no time for the third and most important, one that probably wouldn't be so simple to answer anyway.

"I have to go, ma'am."

"But…"

"I'll be in touch." Tuck picked up the backpack and left the room he'd rented under the name of Sigmund von Hoffen,

German importer-exporter. Down the staircase with its creaks and squeaks and wheezes, past the cigarillo-sucking desk clerk, the lobby full of frayed furniture, and the doorman in his bad, white suit, Tuck walked into the half-lit swelter of midnight in Rio.

TUCK LEFT BRAZIL TWICE THE NEXT DAY—ONCE AS HIMSELF, once as someone else. The first time, he used his own papers to sign up as a junior deckhand on the Trans-Atlantic banana boat, the Alto Robero. A few minutes later, the Alto Robero still moored in the harbor, Tuck dove over the side. This, he knew, would provide scant information and do it slowly enough to foul up anyone trying to find him.

If not the Director and ID, certainly Homeland and any number of others would be after him now that they had proof of life. He knew exactly who Hunter and Clarion had been talking about in the recording, General Giselle "Thunder" Evans, Hunter's semi-boss and senior rival, a woman whose ruthlessness and distaste for religion were legendary. She'd probably suggested the President have him assassinated as a precaution.

Six hours later, under a Polish passport—Jaroslaw Adamczyk—Tuck had boarded a plane to Buenos Aires. The next few days he spent bouncing from airport to airport—Rio to Buenos Aires to Melbourne to Mauritius to Istanbul to Geneva. Once in Switzerland, Tuck got in touch with his uncle Largesse.

"What in Hades, son? There are guys with bad haircuts and cheap suits everywhere. I had to head for the Fortress just to get a little work done." The Fortress was Squiresese for

Squires Cairns, the family's private island off the coast of Nova Scotia. "They told us you were missing, presumed dead, said we weren't to mention you, or give any interviews—even though Wolf View still calls your mother three times a day—said the mission you died on was top secret, something to do with all that jewel thievery and the Russians."

"Sounds about right."

"Didn't I always tell you those Neo-Communists would be up to no good before long?"

"That's just a cover story."

"Oh, sure it is. The godless, Putinite bastards."

"No, seriously, Largesse, none of that's real."

"What is then?"

Tuck considered the question's implications.

"I can't go into that. Not yet."

"All right, all right, if you say so."

"I'm in trouble, Largesse."

"Did I tell you not to get mixed up with those spooks, or didn't I?"

"You told me. But I'd rather not discuss that part of it right now."

"Sure, sorry, Tuck. Damber is crawling with agents. Had to get all the way to Halifax before I was sure there wasn't some robot mannequin trailing me."

"You said this line was safe?"

"I'm at the Fortress."

"Well, then. You know I'm in a bind here and I wouldn't ask if—?"

"You want me to let Puppy know I heard from you? She's a wreck, refusing to admit you're dead. It'd sure brighten up her

Thanksgiving to know you're still alive, especially what with your dad's death and all. You know that's always hard on her."

"No, Largesse. In fact, that's what I want to talk to you about. I want you to tell Mom and Sara Sue that I'm dead."

"But you're not?"

"Yes, I realize that. But I need to disappear. As in, completely. That's the only way I'm going to be able to get to the bottom of this."

"The bottom of what?"

"I'll be in touch, Largesse. But I have no idea when. Until then, I'll just be living the dream."

EPILOGUE:

VIRTUAL JERUSALEM

PLACID SKY AND REFLECTIVE GLASS. AIRPLANES TRAPPED IN pitiless slow-mo hurtling again and again into those stoic towers of steel. Balls of fire flowering like midair cancers. Plumes of thick black gashing the sky. Broken buildings become the ruins of a once-great civilization. People, too, fall. Unable to bear the flames or the fear, they know they're going to their deaths, but take that last step just the same. The lower air soon fills with smoke and debris, screams and dust and death. All of it the work of religion, the fantasy known as God…

Like every American, the Angel knew that day. She knew it as a series of pictures—reality's veneer clipped and edited and sanitized, video captured and digitized, turned into a living record of national loss. Pressed into her brain with the same vivid certainty her mother had once known for scripture, these pictures became the Angel's memories. They became her history.

In the sense that she hadn't wanted this knowledge, that the decision to accept it had been made for her, the images were very much as scripture had been to her mother. They were a thing dreaded and dark from which she would eventually learn to extract light. From fear, we draw courage. From loss, power. From hate, love.

THE ANGEL REMEMBERED LEAVING PHILADELPHIA THAT morning. She remembered driving south on 1, moving away from the chaos only so she could run back to it later. She had known the truth already as she drove. Her older sister, Anne, was dead, taken by the terrorists.

She had gotten the letter just a day before, spent the night reading and re-reading, drinking, shaking, dialing—work cell home, work cell home, work cell home—hoping the whole thing had been an act, a cry for attention, a call for help.

When she woke the next morning, it was a little past ten, the TV still on. The first image she'd seen was of the North Tower being hit. The South Tower followed. Then came speculation. Talking heads. The Towers, North and South, again. And again. And again. Her mother called as the second wave of studio chatter began.

"Have you tried Anne?" her mother asked.

"I can't get through."

"Why would someone do this? So evil. Such a…I can't… such a waste."

"I knew it would come to this. It's religion, Mom. You know that."

"This is not religion."

"No?"

"No, there is no religion. There is only God."

"Jesus?"

"Right?"

"Yes," the Angel said, not because she believed, but because it was what her mother believed, and more than that what she needed to hear.

"I want you to come home."

THE CALL CAME TO THEM IN D.C. TWO DAYS LATER. ANNE had been found face down in her brownstone, roof and walls fallen all around. The attacks on the WTC had killed her. Collateral damage from the blast, the toxic aftermath, maybe a combination.

The Angel knew the truth of course, the truth Anne had hidden from her parents so well—Wall Street had driven her mad like their mother, made her a drunk and an addict like their father. She still had the letter with her in her backpack, had brought it all the way from Philadelphia, the letter that seemed to explain so little. To the Angel, though, it explained too much.

Dearest Sister,

Remember the park. Remember me pushing you on the swings. Remember reading The Little Rabbit Who Could. Remember the good times because they were so very good. But they aren't anymore, not for me. And I know they will never be again.

If there is a God and he made me like this, then he is a fucking bastard. But you've known that for a while, haven't you? That's one of the things I've always loved about you. Take care of Mom and Dad. This will be hard on them.

Love always,

A.

THE TRUTH DIDN'T MATTER. WHAT MATTERED WAS PLAUSIBILITY. And belief. If Anne's life could mean something, if she could be a victim, her mother would accept it. And the Angel would be able to accept it, too. If she could make her sister's death mean something, somehow, some way, no matter how far across the plains of the future…If she could make that happen, things would work out.

Eventually, she returned to Wharton. Her parents had wanted her to follow in Anne's footsteps, to go to Wall Street, to prove them right, validate their hopes and dreams just as Anne had. And she had decided to humor them even though she knew she would never see Wall Street in the way her sister had.

As a family member of a victim of 9/11, as a woman of exceptional abilities, she was contacted and recruited by Internal Defense. She was a model candidate they told her. She would be a field operative for the Shadow CIA, hold secret the greatest of secrets, wield the greatest of power, licensed to kill in the service of America. She would go to the Academy, serve her country. In this way, they said, she could make her sister's death mean something.

BOOK-STUFFED BUILT-INS STRETCHING WALL-TO-WALL, floor-to-ceiling, drapes of crimson crushed-velvet cast wide before her, Hunter sat in the study of the Foxhall Road colonial, one of several houses she'd inherited from her mother. Lights off, Coltrane on, and the night beyond was backlit in platinum; the sort of temporary glamour that might have prettied one of those fuck-me-and-forget-me-nots of the old, silver screen. It had been an hour since she'd left 1600, just enough time to let them get comfortable before she made the call.

"Is the President asleep?" she whispered. Circling her wrist slowly, she watched as the smoky golden liquid lapped from side to side of the tumbler, a cosine in three dimensions, geometry on acid.

"Not yet," said Prentiss. "Once he's down, probably a week."

"You sound like you're talking about a baby." She almost laughed as punctuation, but kept her response to a smile. She still wasn't sure about Prentiss, whether he pursued his own agenda, or the President's.

"He's tired as hell, that's all I'm saying."

"Sure, Prentiss. But you and I both know there'll be a Nobel in it for him, not to mention a second term."

"And Wolf View Kids will be running cartoons with him as the Anti-Christ."

"You haven't been paying attention, have you?"

"Silly me."

"After the way he pulled everyone back, got the Russians and the Chinese on board. After that smooth little trick."

"Guess when it came down to it, not even the theocracies wanted to go down that MAD path."

"Didn't want to or couldn't?"

Prentiss paused, considered, finally continued after a few beats. "Is there a difference?"

"You know there is. How far do you think they would have taken it if they'd been the ones holding trump?"

"Yeah, well…"

"Ring the residence. I need to speak with Himself."

"About?"

"Sorry, Prentiss, for his ears only."

A moment later, a tired, familiar voice crossed the line, "Don't you think you've caused enough trouble this week?" Raglan's tone said he was kidding. Hunter knew that wouldn't last long.

"Yes, sir," she said, laughing without a hint of smile. "It's just, I need to bring something to your attention."

"Something that can't wait?"

"It's a lead on Symmetra."

"Symmetra? There's not supposed to be any Symmetra. Scorsi, the Presence, the agents…you told me they'd all be dead."

"We're not so sure."

There was a long pause before the President answered, "Well, you'd better fucking get sure."

"Yes, sir, I'm sorry. I absolutely understand what you're saying from a disclosure standpoint."

"Disclosure? We'll be back to talking about Congressional hearings if the Republicans get their teeth in this. Impeachment."

"Yes, sir. It's just that we…we've been getting conflicting factuals now, over the last twelve hours."

"Internal?"

"From the Brazilians, sir. They may have tagged one of the agents heading through customs on a Polish passport. Video's bad. We're still scrubbing it."

"Who?"

"Squires."

"The Jesus freak?"

"Yes, sir. But he's back off the Grid. Somehow he got wise to the tracker. He's got family resources. You know, the Squireses?"

"Lunatics. All of them. How did he even find out about the tracker? You told me they were clandestine."

"Probably Clarion."

Hunter hadn't been happy about having to sacrifice Clarion—she'd loved him in her way—but justice was more important than anything or anyone, so important that she would have sacrificed herself if she'd had to.

"How did he…Oh, never mind…And you think Squires is working with the Presence now?"

"It's starting to look that way. But that's not the worst part."

"You're not going to tell me Clarion's alive, too, are you?"

"Worse."

"What could be worse than two turned agents?"

"Squires may have Scorsi with him."

"Meaning the Presence may have both?"

"Yes, sir."

"And do we have any better idea who he is?"

"We still can't be sure."

"Why on Earth would Scorsi have turned?"

Well, let's see, she thought, smiling to herself. "Could be she's pursuing her own agenda, or worse, the Presence's. We just don't have many answers yet."

"Obviously. For God's sake, what is it with these people? I've got half a mind to…"

"What?"

I know what you're thinking. I know what you want. But you'll never come out and say it. You'll make us do that. Which is a lie, of course, because we're making you.

371

"Just fix it," said the President. "And fast."

"You mean—"

"I mean I want a briefing with an action plan. Here, in thirty minutes." With that, Raglan hung up.

That's not all you mean, Hunter thought, as she poured herself a second Dewars, sank back in her chair, and watched the oaks and poplars and dogwoods sway, their jumbled shadows making love in the moonlight. Her driver would have her at the White House in twelve minutes. She had plenty of play.

Like Squires, Hunter had spent her life benefiting from privilege—the chain of tony prep schools and tonier colleges, the houses, the cars and connections. These were all ways in which their lives had been similar, reasons she'd had for thinking she understood him. And she had, just not well enough. She knew that now.

Being a woman, Hunter would never fully comprehend the impact of male privilege layered on top of class privilege; the sort of psychotic ego that might result in someone like Tuckford Jefferson Squires. In the end, this psychosis was what had saved him. His selfishness had overcome his "faith" and even his desire for glory.

Hunter drained her drink and crossed the study, stood looking at the picture of her great grandfather. She stared into the blue eyes that matched her own, and wondered what he would have done in this situation. Clearly, nothing. He hadn't had the foresight to see McCarthy for the scourge that he was. He'd bent when he should have been willing to break. Because all of it from the Cold War on had been about religion, about worlds that weren't real supplanting worlds that were.

She reached for the frame, and used it to draw the picture

away from the wall, almost as if she were opening a storybook. When the sub-retinal was complete, she keyed in the thirteen digits, careful to use the correct finger for each, went slowly enough to allow the touch sensors to read each of the prints. When she finished, she heard the click and subtle sigh of the mechanism releasing.

"Virtual Jerusalem," she said. She heard a second click, imagined a third in her bedroom, and left the study.

Hunter climbed the main staircase and traversed the long hall finally arriving at the double doors to her suite. As she entered she saw her objective, the fireplace at the far end of the bedroom's adjoining sitting area.

At the center point of the white, wooden mantle, practically hidden within a mass of flowers and filigrees, lay a carved diamond with three concentric, progressively smaller diamonds within it. She extended her forefinger, pushed the smallest of the diamonds, and watched all four move outward a few inches, revealing a recessed nook with a clean cell inside. She tapped the cell's sensor, pulled it to her hear, and waited.

"Three," the Vice President said after a few beats.

"Two," said Thunder after a few more.

"One," said Hunter. She paused a second, let it sink in for all of them, then added, "For Virtual Jerusalem."

"And justice." They repeated as one. With that, Hunter killed the call, returned the phone to its hiding place and left the room.

THROUGH THE HOUSE SHE WALKED, TO THE FORMAL DINING room where she would watch for the car to take her to the White House. There, she would sit in the Situation Room with Thunder and the Vice President, watching Raglan squirm. Beyond the window, the streets were quiet, cold and somber in a way that echoed the truth. No one knew, not yet, but they would. Very soon, the Old World and its holy cities would be in flames, the images seared into the consciousness of billions, made counterpoint to those images from Manhattan so many years before. Raglan's diplomacy had thwarted her in the short term, but the President's luck wouldn't last. It couldn't. Hunter would prove that. And when she did Clarion's death would mean something, too; something great, just like Anne's.

Hunter laughed then. She laughed softly, chuckling and nodding as she watched the company car, the black Antares, pull up. She knew how it would have seemed on the surface, that it would have been impossible to explain to someone, to anyone including her associates, why it made sense. But it did. Her whole plan, and more than that her whole life made sense only through the lens of justice, the ability to wield power to make the world right. Which was what she was going to do. And she didn't care if it sounded evil, and she didn't care if it sounded good. These terms were just as passé as faith.

She would prove once and for all that the Apocalypse on which the faithful waited was a fraud. She would give them the Apocalypse in all its glory then ask why the world hadn't ended, why none of the stories had come true. She would ask the Christians for their Jesus. She would ask the Jews for their Messiah. And she would ask the Muslims for their Twelfth Imam. And when none of them appeared the world would see the truth, the illusion of it all, and in that moment humanity would be set free. Yes, Hunter had known Symmetra might have changed the world, but she'd known just as surely that it couldn't save it. Real, physical salvation—the only kind that mattered—was born of deeds, not children's stories about life after death.

ACKNOWLEDGMENTS

SPECIAL, FIRST THANKS MUST GO TO MY FRIEND JAMES REICH, whose Stalking Horse Press decided to take a chance on *Pax Americana*. I can't thank James enough for the way he combines strong editorial guidance with a commitment to realizing an author's vision. I feel so fortunate to have been one of the early authors at Stalking Horse, a press I believe will make a big name for itself in the years ahead.

Thank you to my teachers, the people whose wisdom, kindness, and patience kept me going, kept me returning to the written word despite long absences. Thank you to DeWitt Henry for re-introducing me to Shakespeare and being the best boss I ever had; to Bill Holinger and Ralph Lombreglia, my grad school gurus, for all their encouragement; to Bill Miller, my first writing teacher; and to Steve Goodwin for, among other things, suggesting I might want to read Martin Amis.

Thank you to fellow writers, editors, friends, benefactors, and random good-hearted souls Traci Foust, Greg Olear, Sean Beaudoin, Jonathan Evison, Caroline Leavitt, Shya Scanlon, Thaisa Frank, Ted Heller, Samuel Sattin, Lori Ostlund, Jennifer Haigh, Michael J. Seidlinger, Lincoln Michel, Mike Joyce, Scott Waldyn, Laura Bogart, J. Ryan Stradal, John Domini, Rob McQuilkin, Elisa Petrini, Matt Bialer, Renee Zuckerbrot, Kyle Muntz, Ned Stuckey-French, Meakin Armstrong, D. Foy, Dena Rash Guzman, Sean Murphy, Elissa Schappell, Matt Norman,

Darin Strauss, Chuck Greaves, Brad Listi, Tom Francoeur, Geoff Coffey, Creaghan Trainor, Jennifer Itell, Kris Saknussemm, Mia Avramut, Meg Pokrass, and Heath Paley.

No set of acknowledgements would be complete without one's masters, the literary giants, living and dead, who animate a writer's work, give him or her something to aim for. Though there are many writers who influenced me, these are the most important: Thank you to Martin Amis for his sense of rhythm and blackest of black comic visions; to Kurt Vonnegut for his humor and heart; to Don Delillo for his surgical prose and nihilistic obsession with the American Dream; to Vladimir Nabokov for his raw genius and ambition; to Michael Moorcock for enlivening my youth with his consummate antihero Elric; to Milan Kundera for his philosophy; and to William Shakespeare for the phrasings that color our thoughts often without realization and for the grand, early novels he called plays.

Finally, I want to thank my family for all their love and support, especially my mother, Kathie, to whom this book is dedicated; my father, Jerry, who deserves to have a book dedicated to him and I hope someday will; and my brother, Ian, may he someday write a book of his own.

ABOUT KURT BAUMEISTER

Kurt Baumeister has written for *Salon, Electric Literature, The Weeklings, The Nervous Breakdown, The Rumpus, The Good Men Project,* and others. An Emerson MFA and Contributing Editor with *The Weeklings,* his monthly Review Microbrew column is published by *The Nervous Breakdown. Pax Americana* is his first novel.

www.kurtbaumeister.com